DAWN OF VENGEANCE

Books by Ronie Kendig

DAWN OF VENGEANCE

THE DROSERAN SAGA
BOOK 2

RONIE KENDIG

Dawn of Vengeance

Copyright © 2020 by Ronie Kendig

Published by Enclave Publishing, an imprint of Third Day Books, LLC

Phoenix, Arizona, USA.
www.enclavepublishing.com

ISBN: 978-1-62184-145-6 (printed hardback)
ISBN: 978-1-62184-147-0 (printed softcover)
ISBN: 978-1-62184-146-3 (ebook)

Cover design by Kirk DouPonce, www.DogEaredDesign.com
Interior design and typesetting by Jamie Foley

Printed in the United States of America.

TO
KATHY TYERS

Your name is synonymous with space operas and for decades you have inspired readers and authors—including me. In 2004, I met Steve Laube at my first writer's conference and he recommended I read your Firebird Series. It was through Firebird and Brennen's story that I fell in love with space operas, but it was also through this encounter that I made peace with a deeper question—that I could write fantastical stories about alien creatures and civilizations, and still honor God. In essence, your stories— *you*—helped my creativity find wings and take flight. Thank you for the way you have so graciously poured your wisdom and experience into other writers, offering feedback, encouragement, and endorsements. I'm grateful for your initial feedback in 2012 on *Brand of Light*—grateful that you challenged me to do better, strengthen my craft before I sought publication on this beloved saga. Seven years later, I'm grateful you generously offered an endorsement on it, but most of all, I'm grateful to call you friend. Thank you, Kathy!

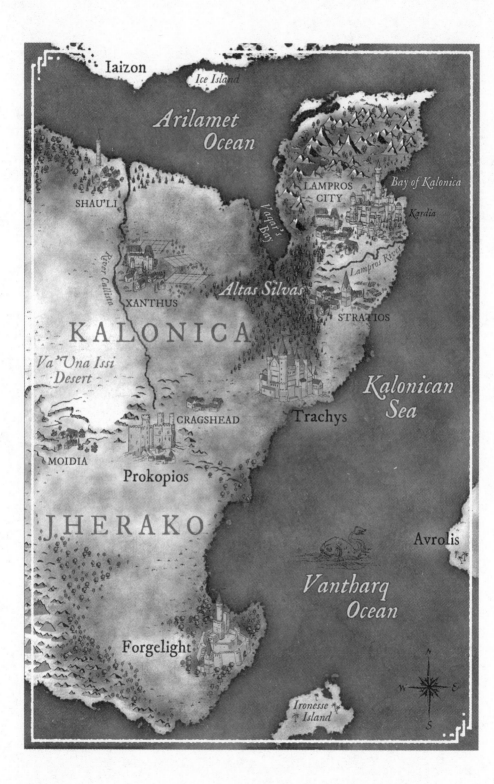

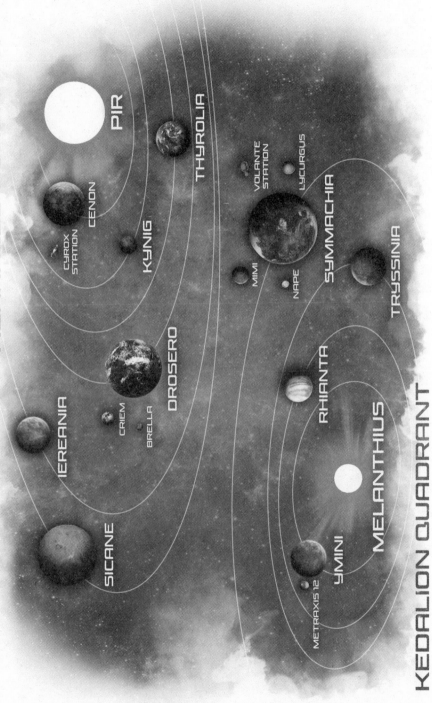

HERAKLES QUADRANT

PIR

THYROLIA

CENON

CYROX STATION

KYNIG

VOLANTE STATION

LYCURGUS

MIMI

NAPE

SYMMACHIA

TRYSSINIA

DROSERO

CRIEM

BRELLA

IEREANIA

RHIANTA

MELANTHIUS

SICANE

YMINI

METRAXIS 12

KEDALION QUADRANT

"Tigo Deken, according to the Codes of Conduct and Ethics set forth by Symmachian Command and the interplanetary Tertian Space Coalition, you are ordered to stand down and present yourself without opposition for punitive action." Commander Benjt Crichton stopped in front of Tigo's cell with Eidolon 225, an elite team of Marines, arching behind him. He motioned his men to release the 215—Tigo's team—from their holding cells.

Tigo had been to the brig dozens of times to stow prisoners, but tonight he sat in a vat of treason and conspiracy that flipped his arcs and made no sense.

Not true. His actions leading to this made sense. Conviction had compelled him to act on behalf of an innocent downworlder. Compelled him to advocate for a brilliant doctor who had pulled the thread of a very big conspiracy infecting Symmachian Command—perhaps even the Tertian Space Coalition and the Council.

How deep was the corruption?

Lieutenant Jez Sidra held her head high, her attitude higher, as she exited her cell. Something telegraphed through her mahogany features that made Tigo wary. Angry, AO, Diggs, and Rhinn were herded together by 225. A smug-looking sergeant prodded AO through the hatch.

Apart from the others, Jez grew preternaturally still and quiet. A familiar mode she adopted when she needed deep focus before—

Tigo lurched. "No!"

With a sharp pivot, she thrust her shoulder into Baedth's chest, sending him flying. She snatched the commander's pulse weapon and fired at Crichton, then wheeled around. Fired twice more, reaching with her free hand to nail the hatch release. The door slammed down between AO and his guard and the rest.

"Jez, no!" Tigo scrambled toward her, but she'd already taken aim at Diggs and Rhinn. What the . . .? He staggered to a stop as she neutralized the two men.

"Go go go!" Jez pitched him into a turn. Shoved him toward the recycle bays.

His father. His team. His career. "I can't." Tigo glanced at Rhinn—saw no gaping wound. Same with Diggs.

"Move!" she growled at him.

"This isn't the way—"

"It's the only way if you want to live." Her expression went black. "Trust me. I know."

He blinked. Saw something in her eyes he'd never seen before—fear. And yet something stronger, bigger, too. He wondered who she was, what she had become. Was it his fault? Her actions here left him bewildered. "Jez—"

"Go. Please." She pushed him backward.

A gust of air drew his attention to bay doors that had opened, revealing drop pods. There weren't supposed to be pods in those bays. He stumbled over to them. "What—"

A hard shove from behind knocked his cheek against the pod. Pain darted down his neck. Scowling, he turned. "What—"

"I'm sorry." Jez seemed strangely tall . . . yet not. Her expression grew conflicted. "I was supposed to do more. I didn't . . . I failed you."

"What're you talking about?" What happened to her that she'd hit their own team? "I was your commander. *I* failed *you*—the team." His gaze hit the others, laid out. "What's going on?"

"Forgive me." Jez planted a hand in the middle of his torso.

Heat rushed into his abdomen, forcing him backward. Shocked, he gaped at her hand—no weapon, yet the heat built. Snatching coherent thought, the burn rose through his chest into his throat. Fear gripped him. "Wh-what is this?"

"Peace." Face oddly serene, Jez nudged him again, then stepped back.

Doors snapped shut, sealing him in. "No," Tigo breathed, then slapped the window. "Jez, no!" Through the small window-like visor, he watched her slip into another pod.

The floor beneath his pod shifted. Gel cocooned his body, suctioning him into place as he accepted the mouthpiece that arced over his face. He bit it, catching one last glimpse of Jez's pod before his dropped. As the *Macedon* ejected it from its innards, the pod rattled and jerked. The great chasm of space welcomed him into its black hold. Thrusters fired, guiding it toward some destination.

Where? Who'd programmed it? Jez? She'd anticipated what he'd refused to accept—the alliance would chew him up and spit him out for helping that Kynigos and the girl, for not idly standing by while an alien race decided humans were expendable.

A bright light shot past his pod, yanking his gaze toward it. Somehow, he knew it was Jez's pod. Why was hers moving so much faster? He watched as the pod rocketed toward Drosero. Of all planets for him to get marooned on . . . it had to be the one without technology.

Maybe that was the point. Jez knew Symmachia couldn't find him here. Doing so would break a dozen intergalactic treaties. But that hadn't stopped them with the Kynigos. Or the Droseran girl.

The sun cresting the planet's curve reached toward her pod as it broke the atmosphere.

Wait. No. That wasn't the pod hitting atmo. It was . . .

No. No no no.

A great ball of fire sparked across the atmosphere, bouncing, eating up the pod.

Tigo watched, heart racing, frantic to stop that pod, save Jez. But he could do nothing. He tried to bang his fists. Useless. The cocooning gel refused to let him move. But it couldn't stop the tears. Or the fire that rushed over his shield and consumed his pod.

"Zacdari! *What* in Void's Embrace are you waiting for?"

Claxons rang in her helmet, a grating noise that made it hard to think. Her heads-up gave a visual on the target station, and another on the left displayed the corvette's actual trajectory. The dots were not aligned.

Lance Corporal Eija Zacdari could handle it. She might be a mere candidate for the Tertian Intergalactic Hyperjump Program for Exploration. She might be a Tryssinian orphan with more scars than fingers. But she wasn't a quitter. Getting onto the *Prevenire*, the first HyPE ship to access the hyperaccelerated slipstream to Kuru System, was her last hope.

She nudged the controls, bringing the corvette into alignment with the great metal flower that was her target.

A wave of heat speared her mind, and with it came a strange visual. A realization. The vectors were wrong. Her angle of approach wrong.

It was all djelling wrong.

And you know that how? Nobody knew Kuru System because nobody had been there. How did Command know this was right? How did anyone? Even her? That alone made her hesitate. Throw this away and she threw away a gift.

"Nobody can know, Eija. Do you understand?"

She glanced up, wide-eyed, at the one offering her the world—a whole new world and life.

The woman wore slacks and a blouse. Nothing fancy. But a lot nicer than anything Eija's orphaned self ever wore. "If they find out, this all goes away. And there will be nothing here to return to. Am I clear?"

"Why me?"

"Look around you, Eija. The others—they're hurting, too. That's what we are supposed to change. They are the ones we need to protect; the ones who can't do anything for themselves." Her bright eyes seemed less blue just then. "So, tell me. Are you the warrior I think you to be?"

"But nobody from Tryss—"

"No. Never mention that place again. Do, and your dream of escape dies as

soon as the name falls from your lips. Do you understand?"

"Yes, Patron."

"So, what are you, then?"

"Napian," she replied obediently.

Napian. By record only. But Eija had grown up on Tryssinia, where everyone was taught from birth to distrust the government, and the Academy was as close to government as one could get out in the black.

"Nice and easy, Z. Guide her in," came the calm, unaffected tone of her flight training instructor, Gunnery Sergeant Sevart "Rhinn" Crafter. "That's right."

His words pushed her attention back to the panels. The simulation said it was right. *So just shut up and do it. Pass the stupid test.* If she failed, she wouldn't get assigned to the *Prevenire*.

Eija's vision blurred, and a thrum of heat against her palms warned her of a fatal mistake. Something beeped. She glanced down. Her thumb slid across the rounded surface of the control instruments. A small but significant gesture that shifted her trajectory.

Beep-beep-beep!

"Zacdari! What're you scuzzing doing?"

Her gaze snapped to the blue ring gliding farther from the white blip of her craft on the screen. No. She couldn't scuz this. Breathing a little harder, she jerked right.

Too hard! Too hard!

The sim ship decelerated sharply, and she could feel it itching for a spin.

Exiting slipstream at Kuru Station One in five . . . four . . .

"C'mon," Eija muttered as she hit thrusters to compensate for the variance in distance. If she didn't get it corrected soon, she'd fling into the atmosphere or collide with the station rings, which guided ships safely through Kuru to the anchor point station, where she'd dock.

According to the intelligence.

Which was slagged.

"Just . . . pass the . . . djelling test," she murmured to herself.

The hard deceleration flipped her couch and pressed hard against her body, fluids snaking into her system to keep her from being crushed alive. The fast-attack craft finished its deceleration. But like everything in her life, it wasn't enough. The first ring was barreling toward her. She tensed. Her sweaty hands slipped off the control. A whimper lashed out, fogging the helmet. "No no no," she muttered.

Warnings glared in red block letters: IMPACT IMMINENT. ALTER COURSE.

Eija tried to comply, but the ship shuddered as if it, too, were appalled by her insanity. The screen flashed searing white. Her fluids went cold, a painful punishment for failing the sim.

Like her own deflating hopes, the couch sagged and lowered her to the deck. Snakes retracted, sucking away her last vestige of self-respect. Growling, Eija pounded her console. With a huff, she extricated herself from the simulator.

"What the slag was that?" barked Gunny as the walls drew up.

A swarm of nerves invaded Eija at the sight of the forbidding former Eidolon charging across the simdeck. "It messed up—"

"No, that's what *you* did!" Gunny growled. "You just blew up everyone on your ship, Corporal!"

"But I—"

"*What* does that readout say?" He towered over her with furor in his eyes.

The bleeding crimson display still flashing in her mind, Eija shoved her gaze to the deck and huffed. Gritted her teeth.

"I'm waiting!"

She jolted. Looked at him. Right. The screen . . .

But the simulator wasn't right. If the intel about this planet they were jumping to was right, then the tactical plans had fundamental flaws. Yet she couldn't justify that assertion with science. She barely passed her modules each week. Flying wasn't a science—not to her. It was instinct. Which frustrated her because she couldn't explain exactly what was wrong, so nobody would listen to her objections.

Lifting her chin, she met the sergeant's hard gaze and—by the stars, she would not let a smug Eidolon-turned-flight-instructor destroy her chance of getting off this forsaken planet. "It's wrong! I don't know where we got the intel on that jump, but it won't work."

"It *does* work—except with you!"

"That's because the simulations are set up with erroneous intel. Based on conditions here, that we're used to, but—"

"Enough!"

"—it's not. We're going to get everyone killed if we—"

"Stand down, Corporal!"

"Why won't you listen?"

"Excuse me?" He moved forward, forcing her to take a step back as he pressed his bulk and authority right into her nose. "This is your last warning,

Zacdari! One more, one little infraction—including breathing wrong when you're near me—and you're out."

Stricken, Eija lifted her head, mouth parting. Dread nauseated her. "But—"

"Got it?"

She tightened her jaw. "Yes, sir."

"Dismissed!"

No more was he Marco Dusan, Kynigos, skilled hunter. A man concerned only with tracking quarry and sorting scents. Finery and frippery choked him as he stood before the full-length mirror in his private residence within Kardia, the royal palace that sat in the heart of Lampros City. The reflection of his black and blue Kynigos cloak taunted as it hung next to the duster behind him. It'd kept him warm on many a hunt in his pursuit of fugitives across the quadrants. His gift had fueled and given him purpose, defined him. Now what purpose did it pose?

He dropped his gaze, rubbing his knuckles, unwilling to don the ornamental sash and sword belt. He could scale a building in a heartbeat, but fight with a sword? Play politics?

Shaking his head, he eyed the waistcoat stitched with the sigil of House Tyrannous—an attacking aetos, wings and claws outstretched in powerful threat. His white sash of nobility atop black slacks tucked with precision—by a sergius—into polished ebony boots. Gold cords ran from one shoulder to the other and tucked beneath gold epaulets that identified him as medora. Balling his fists, he gritted his teeth. This was not him. He wasn't one to wear ornamentation, to adorn himself with regalia. He thought to toss off the extravagances.

Yet he was medora—king. Of a people he did not know. A land he'd forgotten, having been taken from these very halls at the young age of six. Parents, whose blood he carried, were only hazy memories haunting marble floors and columns of this palatial home. What did he know about ruling a people? Deliver justice, aye.

But today was not about him. It was about Kalonica. A realm in need of a ruler, of guidance. For a prophecy—he rotated his right forearm and saw the brand hidden beneath his sleeve glowing faintly—that had chosen him as a boy.

"Your Majesty?" Ixion called from the solar.

Tugging his cuffs, Marco used his enhanced sense of smell—the *anaktesios*—

and detected the respect of a man long used to ruling as elder of a Kalonican province for decades.

"You are late," Ixion said. "To your own coronation."

Marco expelled a heavy breath. "I am ill-suited to diplomacy and pandering."

"The time for those things is long past. Considering the change facing Kalonica and Drosero, you are exactly what the people need."

The words enabled him to draw a breath not pained with inadequacy. "Mayhap." His thoughts drifted to that satellite, the intel handed down by a Symmachian Eidolon, that . . . creature. "After what I've seen, war is very near, and that is . . . overwhelming."

Ixion nodded yet seemed distracted.

"What is it?"

"They rail that you will not use your birth name."

"Achilus is a boy long dead." Marco stretched his neck beneath the starched collar. "Let's get this over with." Heavily burdened yet unbowed, he strode out of the apartments. His regia—royal guard—fell in step behind him. A dozen paces later he caught a scent of surprise. Admiration. Then anger. He slid his gaze to the source and resisted smirking. "Darius."

Tight-lipped yet comfortable in the regalia of heir presumptive, his brother stood at the end of the hall. "By the fires." He drew closer. "You are the image of our father."

A father Marco barely remembered, save a parting moment etched in heartache. He tucked his chin, appreciating yet hating the comparison and knowing he could not live up to the legacy of Tyrannous Zarek. The roiling scents betrayed Darius's agreement with that sentiment.

Distraction came in that beautiful Signature of vanilla and patchouli wafting from the right.

Marco braced as Kersei emerged from the residence she shared with Darius. Attired in a flattering gold gown, she wore a small tiara that did little to control her riot of black curls. Still the most beautiful creature he'd ever set eyes upon.

"Were it not for that brooding look," Kersei said with a smile, "I would scarce recognize you." Though teasing, she couldn't hide her scent leaden with grief and . . . ache.

Marco stowed his feelings lest they betray him. He looked away from them, hating that Kersei stood with his brother, not at his side. "Shall we?"

"Actually," Darius said, "Kersei and I must go first, then you walk alone."

"I only meant—let's get this over with."

Arrogant to the last, Darius turned to Kersei. "My princessa?" His rank gloating fouled the air as he put a possessive arm around her and led her to the stairs.

Anger rattled through Marco. He could flatten the impudent prince.

Ixion manifested at his side. "Easy," he breathed.

Stretching his neck, Marco restrained himself. Stalked to the staircase. A crack sounded from below, startling him to a stop. He peered over the balustrade and his heart thumped—a sea of green waited below. In the grand foyer, there were easily more than a hundred machitis, aerios, regia, nobles, and elders. "I said a *small* gathering."

Today's ceremony was formality, an assurance that he was not a pretender. So he'd wanted as little fuss as possible, allowing only elders and nobles to attend. For now. Later, a celebration for the people. Much later.

"This *is* small," Ixion noted. "It would be greater had not Stratios been lost."

Sobered by the mention of Kersei's people lost in the attack that thrust her into his life, Marco moved down the stairs, spotting the aged iereas, Ypiretis, and his apprentice, Duncan, near the entrance to the great hall. Two machitis opened the throne room door.

Marco entered the columned hall with its mural and Kalonican green.

"Stand true and ready," a caller announced, his voice echoing through the foyer, "for one comes to claim the heart of Kardia and its throne."

Gilt cornices and chandeliers glittered as Marco strode through the crowd. Straight ahead, the elders surrounded the throne dais upon which stood Darius and Kersei.

"Who approaches the altar?" Grand Duke Rhayld demanded. Marco's uncle had little of the Tyrannous bearing so strong in their line.

"I, Marco Dusan, do." He closed the last few yards.

Rhayld's scent trilled with an irritated but quiet acceptance. He had been comfortable in his role as praetor, temporary ruler after Zarek's death more than six months past. "What cause do you have to claim this crown?"

"I was born Tyrannous Achilus, firstborn son and blood heir of Medora Zarek and his kyria, Athina." The words were strange to Marco since years of training had forced a shunning of familial identity and embracing of only one: Kynigos.

"Prince Darius," his stout uncle spoke, "please bring forth the confirmation device, loaned to us by High Lord Kyros"—he nodded to the red-robed iereas with a white mantle—"for the expedience of proof that will remove all doubt regarding this man's claim that he is Zarek's eldest son, long believed dead."

Darius delivered a small black box to the grand duke with a scent of jealous rivalry. It was less than the rage Marco had detected when Darius and Kersei first returned from Iereania two weeks ago. The prince had so wanted to challenge Marco then, but with little grounds, he subsided into sullen acceptance.

"Provide now your proof." Rhayld wafted a strange scent, not doubt of Marco's identity but . . . a tremor of fear, uncertainty.

Why? Believing men should be able to keep their secrets, Marco closed his receptors but not before he caught Kersei's Signature, imbued with awe and grief. His gaze touched hers for a click, appreciating the caress of her brown eyes, as he turned to the pad and pressed his thumb there. A single prick from the device extracted a droplet of blood.

A heavy pause hung over the great hall as Kalonicans waited for the result, which appeared with a blue light. Fitting, considering the blue hue to his now ever-glowing brand that had connected him to Kersei in the Ierean Temple.

"Prince Darius," Rhayld intoned. "Have you a result?"

"Aye, I do, Grand Duke," his brother answered.

"Pray, show it to the elders and claimant, then produce it here to be ever recorded in the annals of the medoras."

Showing the result, Darius walked the line of elders, then turned to Marco, who nodded. He had been accepted as truth when Roman told him, but somehow, seeing the digital proof of his legacy stirred something deep as Darius delivered the device to Rhayld.

"It is confirmed—a 98.9 percent match," Rhayld said triumphantly, and despite Marco's closed receptors, there riffled a scent that bespoke joy with yet another undercurrent of uncertainty. "Nobles, machitis, and elders, before you stands Tyrannous Achilus, son of Zarek. What say you?"

A collective shout went up.

Overwhelmed by the enormity of what was happening, Marco drew up, glancing around. Two months ago, he'd been on a ship, fighting for Kersei's life and—unwittingly—his own. Now he stood before this crowd not as a hunter, but as heir to a throne left vacant when his father died in an attack that led to Symmachia.

"Achilus, now likened Marco, stand ready to receive your vestments." Rhayld motioned Ypiretis and Duncan to bring forward a staff tipped with a gold, attacking aetos, a heavy fur robe, and a thick gold crown. "Marco, face your subjects. Kneel before them and the Ancient who chose you."

Disbelieving that this was happening, Marco turned and knelt on the low padded bench that looked out at the crowd. The faces . . . his subjects. The people he was to rule, be responsible for. His heart punched his ribcage. He opened his receptors and used the anaktesios to ascertain the collective attitude. Relief hit him—most accepted him, even celebrated him. A few were uncertain.

High Lord Kyros glided from the side and, with the help of Ypiretis, set the heavy robe on Marco's shoulders. "A reminder," Kyros pronounced, "of the weight you carry and the protection you provide to the people you serve." He produced the scepter-staff and extended it to Marco. "A symbol of peace and violence, the scepter-staff bears the aetos, which soars above all, so should your character and honor. As a staff it is the weapon of aerios used to defend the realm, and as scepter it signifies your royal blood."

Kyros next raised the crown over Marco's head. Though Dárius and Kersei stood behind him, Marco caught her Signature, laced with approval and delight so terrific.

The rugged diadem had a thick gold band with five arches, each inlaid with a different jewel to represent the four realms, and in the center an aetos gripped the thick band, curled behind the middle arch, and peered over it in a frozen shriek. In its beak lay a massive emerald. Purple diamonds sparked from the eyes, indicative of the Kalonican Sea, which fed the fertile soil.

"Here we lift the crown of Kalonica," Kyros proclaimed, "forged for Atlas, second medora of Kalonica, blessed by the Ladies of Basilikas in the time of Medora Eoghan, worn by every firstborn son in the four-hundred cycles since. By the authority placed in me by the Ancient, Vaqar, and the Ladies of Basilikas who protect and do violence on behalf of the people, you are crowned Marco, Medora of Kalonica and her realms; sovereign over the Northern, Middle, and Southern lands; hand of Vaqar the Protector."

Slowly, reverently, the crown came to rest on Marco's brow with a notable weight and a foreboding that the pain the Lady had spoken of on Iereania was just beginning.

It was not supposed to be this way. Though Kersei remained by Darius, her bound, everything in her was at Marco's side as he was formally set in as medora. He was handsome, with a powerful presence—yet affected so deeply as the crown settled atop his wavy black hair. Pride surged through her as shouts of *hoyzah* rose from the aerios, elders, and nobles. The thick gray fur cloak added to his impressive bearing. Never had there been such a man . . .

Kersei fisted her hands. An ache of longing swelled—Marco had vowed to make her his bound. That they would rule together. Devoted words spoken moments before Darius reappeared, every bit alive and not dead as believed. Ceremonially bound to Darius, Kersei had been forced to leave the man she loved. It was cruel. Forever would he hold her heart.

"You are princessa now. The people will look to you—be of good courage. For them . . . and for my brother's son you now carry." It was impossible for Marco to know about the pregnancy in that painful good-bye on Iereania. Seven weeks since and her monthly had not come—that and the exhaustion brought on by the life growing within her—proving him right.

"Vanko Kalonica!" shouted Darius, fist thrust against his chest.

As Marco rose and took the throne, machitis echoed the shout, and the crowd bowed to him. Though to all here he likely looked comfortable upon the royal seat, Kersei noted the stiff set of his jaw. The spark of annoyance in his blue eyes. He felt out of place in Kardia.

Darius moved forward and summoned the machitis, demanding their oath to serve their new medora. As one, they went to a knee and swore fealty, to hold honor above all else. That was followed by a winnowing of warriors down to the aerios. Then regia vowed their swords and lives were Marco's to do with as he willed, and then they swore to obey every command with extreme prejudice.

Kyros and Ypiretis stepped from the dais, leading Marco from the throne room. The sea of green-and-white-clad aerios again took a knee as he strode past.

When Darius offered his arm, Kersei startled out of her admiration. Together, they exited the hall behind Marco and the iereas, who moved to a small receiving room where they would remove Marco's vestments.

A half ora later, the members of House Tyrannous, which now included her, formed a receiving line into the grand hall. Marco joined them at the front, and the doors were opened to a long queue that continued for what seemed hours as guests filed in and took their designated tables for the celebration feast. Marco might say he was no politician, but he commanded the attention and hearts of the people unlike any she had seen. She did not doubt many nobles sought him for their unmarried daughters.

When they were seated at last, Darius tossed back a glass of wine, startling her. His nostrils flared. "He is every inch our father down to the way they fawn over him."

At the venom in his words, Kersei skidded her gaze over him, his rumpled light-brown hair curling around the circlet he wore. "You sound annoyed."

His blue eyes hit hers, then bounced away.

"Because you thought to be medora?"

"Test me not, Kersei."

"Are you so easily threatened by a query?"

"He rules a kingdom he does not know or love. His heart is not here."

"Marco could not be forced to do anything against his will."

"You seem to know his thoughts well, yet not mine." His lips thinned. "Remember who is your bound, Princessa."

The way he sneered her title smarted. "Reminders I do not need."

"Think me the villain, but he knows nothing of the kingdom he rules. I may not be perfectly versed on political affairs—my father-medora confided in Silvanus on those—but I am more knowledgeable than Marco, as are others in this room." He nodded to the grand duke conversing in the corner with two round-bellied nobles.

Enduring the assault of Marco's character without posing a defense for him proved painful. She focused on the man Darius had indicated. "Your uncle?" There was an implication in his words she did not like. "But he was—"

"Praetor, upon the deaths of Silvanus and Father. It would not be farfetched to think he fancied himself wearing the aetos, especially believing I was dead as well. It is an adjustment to lose the station he enjoyed for months." He lifted a meat pie from the tray and slid it into his mouth. "The man with him in burgundy?"

Kersei found the man with little hair and much ornamentation. "Lord Artlenburg?" She had attended more than one gala with her parents.

"Director of the treasury," Darius noted. "And the man who just joined them . . ."

Kersei saw the shorter arrival, dapper in tails and slicked-back hair. "Artlenburg's heir, Royd."

"Recently returned from Jherako, where he spent a great deal of time with the economists and is said to have had the ear of their king."

Why would Royd seek counsel with a foreign king? "You know this how?" Would Marco need to watch his back already?

Darius gave her a lazy grin. "You sound impressed, my love."

"Your words, if true, are alarming and could suggest a threat against Marco."

Irritation splayed through his features, then shifted. "That is the Kersei I love so much, thinking past lace and pearls, though you wear them both well."

Bristling, she ignored his well-intentioned compliment. "Darius, you must give earnest consideration to this. Think you Artlenburg is planning some . . . insurrection?"

Darius laughed. "Recall that I am the one versed in political affairs, not you with your morbid imaginations." He huffed. "Nay, I do not think they are planning any such event." He squinted. "Yet."

Why must he always rebuff her? "You should speak with Marco about this."

His mirth vanished. "No."

"It is of great import if you think these men would harm Marco."

"I grow weary of your thoughts so fastidiously focused on my brother." Darius cocked his head. "Do remember to refer to him as Medora Marco now, love." He took her hand. Kissed her palm. "If you would pardon me." He nodded to her regia, then strode across the room toward the men he had just discussed.

Annoyed at his condescension but relieved to be alone, she reveled in the solitude. He had been smothering since their return to Kalonica. A yawn seized her. She gained her feet and startled as a man appeared at her side. "Ypiretis."

"Princessa," he said, inclining his head. "How do you fare?"

"Tired," she admitted, smiling at his apprentice, the black-haired youth. "As a girl, these affairs always bored me. I would sneak into the bailey and spar with the aerios, then be punished later by Ma'ma."

A hearty laugh jolted through the hall, fastening her attention on Marco, who stood with Elder Bazyli Sebastiano and his brothers.

"They are so at ease," she noted quietly.

"He has nothing to prove with them."

As he did not with me. Marco's ruggedness seemed a sharp contrast to the medora's doublet and crown, yet it emphasized that persona. And what a figure he cut with the high collar of his official overcloak. The green of his embroidered coat brightened eyes that had so wholly ensnared her on Cenon. As he talked, she tried to catch his words and found herself staring at his mouth. Remembering—

Things she should not. Kersei lowered her head and massaged her neck.

A woman's tittering drew her gaze back. Elegant, carefree Danae Sebastiano now entertained her brothers and Marco, who chuckled and shook his head. When her hand landed on his arm, he barked a laugh.

A black spear of jealousy ripped through Kersei.

Tall with long blonde hair, Danae, the daughter of Ares, former elder of the Xanthus, would secure a strategic alliance for her entoli if they could tether her to Marco. That was surely her intent. Could Marco not see it? Danae did not care for him—the man, the hunter. Only for the crown and how it might benefit the Xanthus.

"When in a position of authority and new to a seat of power, should not one be gracious?" came the soft, not-so-subtle voice of Ypiretis.

"Aye," Kersei said as she averted her focus. "But perhaps he should not enjoy it so much."

Ypiretis smiled. "Have you counted the number of times he has looked to the terratza?"

Kersei glanced at the iereas then Marco—his gaze even now wandering to the gauzy curtains billowing between columns as if he sought escape. He clapped Bazyli's shoulder, nodded curtly to the others, and walked away with his regia, Kaveh Naderi and Edvian Solurto, two steps behind as he left the crowd for the open night.

Kersei was halfway across the great hall before she realized it. Reminding herself it would be unseemly to go to Marco alone, she diverted to a pastry table. Hated herself for wanting to be out there with him when it would be inappropriate. Plate of delicacies in hand, she turned as the curtains fluttered, sneaking her a glimpse of Marco, palms on the balustrade as he stared out to sea.

She eyed Darius—still engaged in conversation—then erased the half dozen paces between her and Marco.

When his regia materialized at each column forbidding her passage, her courage fled. "I only—"

"Beg your mercy, Princessa." Kaveh shouldered into her path. "The medora wills privacy."

Her heart sank. "Of course." She peered over Kaveh's shoulder to Marco, still bent and brooding. But she was not one to give up easily. "I noticed the medora had not eaten, so I thought to offer him—"

"He asked for privacy," he said, more curtly this time.

Kersei tightened her jaw. It was for the best. She did not want a spectacle if Darius—

"Let her pass, Kaveh."

Something about his deep voice reaching from the dark night to grant access sent a shameful thrill through her. Chin tucked, she slipped between the aerios, extending the plate toward Marco as she approached. "You have scarce touched food this droll eve, my medora."

With a smirk, he folded his arms, leaned back against the thick balustrade, and crossed his ankles. "I have little stomach for food or platitudes."

Kersei sighed. "I am of the same mind." She glanced at the plate, telling herself to leave before she did something foolish. She lifted the delicacies. "So, which—"

He flashed a hand. "The only sweet I sought was your company."

Her heart stuttered, throwing heat into her cheeks. Stunned, she found herself captive to his gaze. Thought to speak, tell him her love had not dimmed, that she was sorry for all that happened on Iereania, that she would do anything . . .

Yet, she could not.

Willing her pulse to slow, knowing well how her pheromones thrust her attraction at him, she set down the plate. Touched a sugared confection. "They are too sweet. Making me sick." Brushing off her hands, she braved another look at him, the gold circlet a nice accent to his olive skin, resting on . . . his knotted brow. She reached to brush back the strands—

Marco straightened to his full height. Turned again to the sea, hands shoved into his pockets.

Of course. Though their relationship had been short, she still felt it second nature to touch him, to be with him. He had more honor than her, more strength, and she grieved her own weakness.

Stiff and staring up at the sky, he groaned. "The Lady told us the heartaches would be endless, but I couldn't have imagined"—he motioned between them—"this. Loving you, being so close, and knowing I can never . . ."

Her throat thickened with emotion. "Nor I." The heartache was acute. Too much like that reminding chamber the Symmachians had locked her in. "She said to stand strong." Something Kersei did not feel.

Another snort, and he scratched the side of his face. "When Roman told me who I was—that Zarek was my father—it opened up memories, but I wasn't overwhelmed because . . ." He pressed his fingertips to the stone rail, his voice rough. "Because I thought I would face it with someone who made me want to be a better man. Someone who understood me and the people I was to rule." He swallowed, his jaw muscle jouncing.

Eyes burning with unshed tears, she dared not speak or move. This was tenuous ground that scared her. Reminded her Darius was on the other side of those curtains, as were hundreds of guests. She would not shame their houses, but oh by the Mercies, she would touch him, hold him, feel his strength, and—

"Kersei," he hissed, a low warning as he hung his head.

She remembered herself, her emotions. "I beg your mercy," she whispered, shamed.

He roughed a hand over his mouth and stretched his jaw. "I'm alone." The words seemed to struggle from his throat. "For the first time in my life, I am truly alone. And I don't know what to do. Surrounded by hundreds, an anchor upon my head, and daunted by what is before me. Daunted and alone."

"No." She slipped her hand to his wrist. "No, you are not alone. We are here. I know things are . . . upside down, but you are *not* alone, Marco. I am here. And I will ever be your—"

"*Friend?*" he growled, his eyes narrowing as he rocked. His venom startled her. "The woman I love, the woman I wanted as my bound, lives in my own house, and I cannot touch her. I cannot love her!" He stepped back of a sudden. Something washed through his face, and he nodded. "Good eve, Princessa."

"M—" The call died on her lips when she saw what pushed him away.

Darius. Standing by the columns. He bumped shoulders with Marco, who returned to the festivities. Alone with her, Darius glowered. "What do you here?"

Feeling caught and yet detesting the man who stood before her for what he had made impossible, Kersei lifted the pastries. "It was too humid. I needed air and a good pastry." She forced a smile.

"Is this what it will be like? You slipping off to be with him every time my back is turned?"

She wanted to argue, but that was exactly what she had done.

"Have you no shame? You are my bound, *mine*! Not his."

"I am your bound, aye," she bit out, "but I am not *owned*. I will not be treated like a possession. You overreact, Darius."

"Overreact?" He stabbed toward the gathering. "What am I to say or do when a duke informs me my bound is alone in the night with my brother? In public, you do this!" His voice and temper rose. "Do not cuckold me, Kersei."

She had training. Instincts. But no self-control. Her hand flew true and sharp across his face. "How dare you!" Beads of light sprinkled her vision. She staggered. "How could you . . .?" She blinked to regain her senses. To shake off the dizziness that washed over her.

"Kersei?"

She blinked again, but this time nothing. A shout followed her into the blackness.

Shame. Sadness. Indignation. Anger. Last eve, those scents had rolled into a painful concoction that stopped Marco from taking Kersei into his arms, comforting her—and himself—and pushed him back into the fray of political machinations. When her scent dimmed, he'd pivoted, knowing something was wrong. His heart jolted to find Darius shooting him a fierce scowl as he carried an unconscious Kersei across the hall to a side room. Later, the pharmakeia reported the fainting was due to stress and dehydration. Too much too soon after what Symmachia put her through.

Assuredly the pregnancy contributed to what happened, but that was not yet known to most. Marco had exacerbated things by what he'd allowed to transpire between them at the gala. He thought if he could just be close to her, that would be enough. It wasn't. He'd wanted her in his arms.

"*. . . I love you, Marco.*" The kisses they'd shared on the transport had been passionate and deep, but what existed between them went beyond the physical.

On the balcony of his apartments within Kardia, Marco rotated his arm and stared at his mark. What had once been black as his cloak was now a lingering pale blue that churned beneath his skin.

The futility of this new life rankled. Drove Marco off the balustrade outside his quarters. He launched up and caught the ledge above. Hand over hand, he slid to the right. Held the corner, then dragged himself onto the third-level ledge. He toed the lip and jumped to the side. Hooked a column. Slid a few feet, but found traction and scurried up. A few more leaps delivered him to the turret. He tic-tacked up to the roof, then zigzagged up the steep slope and perched on the spine.

With an expelled breath, he squinted south to the rubble of Stratios Hall. To the southwest and far from sight sat the walled city of the Xanthus. Farther south still was Trachys, and west of them the Prokopios along the *Va'Una Issi*—the desert interrupted only by deep crevasses that ran for leagues. So many people he did not know.

Laughter below drew his thoughts back to Kardia. Kersei. He would know her Signature anywhere. Instinct told him to find her. *Go to her.*

But he could not. Would not. He had nearly compromised his honor once. She was bound to Darius. Carried his child. Which he only knew because of the twin lights in her eyes, an effect of the prophecy that enabled him to see a person's true character.

Laughter persisted from the west lawn, taunting.

Stay where you are. She is not your concern.

As medora, were not all Kalonicans now his concern?

Interference will only hinder an already fractured relationship with Darius.

Did they have a relationship? Hunters weren't concerned with relationships. Only the Code.

Which held honor above all else.

Marco grunted. *I am no longer a hunter.* He hopped up and moved along the handspan-wide peak, lowered into a crouch, and inched closer. The lawn had a garden and, at the most distant edge, a machitis training yard.

There, Kersei walked away from a powerfully built aerios who stood near a hay-packed dummy. "Stand clear." She held a long silver weapon. "You saw how wide my last throw went."

"When you are experienced with it, you will hit an apple from my head."

She laughed again, lining up the throw, then with a hustle, sent the rod downrange.

Marco fisted a hand to his mouth, watching her. So alive. So fiery. So beautiful. So . . . *Kersei.*

"What do you here after what happened last eve?" The barked remonstration came from immediately below, seconds before Darius strode into the sun and across the lawn.

"I would train with this javrod." Kersei's scent flared defiant. "It was a gift from—"

"You are princessa with a contingent of regia at your call. There is no need for you to wield a weapon."

Now anger infused her scent. "You sound like your father."

"He was a wise medora." Darius reached her.

"I-I did not—I beg your mercy," Kersei offered, radiating grief and sorrow. "You know I meant no—"

"Aye." Darius pulled her into his arms. "I know you did not."

The ache in Marco's chest exploded. Twisted and writhed past his honor. He punched the clay roof. Let the rage course through, trying to restrain himself. Decided he could not, so he slanted his legs away and slid down the opposite slope, half willing the dangerous speed to tear him from this torment.

Instead, he sailed off the roof and rotated to catch the cornice. Eyeing the façade, he swung at a window several feet over. Missed the edge. Plummeted, his fingers groping for traction, for a hold.

Shouts below warned he'd been spotted.

Marco caught a brick. Stopped his descent, feeling his fingertips burn. He spidered over to the window. Grabbed the sill and eyed the lower one.

"You could continue acting like the diabolus himself," came a gravelly voice, "or you could come in and stop alarming your regia."

Marco peered up at the window above, which framed none other than Ixion. "And miss my chance to taunt them for not protecting me?"

Ixion winged an eyebrow. "We have lost one medora already this cycle."

With a grunt, Marco used a toehold to shove up. Hiked his legs up and over the ledge. He landed softly on the marble sill. "Unfair, using guilt." Eyeing the Stalker's sweaty brow and scuffed boots, he sniffed. "You were tracking me."

"How would it look if I let you kill yourself?"

Marco sat back on the windowsill, thinking, staring at the hall filled with portraits of his forebears. Medoras on one side, kyrias on the other. When would that vision he'd had on the cliffs come to pass? How wretched to hope for it, since that would mean the death of his brother. Yet how could he give up on Kersei being his, of them having sons? At all hours, day and night, her Signature called to him. No more could he endure it. "Death would be more bearable."

"And more permanent."

Marco stretched his neck as they stalked down the marbled hall, the hand-carved rugs padding his steps as he passed beneath the life-size gazes of his forebears. "That is not as negative as you might believe."

"I must disagree."

Glancing at his First as he turned on the wide landing, he collided with someone. "Sorry." He caught their shoulders and pivoted to avoid injury— then saw the curls. Her eyes. "Kersei." How? She had been on the lawn.

"Your . . . Majesty." After a slight curtsy, she slid a look to the elder and her smile faltered. "Sir Ixion."

"Princessa."

Marco stepped away, searched the hall and lower foyer. "Where is Darius?"

"Tending something with the aerios."

Then not here. "You were practicing."

Surprise leapt into her features and pleasure into her scent. "I was." Her tentative smile obliterated his ability to think. "Jez gave me a new javrod on . . ."

The *Macedon*. That's what she'd been about to say. It'd been where Jez Sidra and Tigo Deken had plotted Kersei's escape from Captain Baric. Apparently, with a weapon.

She drew straight. "I would be proficient with it."

Of course she would. She had looked beautiful in the yard, doing what she loved, and now her countenance was brightened by the exercise. "I am glad for you."

"You are? Darius—" Wide eyes darted away, nervous. "Not many believe women should enjoy such . . . aggressive activities."

"Perhaps that should change."

A grin forced light back into her eyes. "I said as much to Darius." She shrugged, her scent rank with restraint and nerves, which annoyed him. "If we are to face the enemy predicted in the prophecy"—she angled the arm with her half of the pale-blue mark—"we should be prepared."

"Aye." Somehow he had closed the gap between them again, drawn by her fiery nature. The same desire saturated her Signature.

Curse it all! He would be with her. *They* were marked as one. Attraction spiraled between them. Just a touch. To feel her silken cheek . . . sate the fire in his gut. Her breath faltered, like his own.

Ixion cleared his throat.

Frustration coiled, Marco lowered his head. Glanced at his First, whose gaze was on a shadow. It was then Marco realized he'd been so distracted by the wicked lure he had not detected— "Darius, do you not agree with your bound?"

Kersei drew in a quick breath, her scent worried, as she moved aside.

"I do not." Darius swaggered over and kissed her. "Practice and sparring were well enough when she was an elder's daughter, but she is now princessa."

"Exactly." Marco would enjoy this. "Should we not want our enemy and our people to see strength when they look to Kardia?"

"Strength is not only in a weapon or a blow." Darius's nostrils flared. "Father said it often. Had you remained here instead of going off with the Kynigos, he would have taught you the same."

The barb thumped Marco hard. He stared down the insolent pup and itched to take him to ground as he had first-years at the Citadel.

"Darius, please," Kersei whispered.

"What?" He wrapped an arm around her, gloating. "I speak true. He walked out."

"You know not of what you speak," Marco bit out. "You were a squalling babe when the master came for me. Aye, I would've preferred more time with our parents, but I have no regrets for the life the Ancient chose for me."

"No regrets?" Anger drenched Darius's efflux, but there was . . . more. "You hold no regret not knowing the people you rule, the brother who trains your army, the parents who made this realm flourish?" His gaze narrowed. "Do you not realize, *Achilus*, that had you stayed and been raised as father's heir, *you* could have bound with Kersei?"

"Darius!" Kersei hissed.

Fury tightened Marco's shoulders, and he sensed Ixion shift closer.

"She is what you want, aye?" Challenge lurked in his brother's eyes. "Tell me, will I come home one day to find you bedding her?"

Marco lunged but was caught by Ixion's firm grip.

Tears flashing in her eyes, Kersei spun toward their apartments and hurried out of sight.

"Prince Darius," Ixion said, "address our medora like that again—"

"No." Marco snapped up a hand. Angled toward his brother. "You're a fool. You set a dagger to strike me but it found a softer heart. If you injure her again with your callous words . . ." He nodded toward the residence. "Go. See to her."

"Tell me *not* how to take care of—"

"So, it's true," Marco said, letting a long pause linger until he anak'd uncertainty in his brother. "Spoiled princes care only for themselves."

Darius grabbed Marco's shirt.

Regia manifested and wrangled his brother back as Marco stared him down. Watched those wild blue eyes growing more distant. It stung that he did not know his brother—the only two left of their family, and this was their relationship.

"Your Majesty." Ixion moved in, his presence encouraging Marco down the corridor, to his residence.

Marco stalked through his solar to the bedchamber. Yanked open the dressing room doors. Snatched his Kynigos ruck. He stormed around, grabbing pants and tunics.

Ixion eyed the satchel. "Donating to orphans?"

"I cannot stay here another click," Marco grumbled. "The next time he gets in my face, I will do something I regret."

"This is *your* home. The seat of the kingdom *you* rule," Ixion ground out. "Have *them* removed. His petulance is warrant enough, and the way he antagonizes—"

"No."

"It is your right. Do it, for your own sake. I see how it torments you—"

"Kersei is with child."

Ixion pulled up straight. "They have been reunited but a short time. How can you know this?"

Misery held Marco fast as he shook his head. "Since the Temple . . . the *Orasi* . . ." Hating the gift, hating that he knew, Marco returned to packing. "If I touch a person's skin, I can see"—what was it?—"their *adunatos*. By the color of light, I know if they can be trusted. I know not how this is possible. Mayhap it is simply the Lady guiding me. At the Temple, when Kersei bid me farewell, I saw twin lights in her eyes. Hers . . ."

"And a babe." Silver-gray hair, long and plaited, gave Ixion a fierce visage— especially with the scar that bisected the left side of his face and neck. "You are sure? The royal pharmakeia has said nothing—"

"Kersei may not yet have sought confirmation." Marco gathered his gear, the pieces familiar and reassuring. "If I force Darius from Kardia, she must go as well, and the times are too dangerous. Kersei must remain here, safe."

"Is that the true reason?" Ixion challenged.

Marco drew up straight. Stared hard at the man.

"You do this tour, but when you return, she will still be here. Driving you mad."

Though he wanted to argue, Marco sagged. Pinched the bridge of his nose, his receptors closed so he did not have the perpetual taunt of her Signature. "I can no longer endure it, not his pleasure or . . ." He dared not impugn her character by mentioning the attraction still spiraling from her. Nor would he address the other scent, the one budding through Kersei in the rare moments when Darius chained his jealousy and treated her as would a man in love. "As intended, I'll travel the lands my brother so pointedly said I do not know, and I will learn."

"You're a Class-A hardhead who doesn't belong on this team!" Gunny pointed to the doors. "Get out! I warned you last time. Report to your bunk and wait for your expulsion!"

Foul plagues of the universe!

Eija stomped from the simdeck and punched open the door. It bucked and thumped her shoulder. With a growl, she shoved it again, then struck it with her helmet. She pivoted and stormed from the academics hall, heart pounding. Hit the paneled wall. She stopped and tried to catch her breath, forehead against the cool surface. Anger writhed and churned. Erupted— and she directed the full force of her fury at the wall. Kicking it and earning a sickening crack in her toe. But something bigger within her had already broken. She slammed her helmet against the wall. Over and over. Which did nothing to allay the fury. Breathing hard, as if environmentals had failed, she collapsed against the paneling, fighting tears.

A solid thunk of a door warned someone had exited the facility.

The sound spurred Eija toward the residence hall.

"Eija!"

Wind in her ears made it impossible to identify who called. Really, she didn't care who it was.

Patron would be furious with her. She broke into a run, plowed through the doors to housing, and accessed their wing. "Augh!" She flung her helmet across the bunk room. Ripped off her Shepherd tunic and pitched it at the recycle bin. She dropped onto her bunk and buried her face in her hands. Curled her fingers in her hair. Growled a scream. Why? Why couldn't she just do the djelling program? Do what they said was right?

But no, she had to think she was smarter. And it'd cost her everything. Shattered her chance to get on the *Prevenire*. She thought if she kept trying her way, it'd sort itself out. She'd show them the sim wasn't right. Instead, she just . . . scuzzed herself.

"I have to fix this," she whispered. "Prove . . ."

"Yes, you do," Patron said.

Eija jerked up to find the woman standing six paces in front of her. She glanced at the door—how had she come in without a sound? Why hadn't Eija heard the clip of her shoes? "Where did you—"

"Do you remember why I came to you three years ago?"

She swallowed. "To give me this chance." *Which I scuzzed.*

"But why would I do that, Eija? Why would I offer you an escape from that world?"

"You said the universe needed someone like me."

Patron set her hands behind her back and stalked forward, chin lifted, brunette hair neatly coiled into a bun. "Not just someone like you, Eija. They needed *you*. Those instincts that got you your wings in record time. That got you into HyPE." She arched a rueful brow at the Shepherd tunic dangling in the bin. "Are you going to throw it away so easily when I risked *everything* to bring you out of the Pit?"

Somehow, Eija felt the disappointment and frustration coursing through her patron, and it sharpened her own. "I'm sorry," she said, wanting to squeeze the life out of something. "But it's wrong. They're wrong."

"So are you." Patron angled her head and speared her with a glower.

"The physics—"

"Can you prove it?"

Looking into eyes so confident and fierce, Eija grunted. Wilted. "No."

"Then do what they tell you. For now." She was somehow directly in front of Eija. Her touch was like a pulse blast against Eija's skin. "Do whatever it takes to get on that ship. Do not fail us."

"It's too late. I'm shredded. Gunny said as much, told me to wait here—"

The outer door to the barracks opened, and she checked over her shoulder. When she looked back, Patron was gone. What . . .?

"That took some real cranium," came a deep, mocking voice that belonged to annoying golden boy of the fleet—after Tigo Deken vanished—Sergeant Reef Jadon. Most likely to succeed—at everything. Perfect scores. Perfect tactics. Perfect leadership. Perfect smile . . . hair . . . teeth. Always friendly to everyone with that ever-present grin.

"Here to gloat?" She stomped to the bin and shoved the tunic in the rest of the way. "Well, don't worry. I'll be gone soon and won't affect your perfect scores anymore." Not even Patron could fix what she'd screwed up. She retrieved her flex screen, then focused on clearing out her locker. "Now you and the others will have to find someone else to mock."

"You wound me." He placed a hand over his heart.

She had no energy for his games. Packing her few belongings, she heard metal whingeing and glanced aside.

He turned from the bin with her tunic and his infamous rogue grin.

"What're you—"

"You give up too easy." Holding the neck hole, he aimed it at her head. "No matter what Command determines, you're a Shepherd."

"Plagues," she hissed, waving him off. "Shepherds are meant to lead others to safety, not destruction!"

"You'll get there." Insisting she hold still, he threaded the shirt over her head and tugged it down her shoulders. He had this expression in his gray eyes that made her belly flip. Her heart race. What did he want? Surely he—

No, he couldn't. Nobody ever would.

She knocked him back. The bunk clipped his legs. He went down, grabbing for purchase—and caught her tunic. Yanked her forward, right into a headbutt with him.

She yelped and stumbled around to avoid landing on him. Beside him on the bunk, she slapped his shoulder. "What is your malfunction?"

"What's *yours*?" He tipped his head back, holding his bleeding nose.

"Djell." At the crimson sliding over his lip, she grabbed a towel from her ruck and thrust it at him. "I'm sorry. I—" She was sick of apologizing to everyone. "What d'you want? Why are you even here?"

Towel to his nose, he looked up at her and grunted. "I wanted to ask why you thought the sim was wrong."

Eija stilled. "You believe me?"

His gaze buzzed hers, then veered off.

"Right." Of course he didn't—no one on the team did. After again removing the Shepherd's tunic, she grabbed her tattered brown hide jacket and threaded her arms through it.

"Why're you packing?"

"You heard the gunny—I'm out."

"That's not what I heard."

She rolled her eyes, recalling the words from only moments ago. "Okay, fine— 'You're a Class-A hardhead who doesn't belong on this team!'" Arms folded, she cocked her head. "Better?"

"Crafter has an asteroid up his butt after what happened to him," Jadon stated flatly. "He yells at everyone. If you haven't gotten that expulsion order yet—"

Her flex screen chimed. She threw Jadon an arched eyebrow as she grabbed it, ready for the fateful message, and opened said communiqué. "Getting in was always a lost . . ." She frowned at the message. Her pulse skipped a beat.

"What?"

"I'm to report to Lieutenant Diggins's office." Why would he want her there? "Probably plans to make me pay back training costs."

Jadon stood, tossing the bloodied towel in the bin, cleaned his face at a sink, then turned to her. Holy Void, he was gorgeous. "Why d'you think the sim was wrong?"

"Because." Explaining . . . he'd only think her spaced. How did she justify . . . instinct? "It just was."

"But intel—"

"Nobody's been there, so how do they know? Not one person from the science team that developed the sim's jump program or constructed the hyperaccelerated slipstream jump protocols has actually experienced those or been to Kuru System."

"Neither have you," he countered, "so how can *you* know it's wrong?"

Hands curled into fists, she recalled the heat in her palm. She squinted, realizing that if she was about to get spaced anyway, she had nothing to lose. "I could . . . feel it."

Holding her gaze, Jadon slowly nodded. Like he understood. Like he didn't think she was shredded. Then he smiled. "You always were a little weird."

She carried that hurt all the way back to the Academy's admin deck. Outside the lieutenant's door, she paused, took a breath, then stepped forward. The barrier whisked open to reveal Diggins ending a comm call. "Corporal Zacdari reporting as ordered, sir."

His features were dark, darker than Tryssinians. "Come in, Corporal."

Eija entered and took the seat he indicated.

First Lieutenant Diggins flicked his fingers in the air, and a holo sprang between them. A recording of her sim ran, reminding her of every move, every mistake she'd made in the last several weeks. With an apathetic gaze, he dismissed the screen, sat back, and threaded his fingers. Eyes narrowed on her, he didn't say anything for several long, awkward hours. Okay, maybe it was minutes. Or seconds.

The compunction to explain ruptured her control. Told her to beg forgiveness, to promise she'd never do it again . . .

But she would. Because that's who she was, especially with a conviction this deep. Like Jadon said—a little weird.

"Why did you deviate from a near-perfect trajectory in the sim?" He was calm, nothing but his lips moving. "Why did you veer off and then, in a moment of panic, put your corvette in a spin that flung it into the rings, destroying both it and the 'vette?"

"It wasn't panic."

Dark brown eyes challenged her. "You intentionally blew up your ship and crew?"

"Of course not, sir." Eija stared at the air where the vidscreen—and her guilt—had hung.

"Then what?"

She swallowed. "I . . . don't know, sir."

"I think you do," he said firmly. "You see, Corporal Zacdari, I have spent every hour possible perfecting HyPE and its training modules. I am intimately familiar with every Shepherd candidate. I know your every move, your every word. I know *you*." He came forward in his chair and rested his arms on the spotless surface. "You won't do it again—that's what you've said every time you failed a sim." His left eye narrowed. "But you haven't said that to me here."

"I'm gone, sir." It surprised how small her voice sounded. "Sergeant Crafter said I don't belong here. He's right."

The lieutenant frowned and angled his head. "Why aren't you fighting for this?"

She felt punched in the chest. Wondered . . . "Would it do any good?"

"Would it hurt to try?" he asked. "Are you so willing to walk away from this dream? I thought you wanted to get away from here."

She dared not breathe the hope that lingered between them. "I'd do anything to be on the *Prevenire*, sir."

"I was hoping you'd say that."

LAMPROS CITY, KALONICA, DROSERO

She had betrayed the very essence of who she was and whom she loved. Kersei stood on the terratza, looking out at the Kalonican Sea, which seemed in a perpetual state of rage. Just like her heart. Hugging the wrap tighter, she closed her eyes, shutting out the despair she'd felt at the Temple when Marco did nothing as Darius led her away. Took her to the bedchamber. Lay with her.

"Think you this is less a torment for me, detecting my brother's pleasure?"

"Then it pains you?"

"No, it wrenches my gut. Sours my food. Fouls my drink. Skewers my head. Everything has become vile and cruel."

Nothing could be done. By the laws of Kalonica, she had been irrevocably bound to Darius the night of the Delta Presentation, the night her family died and her life forever changed. The ceremony and pronouncement were legally binding, enough to rend her from Marco, no matter how much they loved each other.

"Kersei!" Darius stood on the paved patio and motioned her back inside.

Could she not have a minute's peace? She had thirty paces to shift her dour mood into a smile. "What is it?"

Darius smirked as he tucked her hand in the crook of his arm. "Our medora has left to tour the lands." His meaning was clear—Marco was gone, *from her.*

She buried her heartache. "This pleases you."

Jaw muscle twitching, he stretched his neck.

"Darius, I made my choice at the Temple. I went with you, allowed . . . what happened."

He narrowed his blue eyes, the scars pinking with anger. "Allowed."

"'Tis not a slight, only . . ." She sighed. Touched his hand. "I love Marco and thought . . ." She huffed. "Regardless, I knew you and I were legally bound."

He flung off her hand as he walked. "I do not need my bound to *allow* me anything. And for you to speak of your feelings for my brother—"

"Would you have me lie?" Her heart rammed into her ribs. "I may be your bound, but I am also a woman with feelings and one who has endured great loss. What happened—"

"Is *done*," he hissed, leaning in. "Just because I'm disfigured, doesn't mean—"

"Nay!" she objected, eyeing the marred flesh of his face and neck. "I would never—"

"Yet you even now stare!"

"If you believe I am so wretched as to judge a person's worth on appearance, then you have never known me."

"What of my brother's appearance? Did you not judge him when you cuckolded me?"

Her hand flew fast and true, stinging across his cheek.

Regia Hadrien and Caio shifted, only then making Kersei realize what she'd done. She dropped her gaze and hands, fisting them. "You are heartless!"

"Never again will you be alone with him."

"Aye, since you just said Marco has gone."

"Belak will not leave your side, save when you enter our bedchamber."

She drew up, heart pounding. "Then I am to be a prisoner?"

"I will not have you running off to rendezvous with my brother."

A week of riding could not deliver Marco from the torment. He and Ixion had reached the southwestern territories of Kalonica, a good place to start—the farthest reaches of the realm and still Kersei' scent tormented.

Impossible. No Kynigos could anak that far. Yet . . . he could.

He had endured the hardpacked earth beneath his head at night and the muscled spine of the Great Black named Vahor beneath his legs at day as proof that life was not easy or painless. "This would have been easier," he muttered as they crested a jagged rise overlooking a small village some distance north of Prokopios, "had we used my scout."

"Which would have violated the Droseran-Tertian Accord, the one your father authored and championed."

"I always thought him closed-minded. When I wanted to shoot his bow, he refused."

"Were you not six cycles?"

"Five," Marco chuckled, at home in his long cloak and boots. He detected a bevy of scents. "What village do we near?"

"Cragshead." For the next hour, they rode across the hot, dry land to a small but bustling community. At a tavern, Ixion led them to a table at the back, where they positioned themselves to keep an eye on the door and kitchen passage.

"Mavridis." A burly man with a voice like rocks limped over to them. His efflux was spiked with nerves, fear. "What brings you here, my lord?"

My lord? How had he recognized Marco?

"Supplies and refreshment, for us and the horses, Brak." Ixion glanced around the busy tables.

"Of course, sir."

"I don't see Martul," Ixion said.

Ah. "My lord" referred to the Stalker, who was elder of this entoli.

"Group went down to Hillioke after the last attack. Sent a runner to Prokopios to lodge complaint and get help."

Ixion's face may have been hewn of stone, but his heart was not. A distinct, spiced anger shot out. "Help will come."

"Thank you, Mavridis." Brak spiraled with relief. "What can I get you two gents to drink?"

"Mother's milk," Ixion said.

"Warmed cordi."

The two gave him a cockeyed look, but Brak shrugged and limped away as Ixion rapped his knuckles on the table. "The blue raiders grow more brazen."

"Blue raiders?"

"Irukandji," Ixion clarified. "Bloodthirsty savages from Hirakys who once lived peacefully among the people but slowly, violently became a scourge."

"And Brak sends to your entoli for *one* Stalker." Marco knew the Plisiázon had earned the nickname for the way they stalked the enemy along the border, but what could one do against these raiders?

"My men are effective. Efficient," Ixion said quietly. "Whoever goes will rout the raiders and provide overwatch while they rebuild."

"Only one?" Marco balked.

"It has always been enough. The raiders expect lambs for the slaughter, not men like aetos, vicious and unrelenting."

The tactic mirrored the Kynigos, but hunters were not fighting, only tracking and webbing. It was hard to imagine one Plisiázon against bloodthirsty raiders. "So, villagers remain though attacked?"

"It is their home," Ixion said with an edge. "If we moved every time someone thought to adjust our situation, Kalonica would be the size of a nut."

Brak returned with tankards. "I've sent Tharlie around back to freshen your Blacks. Karolie is in the kitchen packing foodstuffs for you."

Ixion reached into his pocket and paid him. "Thank you, Brak."

Marco lifted his tankard and threw back a mouthful—and nearly gagged. Came up choking. Eyes watering, he tried to catch his breath. "*What* is this?" He cleared his throat.

With a mischievous grin, Ixion switched mugs. "You have mine."

"That's not milk."

"It's Brak's mother's special recipe. A bit of liquor to chase away sickness and something like vitamins for the long, hot ride."

Marco thumped his chest. "Has a burn to it. I'll stick with cordi." He gripped the tankard and gulped. Then shuddered, screwing his face. "Ack!"

"What?"

"It's cold!"

"You're in the desert. Nobody has hot drinks down here." Ixion drained his tankard.

"Maybe water—"

"No," Ixion grunted. "Never get water from Brak. Trust me."

"I almost prefer your 'milk' to cold cordi."

With food and freshened horses, they rode well into the night and camped on a cleft. Up before dawn, they mounted and kept riding. The brutal unrelenting vigor of the sun sent sweat racing down Marco's spine and temples. Heat baked his skin crimson. It packed his senses, thickened scents. Again beneath the starlit night, he fell asleep in the embrace of memories with Kersei, their time on the stardeck. Their kiss . . .

Halfway through the next rise, Marco felt Ixion's gaze and curiosity for a while, then it drifted away. And returned. "On Cenon, I told you to ask what you will of me."

"Just learning the man who is my medora."

"And?"

"Few men are content to be in their own head for hours without a word to the company they keep."

Marco smirked. "And who is the other?"

Ixion frowned.

"You said 'few men.' Since you refer to me and clearly you are of the same mind, who is the third?"

Ixion bit off some jerky. "I have yet to meet him."

They both chuckled but a sharp scent flew through Marco's receptors. He struck out a hand—and it smacked Ixion's. Apparently he, too, had detected trouble. Yet only rocks and scrubland stretched before them. Where was it coming from?

Marco squinted ahead but saw nothing. His keen senses were without error, yet somehow did no good. Where . . .?

To his surprise, Ixion dismounted and dropped the reins to his Black, Tarjax, who trotted away as if sensing the trouble. Marco followed his First and crouch-ran, until they flattened themselves on the ground.

What in the reek . . .?

Marco realized they were at the edge of the gorges, which seemed more like a steep canyon, carved deep and long through the land. From this vantage, he spied numerous rock formations that jutted up but still did not reach ground level. Hewn into the gorge walls and formations were dozens, if not hundreds, of dwellings!

Just before the gorge bent southward, three men stood in an open area with a fourth on his knees before them. This was what Marco's receptors had keyed into. "They're going to kill him." Other villagers lurked out of sight, watching but not participating in—or stopping—this madness.

Ixion remained unmoving and unfazed.

"We should go down, speak to them."

Drenched in disgust and sorrow, Ixion backtracked on his belly, then rose and returned to their horses.

Dumbfounded by his First, Marco considered the men. Thought of going alone to intervene. No obvious path presented itself, but with his skills he didn't need stairs. There, a ledge with a toehold below. If he—

A woman screamed, yanking Marco's gaze back to the scene. The kneeling man lay on the ground, dead, his blood sating the parched earth.

Hands fisted, Marco pushed up and started around to the ledge he'd seen.

A hand caught his shoulder.

Instinct had Marco catch the wrist and drove under the arm, then up and over.

"Do not." Ixion stepped back. "I beg your mercy." He inclined his head, raised his palms. "Come away before you are spotted, and I will explain."

Though reticent, Marco knew the dead man could not be brought back to life. "Is this who you are?" He stalked after Ixion, who whistled for the horses. "Is this what wastelanders allow—killing men by mob? A man who allows injustice—"

Ixion stopped short, rounding on Marco. The nostrils of his arrow-straight nose flared. Fury assailed the air. "You are new to these lands, and my medora, so I will grant mercy for your stinging accusation birthed in ignorance."

Surprised at the acerbic tone, Marco lifted his eyebrows. "Enlighten me."

"You are a trained hunter, are you not?"

Was there a point to the question?

"What does that nose of yours tell? What did you detect?"

Marco considered the question, considered the very knowing gaze. Recalled the attack scent. Which was coupled with intent—rage, bloodlust . . . "Revenge."

"Aye," Ixion said. "Down here there is only one justification for killing in the square." His breathing slowed. "Life for a life. The man took someone's life, so they took his."

Not his favorite measure of justice, but it worked in some societies. Marco eased off. He had wronged Ixion with his assumption, his quick instinct to protect and exact justice.

"Even among wastelanders, there is a code," Ixion said as the horses returned. "We live a hard life with the sun as much our enemy as the Irukandji, but we simply want an honest, peaceful living."

Marco climbed onto Vahor. "What of the courts?"

"The gorges are claimed by Hirakys, and the desert is their court." Ixion retrieved his waterskin and took a sip. "Even Jherakans use desert justice, though their capital is as impressive as Lampros City."

"Hirakys claims land so far into Kalonica?" Each time Marco turned, he learned something new of this realm he ruled, a task that felt more daunting every day. "Did my father know of this?"

"There is little Zarek did not know, but he also knew to choose his battles." Ixion squinted to the south. "The gorges start—or end, depending on your view—in Hirakys, near Greyedge and the fire gorges. They claim the underground cities as theirs, and after decades of bloody skirmishes, we have chosen to leave them to their justice."

"Are they a danger to Kalonica?"

"The Plisiázon ensure Hirakyns remain belowground or behind borders. We offer no mercy when they are found in our land, and they accept our response. Most within the gorges simply want to be left to their own."

"And yet they enact a life-for-life policy."

Ixion rode in silence for a few minutes. "When you find this perfect world you dream of, where justice is not needed, do not invite me."

Marco glanced at him.

"Because if I come, it will no longer be perfect."

"You say the Irukandji are Hirakyn?"

Days later, crouched on a precipice overlooking Va'Una Issi, Marco scanned the rugged terrain. To the west, more desert and rock burned beneath the relentless sun, and the peak of a mountain in the far distance rose as forbidding as the bleakness of space. To the south lay Hirakys, home of the Irukandji.

The slow bob of Ixion's head matched the languorous pace they'd taken since leaving Cragshead. "It is even said the first man marked by the Faa'Cris was a prince of Hirakys. He was sent out of the city and into the most unforgiving parts of the desert. There, evil bred and swarmed into the infestation we now battle."

Somehow, this region amplified the loneliness Marco had felt since coming to Drosero, though he appreciated the time and space Ixion afforded him as they journeyed. It had been seven weeks since they'd departed Iereania, and he had begun to resolve himself to the path set before him.

"Moidia"—Ixion jutted his chin to a cluster of ramshackle buildings just to the south—"den of the lawless."

After another quick swallow from a waterskin, Marco secured the stopper. "I want to go down there."

Ixion's expression went grim. "That is . . . ill advised. The plan was to show you the outlying villages, then journey to Prokopios to—"

"Noted."

"As your First," Ixion said, "it is my duty to protect you so that Kalonica has a medora to rule."

"You doubt me."

Steely eyes pinched as Ixion considered the lands. "I doubt the survival of the realm should you fall without kyria or heir. Your brother will take the throne."

Marco considered Ixion and the bald words, chose to ignore the kyria comment. "What know you of Darius?"

Looking over the lands, Ixion sighed. "Only what your father told me—the prince is soft, pliable, which could be a good thing . . ."

"But to a cunning enemy . . ."

"One cannot help but wonder at what price he was saved from the ruins."

Marco scowled, anak'ing more than his First's rank disapproval. "You suggest he was bought, then betrayed our—"

"I suggest nothing."

Aye, he did. Though Marco would pursue the discussion, the air roiled with trouble. He squinted at the lawless camp still a half league off. Desperation clung to its shadows with a stench that matched the refuse on the southeastern edge. He fisted a hand, unsettled at what he detected. Sadness hung as rank as desperation. Darkness blanketed the most southwestern part of the city. Had they no torches?

"Once," Ixion said as he knelt beside him, "it was a thriving outpost, the last city before entering the Va'Una Issi. But with frequent Irukandji raids, travelers stopped coming, profits plummeted, and poverty came in like ravenous criemwolf."

"Criemwolf?"

"Large gray hounds with a massive appetite, they only hunt at night, so they were named after the large moon. Vicious teeth on them and little tolerance for people. Irukandji and Hirakyns prize the pelts."

"Not you?"

"What need have we for pelt hide so near the fire gorges?"

"For your cold heart," he teased.

"Then you'll want one as well, eh?"

Marco laughed—but a spiked efflux saturated with balsam and cedar struck him. He rotated, coming upright. No longer could it be ignored. "There's trouble."

Ixion straightened. "Where?"

"South."

A trilling whistle came on the wind, carrying alarm and anger. Then another.

Ixion shoved around. "Raiders!" He swung up onto Tarjax.

"You know this how?" Marco asked, as he mounted and gathered his reins.

"Those whistles were my men—there are two here already, which alone warns me there are many Irukandji."

Marco drew up Vahor as an acrid scent hit his nostrils. "Fire." As they spurred their horses down the canyon wall and across the open plain, the evening sky took on an angry crimson hue. Spouts of flame leapt up in the darkened town with the sudden violence of an adder's strike.

"They're burning it!" Ixion shouted as their horses tore up the distance between them and the buildings.

Ahead, a screaming little boy of perhaps three trotted out, his arms hanging straight out as he called for his mother.

"No mercy for the raiders," Ixion shouted. "Or your life will be forfeit."

Marco's gut tightened—it was not a threat but a warning.

A blur of blue, stark in the darkening day, darted into the open and snatched the boy.

Heart in his throat, Marco pressed his chest to Vahor's neck, the Black seeming to sense the urgency, hooves thundering with Marco's pulse. Angling his head, Marco anak'd for the boy . . . found his terrified scent, a taste bitter on his tongue.

The open outskirts quickly surrendered to multi-storied buildings. Ixion pulled into the lead and flew down the narrow street.

Marco went for the boy, darting into an alley—which immediately pitched him into a whirl of chaos. Darkness swooped in. People, animals, and the foul stench of poverty challenged his senses.

Shouts and screams scored his attention. He shouldered into the focus, homing in on the scent.

Ahead, a family of five darted into a thatched-roof hut, the door thwapping shut.

Smart.

Yet their roof came alive with flames.

No! He diverted. Threw himself off the Black. Kicked open the door. "Get out! It's burning!" Even as he ensured the family safe, he was searching for the boy again. But there were too many odors of panic and terror flooding his receptors. He could not close them at a time like this. The itch to go high drove him at a wall. To the roof. There, he caught sight of Ixion.

The Stalker glanced up, the moonslight gleaming silver in his hair, and after a momentary scent of irritation—no doubt because his medora had thrown himself into the fray—he nodded.

Marco might not know this town, but he knew scents, and they never erred. Anak'ing, he raced over buildings, tracking both Ixion and the scents. He jumped across a road and rolled through the landing. Came up. His foot shot through a rotted board.

"Reek!" He hauled himself back up and caught a stinging smell. The smoke . . . was closer.

A swell of rage and sadistic pleasure rushed through the air.

Marco dropped to a knee on the roof. Stared across the road to the darkness of a sanctuary. Peals rang from the bell tower, its reverberation thumping against his chest. An ominous scent rammed his receptors, stilling him. Anticipating raiders, Marco crouched low into the shadows.

Raiders moved through the streets, throwing torches, driving shivs into innocents scrambling for safety. With feral howls they advanced on the sanctuary, their skin alight with glowing blue lines and arcs curling across arms and chests.

His own brand glowed but didn't move beneath his skin like theirs, as if something within sought to loose itself.

Marco swallowed, watching these dark creatures prowl Moidia. He peered across rooftops and spotted two Stalkers moving with ferocious determination against the frenzy of the raiders. Sight and kill, sight and kill seemed to be their method, their movements graceful and lethally beautiful. He was not sure who was more terrifying.

The raiders aimed for the sanctuary, their gazes wild and fevered—yet focused.

There was something discordant here.

They glanced up at the bell tower, the gonging apparently agony to their ears. Or an invitation for another soul to slay. They slammed through the front door, likely heading for the tower to kill whoever sounded the alarm.

Not if he could help it. Marco backed up and pitched himself across the gap to the slanted sanctuary roof. His hands met hot shingles. Letting go, he twisted and flung himself to the side, catching a pipe sticking up out of the wood. He hiked upward. Hopped to his feet, only then anak'ing the discordance again. Perched there, he felt disoriented, lost. What was that? Why . . .?

No scent . . .

A strangled scream from within yanked him forward. He dashed across the tiles and vaulted up, catching the lip of the bell tower's opening. Hanging there, he peeked in to assess the threat. Vibrations from the deafening bells shivered through his body.

The interior was larger than expected. Three raiders wrangled a priest—a woman, a priest*ess*. She twisted, trying to free herself, blonde hair tumbling loose across her shoulders. Roughly forty cycles, face smudged with ash, she yet had her beauty and fight.

He popped over the ledge and landed with a soft thump.

Attention swung toward him, raiders stomped closer.

Spotting him, the woman shouted, "No! You canna' be here!"

A raider leered at him. "You smell too pretty for this pigsty."

"You smell . . . empty." When a blade glinted, Marco lunged in. Caught the man by the throat and pinned him against stucco. Using him as a balance, he swiped feet out from under the second. Another barreled from the side. Knocked Marco to the ground. His breath seared Marco's nostrils—sulfur. A contorted face with yellow eyes filled with bloodlust and . . . pleasure.

Now, a haunting, terrifying scent pulsed, warning Marco if he did not turn this, he would not live to see another rise. He stabbed his hand into the man's throat, crushing his larynx. Choking, the raider fell back.

Seeing another coming up, Marco wrapped his legs around the raider's and brought him down. Grabbed the man's head. Snapped his neck. He understood now Ixion's warning and desert justice—the only form these raiders understood.

Easing his dagger from its sheath, Marco gauged the remaining raider holding the woman. Knew he could hit the raider without injury to the woman.

Her eyes went wild. "*No*." She sagged with a groan, as if pained—was the raider hurting her? "I canna' stay. I must go." The gleam in her green eyes brightened. "It's your turn to look out for her now." She twisted and dropped, freeing herself.

Glad she was free, Marco wasted no time thudding his dagger into the raider's chest. He turned to the woman. "Are you okay?"

With a grim smile, she inexplicably leapt at the ledge. Then over it.

"No!" Marco lunged after the woman, but the thump of her body on the road below reached his ears. It took several painful seconds to reconcile and accept what happened.

Movement erupted behind. Another attack.

Anger spiraled. Marco pivoted to the raider, but the man's momentum carried them out of the tower onto the sloped roof below. His back cracked against a beam and punched air from him. Sliding toward the edge, he released the raider and groped for traction. Slipping closer to his death . . . closer . . .

He caught a beam.

A weight latched onto his leg—the raider!

Marco fought the urge to shake off the creature. If he kicked, he'd lose his tenuous hold and they'd both fall to their deaths. He scanned the slope for a better grip. Down and to his left a pipe jutted through the shingles. Reaching it would require a leap. Couldn't do that with a raider attached to him. He peered down the length of his body to the yellow eyes glowering back. With as little movement as possible, he twitched his leg—hard.

Eyes darkened. Leered. The man produced a knife.

Reading his intent, Marco shoved off the shingles.

The raider fell away, his howl screaming through the night.

Midair, Marco twisted as he dropped. Clapped onto the pipe. Exultation hit his veins. He breathed his relief. Then he felt a groaning in the desiccated wood.

Reek! It was going to break!

Again he gauged the distance to the ground, considered jumping, but it was easily three stories. He'd break a leg, mayhap more.

Crack! The beam shifted, dropped him several inches. Knowing time was short, he inch-walked his hands to a more solid—

Crack. Groaaan.

"A window below you," guided a soft but firm voice.

Marco had no choice but to trust the voice and the affirming scent that came with it. He let go and plummeted, watching for the—

Ledge! He gripped it. Swung to break his momentum, dangling over the road and a dozen intermingling effluxes that disoriented him.

"You are clear," Ixion announced from below.

Where had the other voice gone? Marco let go and landed with a soft thump, his gaze swinging to the woman from the tower sprawled on the cobbles. Thick as the smoke snaked through the streets.

"You are well?" Ixion touched his shoulder.

Slumped against a wall, Marco steadied himself. "No." He watched as locals gathered the dead woman into blankets. "She gave no warning, just jumped. If she'd stayed . . ."

An acrid efflux stabbed from Ixion and was gone just as quick. Never once did his mask of calm falter. So what was this scent . . .?

And who had directed Marco to the window? He scanned the direction the earlier voice had come from but saw only shadows and scurrying villagers.

"Do you detect more danger?" Ixion asked.

Pulled back to the fray, Marco straightened. Let the winds waft over his receptors. "Some, but not many." He peeled off the wall and checked the alley once more for the stray voice that had guided him to safety but only saw a boy scampering past the end of the alley.

"Hey!" Marco hurried after him, broke into the open, and spotted the little guy across the burning market. Smoke billowed and embers popped. His eyes stung, his receptors as well, not only from the fire but the Irukandji rancor. Instinctively, he lifted his face mask seconds before a raider emerged from a nearby hut.

Those ominous writhing marks were marred with the blood of innocents. He saw Marco, then turned his malicious attention on the boy and grinned.

No! *No more.*

Marco sprinted across the market, aware he hadn't been able to retrieve his knife before being knocked out of the bell tower. He toed a cart and vaulted upward. Sighted the raider closing in on the boy. Knew he'd be too late.

The boy fell into the dirt.

Marco tensed as the raider dove at the now-screaming boy.

A whirl of white erupted from the side.

"No!" Marco kept moving, his actions feeling perilously slow.

A woman whipped her arm up toward herself, then arced it out, releasing a gleaming bronze weapon. It whisked across the square and sliced the raider's shoulder. He let out a howl, blood spilling down his arm. The second weapon she'd thrown expunged him from this life.

Stunned, Marco slowed as the raider crumpled to the ground.

She rushed forward and pulled the boy away, hugging him tightly.

An explosion of scents came from behind. Marco pivoted, ready to fight, but saw Ixion and a man wearing a similar baldric emerge from the smoke. The newcomer was one of the Stalkers Marco had watched in action earlier.

"Clear the city," Ixion shouted. "It's burning to the ground!" He strode toward the young woman and lifted the boy into his arms.

The girl caught Ixion's arm in clear panic, said something urgent, then retrieved the bronze, bloodied discs and darted away.

"Shouldn't you stop her?"

"She knows this place better than we do. Come." He rushed in the opposite direction with the boy and the Stalker.

Marco hesitated, glancing after the young woman, but fell into a lope after the Plisiázon. Just beyond the last building, they met with the other Stalker and slowed. "What—"

"Mavridis, we should . . ." The younger Plisiázon assessed Marco with a probing gaze.

"Hushak, Dusan," Ixion introduced them. "And this is Shobi."

Marco clasped arms with the Stalkers, whose effluxes were rank with awe. "Well met."

The younger Stalker inclined his head, then tilted it and looked around.

"What is it?" Marco asked.

Shobi considered him again before relenting, clearly not used to answering to anyone but his elder. "One group attacked the market while the other hit here. I've not seen them coordinate their attack before."

"So that's why the city burns," Ixion muttered. "Never have the Plisiázon lost a city."

Hushak hung his head. "It was . . . impossible. We did everything we could . . ."

Ignoring the rank dolor of failure emanating from the Stalkers, Marco considered the crumbling buildings, the ash-smudged faces of the people as they dragged out belongings before they were consumed. "Money and religion—that's where the Irukandji struck."

"Two of the most powerful influences over a people," Ixion said.

Though Marco tried to focus on the conversation, a stench in the smoky air rifled across his senses. Something was wrong. Panic. Fear. Not the duller, more pervasive scent of the fleeing Moidians, but a dolor spiked, recent. "You're sure the raiders are gone?" He shifted. Glanced away from the Stalkers. Homed in.

Following the efflux, he jogged, avoiding barrels. He zigzagged down alleys and through buildings for quicker movement. The path ended in a field just beyond a dozen new Signatures and the ragged edge of the city. He paused, anak'ing the panicked efflux and an unusual fetor.

Ixion trotted up. "What is it?"

Smoke snaked through the night sky like a threatening specter. Fire erupted, its appetite ravenous along a building's length. Whinnies trilled from the flames. Hay. Wood. Then a scream—that Signature.

"The stables," Ixion said.

Marco tore across the field to the engulfed structure. Roughly two dozen men formed a bucket line, passing water to those fighting an unwinnable battle.

"Is anyone in there?" Ixion shouted

"Neh," a man grunted. "Yeh can't get in there anyhows. It's consumed. One second it was fine, the next it went up with a whoosh."

That was what he'd detected. "They used an accelerant," Marco said.

Surprised, Ixion glanced at him. "More of that coordination Hushak mentioned?"

The air shifted. "Someone's in there!" Marco darted into the barn, moving fast to avoid the flames catching at his cloak. "Hello! Anyone—" He knelt to avoid the hovering thick smoke.

Fifteen paces ahead, a person shuffled beneath a thick blanket. The figure dropped to his hands and knees, coughing.

Marco hurried over. "Come out, man! It's no good."

"I can't." The voice—a woman's!—was roughened by the smoke and coughing—then she slumped to the ground. She'd get herself killed.

Heaving her into his arms, he pushed to his feet. And realized she was the one with the strange weapons who'd saved the boy.

"No!" She writhed as he hurried her out of the barn. "She's in there! The foa—" Coughs choked her words, and her scent found a moment without smoke to smack him.

Marco thrust her at Ixion. "Take her! There's another." He lifted his mask to his face, yet he caught the rife scent of protection and near-grief from Ixion before starting back in.

"Nay!" A man rushed from the side.

Glowering, Marco pushed him away. He could not leave someone to burn to death.

"Here, a wet cloak!"

Appreciating the help, he swung it around his head and shoulders and hurried back in. It was dangerous to close his eyes, but they were no help with the smoke and the nearly searing heat. Anak'ing was the only answer. Angling his head down, he went to all fours and crawled toward the scent tangled in smoke.

Where are you . . .?

Skin tingling from the heat, Marco passed a row of stalls, gates open, horses gone. He continued farther back through the haze. Coughed. Tried to slow his breathing so he took in less smoky air, but that limited anak'ing.

A cry filtered through the thick veil. Flames leaped, reaching for him. Taunting. Threatening. He pulled in the scent, letting it lead him. There, just beneath the roar of the fire and creak of timber came panic and too-soft cries.

He scrabbled forward, yet he saw nothing in the stall. "Hello?" Grit coated his tongue. He spit, trying to work saliva into his throat so he could anak. "*Hello?*"

Hair dusted with ash, dark rivulets carved by tears, a child peered around a rail.

Groooan.

The sound drew his gaze overhead to the main support beam that glowed like sunrise. It shifted, raining embers.

Not good.

Instinct threw him at her. He rolled and came up in a crouch. Found her huddled beside a newborn foal, its legs folded, head down. Eyes closed. *It's dead.* He reached for the girl, but she screamed and shoved away, wrapping her arms around the foal. The furry head lifted.

Grooooaaann.

Behind the girl, a wall glittered with hungry flames.

He crushed her to his chest and gathered the foal as well. The thing came alive with blind panic.

Whoooosh!

With beams falling there was only one way out. Marco shoved off and twisted, throwing his shoulder into the burning wall. Something thumped hard against his skull as he landed, hard, blackness engulfing him. His last thought one of concern for the child and foal.

Pain thumped the black void that held him hostage. Coming aware, Marco groaned and blinked, surprised at the light filtering through his lids.

"About boiling time," Ixion growled.

Marco's head roared. Palm to his temple, he groaned, trying to recall what happened. It came to him in rolling waves of pain. The barn. The fire . . . "The girl!"

"She is well, thanks to you." A man with a nasally voice approached. "I'm the pharmakeia, or as close as you'll get in these parts. You have quite a knot on the back of your head from saving her."

"You were buried by the barn wall." Anger radiated through Ixion's Signature.

But they'd said the girl was well. "What's wrong?" Marco came up off the cot.

"Stay there. I want to check your head and eyes," the man said, leaning in with a glass.

"I'm fine. Thanks." Marco waved him off. He'd had enough instruments probing him to last a lifetime. He shuddered, thinking of that creature on the *Chryzanthe*.

A subtle stirring of air wafted across Marco's receptors seconds before his shoulder was slapped. Surprise leapt through him as he looked at his First. "Did you just smack me?"

"Aye, and I would do more if—"

"If *what*?" Few, save the master hunter, dared issue a challenge, and rarely so openly. Indignation wove through him with a heated charge.

"You endangered yourself. Needlessly."

Marco stopped short, scowling at the tall Plisiázon. "I saved *lives*," he growled. "There is nothing *needless* about that." He motioned to the Moidians. "They are why I am here. Why I have been yanked from the only existence known to me and deposited onto this backwater rock." As he strode into the morning, applause broke out, stopping Marco. He considered the townsfolk in the field, clothes dirty, some singed, others as bedraggled as he felt. Admiration was to be expected toward a noble, but toward a hunter? People ran in fear, they did not shout praises.

A new fear trilled. "Wait, do they—"

"Think you're a hero? Aye." Ixion's voice turned dry. "Fret not. The medora in the north will not hear of your attempt to steal the hearts of his people."

A little blonde thing came flying at Marco. Slamming into his legs, she held on tight. Shocked, he stumbled back and glanced at the child. What was he to do with this?

"That is what happens to heroes," Ixion growled, but something spiked in his scent. "And dogs." With a little less begrudging, "She's the girl you saved in the barn."

Marco had not realized her hair was blonde. He recalled brown hair. *Ashen* hair. He touched the girl's shoulder. She should . . . go. He tried to pry her free. "Where are her parents?"

"Dead." The voice belonged to the woman who had saved the boy and been at the burning barn. Dangling from a braided belt that slanted across her hips were the bronze weapons she'd used against the raider. Not much past twenty cycles, she had the same flaxen hair as the girl. "Sadly, she is now an orphan."

Ixion's efflux went strident. "Her mother was the one from the bell tower."

That stirred Marco's guilt, and he remembered the woman's words. *"It's your turn to look out for her now."* Did she mean the little one? How could she know that? "What will happen to her?" Feeling suddenly responsible for her, he stopped trying to remove her.

"After you dove out with the girl, the barn fire spread fast, and it was not the only one. Food stores are gone, the market is burned, as are most homes. These people, including the child, are destitute." He nodded to the crowd. "All of them."

Marco scanned those gathered. What would they do? The officials and governing body would have an enormous task rebuilding a town, even a small one. A daunting truth weighted his shoulders: *he* was that governing body. "There must be something that can be done, at least for now."

"Hushak sent a bird for help and supplies from Prokopios," Ixion said.

"Help?" Marco frowned. "In the tavern you said one was enough, yet we arrive and there are two. Now the village . . ."

Ixion's jaw muscle jounced as his steel eyes lasered Marco. "The devastation is complete this time." Squinting, he nodded to the rubble that was Moidia.

"Therefore, we will allow a couple of days for the people to recover and salvage what they can from the city, then we will escort them through the badlands to Prokopios."

"No!" A short man strode forward. His well-oiled hair and pretentious suit were spotless. "Moidia is our home. We stay, rebuild. As we always do."

"I agree, Regent Ven'tac," the flaxen-haired woman asserted, her voice and efflux rife with nervous jitters but also a strong, more potent . . . desperation. "We should rebuild. After all, Moidia is the last waystation, the dividing line between civility and lawlessness, no matter the name they set on our heads. You are wise to consider a break so the children and women like me can recover from the shock of the raid and the loss of so many and so much. Thank you, Regent—"

"Never did I speak any such thing!" The round-bellied man sneered. "Go back with the other children, Isa!" His rebuff and foul stench were nauseating.

"Ven'tac," Ixion growled, "the Irukandji have decimated your food, water, and cattle. The town is burned. With what do you intend to rebuild on scorched land?"

The grizzle-faced man lifted his chin. "We have never needed handouts and will not take your charity!"

The arrogance angered Marco. "Then you are content to watch your people starve, the children's bellies bloat with malnutrition? You are their regent. Is that what you will for your people? You with your tailored suit and soft hands!"

"Who are you?" Ven'tac bellowed. "Do not speak to me—"

"See to your people, Ven'tac," Ixion snapped. "We will council after fasts are broken."

The regent sniffed, then stomped off.

"Mavridis," Isa spoke quietly, pulling their attention again, "a tent is prepared for you and your guest." Her gaze danced to Marco, and the air was saturated with a floral aroma of attraction. Curse the reek!

Another scent competed—one of disapproval, protectiveness—from Ixion. There again came that subtle nuance of fetor that he could not decipher.

"Appreciated," Ixion said to the girl. His gaze held something sharp as he nodded to Marco. "This way."

Puzzled, Marco followed his First past the throng of Moidians and entered the large tent. The interior had been configured into three sections—one a narrow meeting area that ran the length of the tent and offered a seating area with rugs and cushions. A large trunk served as a table. The other half was bisected into two compartments with cots and washstands.

"It is not Kardia," Ixion conceded as he snagged a chunk of cheese from a sideboard.

"As a Kynigos, I often slept beneath the stars." And it had suited. "Can we open the walls to afford some air?" Even as Marco spoke, the sides rolled up, and a morning breeze filtered through, along with the curious gazes of the Moidians. "Is it so bad out there that they must truly leave their home?"

Ixion reclined against the cushions. "While you were yet unconscious, Stalkers searched for injured and survivors. A triage is set up not far from here, but there are a great many dead. I also spoke with the businessmen. Most are fed up. Ven'tac might insist on staying, but the people are ready to leave. Some will take convincing—this land is all they've known. Change is hard."

"The girl, Isa, is one? It took courage for her to speak up in opposition to you."

Ixion held his gaze, unflinching—and though Marco wasn't sure why, the Stalker seemed to be working hard to control his reaction and scent.

"The weapons hanging from her belt—what are they?"

"Fire discs," Ixion said, and the tension in the tent released. "An ancient Droseran weapon that's easy to carry and lethal when correctly thrown."

"She correctly threw," Marco chuckled. He lowered to the cushions, only then sensing a profound ache in his shoulder, no doubt from crashing through the barn wall. "Tell me of Ven'tac."

Ixion sipped from a tin cup. "He is spoiled and belligerent, but he understands the land. It would be a mistake for him to stay, yet neither will I force his kind into the polite society of Prokopios." He hooked an arm around his leg. "My greater concern is that those loyal to him may remain, and that would be a problem."

"Agreed. Would it help for them to know . . .?" He did not want to open that vault.

Ixion lifted grapes from a bowl. "No." He ate in quiet, then sighed. "And forget about the girl."

Marco retrieved a fresh cordi. "The orphan I saved? But should we not see her placed—"

"Not that one." Ixion had an edge to his voice.

Marco hesitated, confused by the strange tinge to the Stalker's efflux. What other . . .? His mind swung back to the pretty flaxen-haired young woman, Isa. Signature—sage . . . No, not sage. Something more . . . floral. And the way she flicked those discs . . .

"The two are sisters."

Flinching, Marco struggled with the truth that he'd failed to prevent their mother from jumping off the ledge. "Both orphans then." Something nagged at his receptors and leftover headache. "Will they be situated with a family? The older, Isa, seemed of age—but they will need protection during the exodus. I feel responsible—"

"You are not." Ixion's Signature was firing off a rank odor.

Trying to wade through the dolors proved difficult, since he'd known Mavridis but a short time. Marco thought back to the sisters, wanting to make that right somehow. "There's a sizable age difference between the two. Are there other siblings? The elder could marry—bind, as you call it."

Chewing more grapes, Ixion took his time responding. "No other siblings." Guarded. Defensive. Concealing again.

"What is—"

Sunlight flickered at the entrance, delivering two shapes into the tent—the flaxen-haired Isa and a slightly older woman who backed in with a tray of meats and fruits. Directly below the wood tray was a distinctly round womb. Pregnant.

At the waft of floral against his senses, Marco narrowed his receptors. The scents did naught but make him lightheaded. He must've been struck harder than he'd thought.

Ixion sat straighter. "We need to speak of the route."

"Should not the leaders of Moidia be involved?"

Something flew on the air from the two women. Concern. Surprise. They hesitated, shooting glances at Ixion, then quickly busied themselves, heads down.

Ixion's jaw muscle worked, and it dawned on Marco that the elder of Prokopios set the rules here. What he spoke, the people did without challenge or complaint. And while Marco was medora, neither these two nor the townsfolk were aware of his identity, so his questioning their elder was viewed as a significant breach of protocol.

"I beg your mercy." The phrase helped him to stay in character.

"As seen," Ixion said, "Ven'tac has little concern for anything but himself." He watched the pregnant woman set a platter in front of him. "Thank you, Madame Lasdos. You are most kind, but I am sure Manty would be better served by your attentions."

The pregnant woman paused, a hand going to her rounded belly. Her efflux spiraled with a tangy and bitter pang.

Recognizing her grief, Marco rose. "Madame, I am truly sorry for your loss."

On his feet as well, Ixion touched her shoulder. "Kita, why did you not say?"

She tucked her head. "I beg your mercy. There is naught to be done for it. Weeping will not bring him back, and there is much work to be done."

Ixion gave a nod. "Prokopios will see you protected."

"I am grateful, Elder Mavridis, but we both know there is little to go around."

Isa slipped closer and wrapped her arm across Kita's shoulders. "He speaks it, so it will be."

Meaning sparked fiercely in the Stalker's expression as he spoke with the pregnant woman. "The words have breath."

Madame Lasdos pulled in a shuddering sigh. "And bloom to life."

"And bloom to life," Ixion repeated, a near smile parting his trim beard. Then his stony expression returned. "Have you seen the pharmakeia this rise?"

Hand on her womb, she shook her head. "I . . . couldn't face it." The pang went salty now—she feared her child dead.

The thought cut sideways through Marco, and he anak'd her pheromones. "I can assure you, the child yet lives."

Ixion started, then nodded. "Kita, this is Dusan, and with his gifting—you can trust his words." He turned to Isa. "Take her to the pharmakeia. Set her mind at ease with a good report."

Marco shifted away as they left. The plight of the Moidians smacked his complacency—people were now fighting for their next meal. By Vaqar, how quickly his priorities had fallen.

STRATIOS, KALONICA, DROSERO

Had her heart rent in two the pain would not have been as great. Wind tugging at her curls, Kersei shielded her eyes from the sun. From where she stood in the swalti fields, the grain stalks swishing against her omnir pants, she stared up to the great hulk of black stones collapsed upon one other. The bailey walls had crumbled to nothing, destroyed in the terrible explosion that had shattered her life. Haunting whispers spirited up the path and into her mind. Recalled the day she had hurried into the side of the house, warning Adara not to speak of the sparring match that had bruised Kersei's ribs.

"I heard you the first thousand times," her sister moaned.

Oh sweet Adara . . .

Kersei traced what remained of the stairs, remembering the long journey up each step with an injury that felt like breathing fire.

They're gone. They're truly gone.

Aye. Yet a vain, desperate hope lingered, held captive by painful truths and events, that it might all prove false. A nightmare from which she would wake. Here, that hope had escaped . . . only to die on the black stone from which Stratios Hall had been hewn. Tears pricked as she gazed at the remnants of her family home. The truth of this terrible crime had a violence of its own. How horrible it must've been for her family, seeing the walls come down. Being crushed by them.

Their screams were all too fresh in her mind. Screams she had been forced, over and over, to hear in the reminding chamber on the *Macedon*. Screams not from her own memories, but from Darius's. He had been here when the walls fell.

"Kersei?" A light touch at her shoulder drew her back to Darius, to the present. He was alive and her family was not. Why could it not have been Father who had survived, who had returned with scars?

"Kersei." Darius was firmer this time, worried.

"It is so horrible. You were in there when the walls fell." She turned to him. "It must have been terrifying."

"I try not to think on it."

She pointed to the ruins. "Your father and brother died in there, violently crushed to death! How can you *not* think about that?" A breath shuddered through her. "Whoever did this . . . Murderer!" Conviction fastened onto her. "He will *pay*."

Darius swung around in front of her, the wind riffling his sandy-blond hair. "Kersei?" His brows drew together over those Tyrannous blues. "Was I wrong to bring you here?" He cupped her face, wiping away a tear with his thumb. "I thought it might help."

Even beneath her ragged breathing, she could see his concern. Hear it in his voice. Yet he was here and her family was not . . . and she hated him for it. Wanted to shove him away. Punch the insupportable reality. She balled her fists and shifted her gaze to the ruins. "Where are they buried?"

"In the family cemetery."

"I would see it." Kersei started around the path to the south gardens. The wind ripped at her blue omnir pants. Blue for Stratios, not green for Kardia. She was last of the Stratios and must keep her father's name alive.

Curse the reek!

As night crept in and darkness blanketed the tent-studded plain, Marco gave himself some much-needed solace and invigoration by taking to a section of Moidia where structures had been built off a brick wall that was still standing. Two days had passed since the raid. The painstaking detail that went into organizing an entire city to make a long journey weighted him. The route he and Ixion had taken on horseback to reach Moidia was faster but not suitable for families and wagons. The only road for them would add a dozen days or more—a minimum of two weeks.

He pitched himself at a building that had burned yet stood. Caught a window ledge and swung out to another, catching the lower rooftop. He hiked onto the brick wall and started running.

Laughter trailed him.

Children.

Not again. Speeding up, Marco moved deeper into the city. Losing them was easy, and they soon wandered back to the fields. As he navigated rotted boards and burned roofs, something acrid slowed him to a stop. Angered at what he detected, he drew into the shadows.

Men in search of pleasure.

Another scent—wary, frightened. A young woman.

Wait. He knew that Signature—the older sister, Isa.

"Well, well," came a sneering voice that drew Marco toward it, crouching in the shadow of a crumbling fireplace. "What do we have here?"

Feet skidded on the cobbled road. "Go, Laseria!"

Both girls! Marco spun and threw himself over the other side of the roof. He slid down, landing with a soft thump.

"Leave us alone!" the young woman demanded. "Go back to y—"

"Yer alone in the dark with men that gots needs."

Tucked in a doorway, Marco cupped his hands over his mouth. "Mavridis, over here."

"Scatter," an urgent voice hissed with a panicked efflux.

Marco watched from the shadows as the brigands sprinted in different directions. He waited until the girls escaped down the alley toward the safety of the tents. Using his forearm to swipe the sweat from his face, he stepped into the open and started down the cobbled road. As he did, he caught that Signature again. Lavender and—

Wait. The girls were behind him. How had they backtracked without him knowing? Annoyed, he hurried his steps and reached the field. He was halfway across it when they caught up.

"It was you, wasn't it?" The little one twirled around in front of him as she hustled backward. "You saved me again. Didn't you? I heard your voice—it was you."

"What were you doing in the city at night?" he demanded.

She batted hair from her face. "I had to find Isa."

Marco glanced over his shoulder and met the young woman's eyes. "You have oversight of her and should know better than to be here after dark, considering the Irukandji attack."

Embarrassment and not a little irritation flooded out as she reached for her sister, who jerked away—and fell hard against the ground. She yelped—a spike of pain hitting her Signature, followed by a scream.

Isa drew in a breath as she squatted. "Where are you hurting? If you are pretending—"

"I'm not!" Laseria wailed. "My wrist." She hugged it to herself, crying.

Scenting real distress, Marco knelt and convinced the little one to let him see her arm. He probed it, and when he angled the hand, she let out a yelp. "A sprain, likely." He lifted her and looked to her sister. "Where is the pharmakeia?"

"This way." Isa led them across the plain toward a dark tent. If they were at the Citadel of Kynig, the injury would be quickly repaired, but here, on a planet without technology, it might take weeks.

The pharmakeia gave an exasperated glance when they entered. "Again, Laseria?" He huffed. "Last bed on the right."

Marco deposited the girl on the cot and stepped back as her sister knelt, her golden hair a silken sheet across her shoulder and a striking contrast to green eyes lit by the torch.

Ixion strode in, scowling. "What happened?" The Stalker's scent was thick with disapproval . . . and protectiveness.

Isa came to her feet. "Laseria—we were . . ." Her words trailed off into a vat of fear.

Why does she fear him? Why this protective scent from his First when it was directed toward no others here in the camp?

"The child tripped and injured her arm," Marco supplied.

"Please don't be mad, Mavridis," Laseria said, pouting. "It wasn't on purpose."

Ixion met Marco's gaze, then indicated for him to follow. Wanting answers, he started after the Stalker. Something ensnared his wrist.

In a fluid move that whipped his training to the fore, he flipped the grip, pivoted and drew his right leg back, pulling the person into his personal space, heel of his hand poised to strike. Her weight fell against his chest, and a startled gasp dashed his cheek.

Staring into green eyes, Marco released her and stepped away. "Forgive me. You . . . Most people know not to touch me."

She blinked away her surprise. "I wanted to thank you for covering for Laseria. She knew not to be in the city, but she would follow you."

He searched her for a lie but found only earnestness. An irritated scent smacked him from behind—Ixion. "Excuse me." He stepped into the night for cool air but found none, only more of the smothering heat.

Ixion fell in with him. "You left the tent without word to me."

Feeling no need to explain himself, Marco said nothing.

"I cannot protect you if I do not know where you are."

A valid point.

"I am not a Kynigos. I cannot smell you out."

Marco slowed, tucking aside his irritation. "I am unused to having so many . . . demands on my time and energy. Hunters work alone, one decree at a time. I went into the city for solace, to work off frustration. It was soon obvious I was still not alone."

Ixion smirked. "You are a curiosity to them."

"I am Kynigos." Marco shook his head. "People know to keep their distance."

"Maybe on other planets. Here on Drosero, these people . . ." Ixion shrugged.

"Mayhap they should be taught to."

"Is that how you would have them see you?" Ixion's gaze was sharp as ever. "Think past this point in your life, past what you just lost. Look to the future—not just who you are, but *what* you are. And I do not mean that mark on your nose."

Medora.

"It is not good for them to fear *that* man. Respect, aye. But not fear."

Chastisement forced Marco to reconsider approaching life here as he had on Kynig, as a hunter. But if not that, then . . . what did a normal life look like?

"When the truth of your identity is revealed, what will they think? That they are proud, or that they are afraid?"

This wasn't a browbeating but a bludgeoning. "You should have been named medora."

Ixion gripped Marco's neck and pulled him in. "*Never* speak that again," he hissed, a rancid odor dousing his scent. Just as fast, it vanished, and he pitched Marco back with a glower. Ferocity bled into gray eyes. "We each of us have a purpose. Live yours. Others are counting on it."

Anger borne of humiliation surged through Marco. None save Roman had dared handle him so. He was Kynigos, a hunter. One who never wanted to be medora. He glared at the silver-haired Stalker, ready to strike back, reclaim his pride.

Then, abruptly, the fight went out of him. Though he wanted to argue, Ixion was right. Again. His excuses were already old: this life of attention and leadership was new. He must adjust.

A shout went up in the camp. Over a din, he heard someone telling the people to pack and ready themselves. They would set out at dawn to begin the journey north.

Marco looked to Ixion. "Why have I had no word of this?"

"Because you were too busy skipping rooftops." He jerked toward the tent. "Come. Let me fill you in."

After they had spoken of plans for the morning, they were invited to join the townsfolk in a campfire celebration. It was strange to think of celebrating when so many things were wrong, from the devastation of this town to the conspiracy spanning the stars. When the Brethren were being taken by Symmachia. The thought drove Marco to check his vambrace. Roman had promised to keep him updated, but there was no message, his vambrace's silence just another example of the wrongness.

"We got us a new medora," a young man said near where Marco settled by the fire. "He's younger, better."

"Bah!" his companion balked. "What does he care? He's up in Kardia, sitting pretty." Many of the men around the campfire grunted their agreement amid the rank efflux—drunken.

"Give care, Oxir." Ixion's grave expression was made more stark by the firelight. "You speak of things you do not know."

"I know he's not here," the thick-armed man bit back. "Where was he when the raiders burned our homes and livelihoods?"

It was not just the Kynigos who were in a fight for their existence. Marco eyed the dancing flames, listening—*hearing* their hearts. Feeling overwhelmed.

"Have you met him, Mavridis?" The young woman, Isa, sat on the ground, working her sister's hair into a long plait.

The din around the bonfire quieted, as if everyone awaited their elder's answer.

"Aye," Ixion said, giving attention not to look at Marco. "Confirmed and accepted him, saw him crowned."

"What sort of man is he?" Kita Lasdos asked, a boy tucked against her side, his head resting on her belly.

When Ixion hesitated, Marco grew concerned. Much had happened in the last couple of days. Did his First already think less of him? Temptation arose to anak, but there were times it felt a violation. And this felt like one of those times.

"A good man," Ixion finally said. "A situation came up that I could see no possible means by which he could walk away with his honor intact . . . Yet he did, though it ripped his heart from his chest. I do not think even his father, Zarek, could have done it so honorably."

Marco lowered his head, humbled and relieved by the words.

"What about—"

"Our journey starts early," Ixion said. "I must rest. If you will excuse me." He stood and started from the camp. "Come, Dusan, before they lure you into dancing."

Amid chuckles from the crowd, Marco followed the Stalker, thinking about the people. About their negative view of their ruler.

A scent leapt from behind.

Marco snapped his hand back, catching a wrist. A small wrist. Child.

"See? I told you," a boy gloated to the one whose arm Marco held, then tore off.

The ensnared boy—the same one who'd been with Madame Lasdos—widened eyes that filled with tears. "He dared me to! I didn't do nothing. Honest! Please don't kill me, Mister Hunter." He looked ready to soil his pants.

"Do you always allow others to goad you into trouble?"

"I don't have no goat, Mister."

Melodious laughter floated on the air as Isa glided up with a rueful smile. "Oh, Mnason. Did you let Addar get you in a fix again?" She tussled the boy's hair.

"Use your own mind to make decisions." Marco released him. "If you do not, you'll have no honor."

Firelight caught Isa's long, lithe form as she watched the boy sprint away. She shook her head and turned back to Marco. "He meant no harm. They are curious about"—her gaze struck the Kynigos sigil on his nose—"your kind."

"We hunt by smell, so he will not be able to sneak up on me."

Her eyebrow arched. "Is that a challenge?"

Startled at her audacity, Marco could not look away. People did not react this way to Kynigos. At least, not those who wished to remain free and unmarked. He cringed at the thought of stamping the Kynigos iron into her graceful neck.

That was his previous life. He was no longer a Kynigos. No longer hunting. And she was his—people, that is. These were his people. Which included her.

What in the reek was wrong with him? "Good rest." He pivoted toward the tent.

"Wait. I beg your mercy." She hurried after him.

"Is there something wrong?" Ixion demanded at the tent opening.

Isa drew up short. "No, Mavridis. I-I only wished to say good night." Without another word, she rejoined her friend at the fire.

The strange mixture of scents from Ixion and the girl kept Marco awake well into the night.

KALONICA, DROSERO

Why had it not dissipated?

With a handful of Stalkers, the Moidians had set out two days past, leaving their homes and all they knew to journey northward for a new life. Leading his horse, Marco walked after hours of riding and patrolling with the Stalkers. He stayed vigilant because he could yet smell those rancid Irukandji, along with another strange fetor.

Sinus pounding by the time the sun reached its zenith, he longed for the cloak tucked into his pack. It may well be too hot, but it would stifle the plaguing reek. Would that he could close his receptors, but with the ever-present threat of danger and his lingering doubt that they were alone on this journey, it could not be risked.

A tangle of acrid scents assailed his senses. Groaning at the onslaught, Marco had no trouble sorting the Signatures—Isa and Ixion. Hers that lavender and something . . . outdoorsy with a sense of nostalgia, like coming home. Oak. No, sweeter, so . . . white oak? Aye. He moved on to the next—a woodsy and tangy. Both had hefty doses of anger, hers saturated with hurt and his with . . .

What was that? Fear? Pride?

Brows drawn, Ixion gave her a reproving look, his head jerking as he spoke. He was strangely . . . protective toward her. This seemed more than him being an elder and her a citizen. Marco may not have much knowledge of Ixion and his highly trained Stalkers, but he had the anaktesios, which told him more than their quick responses and sidelong glances. Isa lifted her head, spotted Marco coming toward them, and hurried off, a wake of grief trailing her.

Marco eyed his First, curious about what he smelled and witnessed. What was this girl to him? What he scented wasn't romantic—

"She is upset," Ixion muttered, rankled. "After what happened . . . her mother's death is hard on her." With a curt nod, he stepped back. "I must gather reports from the scouts."

The barn fire. Her mother's death. That explained her grief, but Ixion's . . .

A mischievous scent spiraled from the left, coming in fast. Anticipating the pickpocket, Marco caught his "assailant." Stared down into familiar eyes. "Again, Mnason?" When the boy shoved another and called him a liar, Marco swiveled between them. "What lie this time?"

The boy pouted, trying to extricate himself from Marco's grip. "He said you couldn't do it in daylight."

"Do what?"

"You know . . ." Mnason motioned toward his own nose. "Use your majuk from those lines what you got on your face and know everything."

Majuk. "There is no sorcery here."

"Then how come you always know when we come?" Mnason asked, frustrated. "It ain't natural, that's what I heard them saying."

"Who said?"

"Oxir and Regent Ven'tac."

"And are they who you want to be like?"

"No way! The regent is fat, and Oxir smells."

"Then stop listening to them. They are wrong—my abilities are a gift from Vaqar."

Mnason screwed up his nose. "What? He come down and drew on your face? Or are you like the raiders and it's punishment?"

"A gift, remember?" Marco chuckled again as they walked. "I was just a little older than you when the master hunter came for me."

Sandy-blond hair twitched. "Were you bad like me? And he came to switch your hide?"

"No, the master does not for the errant but for the set apart." It was strange to talk of his Order among those who had no knowledge of the Brethren. "Reclaiming—that's what it's called—is a very good, blessed event. It is an honor to train at the Citadel."

"Can I go?" Mnason's longing drenched the air. "If I was to straighten my ways and promise not to snitch or snatch?"

"That would be a very good start."

He grinned and darted off, shouting for his friend.

"Careful," came a soft voice. Isa. "Keep smiling like that and someone might mistake you for a nice man."

"Am I not?" Marco imagined what it must have been like for her to see him dangling from the tower shortly after her mother's fall to her death. "I beg your mercy if my methods are . . . upsetting."

"Surprising, but not upsetting." She walked for a while in silence. "Are your kind related to the Irukandji?"

"Am I so terrible you would think that?"

"No!" She looked at him—her gaze reflexing away. But he'd seen where her gaze had landed. His face. "It is said for each act that goes against the Ladies, blue marks appear on the raiders' bodies, that they're painful, which is why the raiders are so . . . touched." She tapped her temple.

"You think me touched?"

"No. I—that is not—" She groaned. "I beg your mercy!"

Marco smiled.

Her alarm melted away. "You jest."

He let himself smile. "My sigil does not glow, and it does not appear as punishment from any hand. It is a reward, an outward sign that I live by the Codes." Or had. It was a small distinction and lie for now. "At Mnason's age, we're taken to the Citadel, and once training is complete, we go before the Council and receive the sigil."

"You were seven when you were taken?"

"Six."

Her efflux grew more drenched in grief. "You have my condolences for your loss. I know from experience 'tis hard to . . . lose your parents." She slid her plait over her shoulder. "Did you have siblings?"

Marco tucked his chin. Speak too much and he risked betraying his identity.

"Mercy." She gave a soft laugh as she worried the ties of her vest. "I am told my questions are intrusive—and tiresome. My mother . . ." Her smile and light faded. "I was often in trouble and . . . stubborn." She twisted her hands. "I . . ."

Her embarrassment made him ache for her. "Two brothers," he said. "And no, it was not hard being taken to the Citadel. I found great relief in no longer having to hide what I could do and an even greater confidence in who I was. I also discovered my purpose as I trained to use the anaktesios and the Codes that guide Kynigos in honor and truth."

She smiled. "That sounded like a speech."

He breathed a laugh, nodding. "I suppose it did." He smoothed a hand down the back of his neck. "I hold deep convictions about honor and Vaqar who gifted me."

"So you believe in the Ancient?"

"How can I not when I bear his mark?"

Green eyes considered him, tracing his sigil. Her curiosity spilled into her Signature and ensnared a memory. A painful one—the moment aboard the transport freighter when he stood on the stardeck with Kersei touching his sigil. Their first kiss.

"If you will excuse me . . ." Marco strode from her questions. Flinging himself onto his mount, he shoved that memory back into the vault in which it belonged. All these weeks managing to keep the torment at bay . . . He broke from the main road and made his way up onto a small rise that flanked the road through the desert.

He and Kersei were meant for each other. Why had their lives been torn apart? He reached out with his receptors, searching the bitter, hot land. Up past thick air—humid. Lakes—no, there was salt, so the sea. Up the grassy hills, northeastward. He angled his head, eyes closed as he breathed in deep and—

Ahhh. Blessed, sweet relief. She was there, amazingly. Unbelievably.

It is your imagination. He was too far away. This distance impossible to anak her. Yet, he lifted his face as if a breeze wafted over his receptors. That he could keep her scent here. Memorize it deeper. Vanilla, patchouli.

My love . . .

Like a crack of thunder, a different scent struck—malodorous. His hunter training forced Marco to dismount and send the Black away. He dropped to a knee, fingertips to the rugged, sun-warmed terrain and angled his head down and to the side. Where was it coming from? Alert, he caught the scent.

Behind. He scurried along the ridge, guided by the rancor. The scent of . . . "Raiders," he whispered, then spun back toward his First. "Ixion!"

"Plisiázon!" A shout from the front of the line swallowed Marco's call. The wagon train came to a lumbering halt. Horsemen approached the head of the caravan from the southeast, more Stalkers patrolling cross-country.

Marco cursed himself for not learning the Stalkers' whistles. The rancor was stronger, closer. If he called again, he'd betray himself, and the raider would escape. Hunched near a scraggly scrub, he glanced around. Gauged his position. The scent from the south.

Exultant cries erupted from the Moidians as more Stalkers joined them. He watched Ixion greet the newcomers, then saw scrubs shifting near the road. The Irukandji were close! Much closer than he'd realized.

Marco eyed the last wagons with sick, elderly, children.

His heart thumped. No time for help. Using the brush and jagged terrain to hide his movements, he followed the ridge that banked away from the road, arcing down, and then veering sharply back to the end of the train.

Stilled, he picked up more scents. Three, maybe four. Concern wedged into the knots of his shoulders. Shadowy forms darted toward the wagons.

"Raiders!" Marco shouted as he sprinted after them.

Backtracking and coming upwind, he looked for Ixion, but the elder apparently hadn't heard him. Marco toed a wagon's frame, left-right-left up, up to the spines supporting canvas. As he leapt across each that gave a little, he spotted a raider creeping toward a group of children.

Savages. Marco vaulted for a large cart crossbar. Swung out, dipped, and nailed the raider in the head. Hearing him thump to the ground, Marco dropped, focused on the next one. Rolled beneath the cart and spied boots on the other side. Gripping the undercarriage, he flung around, swiping his feet.

Head hitting with a solid thwack, the raider groaned and went unconscious. A small trail of blood marred his temple.

The workhorse whinnied and stamped its hooves. Marco smoothed a hand along its thick neck. Eyes afire with panic, the horse *smelled* the trouble. Just like Marco had. As he tried to steady the beast, he caught a shrill scent.

Pain scored his temple. His teeth rattled. He staggered—catching himself. Legs like gelatin, he wobbled. Buckled to a knee. Felt more than saw another blow coming. Fire exploded through his shoulder. He dove into the threat. Caught legs. Went down.

"The horses!"

At the distant shout, Ixion shifted to the rear of the caravan, searching for his new medora. As if a river escaping a broken dam, crying women and children flooded away from stamping horses and plumes of dust.

A shape leapt over the wagon, using canvas in lieu of a road.

"Dusan!" Hushak's gaze flicked to Ixion with concern.

The man had a death wish. With a piercing whistle, Ixion flew like the wind, his Stalkers as quick and swift as the diabolus plaguing the wastelands. He gave another signal, this an order to settle the pack horses so they didn't berserk. Even as he closed the distance, he saw Marco spring over a horse. What in the Ancient's name was he doing?

A blur of blue streaked across Ixion's path, making his destrier rear. A bloodied Marco stumbled after the blue raider.

Isa was there, flinging her discs to eliminate a raider.

"Irukandji!" Pulling around, he leaned into Tarjax. "*Frei-hah*!" Muscle and sinew contracted beneath Ixion's thighs. The Black surged forward and tore down the road after the raider, the impact of hooves jarring but familiar. As they slid down the embankment, Ixion leaned back, his spine mirroring Tarjax's. From his belt, he removed the manriki. Holding one of the weighted ends, he whirled it overhead, the chain singing. He sighted the raider.

The fool spun, turned—stopped. Saw what Ixion wielded, widened his eyes, and yanked something from a leg holster. Pointed it. A beam of light shot out and seared Ixion's leg.

Angered, Ixion focused on eradicating this accursed dog of Hirakys.

The savage spun, legs tangling. He tumbled, great sandy plumes billowing. "*Siel-hah*!" Ixion whispered to the Great Black.

Tarjax's hooves plowed into the ground, stopping. Dirt and rock sprayed upward as the destrier lowered his head and shoulders. Momentum vaulted Ixion off his back.

Wind tore at him as he sailed over Tarjax's head. Twisting in the air, he locked onto the raider and stretched out the manriki. Swung his arms down as he did an aerial maneuver. In the split second that his boots hit the ground, Ixion made a great circular motion with his upper body, crossing his arms over one another, and then he yanked his arms apart.

Marco had not needed a mount or closer proximity to know Ixion slew the Irukandji raider. Without hesitation or remorse. With a precision that left him both awed and sickened. "You killed—decapitated him!"

"And he won't be the last," Ixion hissed, blood on his tunic and pants as he stalked back to the caravan.

Marco caught his arm.

Like a great storm, Ixion whirled. Shoved up against Marco with a rage unlike any before. He glared from beneath white-blond brows, his gray eyes razor sharp. "Do not challenge me in this."

Stunned at the wildness, Marco held his ground. Scents assailed—shock, trepidation, outright fear, panic—from the people and Stalkers who gave witness to their confrontation. "Your people watch you."

A nearly imperceptible shift slid through Ixion's face. "And you." He stepped back, removed his gaze to the ground. "You know not what you challenge here."

"What makes you both jury and executioner? Where is justice?"

"*Where?*" Ixion gritted out. "Sitting in a palace leagues away and largely unaware of the evil we fight from risen sun to fallen."

The well-placed words struck true. "That was before . . ."

"Your challenge of my actions speaks that it is still true." His gaze hit Marco's wound. "You are injured."

"A scrape." He would not be deterred. "Desert justice—"

"Is needed." Ixion pushed something against his chest. "Especially now."

Marco caught it and glanced down, surprised. "A pulse pistol."

"The raider you defend had it."

"Not defend," Marco countered, watching men moving with deadly intent among the horses and wagons, searching for raiders. "I only—"

"Mavridis." The sandy-haired Plisiázon had a jagged scar that ran the length of his jaw and neck. "Stopped two more down the ridge. Three others among the caravan. Hushak and Shobi are tracking a band fleeing west."

"So many . . ." Ixion clapped the young man's shoulder. "Well done, Axeon." His jaw muscle jounced. "We will set up camp here."

"This early?"

"They are shaken," Ixion said. "Rest is better than beating them into the ground with fear hounding our steps."

As Axeon trotted off, Ixion seemed focused on something . . . Isa, who watched them. A strange mixture of scents clogged the air.

Marco strode toward her. "It seems you are much the warrior with those." He indicated to the bronze discs she was cleaning then touched his temple, where the raider had struck him. "I owe you thanks for intervening."

She slung the weapons on a leather thong, then rubbed the material of her vest over her hands, using the fabric to clean something off. "No thanks is appropriate in taking a life." She rubbed harder, violently.

Marco anak'd her efflux, which was awash in grief. He stilled her frantic movements. "Take comfort in protecting the innocent. Give the rest to Vaqar." He nodded for emphasis. "You did well. And my still-attached head thanks you."

A smile tugged at one side of her mouth. "It seemed necessary to keep it in place."

"I would agree. Heartily."

Ixion's irritation preceded his words by seconds. "Life is precious here in the wastelands. Grieve what is lost, celebrate what is not." He touched her shoulder. It was nothing untoward. So what was it between them?

Stinging drew Marco's attention to his scrape. He untied the cloth. Saw bubbling flesh. His mind zipped to the pulse pistol Ixion had taken from the raider. Were more raiders armed in similar fashion? How? Technology did not belong on Drosero. He mentally backtracked to the fires that had leveled Moidia. So much damage so quickly. The attack here—a half dozen slipping into the caravan unnoticed. The unusual coordinated strategy mentioned by the Stalkers. This wasn't simply a savage attack.

The dark realization pitched him across the road. "Mavridis, we should talk." Though his First glowered, Marco pushed on. "I have a suspicion to discuss."

Ixion reluctantly met his gaze, efflux rife with insult. Axeon and Hushak drew to his side, which seemed to bolster the indignation. The Stalkers resented his familiar address and intrusion into a long-established order.

Hushak eyed Marco but spoke quietly to his elder, "The tent is ready."

"In private," Ixion said to Marco, then headed across the road and into a tan-and-brown tent, where Isa was preparing a meal. He stopped and eyed her. "You are injured. Go rest."

It was not his words but the roiling scent that again made Marco pause.

In the sitting area, Isa shrugged. "It is nearly ready."

"It can wait," Ixion bit out.

She acquiesced, leaving without a word.

Marco wanted to respect their relationship but what hung in the air . . . "I would have an explanation." His First did not like being challenged, something Marco had unintentionally done several times in the last ora. This time was intentional.

"For what?" Ixion gritted out.

"Isa."

Hands fisted, Ixion stood firm, then sagged. Defeat clogged his scent as he turned to the sideboard where the food waited. He seemed to hover over the secret he held. Then freed it. "It's a nickname . . . started by her little sister who cannot pronounce her given name."

"I care not about nicknames," Marco scoffed. "I—"

"Her name is Isaura."

Marco's mind whiplashed to his last hunt. "You gave Kersei that name to get her off Cenon. You said it—" This time, he drew up. "Oh."

The cockeyed nod seemed as much acknowledgement as regret. "My daughter." On a crate, Ixion sat with elbows on his knees. "I do not speak of this, but I should have known from you it could not be hidden."

"Why the ruse?"

"It is for her protection."

"Against what?"

"Few know of our"—Ixion rubbed his knuckles—"connection."

"Connection? She is your *daughter*!"

That storm returned. Ixion unfolded to his full height, seeming to take on stature and breadth. "I do not need you to tell me—"

"I think you do. What sort of father will not acknowledge his own child?"

"The kind who has seen depravity and would not wish it upon his family. The kind willing to do anything, including send her away, so she could yet live." Rage shoved aside grief and flooded the room with a rank dolor. But Ixion did not go on.

"There is more," Marco said. "Forgive me, but I must press. There are things at play here that—"

"Her mother was . . . touched."

The woman from the bell tower—aye, Marco had guessed that.

"Lost in her confusion, she . . . cuckolded me." Ixion studied the ground. "Repeatedly. Made a mockery of my name and house. My position as elder." He ran a hand over his head. "It was a disaster I endured as long as she did no harm."

The scent spinning out warned that very thing came to pass. "But she did."

"She killed our son shortly after his birth." Grief tore at the man. He worked his jaw, trying to keep himself in check. "Pitched him from the heights of our home, shrieking that he had an evil heart."

Marco lowered his head at the sickening weight of that revelation.

"The Prokopian and Kalonican councils ordered me to have her executed, fearing she would turn against me." He roughed a hand over his face. "I could not do it. During one of her lucid moments when the agony of what she'd done to our son ripped her in two, we agreed in secret that she would escape to Moidia, start a new life. But I knew—she knew—she could not survive alone." He balled his hand. "Isaura, Ladies bless her, was the only one who could soothe her mother. Even at the tender age of four she had a way about her. So I sent her away with Deliontress."

"What I experienced in the six short years of life with my bound is nothing compared to what Isaura has endured learning to handle a madwoman. Being the brunt of jokes and vicious words . . ." Grief coated his anger, strengthening it. His gray eyes pummeled Marco, as if trying to impress additional meaning. "Careless words do far more damage than cruel intent."

Marco felt the smack in his scent. "You refer to me."

Crossing his arms, Ixion paced. "You question desert justice and my use of it—*their* use of it. Moidia may be called Camp of the Lawless, but it is not the only area where the lawless exist. Much of this land you rule is riddled with those driven to desperation, seeking a better life, no matter the cost to themselves or others." He rubbed his knuckles again, a move that flexed his biceps. "The people look to me and the Plisiázon for protection but also for guidance. I have worked hard many cycles to gain their trust, to do everything in my power to ensure a man does not need fear for his life going to the chicken coop, or a girl for her virtue when she fetches water from the wells."

"I have seen that trust," Marco said with a nod. "They trust you."

"Aye." Ixion turned that terrible gaze on him.

It came together for him then, what he'd already seen but had not fully realized. The import of his hastily spoken words. He'd challenged Ixion, aye.

But he had done more than that. "I overstepped."

"Nay." Ixion sniffed, shaking his head again. "You have not—you are medora. It is required of me to do your will and bend mine to yours. To do whatever is asked of me—and more. To lay down my life, should the need arise. I recognize this task and honor." He indicated to the camp. "But they do not know."

"So, when I challenged you for killing the raider . . ."

"You had every right, unused to it as I may be."

Marco thought of the shocked scents when he challenged Ixion. "But in the eyes of your people, I have wronged you."

"Never have I let a challenge go unanswered," Ixion said. "I cannot afford to or every man with a grievance will do the same. Your rules of civility and those Kynigos Codes are commendable and have served you well. Yet they are ineffective where raiders raze cities and slaughter people for sport." Leaning to the side, he plucked a chunk of meat from the tray and ate it. "Kalonicans are not without our own codes, and you will find laws of civility absurdly high in Kardia, but Stalkers confront the evil ravaging our lands with as much violence as it wreaks. We must. Or we will cease to draw breath, to exist."

"I will never forget watching you behead that raider." The way Ixion floated in the air, rotating over the man, his skill with the manriki, had left Marco in awe. "I have a new respect for you."

"I fear you lost as much as you gained seeing that." Ixion looked down. "What I do—what the Plisiázon do—to protect these lands is not pretty. Nor comfortable. But comfort *is* found for our people knowing we stalk the terror that hunts them. That method of killing is swift and painless. Raiders are cruel and vicious, so I act without mercy."

"How do I right this?"

Somber eyes held his as he sat again. "Without compromising your identity and thereby your safety? I know not." Ixion shook his head. "Considering the encounters with the raiders, I think it too heavy a risk to divulge the truth until we are leagues farther north, where the aerios and regia will join us."

Regia. Darius, praefectus of the Kalonican army. Surely he would not venture from Kardia. Darius had better not come—Kersei needed protection. No, he would send his commander, Theilig of Vereil.

A stale smell filtered through the tent, pushing his gaze back to forlorn eyes. "What?"

"It is not my place—"

"You are my First. If not yours, then whose?"

Ixion nodded with an arc of his eyebrow. "Very well. I will speak plainly."
He planted a hand on his leg and peered at Marco. "You should be in Kardia,
courting some noblewoman with thought to gain a kyria and an heir, not
here where the wilds are tame compared to the dangers we confront. You
run from what you cannot change, what you have lost, putting everything
in jeopardy."

"I have no desire to court—"

"Be that as it may, you have an uncle from whose gnarled fingers we had to
wrest the throne in order to crown you, and a brother all too eager to assume
what does not belong to him. A bound and heir will enact *Os Foní Tou*."

"What's that?"

"It means 'as his voice' and guarantees your throne if you are injured, or as
happened with Medora Eoghan, captured in battle. With that Council order,
his kyria, Valona, was empowered to rule until his return, saving the realm
from his ruthless brother."

"You fear I will be killed? That Darius—"

"You have proven the mettle to confront danger, but sadly, it is rarely
kind enough to operate according to our intention." Ixion gave him a tired
smile. "I appreciate your fervor and courage, Marco, but I need—this realm
needs—its medora. Putting yourself in danger out here will not change what
happened on Iereania. Stop running from what you cannot change. Return
to Kardia."

If Ixion had any idea what it was like for Marco . . . The smells that
betrayed everything. Tormented and taunted. Though his heart railed, he
could not argue. "I will return," he said quietly. "But not yet."

"The longer you avoid this, the more power you give it."

"I would say the same of you."

"How so?"

"Isaura," Marco stated. "She is now motherless. Will you take her to
Prokopios?"

Grief again infested the man's scent. "Prokopios believes my daughter
died in a house fire with my bound."

"What for her then?"

"I am thinking on it." Ixion's face twitched with irritation, but he turned
away. Picked up fruit. "The point of this meeting was a suspicion you had."

Marco huffed at the redirection, but neither was he willing to hear more
of finding a wife. He shirked off the idea. "I think the raiders are being
encouraged by Symmachia. Mayhap championed."

"The weapon we retrieved."

"The technology is Symmachian." Nodding, Marco bit into some cheese. "And the attack on Moidia—your men commented the raiders were organized, that there was a change in pattern."

Ixion set aside the fruit and leaned back. "Raiders are notorious for being vicious, erratic—but not intelligent. The marks on their bodies are burned into their flesh by the Faa'Cris. The constant pain drives them to savagery. But of late, there is a cunning to their methods that we have not been able to understand."

Marco narrowed his eyes in thought as he sipped from a cup, then let out a strangled cry and held the cup so he could look into it.

Ixion came forward. "What is it?"

"Cordi!" Marco exclaimed. "*Warmed*." He grinned. "Did you do this?"

"Why would I pander to a spoiled hunter visiting my lands?"

The only way the newborn would survive was if Isaura could get through to Ma'ma, bring her out of the vague reality that held her hostage. To the side, she whispered to Laseria. "From my bag—steam the satchel." It was a special herbal concoction of lavender and vanilla. For some reason, it always seemed to help.

Listening to her ma'ma muttering something over and over, Isaura drew closer. Motioned Laseria away. She eased onto the wide ledge. "What have you here, Ma'ma?"

Cloudy eyes stared straight ahead, out the window to the bell tower. "Gong, gong, the bell will drone, as she calls her children home."

"Ma'ma," she said, firming her voice, "is that Hieropyla's baby you're holding?"

Though her gaze drifted downward, Ma'ma remained locked in confusion. "Far, far the little boys will stay, as the stars do drift away. Cry, cry, come their anguished pleas, torn apart by sacred decree. To their deaths, down down down they go, the darkness all they will ever know."

Isaura smoothed her hand over the little boy's downy head. "He's beautiful, isn't he? Let me hold him."

Ma'ma's eyes came to hers. A crooked smile. "Yes, yes. You must." She shifted the babe from her arms, and Isaura wondered if she'd come back, found lucidity. Yet in her gaze there was no awareness, no recognition. "Soon my days will be all gone, and in his arms your heart undone." She smiled, a haunting emptiness in her brown eyes.

All Isaura cared about was protecting the baby. She felt his lightweight body rest in her arms and relaxed.

Then something shifted. Changed.

Ma'ma blinked. A terrifying chill ran through Isaura. She gripped tighter, anticipating what came next—her mother tried to pull the babe back. She stood, stepped back. "Ma'ma, I think—"

"Not in your arms. Not your babe. Not yet. You can't. He hasn't come."

Two men tackled her ma'ma, and though Isaura yelped, she hurried the babe to Kita, who rushed from the room with the now-wailing infant.

Shrieks filled the rectory, and Isaura turned, but not before she caught sight of a familiar blue uniform coming up the stairs. Hushak. She shut the door and rushed back to where men were wrangling her flailing ma'ma.

"Leave her," Isaura said, swinging her braid back over her shoulder.

The men grunted and muttered curses.

"We'd all be better off if she was gone," one said.

"Down he comes, fly fly fly. Right down from the sky," Ma'ma wailed, pulling herself into the corner and hugging her knees. "He's come, he's come, to make it undone."

Isaura knelt beside her mother and pulled the slip of a woman against her chest. Cradled her head. "Shh," she whispered. "It's me, Ma'ma. It's me."

Bony hands clung to her as she smoothed the disheveled hair. "Isaura," her mother breathed. The rigidity rushed out of her. Sobs soon shook thin shoulders, her hands digging into Isaura's dress. "Oh, please . . . please tell me I didn't hurt him."

Relieved at the desperation she heard, Isaura knew her mother had finally emerged from the cloud that had consumed her far too often. "You did not," she whispered, her own tears slipping free. "He's safe."

Once the sobs subsided, Isaura felt the acute loneliness that always manifested after these spells and her own tears fell. The room had emptied, the people now gathered on the street below, likely discussing whether Delirious Deliontress should be allowed to continue—practicing her healing arts, or even living.

Heaviness blanketed Isaura, trapped in a world not of her own making. Accepting this was what the Ladies asked of her. She dared not dream for more— only disappointment lay therein. Friends were few, taunts were many. With a mad mother, no man would set petition for her.

Ma'ma tilted her head back. Eyes red and face splotchy, she reached up and framed Isaura's face. With fresh tears that made Isaura cry more, she smiled at her. "Oh, but he is coming. With fire in his arms and war in his eyes. He is coming."

"Fire in his eyes, you mean."

But true to Ma'ma's delirium, she had misspoken the phrase. After all, how could someone have fire in his arms? She had proof, however, that men could have fire in their eyes—Dusan was evidence of such.

Nerves aplenty, she gripped the metal charm that hung at her throat and paused in front of the outside food table. What was this timidity? She had never been timid—could not afford it with her mother. Yet . . . blood and boil, concentrating proved difficult around Dusan, especially with Mavridis at his side.

"Need help?" Hushak grinned.

"Have I ever needed your help?" she teased, lifting the food tray. "You should be aiding the women break camp."

When he grunted and left, Isaura turned to the flap. Sunrays peeked across her shoulder into the tent, as if it, too, were anxious to see him again. Both rooms were still shrouded, but she heard Mavridis moving about.

Knowing the caravan would set out soon, she made quick work of packing items not necessary for them to break their fast.

"Morning." Mavridis strode past her, grabbed a cordi, then headed out, his terse commands strafing the air.

Isaura collapsed the table and set it near the entrance. Standing on a footstool, she unhooked the curtain from Mavridis's chamber. It snagged, so she tried to ruffle it free. When it defied her attempt, she snapped it. The curtain came free—but swung and caught the other side. The whole line dividing the interior came down with a whoosh.

A stunned Dusan stood shirtless at the washstand. His back, tanned, strong, and sinewy, rippled as he turned.

Isaura gasped and leapt off the stool, turning, but not before she saw his corded chest and the strange mark on his inner forearm that glowed blue. Like raiders. Alarm clapped through her. Was he one of them? Should she run? Alert Mavridis?

Fire in his arms . . . She stopped cold.

No. No, it was not . . . could not . . .

Dusan blurred to her side and clasped her arm, which drew her gaze again to his. The blue . . . fire. "Speak not of it." His words were a breath against her cheek.

Peering into his blue eyes, she tried not to think of the fact that he still wore no tunic, and forbade herself from looking at his bare chest.

"Promise it, Isaura."

She jolted. Not Isa, but *Isaura*. "You know?" She searched his face, wondering who he was that Mavridis would break the vow held these long cycles regarding their connection. What manner of man evoked that depth of loyalty from one who so rarely gave it?

The brooding hunter made her stomach churn as no man before with his beautiful, pale eyes, dark hair, and olive skin. Yet it was more than that—the way Mavridis deferred to him. Respected him. *Who are you?*

"I see in your face the same fear that would darken the thoughts of many here in the camp—that I am the same as the raiders. However, I assure you, I am not."

No . . . no, she knew he was not.

"We must bear each other's secrets with absolute solemnity." His hand shifted from one of restraint to . . . something gentler. "Have I your word?"

He was close enough for her to smell the soap he'd used to wash before her interruption. She considered him—his skin a darker complexion like Jherakans, black wavy hair curling around his collar, and pale eyes that saw all the way down to her adunatos.

"Isaura?"

Startled out of her musings, she liked the lilt of her name with his accent. "You have my word."

"Thank you."

"For now."

Frowning, he retrieved his tunic from the cot and donned it. Pausing only to take a hunk of cheese and a ripe fruit from the tray she'd brought, he picked up his pack and strode from the tent.

Secrets. Everyone had secrets. She had lived with them all her life, being treated as one thing when she was another. Daughter of an elder relegated to the tattered cot of a madwoman's shanty. She must not begrudge it, for that secret protected Mavridis, and she would never do him injury. How many others did she protect with her silence? Ma'ma. Laseria. Now Dusan. Folding his blanket, she thought of the mark he bore. Had Ma'ma been right in her head when she mentioned the fire in his arms?

Of course not. It wasn't fire really. Yet . . . what was it? The scent of him wafted from the blanket she was folding, drawing out a smile.

"Isaura." Mavridis stood just inside the tent as Hushak and Shobi pulled away the outer canvas. "'Tis time."

They were quickly under way, racing the sun, it seemed. As she walked, Isaura thought of the disapproval she always felt from Mavridis, and now from Dusan. What must he think of her, pulling down his curtain while he bathed? Then staring at him so baldly . . .

"You are lost in thought."

Isaura glanced to where Kita walked beside her. "I am lost, but whether in thought or adunatos . . ."

"You are far too sweet to have lost your adunatos." Kita's thick red hair was tied back, but curly sprigs defied restraint. "Is it Dusan who has your mind tangled?"

Isaura startled at how easily her friend had guessed.

Rubbing her swollen belly, Kita laughed. "He is very handsome, heroic, and has the approval of Mavridis. It is no wonder you stare."

It is more than approval. "I am but a child to him, one who inadvertently saw him bathing."

Though Isaura hurried to explain the innocent mistake, her friend's infectious laughter had them both in fits. Eventually, they settled into a quieter, casual pace for the journey. Soon, they heard the giggles of the children—racing in and out.

Isaura caught her sister's arm when she tried to dash past them. "What are you about?"

Little spry Mnason circled back to his ma'ma, his cheeks ruddied from racing up and down the line. "We want to show Iason how you can't sneak up on Dusan." There was more than a little excitement. "He doesn't believe us."

Oh Mercies. "The friend of Mavridis is very busy." Isaura hoped mentioning his connection to the Plisiázon elder would dampen the boy's curiosity.

"No, he's not," Mnason argued. "He's riding a Great Black and doing nothing for leagues but watching what clouds go by."

"Then all the more reason to avoid approaching—those beasts will crush you." But it was too late. The children gave triumphant shouts and bolted away.

Kita groaned. "The last thing I need is for Mavridis to think us a problem, and with those raiders sneaking into the caravan . . ." She started forward, but in her condition, she would never catch up.

"I will go." Isaura hurried to stop the children darting through the Moidians. More than halfway up, she lost sight of them. She slowed and turned, searching, but it was of no use. A higher vantage was needed. There—a small knoll with shrubs. Down the gully and up the rise, she clambered to the top. Fingers above her eyes, she scanned the line.

"Seems we had the same idea."

The resonating voice behind her churned Isaura's stomach. She whirled right into him. "I didn't see you."

Dusan steadied her. "Clearly."

Suddenly aware *she* was holding *him*, Isaura jerked away. "I beg your mercy."

"No need." Unaffected, he moved his gaze past her to the dusty road and its travelers.

"Are you well? After the blow you took, I mean?"

"A headache, no more." He squinted, then angled his eyes in her direction but didn't meet her gaze. "Who were you looking for?"

"My sister and Mnason." Isaura watched him taking in the people, the horses, the wagons. His strong jaw and olive skin were smooth against pale-as-the-sky eyes that took in the Moidians. By the Ladies, he must have been touched by Vaqar himself.

Curse her foolish self. She forced her thoughts back to Mnason and his troublemaking. Then recalled how the spry guy made sport of touching Dusan without being caught. And she could not help but wonder . . . Could he truly not be surprised? Would he catch her, if she tried? Had she not more skill than a child?

Heart pounding, she stretched out her hand—

Dusan peered over his shoulder and lifted an eyebrow.

His expression burst her tension, releasing a nervous bubble of laughter. "I had to try." When he looked back to the terrain, she was amazed he had not chastised. Mavridis would have. "How *do* you know?"

"Has Mavridis not explained about my kind?"

"Mavridis rarely *explains* anything."

"I am a Kynigos, a hunter." He tapped the bridge of his nose where black lines were scrawled. "Here, we bear the mark of our Order because we use it to hunt. We have enhanced smell. I can literally smell those around me."

Curious! "Like a dog or horse?"

His lips tightened. "Some have dared called the Brethren dogs."

Blood and boil—her tongue again! "I meant no offense."

"Our gift is from Vaqar. We can smell fear or mischief as easily as you detect cattle dung." Hot winds teased black curls that hung to his shoulders. Then his gaze narrowed, and keen, discerning eyes probed the distance. "You have your weapons, those discs?"

She shifted her leg to reveal the bronze weight there. "Always. Why?"

"Good. Go down." An edge climbed into his words. "Now."

Something changed. What had he seen? "Is everything well?"

"The children—they're there." He pointed at where they hid in the bushes. "Get them into the wagons." How had he found them so easily? "Go!" With that, he sprinted toward the front of the line.

LAMPROS CITY, KALONICA, DROSERO

"It is confirmed—your womb is consistent with at least two months' gestation." The pharmakeia moved around the drawn bed curtains. "I am done. You can dress." Soon came the splash of the water basin.

Kersei lifted herself from the bed and slid on her omnirs. Having Marco announce it to her on Iereania was one thing, but having a pharmakeia verify the pregnancy . . . She touched her belly in wonder. There was a life in her!

"The prince will be most pleased!" he exclaimed. "It will be a wonderful celebration, I have no doubt, especially with the loss of the medora and Prince Silvanus."

"Perhaps, but . . ." Kersei stepped into the open. "Please, I would hold this secret a little longer."

He frowned. "I do not—"

"For a while," she insisted. "Till I am sure . . ."

"There is no doubt, Princessa. You yourself stated your menses has been missed now these two months and your womb is swollen with the heir growing in you."

The heir. A son . . . "Aye," Kersei said. "Yet in light of the great strain of these last weeks, I would be sure before elevating the prince's hopes." When he did not agree, she added, "I insist."

He hesitated, then nodded. "As you will, but as the official pharmakeia of House Tyrannous, I am obligated to report a royal pregnancy within a reasonable time. I would face an uproar if Prince Darius learned I withheld news of his heir!" His face reddened with distress. "I could lose my position, my la—"

"I will not allow that," she assured him. "Have I your word, then?"

He huffed. "As you will." He moved to the door as if he would be away from her and her deception. "No more than a month, however."

"Thank you." Kersei closed the door behind him and turned into the parlor where she eased onto the settee. Again, she touched her stomach, wondering at the little one there. She felt joy, of course, but also a measure of grief . . .

Marco, where are you?

She moved to the windows and peered across the lands. Past the rubble that was Stratios Hall. Much farther south. At least, that had been the last report.

"Kersei?" Darius rushed across the solar, his very presence a storm that made her brace. "Why was the pharmakeia here? Are you well? What ails you?"

She returned to the settee. "I simply ate something a little off." She felt bad for the lie. "Never fear—I am well enough."

Darius frowned. "You summoned the pharmakeia for food illness when you let bruised ribs from sparring with Myles go unattended?"

She shrugged. "After losing my family to an attack, I felt it worth investigating to be sure I had not been poisoned." A terrible lie, but she must divert his attention. That's when she noticed something in his bearing . . . "What of you? You seem concerned—and not just about me."

He faced the windows. "There is word from Elder Mavridis." Shoulders drew into a ball of tension, then lowered slowly. "Of our medora."

Her heart skipped a little. "All is well?" She tried to keep her voice neutral.

He pivoted back to her, intensity radiating from his gaze. "There have been skirmishes with the Hirakyns. Moidia is razed, and Marco was injured."

She came to her feet, unable to prevent herself. "Injured how?"

"Unknown, but since Bazyli was here when the messenger arrived with the news, it was decided he will locate Marco and escort him back to Kardia."

Likely Marco would not appreciate that. "Is that his will?"

"I care not." Darius furrowed his brow. "He is medora, and the duty of every man in this realm is to protect him. It cannot be helped that he was so foolish to go out unprotected, and I will have words with Ixion for allowing such."

"He reports to Marco, does he not?" Kersei could not stop the small laugh that escaped her. "In earnest, do you think Elder Mavridis had much say in what Marco did? He's a hunter, used to doing whatever he believes necessary."

"But it wasn't necessary, was it?" His eyes sparked, betraying his anger. "Marco did not leave for any purpose related to the crown."

"You condemn him easily."

"Easily?" He sniffed. "Nay, but I know his reason had little to do with desiring a better acquaintance with the people."

"I think you misjudge him."

"I think not," he sneered, all but pouncing on her words.

Kersei drew back, realizing he not only anticipated her words but . . . "You provoke me." Disbelief wrapped a tight cord around her chest, anger rising at the dark accusation he made no effort to deny. "You deliberately spoke those words to see what I would say."

"Aye, and you did not disappoint."

"Am I to easily carve so deep a feeling out of my heart?" Her throat thickened with the rawness of what she felt, what she had lost. "Am I to be a creature so calloused and so . . . so selfish that I give little care for a man who has had to rewrite every piece of history he knows and step into the most powerful position on our world? With a brother who would as soon put a dagger in his back as accept him as family."

"How you defend him and make me the villain!"

"He is my medora, and you—" Indignation constricted her breath. She swallowed the rebuke. "I have seen no ill in him as I have in so many others in this wretched palace."

"Wretched palace?" he balked. "Would you rather live among the ruins of Stratios, exposed to the elements and poverty?"

"I would rather poverty of pocket than one of the adunatos." Breathing became a chore, and she reminded herself to calm. Think of the child. She should tell him.

Nay! Not until he showed himself of a more compassionate nature.

"Is that what you think of me?" He advanced, his blue eyes dark with more of that masked anger. "That I have no adunatos?"

Kersei perched on the edge of the settee, folding her shaking hands. "It is what you have shown, not only to me but to . . . others."

Angry, he stomped to the doors, then stopped. "Tonight we dine with the ambassador from Avrolis. I would have—"

"I cannot." Petulance never looked good on a lady, ma'ma had said, but it worked very well for Kersei this eve. "I arranged a visit to Stratios." How many lies had she told him today alone?

"Belak will escort you and tonight—"

"I am not a child who needs—"

"You are my bound and the princessa of this realm!"

"And quite capable of visiting my family's home."

"*This* is your home!"

"No, this is a cage!"

Even amid thousands, Marco would know that fetor anywhere. It was distinct, mechanical, and unusual for this non-tech planet.

Earning some unpleasant glowers from the Moidians, he vaulted onto a Black so he could move faster and see above their heads. He felt bad that his instruction to Isaura alarmed her, but he needed to be sure the children didn't give chase.

Heart alight as he chased the scent, he worked to ascertain which direction the smell was strongest. They were here. He was certain. Riding to the highest vantage of the gently sloping land, he scanned the surrounding terrain for sign of the unique scent infiltrating his receptors.

In the far distance, a copse of gnarled trees bent and shivered beneath some unseen force. Like a heat wake. Once sure he was not visible to Moidians, he removed his vambrace monocle and lifted it to his eye. Peered across the badlands to the copse. Adorned with a few brave leaves, the branches vibrated.

Marco lowered the monocle, smirking, and picked up the scent of Ixion's approach.

"What is it?"

"A ship."

Ixion's scent went foul. "Symmachians?"

"Nay." Though uncertain whether to be pleased or concerned—mayhap both—at who owned the vessel hiding here he stowed the piece. "I'm going closer."

"Not alone you aren't." Ixion silenced him with a look when he started to object. "You are medora, and I already fear the Council's wrath after your injuries in Moidia."

"You should fear mine more for disregarding my will."

The Stalker gave him a knowing look. "Not a cycle as medora and already you don the arrogance of nobility." He nodded ahead of them. "The land is open and parched. The Black will give you away."

Mavridis was right and, in fact, had already fallen into a light jog.

Marco slid off the mount and sprinted to catch up, earning a wry smile from the Stalker. They headed south, using the rise that abutted the copse to conceal their approach. It took them just under an ora to reach the trees. Leaves jittered, and the distinct fetor of engine fuel rankled his receptors. Definitely familiar.

Marco ran the jutting cleft that rose straight up fifteen meters. The jagged, unforgiving slope forced him into a climb, as if it were a wall at the Citadel. The workout felt good, rigorous, appreciated.

Atop the flat outcrop, he stretched prone and crawled forward until he spied the hull of a scout. He stood, backed up, and pitched himself out into the air. Landed on the hull with a thud that couldn't be helped. Quickly, he accessed the hatch and dropped through it onto the upper deck of the interior.

A stiff, slow clap echoed through the scout, coming from the galley. "We detected you a klick out and had time to sup and meditate. Tell me, has your time among the Kalonicans dulled that nose so much you wish to be dead?"

Marco grinned, his chest swelling with more pleasure than he'd felt in months. He strode forward, and the large man stood, catching his forearm in the familiar greeting. "Master." They slapped shoulders. "You are a sight for dry, tired eyes."

"What of the silver fox sneaking around our aft thrusters?" came the voice of Rico from the cockpit. "Should I light it up?"

"By fox, I suppose you mean the one that is near two meters tall?" Marco chuckled. "Since he is my protector, it's probably best to keep him alive."

"As you say." Rico shrugged and made his way belowdecks.

Marco slid onto a seat at the small table and let out a breath as he looked around the ship, recalling many years on his own scout—spending so much time in her that he could tell when atmospherics were low. Feel when she needed maintenance.

"How are you?" Roman's perceptive gaze probed.

"Alive."

"That good, eh?" Roman rested his arms on the small surface between them. At least, it always seemed small with the master hunter. "Searching for you, we were surprised to find you so far from your throne."

Marco grunted again. Knew his feelings could not be hidden from a Kynigos with twice as many years hunting. The grave loss of Kersei . . . the ache he yet felt for her . . .

"I tried to warn you," Roman said quietly. "It was not yours to be with the Dragoumis heir."

Anger sprouted roots from every objection and injustice on this perilous path. "She's with child. *His* child." Miserable, he shook his head. "I could no longer remain there and keep my sanity."

Roman nodded his understanding. "House Tyrannous owns half the land in Kalonica. Does the prince not have his own property? Why must they remain there?"

"Kardia is the safest fortress in the realm." Marco detected an irritated scent from Ixion and guessed he was being kept below. "I did not want her anywhere else until I learned what trouble plagued the land and resulted in an entire clan being wiped out."

"She beds your brother, and still you protect her."

Those roots dug deeper, twisting and coiling. No more would he speak of this. "What purpose have you for breaking the intergalactic pact with Drosero?" He grinned and eased forward, refusing to lick the festering wound. "How did you descend without being seen?"

"Broke atmo above the oceans in the far west, then dropped hard and fast until we could skim the surface. Let guidance navigate along canyons and gorges to the cliffs and hills that shielded our approach." He nodded. "Rico did not think with the stench of horses and that many people that you'd detect us, but I knew better."

"That was a lot of work and risk when you could have thumped me." He referred to his behind-the-ear implant the Kynigos used to maintain contact with hunters.

Roman grew somber. "Our communications are being monitored."

"Symmachia."

"Who else?" Roman downed the last of his drink. "More Brethren are missing."

Though he detected the obnoxious dolor emanating from the hold—Ixion was getting angry—Marco shouldered it aside. "How many?"

"Five last month, then this . . ." Roman set a data channeler between them and let it play. The training yard of the Citadel appeared, then the camera swung to the outlying fields and hills, which eventually morphed into the colossal range of Vaqarius that stretched for leagues and ended at the Sea of Eleftheria. Recruits did klicks-long runs there. The channeler's image was serene and quiet . . . until out of the trees rose three corvettes. "Twenty recruits rounded up during their run and taken."

Marco uttered an oath.

"The 'vettes were cloaked and had apparently come in the night to lie in wait."

"Someone knew our routine."

"Likely they've been monitoring Kynig to learn our movements." Roman cocked his head. "It's only a matter of time until they attempt to breach the Citadel, a violation so egregious it will be deemed an act of war. While Kynig is small, our allies are not, and the Symmachians seem unconcerned about turning the favor of Herakles against themselves."

"Especially with the *Chryzanthe* arguably in this quadrant." The station had been built so close to the Kedalion-Herakles border that it was now in dispute who owned it, since the TSC had no formal right to build stations or outposts in Herakles.

Roman nodded. "We cannot and will not risk the Brethren."

There was a message behind those words that pulled Marco nearer, anticipating what the master would say next.

"There is talk among the masters of going into hiding."

Questions erupted, and Marco had trouble picking where to start. "Just the masters?" No, they would not be that selfish. Yet if it was everyone . . . "The Citadel has never been abandoned since its inception!"

"All Kynigos would go, and for that reason this decision is not lightly made." Roman shouldered in, his intensity roiling. "You saw what they are doing—"

"Saw? I *experienced* it! No matter the purpose that creature had"—he'd never learned the truth behind that—"it's downright horrific." But what purpose did Roman have in telling him this? Though the masters had not applied Revocation to Marco, he was no longer a hunter. "Why tell me? If it is Sanctuary you need—you have it!" He smirked. "I know the medora of this land."

"The offer is appreciated, but our purpose here is . . . darker." He met Marco's gaze. "Your name and this planet have been mentioned in Symmachian communiqués."

Thinking of the land he'd traveled the last week, its people—*his people*—Marco scowled. "I don't understand Symmachia's obsession with this planet or me. And yet . . ." Even as he heard boots on the steel steps, he recalled the blue raider who'd shot him. "Have you heard of the Irukandji?"

Roman shrugged. "Raiders, savages."

"They are marked as I am, save that mine is prophetic. Theirs, I'm told, is punishment and borne all across the body. I recently encountered one with a pulse pistol." He leaned forward. "Technology on a non-tech planet."

Roman squinted. "Tell me more of them."

"They—"

"They are wild men." Ixion's firm, annoyed voice overrode Marco's. He and Roman seemed to measure each other with invisible scales that made Marco shift. "Men whose minds are ravaged by the wilds of the desert and fire gorges. The marks come with excruciating pain. An eternal punishment, it is said, for every wicked act they perpetrate."

"The Irukandji are conducting raids in a manner not usual to them," Marco said.

The master slid a look to the Stalker. "This is true?"

Ixion nodded. "They are cruel and vicious, with but one intent: to pillage and kill all in their path."

"The Tertian Space Coalition has never been quiet about their desire to colonize Drosero." Rico moved past Ixion and leaned against the bulkhead. "It'd be shrewd of Symmachia to align with a kingdom here, arm them, teach them strategy. If they can shift the tide of power—"

"The Irukandji—even the Hirakyns—are no more than savages," Ixion countered. "Your space army may provide weapons, but do not think it will be more than that. Their thirst is for blood and gold."

"What more can be said of most kings who subdue nations for power?" Rico noted.

"And is that the way of your brother here?" Ixion indicated to Marco. "Who is a king, medora of Kalonica."

Rico scowled. "I said *most* kings."

"As stated," Roman asserted, resuming control of the conversation, "obviously there is an element here that would embrace a Symmachian colonization, no matter the will of the majority."

"The majority will push back," Ixion warned tersely. "Symmachian interference is not wanted. We made that clear with the Tertian-Droseran Accord. Our people are not yet ready for such a leap when we still light our halls with touchstones and torches."

"There are a dozen planets in Herakles and Kedalion alone—and twice that number of moons and stations. I fear Drosero is vastly outnumbered, Stalker." Rico's words were calm, and when Ixion scowled, he lifted a hand. "I don't say that in challenge, but to point out the odds against you. Considering what Symmachia is doing with our Brethren, I would not count on them honoring the pact made with now-dead leaders."

"Zarek may be dead," Marco said, "but his son is not. And I will protect

Drosero."

"Foolspeak!" Roman growled, pounding the table. "With that brand fulfilled, you are more temptation for that Khatriza creature than ever before. If they know you are here, they will raze this planet to regain you."

Marco did not want to think of being in the clutches of that creature. He turned away, more to shake off the chill he invariably felt in his mind at the lingering impression of her. "Kynigos are a prize to them, but one does not hold her favor more than another. Evidence of that lies in the snatching of the recruits."

"You are not so weak-minded to believe that," Roman hissed, his efflux saturated with disappointment and irritation. "Do you not recall that it was said you were stronger, that is why they tracked you across Herakles and took you back to that satellite."

Marco gritted his teeth, searching for a truth that would deliver him from this nightmare. None came, but he was reminded of where the Lady had sent him. His role. His purpose. "It's imperative that I remain here. Figure out what's happening, who's behind it, and how to stop it."

"We know who's behind it—"

"Symmachians, aye," Marco agreed, with a sigh, "but with whom are they in league? I would rout those blackhearted traitors."

Nodding, Roman stood. "We should go."

"We as well," Marco said, clasping his master's forearm. "Know my heart, Master. I would not argue—"

"Aye." With a hint of a smile, Roman clapped his back. "You have long made me proud and that is unaltered this day." He rested his hand on Marco's shoulder. "Should you need shelter, thump me. The journey is not far to safety."

"Likewise." Even as they said farewells, Marco could not shake the belief that if what he anak'd in the hot air held true—too many raiders on Kalonican soil—safety was but an illusion. There would be war.

Her heart could take no more.

How vast the change of Stratios from when she had strolled these streets before the attack. Where once there were smiles and waves between friends as they carried out errands and work, now heads were tucked and spirits low.

Kersei slipped to the ground, took Bastien's reins, and walked once more among her people. It was good to be here, to see familiar faces, yet she felt a stranger now. Neighbors hurried away from her, heads down. Girls she'd once played with would not meet her gaze. But then an old friend emerged from a shop with a small brown bag.

"Confections again, Erelia?" Kersei teased, moving to intercept her, but the girl scurried off. Stricken, Kersei watched her go. Why were they acting as if she had the plague? Was she to lose both family *and* friend? There were not many left . . .

"We should return to Kardia." Darius's grim voice intruded on her grief.

Kersei determined to find one among the remnant of her people who would speak to her. Treat her as Kersei, daughter of Xylander, not the bound of Darius.

Ahead, several laughing men stumbled from the Great Black, the lone tavern and pub in the city that offered a place for Stratios fieldworkers to get a warm meal and ale after a hard day's work. It was not a bad place, her father had said, but still he forbade her from entering. Two girls ambled toward it, and one glanced her way.

Kersei started. *I know that face!* Rakel. Her longtime friend bounced her gaze up over Kersei. To Darius. With another quick look to Kersei, she scuttled into the tavern.

Plucking off her gloves, Kersei nodded to the contingent but spoke to Darius. "I shall return."

"Kersei, what are you at?" Darius demanded.

She started for the tavern and crossed the cobbled road.

Boots thumped behind her, then a hand hooked her arm. "We should not—"

"Release me." Anger flashing, she glowered at Darius for his manhandling. "If you ever want my heart, it does not begin with accosting me publicly like a dog needing to be domesticated."

He loosened his grip, face slack with shock. "I meant no such dishonor, only to remind you that we have a guest for dinner."

"*You* have a guest."

He frowned. "This dinner is important. We must meet—"

"And *this* is important to me. I have lost everything. These remnant"—she motioned to the people feigning ignorance of the argument—"are all that is left of my family and many friends. Stratios is a quarter of what we were. I have no home, no parents, no sisters, and no friends." It tugged at her conscience the way injury pinched his face, but Kersei would not surrender. "I need to make myself known to them. For months, my people have had no elder or representation of their needs before the court."

"*We* are the court."

"Aye," she said, "and now I am their representative. These are my people, and I must renew their faith in me and in the crown."

He scowled, drawing up. "What has the crown done?"

"To be sure, that question has been on every tongue these last months since their entoli was decimated."

He hesitated, then lowered his gaze. "Kaveh will remain with Thorolf and Belak."

"Thank you." She set her mouth in a grim line and started away, the precise steps of the regia behind her. At the door to the Great Black, she glanced over her shoulder. "You will wait here."

Kaveh frowned. "That is not wise—"

"I did not ask for an opinion, only your compliance." Cringing at her sharp tone, she stepped into the dim surroundings.

The thick stench of sweaty bodies and ale assaulted her. She paused long enough to let her vision adjust and locate Rakel. Halfway across the wood floors, she noticed with each step the thrum of conversation quieted. She quickly deposited herself at the table with the girls and let out a breath.

Rakel's face went white. "Princessa!" She darted a glance around.

"No, Rakel," Kersei said. "No titles. Remember, we agreed."

"We were ten and angry with that sniveling prin—" Rakel bit off her words. "I beg your mercy. I did not mean—"

"No offense." Kersei sniffed. "He can be quite querulous."

The eyes of her table companions widened. Rakel shared a look with the other girl, who had leaned away. It was just that move which awakened recognition.

"Eaddra?" Kersei laughed and eased forward. "I barely recognized you. I thought your family had gone to Valden ages ago."

Eaddra's expression tightened, and the girls again fell silent.

Clearly something had transpired, though it seemed neither girl would enlighten Kersei. "Would you speak plainly to me? I am without friend or ally." She touched Rakel's arm as the space around her seemed to brighten.

"What of the prince?" Rakel inquired, her tone laced with jealousy and anger. Yet there was a lightness about her that somehow invited Kersei in.

"He is not here. And I am."

"But . . . of course he would want you there and not here?" Eaddra asked. "He seemed something fierce out there."

"He is . . . concerned, aye." Kersei let out a heavy breath. "However, I miss my family and entoli fervently. Since returning, I have felt alone . . . empty."

"You don' look empty, what with those clothes and jewels." Venom doused Eaddra's words and stung the dingy, stained air.

Kersei had never been one for finery, but saying that would do no good. Especially with the Tyrannous royal ring on her hand that pressed heavily against her conscience. Then there was her luxurious attire—omnirs embroidered with daisies and her silk brocade bliaut. "It is ridiculous, is it not?"

"There was a time you wouldn't be caught with your hair done up," Rakel said softly, glancing at her slyly. "And he'd always catch your curls. Remember when you—"

"—chopped it off so he had nowhere to grasp?" Kersei giggled, her hand even now going to her thick coils secured with a brooch. "My father was so angry."

Rakel tucked her head to hide the smile.

"Ma'ma caught Adara sawing at her own . . ." The words made her throat raw. Her chin trembled as she fought the tears. Fought the memory of her precious little sister.

"I . . . grieve for you," Rakel whispered. "We heard the skycrawlers made you stare at their dead bodies for days."

Kersei nodded around her tears. "Horrific. Worse than the nightmares."

"What are you doing in here?" growled a man, loud and demanding. "You ain't got none business here!"

Startled, Kersei turned—only to find all eyes on her and the man standing over her, his beard mottled with foam, most likely from ale. His eyes were as dark as his hatred was focused. Behind him stood two others, their arms crossed over burly chests.

"Sit down, Malner," the tavern owner groused, motioning around the large room. "The rest of you, back to your ale."

Malner yanked away, stumbling. "Go back where you belong! Before you get the rest of us blown up!"

When he started toward her, Kersei stood. Tripped moving away from her chair. Her hand rested on the metal tube strapped to her hip—the collapsible javrod Jez Sidra had given her—and she eased a foot back for balance. Not a sparring stance, but near enough. Fighting these men was not the way to win their loyalty, but she would defend herself—and her babe. "I have no quarrel with you."

"But we've one or two with you," he jeered.

She unclipped the weapon but did not deploy it.

The men hesitated, shifting on their feet, then they looked down—and turned away, the rage and bloodlust gone, despite the furtive glances that said they still wanted a fight.

What . . .? Kersei saw then that their gazes had fixed on something behind her. She glanced over her shoulder. In the far corner, a shadow took the shape of a man. A very beefy man who shoved open a side door. Light blinded her as it spirited him away.

Kersei jolted at that large, familiar build. *I know him!* She hurried for the door and thrust it open. Hustling down a step, she glanced about, searching the dank alley for him, keenly aware the regia were on the other side of the building. Out of earshot. If anything went awry . . .

But a realization struck her mute. This street fed onto Horn Street, the main road between the village center and Stratios Hall. Her home. The ruins. Nothing but darkness waited at the end of the cobbled pavers. So where had he gone?

Palms sweating, she started down it, scanning side streets and alcoves. The darkening day made it difficult to see, jouncing her nerves. Running about after dusk in a town that no longer wanted her may not have been her brightest idea, especially since she had inadvertently abandoned her regia. But if she was right about who this man was, then she must . . .

Something darted from the side.

Snatching in a breath, Kersei yanked to a stop. The scritching drew closer, louder.

A small dog scurried across her path in pursuit of some critter.

She released the breath she held and laughed, smoothing her bliaut. Another quick scan of the road revealed nothing but shadows. Perhaps the better course was to return—

Steps hurried from the rear. An ambush, and she had walked right into it! She could hear their steps, sense the way the alley darkened with the presence of the loud-breathing man behind her.

Turning, Kersei flicked her wrist as taught by Jez and AO. The javrod telescoped out with a subtle *thunk*.

"Look at that, lads," Malner jeered, stalking closer. "Little girl's got her a stick. Maybe that's how she escaped and let Xylander die." He snarled again. "You need to pay for what you done."

Kersei stepped into a fighting stance. "I would never harm my family! My life was destroyed that day."

"You alive and they ain't." A second man closed in and lifted his hands as if he'd proven his point.

"Now you got that fancy prince and fancy clothes and jewels. And what we got? Nothin'!" Malner advanced with a sneer. "'Magine we could get a pretty coin with that." He lunged.

Kersei snapped out her rod, striking as trained—head, shin, gut. Three quick thwacks that made the man trip and go to his knees. She hopped away to ready herself for the next, already coming at her. Twirling the rod in a figure eight, Kersei advanced, watching not just the second, but Malner, whose gaze warned they'd both attack. The figure eight kept them both at bay long enough for her to figure out her plan. Two resounding cracks to the second man's head gave her little time to come round.

Malner was surging forward.

Kersei pivoted, putting her back to him, and drove the rod straight back. Caught him in the gut. She pivoted and leapt back, again assuming the stance. Though two of them now bore telltale marks of her skill and one quite a bit of blood, they both gained their feet and grouped up on her.

She had been trained by the best and with the best but . . . three to one?

She stretched her jaw. Never had she been one to give up. She struck out with the rod—but he caught the end, his palm no doubt stinging. Surprise rattled through her as they dove at her. Shoved her backward. Her head bounced off the brick, eliciting a yelp.

As Malner's fat girth plastered her against the wall, panic clawed. She could not die here—her baby! "No!"

Fingers closed in her hair. He yanked back her head.

She yelped but had to get her wits about her. When his hands encircled her throat, her anger vaulted over her fear. She dropped, twisting as she did, and broke his hold.

Kersei threaded her fingers, then drove her elbow backward, hard into his gut.

Another shove sent her headlong into the wall. Her teeth clacked. She bit her tongue and winced, feeling his hands where no hands should go.

Crack! Oof!

Malner pressed against her.

Kersei cried out and thrashed—amazingly coming free of him. She stumbled back and tripped—over Malner, who was collapsed on the ground. Heart pounding, she hesitated. *What . . .?*

The other two were laid out in the alley.

What happened? How had they been felled?

She looked up in time to catch the retreating shape of that familiar build. Shocked, she realized *he* had leveled these men. "Myles!" Foolish to think she had knocked these men down. That had been the handiwork of him— Aerios Myles. The fiercest of her father's warriors. "Please, wait!" She darted after him.

Wait, her javrod. Kersei cast around for it but could not afford to lose him. She pivoted and lurched into a massive wall of chest. She thumped off him and shuffled back. Looked up into brown eyes. "Myles," she laughed.

His dark, grim expression silenced her. He looked ready to kill—perhaps had killed to defend her.

"You're alive," she said, her exultation at finding him still bubbling. She shook her head. "How? How are you here? You were at the hall that night."

He glanced at the javrod in his hand, frowned, then returned it to her.

She flickered her wrist and collapsed the rod, earning a curious squint from him as he watched her deposit it in the leather holster at her hip. "It was a gift . . . from the people who helped me escape the Symmachians."

Something deep and sad furrowed through his features. Shoulders with corded muscles drooped. He lowered his head and started back down the road.

"Myles, please." Kersei hustled after him, wondering why he went this way, toward the ruins. "I would have word with you." She rounded the corner and again stopped cold at the dark shadows and empty street that stretched into the night. Groaning, she had naught to do but search him out—again.

After the better part of a half ora searching for him to no avail, Kersei found herself on the southernmost edge of Stratios Hall. She slipped through the stone gate marked with rearing Great Blacks and twisted vines crawling up the ironwork. Knee-high grass was evidence of the emptiness here. She tucked herself to the side and leaned against the stone wall, eyeing what had once been her home—a very grand one.

In her mind, she saw the hall as it had been—tall and formidable. *Like Father*. Lights glittered in the uppermost rooms as Ma'ma combed and braided Adara's hair. Told stories by the fire of Ladies who had won hearts of kings and nobles. The window to Lexina's room would be about there, just to the right. How they had fought and argued, hated each other! Over petty, trivial matters.

Kersei slid to the ground, letting the tears come. Letting grief leak into the earth that had swallowed her family's remains. After the sobs subsided, she lay there, willing the ground to take her, too—anything to ease this horrible ache that twisted in her chest.

Something whispered on the wind, startling her. Sensing she was not alone brought her up, seeking the intruder or danger. In the darkness and naught but shadow squatted a form. Arms resting casually on his knees. Waiting. Watching.

How long had he been there? She came to her feet, and he rose, too, his face coming into the moonslight. "Myles," she breathed, relieved and yet a bit unsettled.

"I will deliver you to the gates of Kardia, no farther."

She frowned. "How are you alive, Myles?"

"How are *you*, Princessa?"

The stench of death stung his nostrils. Marco scanned the terrain, which had changed in the four days of journeying since meeting with Rico and Roman. The following morning, Moidians had gotten under way at first light and traveled nonstop. Day after day. Yet he could still detect the fetor of fuel. Why did it linger?

As the sun neared the horizon, the thickness in the air made Marco's gut clench. He could not ignore it any longer. "Something is wrong."

Ixion scanned the dusty road. "Raiders?"

Marco squinted, anak'd. "Mayhap, but . . . wrong somehow."

"Fear not, my friend. Consider the men you keep company with and know we stay vigilant." He slapped Marco's shoulder. "Come, we will break for camp."

The Moidians, exhausted from the prolonged march, again set up tents and started fires. After seeing to Vahor, Marco stretched out before a fire, a log at his back and his conscience heavy with the news delivered by his brethren. Thoughts of the missing Kynigos and that creature torturing them left Marco in a foul mood and his heart leaden, especially knowing he was being hunted on his own world, putting the people in danger. Add the slowness of the caravan and the intermittent Irukandji stench stinging his nostrils . . .

He shifted closer to the fire pit in the hopes of drying out his receptors and filling them with the fragrance of cooking meat and bread. The rancor of the raiders was persistent, growing as painful as his ability to scent Kersei from this distance. With a sigh, he sliced a cordi.

Thunk!

Marco flicked his gaze toward the sound, a nearby tree from which Isa—Isaura—retrieved her bronze disc. Tucking a slice into his mouth, he tracked her pace back to where Hushak stood, giving her technique tips. Interesting.

It was unfair, he supposed, for him to know via her scents of both appreciation and annoyance, that she wanted to better her technique yet likely did not enjoy the attention of the Stalker. Isaura had been through much and yet still fought hard to be strong.

Smirking as he cut off another chunk of fruit, he watched her spin—her hair like a golden disc itself, flaring out against the firelight—and fling the disc with an effortless grace that made him still.

Thunk!

Even against the darkness of night her green eyes shone with victory as she retrieved the metal discs again. And her laughter . . .

"I gave her the discs for her tenth birthday," Ixion said as he joined Marco, stretching his legs out. "It would seem she has trained tirelessly with them. I daresay she is more proficient than any man I know."

"I'm not familiar with the discs. Where are they from?"

"Ancient weapons of the Faa'Cris, or so the legend goes," he said with a shrug, biting into a hank of meat.

The wind blew smoke from the fire their way. With it came a thick waft of that rancor. Marco tried to block the stench, hating it. Yet . . . His gaze rose in that direction. The scent was stronger, closer. "What's out that way?"

Ixion squinted and hesitated. "Near—a few houses. Farther out, Shau'li land. The city houses the seat of Elder Durjan."

So, firmly within the Kalonican realm. Marco hesitated, glancing to the northwest again. "And how far are we from Prokopios?"

"At this pace, perhaps a sabbaton."

Seven days. He chewed the cordi and homed his receptors on those scents. He'd thought he merely sensed the scattered remnants of the band that had attacked two days ago. But . . . there were too many, and they were drawing closer. The scent clearer. Did they know of the caravan, or was Prokopios their intended target? Did it matter? Out here on the plain, once raiders spotted the caravan, the Moidians would be sheep for the slaughter.

After cleaning and sheathing his blade, Marco walked to the other side of the line. There were no ridges out here, but there was a cluster of hoodoos just off the road. He jogged to the nearest one and tic-tacked up the warm, smooth rock and hauled himself atop its pinnacle. Through the monocle, he probed the direction from which he'd anak'd the scent.

Moonslight was stingy this night, unwilling to betray secrets. Yet with his gifting, he soon made out a thick shadow moving toward them and startled. The scent he anak'd was strong, but not that strong—the shadow in the far distance indicated nearly twice the number he'd expected. Too far out to be distinct, but coupled with his anak'ing, he had no doubt what the shadow meant. There'd be little hope if they fell upon the Moidians out here. He muttered an oath.

"What?"

He glanced to the road where Ixion stood with Hushak and Shobi. "We should push through the night."

Gray eyes probed him. "What trouble?"

Marco looked back to the camp, where laughter and merriment still carried loudly. If they knew the danger . . . "A band of Irukandji from the north."

"Impossible," Ixion scoffed, then his gaze flashed. "That's why you asked about the Shau'li—same direction." Incredulity darkened his features. "Raiders cannot be that far into Kalonica."

"Would that I were mistaken," Marco said, "but the anaktesios is never wrong, and the shapes sailing across the valley are neither animals nor allies."

"How long do we have?"

Marco dropped to the ground. "Unless we change our pace, four days at best."

Ixion considered him for a long second. "Your master said the alien hunts you, so I will not risk your life. We push through the night and make for the city. Hushak will go ahead to warn the city and dispatch aerios."

Stalkers trotted over, intention in their every move and eyes glittering with readiness.

Trailing Ixion, Marco took inventory of the people, their spirits, their exhaustion. "Some won't be able to move fast."

"They move or die at the hands of those savages." Ixion climbed up on a wagon and addressed the Moidians. "Gather round." He motioned the people closer. "Spread word through the line—we strike camp and get under way."

A collective groan went up, along with shouts of disapproval.

"Raiders are at our heels," Ixion said, "Staying here guarantees death. I know we are all tired, but we must press on." His tanned face betrayed no stress. "Children and elderly into the wagons. Women who can ride take a Black, mule, or workhorse. Men of age or near enough will run and switch with the remaining riders. Push hard and share the burden." He nodded. "Sup if you have not, for we set out within the ora."

"Who were they?"

The quiet question came from behind Marco, pulling him around.

Isaura's scent filled with surprise and regret—then rushed into a mixture of defiance and that accursed attraction. "I . . . saw the ship."

Marco kept walking, and when she stayed with him, he answered,

"Offworlders."

"Did they bring bad news?" Her persistence had iron. "Ever have you been concerned since they flew away."

How could she know that?

Never mind. He needed to talk with Ixion.

"You trust Mavridis enough to let him into your inner circle," she said, keeping pace with him. "To not argue when he says things you disagree with."

"He is the elder."

"Yet it is more than you binding your tongue."

Marco stopped short, and she stumbled into him. "What do you want from me, Isaura?"

"I . . . Truth. Honesty."

It was a good answer, but anak'ing her Signature said she desired much more. He needed to quell her questions and dull her tenacity in pursuing him. "Then I would seek your trust."

"You have long had it." Her expression was so guileless, so filled with worry. "Did your friends bring bad news? I do not mean to be so direct, but you seemed distressed then, and even more so now." Her green eyes held his. "These are my people, Dusan."

"The men who came were more than friends," he said. "And aye, there is trouble. I fear for the littles and the women. What trails us . . ."

"I see." Glancing to the caravan, she seemed to understand better than she should. "I will help with the children and elderly. The infirm are already on wagons. There should be singing to keep them calm."

Marco appreciated her burden for others—that was the way of her, giving little thought to herself—but singing could be trouble. "Mayhap not."

"Singing carries on the wind," she whispered, her gaze traveling the desert plains. "I see." She peered over her shoulder to the Moidians. Moonslight traced her oval face, the curve of her cheek and neck. "Kita will need help. Her time is nearing."

Spiraling out of her, fear and dread assaulted Marco's receptors. Drew him closer. No doubt she imagined what her pregnant friend would endure should the raiders attack—the woman had already lost her bound to them.

He touched her arm. A shaft of violet shot through her irises, sending a deluge of warmth into his gut. Though he had touched her before, he'd worn his gloves. And this pure of an *Orasi* he'd only seen in one other person.

She caught his arm, angling her head. "You are well?"

He cleared his thoughts. Shook off the shock. "We will take care of them."

Breaking away from him with a smile, Isaura gathered children in groups, situating one here and another there. Marco watched, wondering about her logic in positioning the younglings. After helping Mnason and another little boy into a wagon, she moved toward a family group. The father waved her off with a sneer. Disgust wafted from the haggard farmer, but Isaura merely continued on without a word to assist a group of young women. They turned up their noses at her as if she were lesser, when she was clearly their equal if not their better. The arrogance when she only sought to serve . . .

"Have you eaten?" A woman stood before him.

Marco blinked. "Yes. Thank you, Kita."

She looked at Isaura, who was now with children again, her face alight as she laughed with them.

"Why do the adults spurn her?"

"Because of her mother. Delirious Deliontress. The woman"—she shook her head—"had many problems. She screamed from the square that they would all burn and spoke of things that could not be known, yet she did. Deliontress once attempted to burn the wickedness out of a child." Rubbing her belly, she sighed. "Isaura was the only one who could calm her."

"So Mavridis said."

"But now they have taken to calling her Insane Isa."

He wavered. "Is she . . .?"

"Touched, like Deliontress?" Kita narrowed her gaze on her friend. "No, but . . ." She huffed. "Though demure most times, Isaura speaks her mind when she feels she must. If she believes a thing should be done, she will be relentless about it. A woman unafraid to speak her mind is not something most men can appreciate."

Marco's thoughts drifted to Kersei, to the forced binding with Darius. "Seems a lot of things should change in this realm." He located Ixion with his Stalkers, swinging supplies up into the wagons. Next to him, Hushak stared out of their little circle. Marco traced the man's line of sight. Connected it with Isaura, and did not like what he detected.

"Hushak is the exception. He has long wanted Isaura for his bound."

"I would say they were a good match . . ." Marco let the rest fall dead at his feet.

"But?" Kita persisted.

The man was not suited for someone like her. "I will hold my own counsel."

Kita laughed. "Isaura has refused him twice."

The thought of that man seeking her out reeked.

"She has a fancy for someone else now," Kita added quietly.

Marco understood her insinuation but said nothing. Yet his gaze wandered to Isaura, who seemed to have heard them, for her green eyes lifted and met his. "She would do well to seek affection elsewhere. My heart is otherwise engaged."

"Are you certain?"

The question did not need an answer. "It is time to set out."

PROKOPIOS, KALONICA, DROSERO

Four nights after Dusan spotted the oncoming horde, relief rippled through the exhausted Moidians as the city lights of Prokopios appeared in the distance, pinpricks in the black canvas of night. It should give her joy—hope—but Isaura recalled what Ma'ma said of this ancient, prejudiced city, and her hand closed involuntarily around her pendant.

From her perch on the wagon with her little sister, Isaura looked to Mavridis—this was his city, the one he ruled. Straight-backed, he had jogged alongside the caravan without tiring and with an unwavering confidence that warned he would confront any threat.

Ma'ma had never spoken ill of Mavridis, even when he relocated them to Moidia. "It was for our safety," she'd insisted time and again.

He protected the city—why could he not protect her, his family? Why had it been necessary to remove her and her mother from his home and life? His affection? Though he had made political visits to Moidia, she had never known the love of a father.

Shouts went up from the rear of the line. A long, shrill whistle sounded from Hushak. Heart racing, Isaura did not know all the whistles, but she had been through enough attacks to know that one.

Mavridis stilled, then nodded to Dusan. Stalkers bled from the caravan, moving to strategic positions. Alarm rippled through the people.

Laseria clung to her. "What is wrong, Isa?"

"Nothing. Just rest."

Her sister hung her arms over the side of the wagon. "I'm not tired."

As Shobi sprinted past their wagon, Isaura pulled her back and watched until he was naught but shadows.

"Douse the lanterns!" Mavridis shouted.

"Why are you running away, abandoning us?" demanded Ven'tac.

It was a wonder the churlish man had ever become regent. "Quiet," Isaura hissed back. "They run not from us but to danger!" She drew down the wick on the lantern, dropping them deeper in darkness.

"I'm scared," Laseria complained, hugging Isaura's waist.

"Riders and drivers," Mavridis called, "make hard for Prokopios. Use the city lights as your beacon. Stop for no one."

Sucking in a hard breath, Isaura hugged her sister close and felt motherless Oxir press against her other side. "Be brave and strong." She coddled them both.

Kita gathered Mnason to herself, her round belly a reminder of what was at stake—their very future.

The wagon lurched forward, and Isaura braced. Rattling over the rocky terrain, even the wheels seemed frantic as they raced toward safety. Holding her sister tight, she felt panic and desperation—she did not want to die!

The wagon jerked hard left and dived straight down. Jamming her foot against the buckboard, she fought to stay in place, to hold her sister. But she felt Laseria slipping and her panic increasing. She collided with a burly man and his elderly mother. The steep, jarring angle forbade her from prying free.

A hard jolt popped Isaura into the air and dropped her hard against the wagon. Her teeth clacked. Scared, she peered around the others and saw that the wagon driver had left the road to make straight for Prokopios.

Behind them snapped shouts. She glanced back.

Stalkers raced toward them, their faces a mixture of panic and alarm, their words lost to the thundering pace, the wind, children's screams, and her own pounding heart. Something nagged about the way they were pursuing them.

Concerned, she checked the driver again. Then the gaining Stalkers. Though unsure, she thought she heard them shouting to turn back.

"*The crop* . . ." she heard them call.

What crops? Even as she tried to sort the meaning, Isaura saw a long swath of pitch black ahead. Suddenly, she understood. Not crop—drop!

Her heart lurched into her throat. "No!" she shouted to their driver. "No, stop! It's a cliff!" She clambered forward, but the children held her back. "*No!*" she screamed. Why couldn't he see it? "*Stooop!*"

A sudden stillness trapped her. She felt nothing below her. Something tore at her skirts. Sharp pain lanced her head. Blackness embraced her. Swallowed her whole. Suddenly, she was falling!

"Curse the reek!" Marco skidded to a stop at the edge of the cliff, searching the dark depths for the wagon that had careened over the edge. Wood littered the bottom of the gorge. Swarmed with panicked, pained scents, he pitched himself down, slipping and sliding. The stench of death assaulted his receptors.

Ancient, have mercy! Not Isaura, not the children.

Marco probed for that white oak and lavender scent. "Where is she?" He'd seen her go airborne—pitched away from the others.

He lurched free of the debris, rolled his shoulders and tucked his chin, anak'ing around the dead horse and driver. Saw a man helping a woman from the wreckage. Pain and fear drew him to a boy pinned beneath a woman's body. Kita! Tensing as he gathered the petite shoulders to draw her off, Marco heaved her backward.

The woman cried out, went rigid, then collapsed in his arms. The boy—Mnason—scrambled up, throwing himself at his mother.

"Does she live?" Mavridis finally reached them.

"Aye," Marco said, as the older man moved in to help with Kita.

Panic and terror snapped out—Isaura's efflux! He launched to his feet as a scream assaulted the air. Finally, he spotted her a dozen feet away. "Isaura!"

She clambered onto all fours and scrabbled to her sister, gathering her into a hug with a heartrending wail. "No no no!"

Marco slowed, realizing the truth. Seeing the broken body of the little one. He swallowed hard.

"Noo!" Isaura wailed, rocking her sister. Cradled her bloody head and limp body.

He went to a knee at Isaura's side. Touched Laseria's shoulder, though the absence of her Signature already told him she was dead.

Green eyes pooled with desperate grief as Isaura looked at him. "Please . . . do something."

Powerless, stricken by her grief, Marco lowered his gaze. "I am sorry." When she sobbed—a punch to his gut—he hooked an arm around her shoulders. Let her fall against his chest, her tears soaking his tunic.

"Isaura," Ixion said in a rough, raw tone. "We must go." He lifted Laseria's body from her arms. "They will slaughter us if we stay."

Marco shifted back and pushed to his feet, helping her to her feet. Blood covered her bliaut.

Stalkers descended, rushing to them. "Raiders less than a league behind. Hushak and Axeon are staving them off, but there are too many."

"Take the boy," Ixion instructed his man, then he drew Isaura to himself and nodded to Marco. "Assist Kita."

The strident scent from Ixion pushed Marco back a step. Though the instruction annoyed him, he turned toward the pregnant woman. He guided her around debris to the path. As they started up, he felt her draw back and give a low, terrible moan. "Is it your time?"

"No." She rallied, squeezing his hand hard as they trudged up the rocky slope. "Not for weeks."

He would carry her, but the steep incline and loose rocks made it impossible. The climb took long to reach the top, but when they did, there were two horses waiting.

Shrieks and screams peppered the night, drawing his gaze back to the road. Despite the dark hour and only moons for light, they saw what seemed a sea of shifting shapes flooding across the plain. Dread churned through him at the threat.

"Isaura," Ixion said, "mount with Mnason and Kita. You'll ride hard—"

"No, please—I can't. Laseria . . ." Isaura pleaded through her tears, reaching for her sister, whose body lay to the side. Her grief was noxious, stinging his receptors as Marco helped Kita onto the Black.

"Think outside yourself." Ixion's admonishment was hard, but his expression softened. "Kita and Mnason need you." He hoisted the boy onto the second Black, then Isaura. "To the gates! Do not stop!"

Again Kita doubled, sliding off the destrier.

Marco caught and lowered her to the ground.

Ixion slapped the other horse's flank, and it shot off with Isaura and Mnason.

"I think the baby—" Kita groaned.

"She needs a wagon. She cannot ride," Marco said.

"Hushak, take her up the line." Once they departed, Ixion glanced to the little girl's broken body with sorrow. "She was so much like her sister . . ."

His palpable grief nudged Marco back, feeling somehow responsible for not protecting the child. The thought forced him to give Ixion some space. Even as he did, a wake assaulted his back and shoulders—not a heat wake. Or even the wind. But an entire line of hatred and rage. "Irukandji," he breathed, glancing to the northwest. They were there, eating up the distance between them, but a contingent had diverted toward—

A panicked, terrified scent yanked Marco's attention, jarring, and rolled into a familiar Signature he knew too well. "Isaura!"

Ixion pivoted.

Somehow in the ebony void of night and the frenetic pace of the destrier, Marco saw the horse thundering toward Prokopios. Isaura's long golden hair caught moonlight like a beacon.

Then a scream—inhuman. The terrible truth revealed itself somehow, as if it were morning with full light. As if he stood within reach of her. The Great Black had gone down under the power of a spear. Isaura struggled to her feet, frantic, hugging Mnason close. Oh no. Not the boy, too.

Wait. *How can I see this?* Only then did he realize his brand had warmed, the arcs alight—more than usual. Gaze back on Isaura, he measured the distance between her and the raiders. Too close, and they seemed focused on her.

Rage flung him around to alert her Stalker father, but he was dealing with others, too far to help, so Marco grabbed the nearest Black. Vaulted onto its back. As the horse bolted forward, Marco locked onto Isaura and the boy.

She struggled to run.

A swarm descended toward her, tightening the gap quickly. Too quickly. She would not make it to the gate. The aerios on the city wall unleashed arrows, but they could not risk firing so close to her without endangering Isaura.

"Hiyah!" Marco urged his destrier faster. It galloped, the thunder of hooves like a rhythmic applause as they closed the distance. Trusted Vaqar to help him reach them in time. Razor-sharp edge of wicked intent slashed at Marco's heels.

Night breathed the venom of dark souls in pursuit. The raiders were insanely fast, and the Stalkers battled with a similar fury.

Isaura whirled, Mnason in her arms, and her gaze collided with Marco's. A halo wreathed her, as if the moons themselves bestowed their glow on her. It guided Marco, focused him.

"What is illuminated in your sight will be your burden and your measure . . ." the voice of the Lady sang in his head. Scattering his doubts. Obliterating the fear. Speeding him.

At his right hand—chaos. At his left, war.

He would give it to them.

17

THE ACADEMY, CAPITAL CITY, SYMMACHIA

"You slagging me, Diggs?"

Lieutenant Theodore Diggins looked up from the handheld on which he reviewed candidate scores to the door and his buddy. They'd also been a part of Eidolon 215 before Tigo and Jez burned them and earned them desk jobs. "Excuse me?"

"Why's she back on the list?" Rhinn's grizzled features were darker than normal.

"What list? Who?"

"That twig." Rhinn thumbed over his shoulder, though no one was behind him. "Why'd you put her back on the first launch team? Thought we agreed she was a liability. She doesn't know how to follow orders or read her ship. That's dangerous, especially—"

"Hold up." Theo set aside his handheld. "Are you talking about Zacdari?"

"Even you said she's trouble, so why go against me? Just because they stuck those orbs on you doesn't mean you should overrule my expertise or experience with this team." Rhinn huffed a breath. "Not only does it make me look bad, it puts the others and the whole slagging mission in danger."

"What're you talking about? She's on Charlie One." Theo pulled up the rosters. "Didn't even put her on Beta, afraid she—" He frowned at the screen. That wasn't right.

"Tell me you didn't do that."

Staring at her clear assignment to the Alpha launch team, he shook his head. "It's a mistake. She's not going on the maiden jump. I'll fix this right now." He returned to his desk and called up the team liaison for HyPE. "Corporal Setius, this is Lieutenant Diggins. In reviewing the rosters for the jump teams, I've found a mistake on personnel assignments that needs to be immediately rectified."

"Yes, Lieutenant. Let me pull that up." Subtle tapping carried through her mic. "Ready, sir. Which roster?"

"Alpha One."

"Which candidate?"

"Zacdari, Eija. Lance Corporal. She should be on *Charlie* One, not Alpha One."

"Okay, not a problem. Let me—oh. Hm . . ."

Theo looked up, catching Rhinn's terse expression. "There a problem, Corporal?"

"Well, I didn't think so, but . . . Let me try something else." A few seconds ticked by before she grunted. "I'm afraid I can't make the change. There's a Command-level authorization needed for that, sir."

"Corporal. *I'm* the commanding officer of the training program."

"I meant Tertian Space Coalition. Not HyPE. Sorry, sir."

"Why would there be a TSC-1 level clearance attached to her file?"

"No idea, sir. You'll have to ask Tascan Command. I did see Admiral Krissos here earlier today, if you want to talk with him."

Krissos was at the Academy? "Thanks." After ending the comm, Theo straightened. "That makes no sense." He grabbed his jacket and stuffed it on. "I'm going to find Krissos."

"Light and easy," Rhinn said, following him out of the office. "We aren't exactly favorites around here since Tigo."

"I'm aware and reminded often by the brass." Theo headed to the Command offices, anticipating that's where he'd find Krissos or learn his location. The five-minute walk felt like an hour, the urgency of this situation making him feel as if he were running in water.

He entered the offices and nodded at the receptionist. "Morning, John."

"Lieutenant Diggins," he said with a nod. "What brings you up here?"

"Looking for Admiral Krissos. HyPE tech services said he was here."

"Uh, he is, but he's in a meeting."

Theo saw a familiar, welcoming smile. "Thanks. I'll just catch Colonel Galt." Tigo had said she was a friend, that she'd helped him when this trouble started, so maybe . . .

John lifted a hand in objection. "I—"

"Colonel Galt." Theo strode across the foyer to her. "How are you, ma'am?"

She arched an eyebrow. "Surprisingly, still not court martialed." She indicated toward the corridor. "Walk with me, Lieutenant." They entered her office, where she docked a flex screen. "I hear you're making good progress with the candidates."

"Yes, ma'am. That's part of why I'm here."

She took her seat behind the desk. "Shut the door."

Theo did as ordered and sat down across from her.

"Seriously," she whispered, folding her arms over her desk. "Any word from Tigo?"

"Ma'am?"

"I overheard Admiral Deken speaking with Admiral Waring." She arched her eyebrow again. "They think he's still alive, that he escaped the *Macedon* in a drop pod."

"His implant registered in a fire gorge on Drosero but was lost on impact." For weeks the remnant of 215 held hope that Jez or Tigo had survived, but after being reassigned and watching the days tick by without word of them, he'd accepted reality.

"What do you think of Xisya?" Galt asked suddenly, leaning back.

The Khatriza alien, the one who'd speared her tentacle-like appendages into the hunter. The same hunter who had blown their entire careers.

Theo gave an involuntary shudder. "Haunting." Why was she asking about that thing?

Her expression was implacable, unreadable as she nodded. "So what's brought you here, Lieutenant?" Galt reached for her flex screen.

About time. Theo shifted to the edge of his seat. "A candidate I placed on Charlie One was reassigned without my knowledge or permission to Alpha One."

She stilled, re-docked the screen without looking at it. "The roster stays as is."

Theo knew to just nod and salute, but his body disobeyed that order. "Ma'am, perhaps you're not aware of the candidate in question. I can assure you, there has been a mistake."

"So you're saying you know more about this program than I do? That your knowledge is to be more heavily considered than that of a superior officer who was integral in the origin of the program in the first place?"

Theo knew he was treading on sacred ground, but he couldn't believe she had a full awareness of the situation. "With respect, ma'am, yes. Zacdari repeatedly made elementary mistakes that had catastrophic repercussions. It's dangerous to have her on the *Prevenire*." He felt his anger rising and warned himself to calm down. "If something happens, I could be held accountable. I take my responsibility very seriously."

"So your reputation is what you're concerned about."

"The entire crew of the *Prevenire* is my concern."

"Be very careful, Lieutenant Diggins. Don't bite the hand that feeds you."

He frowned, and somehow it struck him that he was sitting in front of the reason he was able to get on the *Prevenire* project at all. "You . . ."

Galt's air of gravitas seemed to expand, pressing against his assumptions and concerns. "Roster remains as is."

PROKOPIOS, KALONICA, DROSERO

Behind him, Marco heard the first raider closing in. The thunder of hooves, the stench of murderous breath. He slid his gaze left, a horse's head bobbing into view. Marco let the Black slow, a move that brought him slightly behind the rider, surprising the raider, who thought to gain the supposed advantage and leaned out to strike him.

Shouts from the city wall warned archers to hold their arrows.

Marco grabbed the raider's arm and threw himself from the horse, bringing them both to ground. He caught the head in one hand, his shoulder in another. Jerked in opposite directions. With a definitive crack of his neck, the raider went limp.

They were yet forty meters from the outer wall and gate where aerios were pouring out to give chase to the raiders.

Marco sprinted after the horse, only to find Isaura had caught it. "Get on!" He reached her, but she turned for Mnason. "Up! I'll get him." When she gripped the horse's mane and hiked, he gave her an unceremonious shove. Then he lifted the boy to pass him up, but the horse whinnied and rose on its hind legs.

Alarmed, Marco shifted back as Isaura clung on with hands and legs. As soon as hooves touched ground, Marco thrust the boy onto the Black, but now it staggered and went to its knees. The beast slumped onto its side, a long shaft protruding from its chest.

Marco muttered an oath.

Isaura stumbled free of the dying animal, catching his arm as she whimpered at the blood gushing from the magnificent destrier.

Hoisting Mnason into a firmer hold, Marco turned toward the gate. "Do you have your discs?"

"No, they were in my bag," she cried.

"To the gate!" As they started that way, four more raiders rushed from the right. Aerios were coming but weren't close enough to help them.

After passing Mnason to Isaura, Marco nudged Isaura behind him, noting the way she clutched his shirt and held on tight. Her breaths were short and ragged, laced with the heady scent of terror. It angered him—the raiders so far north and Isaura in danger. Him to blame, since the raiders were after him.

Around them, a dozen Stalkers and aerios confronted raiders, who were fighting with a viciousness Marco had not thought possible. Daggers slashed. Garrotes choked. Hatchets hacked. No method was too horrible, no manner too dark for the blue raiders. There was a slaughter of both defenders and raiders, but even with the influx of aerios from the city, the Plisiázon were easily outnumbered five to one. The raiders would run out of bodies to break.

Looking for a horse, Marco heard a piercing screech from his right. A raider stood in the blood of a fallen Stalker and shrieked like a wild beast. Blue-laced skin seemed to smoke and smolder, the man writhing as a new symbol appeared on his neck.

There was no way to reach the city gate. *Curse the reek!*

Marco pulled Isaura against his back, Mnason between them, his little arms in a near stranglehold on her neck and his body rigid. Around them, he sensed the cocooning of savages. Suddenly his feet were numb with vibrations, a strange and confusing sensation. A foreign odor rose in the air. What was that?

"Something's happening." Isaura's words were fragranced with her confidence in him, her trust—yet her fear. "The ground . . . my feet . . ."

He looked to the side, trying to focus, sort the strangeness from the imminent threat as the snarling, snapping raiders chomped closer. As the trembling increased, his gaze went to the ridges above, widening as a landslide cascaded down one. Shouts went up on both sides. An enormous creature plowed through the horde of raiders with a decidedly pleased moan. Its thick hide had sprigs of hair jutting up between rock-like scales that armored a tri-horned head. Short, thick legs set it low to the ground, but the pads of its feet left massive depressions in the dry earth.

Isaura gasped, flatting herself against him. "A rhinnock." Her breathed words were hot against his neck. "They never come this far north."

Just like the raiders.

Three rhinnocks barreled through the melee, stamping raiders into the ground the way ants were crushed beneath boots. Marco tensed as the distance between them vanished and he came to the daunting realization:

there was nowhere to run.

A horn blew from the city wall, a piercing warning.

The rhinnocks charged full speed.

Marco stumbled backward, nearly tripping over Isaura. He gave a shout, and the closest beast skidded to a stop, flattening the four nearest raiders. The other two beasts swung around, their spiked tails lashing out.

Marco ducked and rotated, pulling Isaura around with him. The beast's powerful move slapped Marco's hair into his face. But no pain. No attack. Just a thick haze of dust and dirt that peppered them. Holding Isaura close, Mnason still clinging to her neck, Marco peered through the settling haze, stunned to find hard rhinnock hide forming a perimeter around him. To protect, or to shut them off?

Over his shoulder, he peered past one of the beasts to the gate.

Atop the rhinnocks, the riders stared out over the field. The men had long black hair twisted through with leather. Well-muscled, hard-edged, their dark torsos were bare save white tattoos on their shoulders and left arms.

"Hirakyns." Isaura was more than a little awed—and fearful.

"Who are you that you attack without provocation?" Ixion demanded from the other side of the rhinnocks.

"*Attack?*" The stout man atop the center rhinnock, his armored scales splotched with blood, rested a hand casually on his thigh. "I offer protection and you accuse? No wonder our lands have been at war so long."

"Why else would you be this far north with these beasts and the raiders?"

"*With* raiders? Neh. But how 'bout you offer me some ale and bread, and we can talk?"

"As Hirakyns, you know desert justice and the price for entering Kalonican lands," Ixion growled. "Leave so we are not forced to end your lives here and now."

"End our lives?" The man laughed again. "We have done nothing to warrant killing. In our lands, that is called murder. Desert justice is an eye for an eye, a life for a life. Is that the challenge you set before me, Stalker?"

"No," Marco spoke up. "We are grateful for your aid"—he swallowed, understanding the tension, the hatred—"and your protection." It was said the raiders had been spawned from Hirakyns, yet there was little resemblance between these men and the monsters dead at their feet.

The Hirakyn shifted the rhinnock aside to face Marco and grinned. "At last, someone with mind and manners." He clasped his own sword arm. "I am Crey of Greyedge."

"Dusan," Marco said with a nod.

"Your mark," Crey said, pointing to his nose. "I have seen that before."

"I think not."

He smirked. "So not only am I unwanted here despite the obvious protection I just provided for you and your lady, but now I am a liar as well."

Your lady? Marco resisted the urge to look at Isaura. "I beg your mercy—"

"I have no mercy and will have no begging. Just a meal and word with you."

Sensing Ixion's intent to refuse—a mistake, to be sure—Marco replied, "Agreed."

"Then you will be on your way," Ixion said, slipping past the rhinnocks with two Stalkers to secure Marco's side. "The armies of Kalonica are drawing near, and we would hate to start a battle when you are so outnumbered."

"Sometimes, Stalker," Crey said with more than a little acid in his tone, "strength is not found in numbers but in strategy. Say . . . your soft bones to my rhinnock's clumsy gait." He shrugged. "It would be painless."

Crey's men snickered.

Irritation rippled through Ixion's expression. He turned to Marco and Isaura. "Are you well?"

Nodding, Marco looked to her, Mnason still wrapped around her torso, eyes closed and tear tracks on his cheeks. Scared, but safe. Thanks, in large part to the Hirakyn. He eyed the man perched high above on the rhinnock. "I owe you a life debt, Crey of Greyedge."

Ixion caught his arm. "No!" His gaze flicked to the rhinnock. "Dusan is not from here; hold him not to his oath." He gave a grim nod. "Sup with us, then depart at first light."

Shrewd eyes held them. "Agreed."

Oh, Laseria . . .

Unable to forget her sister's vacant stare as she slipped from this life, Isaura stood at the edge of the large market square, already peppered with tents and campfires for the Moidians. She had been helping Kita, still having pains in her stomach, and Mnason to the pharmakeia when two aerios intercepted them, saying the medical tent was too crowded for those not injured. Did her heart count? It bled with grief for the loss and terror she had experienced this night. Dusan, Mavridis, and the Stalkers went in another direction, leaving Isaura alone and sad. A kind lady offered her a clean dress and Isaura changed, though the dress did not fit and its hem frayed.

"Mistress?" a voice called.

Isaura sighed and rubbed her shoulder, shifting to the side and trying to figure out where she belonged here. No ma'ma, no sister . . .

"Mistress!" Shobi appeared in front of her, his expression bemused and earnest. "Did you not hear me?"

Surprised that anyone, let alone one of her father's Stalkers, would address her as "mistress," she frowned. "I did not realize . . ."

"Come. He's sent for you."

"Who?" she asked, moving before he answered.

"Elder Mavridis. You're to be his guest at the mansion."

Dumbfounded, she gaped after him as he strode the cobbled road, then hurried to catch up. "You are sure? He asked for *me*?"

"Asked? No," Shobi said with a smirk. "Insisted."

She followed the dark-haired Stalker, not allowing herself to believe this was real. Mavridis may have sent for her, but not for her to be a guest. To serve him, more like. As they made their way up the tangle of streets, she could not help but admire the milky-white walls and buildings that pervaded the city. She liked a great many things about Prokopios—it was large, the streets cobbled, lanterns lit the roads, flowers grew stubbornly defiant among the stones. They headed up the small hill from the town square to the grand home nestled on a grassy knoll.

"By the Ladies," she whispered in awe as they passed through the gate.

"Bet you haven't seen the inside of something like this before," Shobi said with a grin.

But she had. When Isaura was little, she once lived within these very walls, though she recalled none of it. In truth, it felt as if she were seeing it for the first time.

"Some claim the Sanctuary is the prettiest building in Prokopios, but the only people who say that haven't been inside the elder's home."

As he ushered her through a wrought-iron gate with gilt accents, Isaura wished for a shawl to wrap about her shoulders, anything to protect her from the pervasive dread that seeped into her bones. They would enter the house and be told it was a mistake; she wasn't welcome here. How she wanted to return to the camp, to the bell tower with Ma'ma and Laseria. Her family.

Even as they wound their way up the path, she spotted a wider side path—road, really. Likely for horses, since the stables were at the back of the house. It was odd, knowing he had so much, when all these years . . .

It does no good. Release it. Bitterness rots the bones.

Hushak appeared in the open door of the grand home and held it as she stepped inside. Floors of veined stone stretched smooth and shiny. Paint and pictures covered the walls. Where there were no paintings, tapestries hung. Rich brocade draped windows. Marble columns. Thickly padded furniture and gilt tables.

Shobi escorted her past a large, empty room that seemed in the midst of renovation, then up an arching staircase to the second level. A massive chandelier with dozens of candles hung overhead and made her cringe that the wax might drip or the ceiling catch with that much flame.

Voices seemed to draw them into a long, narrow room that held a table with sixteen chairs—seven on the sides and one at each end. All seats were occupied and many more men stood around the room with plates of food or drink in hand.

What could this be about, having her brought here?

"Let me find Mavridis," Shobi said as they entered the packed room.

Conversations quieted, and a few chairs scraped as aerios came to their feet, their green uniforms vibrant against the stark gray leathered cuirasses of the Stalkers.

Alone and uncomfortable, Isaura frowned. Nobody stood for her. She held her spot, exhaustion settling into her limbs. They did stare . . . Relief wound through her as conversations and seats were resumed.

A familiar form slipped around the standing aerios and approached. "How do you fare?" Dusan, too, looked tired but in better spirits than when they'd been outside the wall.

"Tired, but well. I look forward to a bath and good rest," Isaura said quietly.

"I think we all do," mumbled a man with blond hair, the sides plaited away from his face. He wore Xanthus leathered armor and looked familiar with both blade and authority.

It was then she noticed Hirakyns also sat at the table. A miracle, since Mavridis once said the only purpose for a Hirakyn on Kalonican soil was to slicken his dagger. Admittedly, having lived so close to their lands and seen too much of the raiders' violence, Isaura was not sure what she thought of the Hirakyns being here.

"Eat, Isaura," Mavridis said as he motioned her to a chair a Stalker was vacating. "Then we'll see to the other needs."

Shifting, she hesitated. She did not belong here among the machitis. With a man who had refused to claim her as his own blood.

"Mayhap this is too much," Dusan said. "She could rest and refresh first maybe."

Mavridis considered them both, nodding. "Agreed." He started toward her. "Come."

She smiled her thanks to Dusan before following Mavridis into the hall and up the arching staircase. Thick carpet padded her feet as they passed several rooms. Benches and paintings lined the walls that had several torches spaced every few feet, throwing warm light over the faces of his forebears. Wonder speared her, seeing the many different styles of dress and coifs, marking hundreds of cycles.

He nudged open a door where light and warmth spilled out. "Lounge and"—he crossed the room and threw open double doors—"the bedchamber should do well, I think."

My own room? That had never been so.

Mavridis pointed to a table and chairs near a beveled window. "Nooning tray is there." He moved to a wardrobe and opened it. "Clothes here."

Startled that he had thought at all of her needs, she scrambled to think of something to say. "This is . . . overwhelming. Thank you."

His expression softened and he touched her arm. "I am grieved over Laseria."

Isaura considered him, the man she had seen a thousand times when he ventured to Moidia, but today . . . she *saw* him. Surprised by his consideration. This gesture of kindness. She wanted to ask why he would do this, why now? But the answer was obvious, was it not? She was an orphan now, and somehow, that played against his aloofness.

"Sergii will be along at the top of the ora to help you with a bath." He started for the door. "If you need anything, pull the tassel. Fen or Dart will come." Hand on the doorknob, he hesitated. Glanced back. "Stay in the room. Guests are about, and I would not have incidents."

"You fear the Hirakyns," Isaura guessed.

"Fear?" He seemed affronted. "No. But neither do I trust them." A shadow passed across his eyes. "Forget not—they are responsible for your ma'ma's death." He considered her for a moment. "Be smart and stay safe."

She inclined her head. As the door closed, she felt the grief of it all. The loneliness, being cut off from everything and everyone she loved. Fear had stalked them all the way from Moidia and even now camped at the gates.

Turning, she took in the room, the furnishings, the tapestries, the massive bed with curtains as if they were royals. So much luxury. How she wished Laseria could have seen this! She could hear her exclamations. *"It's the most beautifulest thing I've seen!"*

But never again would Laseria see beauty.

Thick blankets covered the mattress, which even had a skirt. Half the walls were paneled with wood, the rest papered. Windows were tall and narrow—but many, so the morning light pushed through with equal parts defiance and beauty.

A feast waited on a large round table by the hearth.

Laseria would love this, too. Likely, she would ask for one of everything. Isaura, however, had little appetite. After filling a glass with cordi, she took a gulp, selected a chunk of roast, and walked the room, eyeing paintings and tapestries. An entire bookcase built into the wall! She traced the spines.

She went to the wardrobe and opened it. The sight stole her breath. "Never have I . . ." Touching the luxurious gowns felt like a betrayal of their elegance, with her hands dirtied and scratched from the wagon crash. Her heart broken with Laseria's death. They seemed . . . ridiculous in light of the situation. The gravity of the lives lost.

Her hand fell on a light blue one with a sheer overlay and crystals dangling from a high waist. The green one with lacy sleeves and skirt. One stole her breath—it seemed the color of the rising sun. A soft coral satin—sleeves just to the elbows, then sheer fabric spilling to the knees. An embroidered lace overcoat fastened in the center with swaths of the sheer gathered from the buttons and sweeping up over the bosom to bows tied at the shoulders. From there it fell free down the back. It reminded her of the fields of Moidia for some reason. But far grander. More beautiful. So perhaps not Moidia. Maybe this was more like Kardia, where Medora Marco lived.

Overwhelmed at the extravagance, Isaura swished it aside. A pang stole across her heart. It had been her secret dream that Mavridis would come to Moidia and claim her as his heir one day. Strange how bitter that wound, when long ago she thought that fantasy had been surrendered. This—the room, food, and clothing—was not about doing nice things for Isaura. This was about not embarrassing Mavridis, who ruled Prokopios. "It would not do for him to have paupers from Moidia looking like street beggars in his own home." The thought tightened her stomach. All that she loved of Moidia was gone, and now she had no home, no family. Eventually, Mavridis would send her away.

"Speak not of the oath you swore," Ixion warned as they gathered that evening in the salon.

"Oath?" Marco frowned at the elder of Prokopios—he must think of him as such, for he had more recognized power here than his own apparent status as merely a hunter.

"You took him into your circle when you said you owed him a life debt."

"It was a figure of speech, no more."

Ixion gave a grim nod. "Not on Drosero." He lifted a snifter and sipped. "With those words, that man is bound to you, and you to him."

"Bound?"

"Not as a man and woman." Ixion nearly smiled. "But with the same responsibility. Since it was spoken before witnesses . . ." Ixion tucked his chin. "And if he were to learn who you are . . . We shall speak more later, but . . . perhaps stick to the weather, aye?" He moved away, joining the Stalkers in quiet discussion.

Marco glanced at his cup, irritated. That he so poorly understood the customs of his own people, that he nearly died surrounded by smelly beasts and had to be saved by the enemy of his father's kingdom. That there was no reeking *warmed* cordi in this accursed place. Uncivilized!

He set down the chilled drink. Roughed hands over his face and sought the solace of the garden beyond the glass doors. He stepped into the night, ready for crisp air and quiet. Instead, he was slapped with hot air rife with the odor of thousands of bodies, animals, and the rank discord of many people in such close proximity. Then there was the lone man lurking in the shadows. If Marco withdrew now, could he feign ignorance?

"I see I am not the only one who does not enjoy cramped quarters."

Marco twitched, annoyed with himself for debating. Now he must find a graceful exit from the one seated on the balustrade, a foot up on the stone, the other dangling in casual indifference.

Marco leaned on the barrier, but the crowded city afforded no view save building stacked atop building. It was grand, if one enjoyed suffocating cities.

"Kynigos, aye?" the Hirakyn said, lowering his leg and standing.

Marco turned and reclined against the stone rail. "How do you know my kind, Crey of Greyedge?"

"Six months back there was some trouble in the gorges," Crey said, his gaze strafing the walls as if he could see past them. "Protecting the outlying settlements and camps is our responsibility. On one of our patrols, we happened upon a damaged craft that had crashed."

"Kynigos do not hunt on Drosero."

"I did not say he was hunting." Crey's sharp eyes watched him closely. "Actually, he said *he* was being hunted, that he needed to hide."

Marco's heart thumped.

"We led him to some caves. Buried the craft."

"Buried?" Marco laughed. "A scout could not be buried."

"It was more than half dug in the gorge already. Not so difficult a task to finish it off."

Steadying his breathing as he'd been taught to avoid betraying his thoughts, Marco peered into the man's gray eyes. "Where is this Kynigos now?"

A lazy shrug bounced the man's thick shoulders. "No idea. He was gone when we returned a few days later."

"And the craft?"

"I already told you."

"*Where* is it buried?"

Crey barked a laugh. "In the gorge." He shook his head. "I wonder at your listening skills, Kynigos. Guess it's not a bother when you can smell your way around a political table."

Impatience knotted Marco's shoulders. Could the downed Kynigos have been Tulio or Siseal, who had never been found? His bigger, growing concern was that this Hirakyn taunted him, that mayhap he knew exactly what happened to the hunter. Yet, he detected no sour note to Crey's efflux. Regardless, he would need to inquire of Roman. "Why tell me this?"

"At first, I thought you might be looking for him. As you said, Kynigos do not hunt on Drosero. And it was six months . . . So, one wonders . . ." He trailed off. "Wind and fire," Crey breathed.

The scent roiling off the man—admiration, attraction, a hint of lust— forced Marco to follow his gaze to something back in the salon. Through the glass doors came a burst of color that stood out among the grays and browns of the gathered men.

Coral—the color of cordi—wreathed a curvy figure and accented blonde hair. Ixion had no bound, so Marco shifted to see who his First was introducing to the room. When he saw her face, he started.

Isaura. Bathed, her scrapes tended, the cut on her lip barely noticeable, she was a vision. Her hair seemed more golden than he recalled and hung in gentle waves across her shoulder. She smiled, her cheeks gaining color that matched her rosied lips as the men closed ranks, apparently introducing themselves.

Something twisted in Marco.

Crey had an eagerness that left no doubt about his intent. "Will I have to fight you for this beauty then, Kynigos?"

Scowling, Marco sniffed. "*This beauty* is the guest of your host. I would give care lest you tempt the rage of Mavridis."

"So, not his daughter." Crey sent an appreciative smile toward Isaura. "Then also not bound. Promised to anyone?"

Rankled, Marco gritted his teeth. "Not to my knowledge."

"And you—you have this 'knowledge' because you are so great a friend to the Plisiázon?" His gaze swiped up and down Marco. "Is the girl his ward?"

"What concern is that of yours?"

"Much." Crey laughed. "Mayhap an alliance between our lands."

"Dusan." Ixion stood at the door and shot a glower at the Hirakyn. "A word."

With a nod to Crey that felt a little smug, Marco strode inside.

His First shouldered closer. "You are well?"

Besides being annoyed with the Hirakyn's insinuations over Isaura? "Aye."

"That Hirakyn had cornered you . . ."

"We were . . . talking."

"Aye. I saw his lecherous gaze on Isaura."

"He suggested an alliance."

"Not on his dead corpse," Ixion hissed. Though he refused to name Isaura his daughter, he would act the father. Assume anger and protection that were his, though unclaimed.

The sad irony worked against Marco's attempt to not react.

"What?" Ixion stretched his neck.

"Nothing." Marco glanced toward Hushak and Shobi, who stayed close to Isaura, their scents equal parts attraction and protection.

Ixion's jaw muscle twitched, most likely from the restraint he exercised over his tongue. "You think I—"

"It's generous of you to bring her into your home, give her shelter and food."

"But you condemn me for not claiming her."

"I do not." Marco felt his heart pinch a little at the near-lie. "Nor do I understand it, but as was made plain earlier, I am lacking in an understanding of Kalonican traditions. However—" He bit off the words. "Never mind."

"Speak it."

"Nay, I would rather you friend than foe."

Something new spread through the room, a scent that spoke of admiration and respect, and perhaps a bit of jealousy. It drove Marco's gaze to the door of the salon where three Xanthus stood, their jerkins and britches fresh, the blue leather armor oiled and lustrous. His own regia stood with them, and he prayed they would not betray his identity.

"Bazyli!" Ixion moved to the newcomers. "Brothers, welcome! Come— enjoy a drink. Soon, we sup."

"Your food is too soft and spiced, Ixion." Bazyli did not smile, though there was amusement in his scent. His gaze hit Marco. "Ah, M—"

"You recall Dusan," Ixion said loudly. "He travels with me these last weeks."

"Does he?" Bazyli slowed his approach and words, no doubt wondering at the diversion. But he was clever and adaptive. "A Kynigos on Drosero." He arched an eyebrow.

"Unusual, is it not?" Marco appreciated the waft of respect that splashed him as they clasped arms and shoulders.

"Well met, Dusan." He looked into Marco's eyes. "How do you find our realm?"

Marco's realm. "Tumultuous, but beautiful."

"Sad but true," Bazyli said, turning toward those with him. "Remember my brother, Galen, whom you met on the transport? And the others are Aerios Kaveh and Edvian."

Aye, Marco recalled the pup who attacked him to defend Kersei. The bad blood still hung between them. Marco nodded to the aerios, appreciating the way the Xanthus elder handled the secrecy. "Well met," he said to the regia.

Bazyli grunted, but his gaze caught something in the corner, and the dolor stung Marco's nostrils. "Hirakyn. You missed the border by leagues." There came a grim shift in the Xanthus elder, who was grizzled in appearance yet young enough not to be considered old. All the same, there was no doubt of the authority or confidence he wielded. "You are in Kalonican lands now."

"Am I? Is that why this bloodgroot tastes off?" Crey held up a cup of chilled cordi. As his men grouped around him, he grinned. "Must have tripped and blinked when we were scouting the gorges. Landed in the wrong kingdom."

Spirited irritation struck Bazyli's scent as he considered the nearly bare-chested men. "Have you no respect for our customs that you attend a social without jerkin?"

"Are ye worried the pretty lass will see our muscles and realize you are lacking?"

Though the others in the room tensed, no anger infused the Xanthus elder, who kept his gaze firmly locked on the man for whom he clearly had little regard. "Bazyli Sebastiano." He extended his arm.

"Sebastiano." Though the Hirakyn stared at the hand for several long seconds, nearly inciting an offense if the trilling scents were indication, he did finally catch it. "Xanthus."

Bazyli said nothing nor moved, but his scent roiled with challenge.

"You are elder," Crey said with a nod. "Who else would the Plisiázon have in his home? I am Crey of Greyedge."

Bazyli's gaze sharpened. "Greyedge." He angled his head to the side. "You are sure?"

Nervousness tittered around Crey's strong Signature. "Sure of where I was born?" A weak laugh. "Aye."

The room had gone ominously quiet, drawing the attention of Stalkers and aerios, shoring up behind Ixion and Bazyli. The tension was tightening, and Marco considered intervening. But these were men. And a lady was present.

"You were in the Outlands," Bazyli stated.

Crey's smile waned, his wariness growing. "Yeh, as I told them both"—his gaze struck Ixion and Marco—"we were patrolling—"

"Patrolling," Bazyli repeated, unrelenting in his interrogation. "That is the job of the mu'harib, is it not?"

Crey lifted his chin. "For a Kalonican, you are well-versed in Hirakyn ways."

"You all appear to have the same age." Bazyli squinted at each of the Hirakyns. "Are you Qicien?"

Something pained and sour darted through Crey's Signature. "I am not." His scent conveyed both truth and lie.

"Come, if we are to be friends, would you not give honest answers?"

Crey's expression darkened. "That is the second time you Kalonicans have asserted I am a liar." His nostrils flared.

"Your eyes betray you, Raider."

Crey lunged—as did every man in the room—then caught himself.

"*Never* call me that," he growled. "We are *not* raiders. We are mu'harib, and there is as much difference between us and those savages as there is between you and me."

"So you *are* Qicien."

Certain there were simple misunderstandings happening here, most borne out of the mutual distrust and bitterness between the two countries, Marco shifted. "As a newcomer to these lands," he spoke into the thick quiet, "what is kiss . . ."

"Qicien," Crey corrected, giving him a sidelong glance. "It means Fathered-One. In Vysien, when a male heir is born to the rex, all males of the same age in the city are taken from their families and raised in the Outlands. We are trained to hunt, to track, and above all, protect." This time he did sneer. "If this one had done his research better, he would know that Rex Kederac claimed his son three months past. As such, we are no longer Qicien." There was some acrid odor to those last-spoken words that made Marco wonder.

Bazyli peered at Ixion. "That news has not come north."

"It has now," Crey said.

"Then speak to why *you* are north of the border," Bazyli demanded, his pretense of civility falling away.

"Not a day past, I saved the life of your man there, and you challenge me?"

"Aye, we do!" Ixion barked. "Your people are slaughtering ours and razing cities—so, aye, we question your presence. Are you a scouting party? Spies?"

"*Spies?*" Crey spat. "Is that what you now name us? Think you—"

"What other answer is there?"

Crey growled emphatically. "We have not slaughtered anyone. That would be the Irukandji. Would it not cross your mind that we might be here trying to deal with those feral raiders? The horde that attacked you is one we have been tracking these long weeks." His tone was defiant, his scent . . . discordant.

Wanting a clearer view of the man's face to better pair the scent, Marco circled around and stood to the side, anak'ing. There was irritation—likely over being interrogated—and annoyance, probably unused to having his motives challenged or questioned. But there was something else, something . . .

Fear.

Not fear of harm from these in the room.

A deeper, thick-rooted one.

What terrifies you, Crey of Greyedge?

PROKOPIOS, KALONICA, DROSERO

Why would the medora send his personal guard with Bazyli?

How intriguing that of the men who had arrived with Elder Sebastiano, two were not simply aerios as they'd been introduced. Though they were not in their white-and-greens, the attacking aetos emblem on their tunics indicated they were regia—royal guard.

More intriguing to Isaura was that they remained close to Dusan, who was yet near enough for her to touch. So changed was he from the man who traveled with her and the Moidians. Though exhaustion yet marked his visage—as it did for most of the weary travelers—he had washed his hair and queued it back, save the curls that sprang free around his face, giving him a wild appearance. He now wore a black doublet and pants like Mavridis. His earthy wildness was amplified by that mark across his nose, which seemed to constantly emphasize his pale eyes that darkened while listening to the tense exchange between Kalonicans and Hirakyns.

The Stalkers were on edge over the Hirakyns, who stood their ground with a determination that reminded her of most Moidians. After the initial attention she'd drawn, Isaura observed silently the posturing, the way one remarked about a kill and another had to one-up that. For the most part, Dusan remained quiet, responding only when his opinion was solicited.

Brawny Crey of Greyedge nudged Dusan, said something, then barked a laugh. The smile that appeared on Dusan's face was forced, though she doubted the rough-edged Hirakyn noticed. Of more interest to Isaura was the way the Hirakyn's leather vest shifted, revealing marred, ridged flesh on his shoulder. A battle scar, perhaps? But no, she glimpsed a remnant of white tattoo, the lines coming together just so. A sick feeling dropped into her stomach. That mark—

It could not be. After all, Mavridis and the Stalkers would surely have seen and recognized it—as they clearly had not because they would have tossed the man out the city gates, if not over the wall from these windows.

Yet . . . she was certain . . . Having lived in Moidia, so close to the border where Hirakyns took refuge in taverns and inns, she knew that mark. What concerned her even more was that if this mark had gone unnoticed, did that mean Mavridis yet entertained an enemy spy?

It was not often she had information of importance to Mavridis, but if she spoke . . . what would it do to the tenor of the room? Then again, were their lives in danger? How could she ascertain the truth of this?

Isaura stepped aside to see them better. Someone bumped her shoulder a bit. "I beg your mercy," she whispered.

Dusan's pale gaze struck hers, and he inclined his head in apology. But wait. There was a meaning in his eyes. Did he . . .?

"Know you how we hunt?" His question returned to her, along with his explanation. Did he know about Crey?

Dusan tucked his chin and seemed to roll his shoulders forward in a predatory manner. Was he smelling trouble? That arrow-straight nose pointed to his thinned lips and a tense, stubbled jaw. It was his brows that either turned his visage friendly or fierce. This moment, fierce.

Isaura edged closer.

He moved little to show that he was aware of her presence—just the slight angling of his head in her direction, as if ready to hear her thoughts.

"The mark," she whispered.

Dusan said nothing and did not react. Was she wrong to mention it? Was he annoyed by her intrusion into his thoughts?

"The mark below his collarbone."

This time, though he still didn't speak, he nodded slightly.

She drifted behind him to avoid drawing attention. Before going on, she peered over his shoulder at the men to ensure they were still in conversation. "It's the sigil of House Vasiliádes."

"Aye . . .?"

"The royal house of Hirakys. Yet, he said he was no longer Qicien, so why would he bear the mark of the court? Why him and none of the others?"

Dusan shifted to meet her gaze. "You are sure—of the mark?"

She braved a look back to Crey's shoulder. Aye, there was no doubt. Her heart jolted when she realized the Hirakyn was watching her, too—a keen awareness in his dark eyes.

Isaura dropped her gaze and turned to the side, thereby facing Dusan. "Yes, but . . ."

Dusan's touch on her arm was light as he nudged her toward the back of the room. "Give care to the answer you give. What you suggest is no light thing."

"I know," she said, lowering her hands and straightening. "The skin is ridged, marred—as if he tried to burn it off."

"What makes you certain?"

Isaura thought he questioned her, but his eyes only bespoke sincerity, and his tone, while firm, seemed only to search for facts. "The heraldic animal of Vasiliádes is the rhinnock—in profile. And there are three lines not ruined by the marring of the flesh that perfectly match the beast on their sigil."

Dusan again studied the Hirakyns.

"I only mention the mark to ask if there is anything amiss that you . . . sense."

The hint of a smile started in his eyes.

"Does the Kynigos keep the lass to himself?" Crey's voice boomed through the crowded room.

Startled as attention swung in their direction, aware of the inappropriateness of standing so close, of his touch on her arm, Isaura drew back, but his grip firmed, holding her in place.

"Have you not heard?" Dusan said without missing a beat as his hand fell away. "There are dangerous enemies about these halls." Though he seemed amused, he wore no smile.

"You think to protect her from us?" laughed Crey.

"Protect her?" He sniffed. "Nay, I protect *you* from her. Have you seen her wield the discs?"

Laughter filtered through the room, but then slowly died when Dusan did not laugh or move from her side. The men cast wary glances over her, considering her in a new light. It surprised even her that Dusan proclaimed her skill to the others.

Something sharpened in Crey's expression and he crossed the room.

An action that had Dusan shift to position himself protectively in front of her.

Crey's dark eyes probed her in a way that left her chilled. "Would you introduce us, Kynigos?"

"Of course. I am Dusan of—"

"Your wit compels me to like you, though you make sport of me."

Dusan inclined his head, his amusement peeking from that stern brow.

"Give care, Hirakyn," Shobi said. "The lady is under the protection of Mavridis."

"Protection!" Crey balked. "From Dusan's tell, she does not need it. In fact, she would do well in the sands of Hirakys, as a wife to one like me."

Repulsed at the idea, Isaura wanted to leave. Feared that perhaps Crey misread her attention of his mark as interest *in him*. New tension radiated through the room and seemed to make the air dance.

Isaura touched her brow, the humiliation acute.

"I make her swoon," Crey taunted. When the Stalkers and Mavridis glowered at him, he persisted. "Perhaps she should sit down before my good looks sweep her off her feet."

Mavridis surged into the man's face. "Mind how you speak about those under my roof." He stepped back, his expression forbidding as he looked to Hushak. "The mistress would leave. Escort her to her room."

Isaura eyed Dusan, who gave her another nearly imperceptible nod. Embarrassed at the events that had turned sour, she was grateful to leave, but she had wanted to inquire of Dusan's thoughts. Talk to him about what he could perceive. Convinced Crey might hold a terrible secret, she gave Dusan one more look and pushed as much warning into it as she could.

Telegraphing emotions was most often done innocently, but curse the reek—that girl somehow knew a way to channel it into a spear-like instrument that struck Marco's receptors with pinpoint accuracy. Though she did not voice such sentiment, her desire to leave the room was clear and helped him understand the discordant scents from Crey. If he was a traitor or spy, the answer would be routed.

As if on some cue to reduce tensions, sergii entered with serving trays of steaming food. "Please," Ixion said, motioning to the tables. "We sup!" He glowered at Marco as they took seats, and well could his irritation be detected.

Marco assumed a seat between Hushak and Bazyli. Across from them were Crey and Ixion, the rest of the men filling in around them. The pretentiousness—sergii delivering plates and filling glasses—annoyed, but he had learned in Kardia to smile and thank those who served.

They were well into their third course, the conversation seeming to dance around the tension that yet lingered, when he felt a presence press against him.

"Might I offer you a piece of advice?" Bazyli said quietly as he tore a chunk of bread from a loaf.

Marco kept his gaze on his food. "I would appreciate it."

Bazyli grunted a laugh. "You may not once I speak."

Now he gave the man his attention, aware that those around them seemed to go quiet.

"You were raised most of your life among hunters, seeking out fugitives, tracking down trouble," he said and waited until Marco nodded, "so you may not be aware of the great importance propriety carries in this land."

What was his point?

"A simple touch, a whispered word in a corner . . . with a young woman"—he paused once more, seeming to want something from Marco again—"is not appropriate and could endanger your reputation and name—and ruin her."

Shock slammed Marco's gaze into Bazyli's. "You suggest—"

"That it is wise to be cautious and discreet, especially considering your role here."

"And what role would that be?" Crey barked from the other side of the table.

Marco flicked his gaze to the Hirakyn. Despite the challenge in Crey's scent, he would not be cowed by it. "Hunter."

"But you said your kind do not hunt here."

"It does not change what I am."

"So you *are* hunting something here?" Crey rested his forearm on the table. "I mean, what else would bring a mighty Kynigos here?"

"You are right," Marco said, enjoying the presumed gloating from the Hirakyn. "I do hunt here—I hunt truth." He eased back in his chair and eyed the man in his vest and long black hair, so untamed compared to the extreme civility of the Kalonicans. "Tell me about the Qicien process." He lifted a hand in innocence. "I would understand this unusual aspect to the way rulers are chosen among your people."

"They are not *chosen*," one of the other Hirakyns snarled.

"Ikku, they are not familiar with our ways." The words belied the way Crey's smile and mirth vanished. "As said, *Kynigos*, when an heir is born to the rex, he is removed from the life of luxury and forced to live off the land, learn its hardships, its dangers. Protect those in his charge. Then the rex calls back the Qicien and names his son. Only then can the next rex be trusted with the wealth and power of the land." He tossed back a drink.

"Is there not some form of co-ruling?" Bazyli asked, his expression keen.

"Aye." Something rippled through Crey's piney Signature. "Brought in from the desert, the heir undergoes an intensive education on the laws, histories, and geography of not only Hirakys, but our entire world. After completion of that, he co-rules with the rex."

"Or should," muttered a Hirakyn. He lifted a cup and took a long draught.

Ixion eased into the conversation, picking up on the snarled message from another of the Hirakyns. "Is there a reason he wouldn't?"

"Kakuzo had hoped for the throne himself," Crey taunted his fellow Hirakyn.

And yet, the scent said there was more to it than that.

"Would not you all?" suggested Bazyli's younger brother, regal in his green-and-white uniform. "I mean, why spend years in the desert guarding the Outlands if you did not intend and hope to sit on the throne as rex?"

"It is a duty for all men of Hirakys, not just Qicien. That adds to the weight but does not altogether alter them."

"Or shouldn't," Kakuzo growled. The man seemed to have plenty of grievances.

The scents pinging through the room made Marco's head ache. "What is the undercurrent I detect here, Crey? Give us an honest answer since you were so adamant about telling all when we met on the plain."

Crey pinned him with a look of someone cornered. "It's simple—if the rex dies, no matter what stage the Claimed One is at in his training, he becomes rex."

"It's a good thing Rex Kederac is alive then," Bazyli said.

Crey's scent betrayed him.

"Or is he?" Marco asked.

"No word has come from Vysien about his death," Crey stated flatly.

That was not a definitive answer. "What can you tell us of the claimed heir?" Marco felt the resonance of emotion swell from all sides. He tried to steel himself, but the wafting was thick and fetid. Yet for four of the five Hirakyns, there was no visible sign of what their body chemistry revealed.

"Theule," the thinner, scragglier Hirakyn all but growled the name.

"Ikku." Sharp and short, Crey silenced the man, and all the bronzed heads bowed, their attention suddenly focused on the food.

"Is it so great a secret?" Marco asked, confused at their sudden silence.

Crey sighed. "The heir is not named publicly until he is set in to co-rule."

"Or the rex dies," Bazyli suggested, then shrugged when everyone looked at him. "I mean, if the rex died unexpectedly, the capital would have to announce his successor. Would they not?"

"But there is more about this Theule." Resting his arm on the table, Marco let the scent lead. Probed them. Let the taste linger in the back of his throat. They did not need to speak—their effluxes warned that something was amiss.

Crey considered him with a long, hard look. "He was one of us."

Scents assailed the air: cedarwood, pepper, frankincense, balsam . . . Hatred, anger, jealousy. Disgust. "A Qicien?" Marco feigned ignorance of his meaning.

Irritation pinched the edges of Crey's eyes. "No. One of *us*"—he motioned to himself and his five—"from this group. When we are sent out to the lands, we are divided into patrols of six. Theule was with us."

That explained a lot. The jealousy, the anger. But it did not explain why he had the mark and the others did not. "Can you tell us of that mark on your collarbone?"

Crey's lips thinned. "It was a mistake." His hooded eyes tried to portray boredom, but there was now a feral stench to his Signature.

There was something to the claiming of Theule as heir. Something none of these men liked or were willing to speak of. But even as Marco mulled the facts, mulled Isaura's comments about it being a mark of the royal house, Bazyli and Ixion assumed control of the dialogue, inquiring about numbers of Irukandji, methods best to attack them. Galen Sebastiano, however, seemed entranced with the Qicien concept, asking how they summon the men back for the rex to claim them, how they prove the heir is legitimate, what happens to the remaining men—offered positions in the army, which Crey and the five at the table rejected.

That was interesting. "Why reject what you have trained your whole life for?" Galen asked.

The Hirakyns shifted, glancing at their leader, who tightened his jaw, the muscle twitching.

"Come," Ixion said, his irritation growing. "You said you would tell us—yet you sit there and hold fast to the truth, throwing breadcrumbs as if we were dogs to catch your scraps."

A near smile hit Crey's dark eyes. "It would seem I am not the only one holding fast to truths which are not meant for all ears."

Galen punched to his feet. "You dare challenge us? Accuse us of lying?"

Ikku and Kakuzo were on their feet, too. The elders ordered the younger men to sit down. For Marco, it was enough. His head and body ached. Exhaustion called him to retire. To find a quiet place to sift through what was discussed here. What secret Crey held.

As the tensions vibrated, Marco patted Bazyli's shoulder. "I need quiet and clean air—mayhap a bed, too." He left the room, immediately grateful for the cooler air and the quiet of the marbled halls. The blessed, glorious quiet.

She hung on the wall with refined glory.

Well, not Isaura, but Aelinor Mavridis. Seated on a padded bench in the gallery, a hall that spanned the length of the enormous staircase and separated two wings of the mansion, Isaura stared up at the painting of the noblewoman. In a rich crimson brocade gown and golden hair, she seemed to watch over the whole of this grand home.

Isaura supposed she should have some recollection of this hall or more of the home, but she did not. How different her life had she remained here! To have been raised under these stern but loving eyes?

Steps thudded on the marbled floors, sounding casual and . . . lost. Not like sergii, whose clipped steps had moved past her a few times already. After finishing her meal in her room, she had grown bored, so she found the library, borrowed a book, and ended up here.

Dark shadows delivered the tall, powerful build of a man into the gallery. Head down, rubbing the back of his neck, Dusan strode purposefully through the dimly lit hall.

Still a little embarrassed over the way Mavridis had removed her from the receiving hall, she froze. Perhaps he would not notice her—she was well enough in the shadows. What if he did? Should she inquire if he'd learned anything about the Hirakyn?

Yet, they would be alone. And that was not proper. *Leave*, she urged herself.

Dusan slowed, his head lifting. He came to a stop as his gaze met hers. "Isaura."

It was incredible, his ability to know she was there even before he located her on the bench and even though she had done her best to blend in. A foolish endeavor in light of the man who stood before her.

She rose and clutched the book to her chest. "Dusan." To call him by his proper name felt improper all of a sudden. But what other name did he have?

His gaze drifted away, as if searching for an escape. "What are you doing here?"

"I was admiring the portraits." She felt silly stating the obvious.

He took in the paintings with a nod and something played in his features as he lingered on an older one behind her. She angled out and turned, glancing up. Two men—a medora and an elder. Earlier she'd read the nameplate, amazed at how long the Mavridis family had protected Prokopios. "It's Medora Garai and Lorentz Mavridis—they were good friends."

"Apparently," Dusan said, giving the painting one last glance before he bobbed his head sharply. "Good eve, Is—"

"I would ask," she said, stopping him, "did you learn anything of the mark after I left?"

Stiffly, he again nodded. "Little, but enough to warrant suspicion and more questions later. They yet talk, but . . . I needed rest."

She stepped back. "Of course. I beg your mercy for stopping you."

Yet another nod before he started away, but he hesitated again. Glanced back. "Thank you—for the information earlier. For telling me what you saw."

"Then it was important? I was right?"

"Important, yes, but Crey would not speak of the mark, which tells me you were right to point it out." Dusan shifted, the scant torchlight catching his pale eyes. "I believe he was aware you'd recognized it, so he sought to distract the room . . . *me* from the truth of it."

"I was afraid you would think . . ." She straightened. "I knew I could trust you, that you would listen," she said around a half smile. "But when I was hastily removed, I thought you might say something. Yet you kept your silence and I worried . . . Most men . . . Mavridis . . . after my ma'ma . . ."

Why was everything getting jumbled up? Because she was afraid he would see her the same way everyone else did. "I beg your mercy. I will leave—"

"Isaura." He touched her elbow, drawing her to a stop. When his gaze caught hers, he started, then his hand fell away. Conflict seemed to churn through him, though she could not guess its source. He rubbed his jaw and looked back down the hall before speaking. "I must beg *your* mercy. Quickly will you learn I am neither politician nor . . . gentleman, not in the broader form." His expression flushed. "Hunting, anak'ing, tracking—in those, I am unparalleled. Yet the intricacies of politics or diplomacy—or even knowing how well to treat a lady—there I fail."

Rejection perched on her lips.

"What was I to say when Ixion—your father, their elder and leader— had you removed? I dare not counter him again in public. I have made the mistake too often." A softness filled his roughened features. "But think not for one tick that I wanted you removed. You saw things in there that nobody, not even I, did. Yours is counsel I trust and would seek in need."

Validation spilled over Isaura with his words. She widened her eyes at how they were so earnestly spoken, so rare from a man's lips. And the accursed thought forced her to pay mind to said lips, their near-perfect shape, the way they seemed to mimic the lines and arcs inked across his nose.

Dusan roughed a hand over his jaw.

"No man has spoken so generously to me," she admitted, then thought of Hushak. "Save those in want of . . . things." Her breath caught at the poorly chosen words that held accusation against him. She jerked. "I did not mean—that is, I . . . my words—"

Plagues, was there no brain in her head this night?

Rather than scowl at her, Dusan smiled, shooting warmth through her stomach and chest. "You have had a hard life, yet you are resilient and strong, shrugging off bitterness. Why would I not hear and consider your words?" Then his gaze rose to a painting—this one on the opposite wall from the other he'd noted. The one she had admired for the last ora, of a lady in jewels and elegance so refined, her beauty so rare.

Dusan eyed the plate on the wall. "Lady Aelinor Mavridis." Now he gazed at her in surprise and shock. "Mavridis's mother."

"So it would seem."

Hair coiled in plaits atop her head with soft curls about her oval face, compassion wreathed her pale complexion. Resting with casual grace on the gold strands so like Isaura's was a delicate, bejeweled tiara fashioned into flowers.

"Oh, to be so grand a lady and so lovely," Isaura whispered.

"You are the image of her!"

Absurd! That he would think her as lovely as the lady who had graced the halls of this grand home and given birth to one of the mightiest men of Kalonica.

He angled his head. "If this is Ixion's mother, then she is your—"

"Say it not!" Surging at him, Isaura covered his mouth. When his eyes widened above her fingers, she realized her mistake and snatched back her hand. "I beg your mercy."

"Have no fear of me, Isaura. But . . . tell me you can see the resemblance." He laughed. "It must be good to be here, seeing as this is where you belong. It's your home, your family—"

"No!" Her objection echoed in the hall. "It is not. Do not put into my head words that do nothing but stir the heartache of these many years."

"I am sorry."

Worrying the sheer fabric of her sleeves, she kept her gaze on the buttons of his doublet. Not on the eyes that saw into her deepest parts. But her pulse pounded like the drums of war. In truth, there was war—in her heart. "Would that I could be like her . . ." Her gaze again found Lady Aelinor. She wanted to be that woman, to be elegance and grace. Especially in the eyes of one like Dusan, who sat in a council of elders, who had seen worlds beyond this one, who . . . she knew not what else. Only that he was a great man. A revered man. And aye, a handsome one.

"The dishonor done you these many years cannot steal what was given to you by blood." Soft were his words and tender his gaze. "It pains me that you cannot see you are every bit the lady as his mother. A dress or jewels or a portrait do not make a lady, Isaura." He searched her face, studying her, taking her in. "The woman who saw past armor and leathers in the room below, who thought with care and deliberation—she is one who deserves to be on canvas and admired in halls for decades." He tipped up her chin, forcing her to look into his beautiful eyes. "You are that!"

Tears spilled, so relieved to have acknowledged what she had longed these many years to hear. Not from Dusan, but from her own father. They were a balm. That a man of his caliber would speak them—never had she dreamed. "In earnest, I understand why he cannot acknowledge me, but the ache of it, the injustice when I have done nothing to deserve his censure or rejection . . . I would—just once—have him call me 'daughter.'" Through blurred vision, she looked at him. "Is that much to ask?"

He shook his head, his expression forlorn.

"I would have it. I need it," she said, her words choked off by another sob. "Especially now—I am alone. So very alone." She felt Dusan draw her face to his shoulder. The tears came true and hard, pounding out the dents rejection had beaten into her.

"He does not see how it wounds," Dusan whispered against her ear. "He thinks it protects you. Keeps you safe."

"It is a falsehood meant to appease his conscience," she hissed into his doublet, her voice taking an edge not intended. She straightened. "My words are birthed in anger, not reason."

"A little of both, mayhap." He offered a handkerchief. "I will speak to him."

"In earnest?" She blinked free the tears, and keen awareness flared at how close they stood. The way she clung to his doublet, completely scandalous for a lady and a man not bound. But his probing pale eyes . . . so wholly on her . . .

"Yes." It was but a whisper, a promise that caressed her cheek. His face so close, a kiss so near. Yet, like a cold north wind, he stepped away and ran a hand through his hair.

"Dusan?" a querulous voice intruded seconds before a man appeared, shadowed with the light of the hall chandelier behind. "Ah. What are . . ." The words faded as Elder Sebastiano came down the hall, considering them as he closed the gap. Anger brightened his expression as he turned to Isaura. "You are well, my lady?" His question and lips were tight.

"Yes, much—thanks to Dusan." Isaura forced herself to sound confident. "I thank you, Elder Sebastiano." She gave a curt nod. "Now, I must rest."

"You are in the wrong hall, mistress." Elder Sebastiano indicated the direction from which he'd come. "Your chambers are to the left of the stairs, not the right."

Isaura started. "Of course." She hugged herself. "It is all so foreign to me." She inclined her head and hurried away, but as she reached the staircase, she heard harsh words assault Dusan.

"Why did you not heed my words from supper?"

Marco had detected the approaching Xanthus too late and cursed himself for the lapse. "There was nothing inappropriate in my conversation with the mistress."

"Aye, there was," Bazyli said. "A clear one. I must inform Mavridis."

Marco snorted. "There was no breach of etiquette."

"She was in your arms!"

"*Crying*," Marco explained. "I offered solace. Nothing more. If you could detect what I—"

"I do not need heightened senses to know when a man abuses his host's generosity!"

Honor questioned, Marco drew straight. "Guard your tongue," he said evenly. "I abused *nothing*." Yet, hadn't he? Truly, he felt lecherous for the weakness of flesh. Nigh on seven weeks since departing Kardia, four months since he last held Kersei . . . and already he . . . "It was a mistake."

Bazyli's eyes flashed.

"Not that!" Marco let the argument fall away. "There is a wound between her and Ixion."

"I saw no room between you and her for Mavridis," Bazyli challenged, his innuendo clear. There was plenty more on his mind, yet the Xanthus elder restrained himself.

Clearly because he understood whom he addressed. Which was all the more reason for Marco not to sully his honor. "Speak your piece. I will not begrudge you."

Bazyli glanced down, the beads in his hair clacking. How had Marco missed that sound upon his approach? "It is . . ." He scratched his beard. "One would be inclined to wonder at your . . . honor"—his eyes were waiting to capture Marco's—"when you were, in my presence not many months past, so ardent in your affection for another." He looked away, none liking the words he spoke.

Neither did Marco, but they were true and well placed.

"What happened with you and Kersei is foul and cruel. Had I not witnessed your rage the following morning, I would question your character. Yet," he said quietly, looking about the passage, "here I find you with another and so intimately set, immediately after I warned you of our laws of society and culture." He cocked his head. "Granted, I cannot fault you—she's a lovely one."

Marco scowled.

"Good," Bazyli said. "I see your honor is still somewhere under all that brooding. This will remain between us, but if it happens again—"

"It will not." Marco drew in a long breath and slowly let it out. "Your words are well placed, Bazyli. Had I an excuse, I would give it." Head down, he recalled too well the image of her lips. Their cordi color, much like the soft gown she wore. That he felt the irrevocable draw to her angered him. "I shamed myself, but not in the way you charge. Still, it is a good strike against a complacency that has gripped me of late."

Only a Kynigos could understand the draw, the powerful way an attraction scent tangled and suffocated reason. Being a man before such beauty was difficult enough, but add to that the heaping measure of an efflux . . . Well, it was sticky honey to a fly.

Bazyli caught his shoulder. "Find a kyria. Get an heir to secure the throne."

"It would wrong a woman if I took her to my bed with my heart so wholly another's."

"I beg your mercy," Bazyli said, a slight edge to his voice, "but not so wholly. Were it so, that one"—he bobbed his head down the hall again—"would not have tempted you." His steely eyes considered Marco for several long ticks. "Isaura is a good choice."

The realization of what the elder suggested jolted him. "No."

"Do it right, with honor. Set petition for her."

Petition. The very thing that ripped Kersei from him, against both of their wills. "I will not." He needed out of this passage and conversation. "You put too much weight on a perceived indiscretion. I meant only to console the girl after the loss of so much. Naught else happened." He turned toward the stairs. "Good rest, Bazyli."

"My liege." The elder inclined his head, but there was now a stiffness to his moves.

"Recall, I am no liege here. I—"

"Kalonica needs you. Now more than ever."

"In time." He stalked away, feeling the shame of his action and words. He hated himself. Hated what he felt. But he would not violate the vow to Kersei carved in the thick agony of their rending.

It was her solace to retreat to the rubble, black with soot and ashes. In the months since the explosion collapsed walls once thought indestructible, Stratios men had removed bodies, excavated the ruins, and lined the stones worthy of reuse along the north plain.

Kersei stood on the bricked terratza, the same one she had fled to that night when air and hope were thin. Hugging herself, she looked toward the river, though she could not see its sparkling waters. A breeze tussled her hair and brushed across her face, gentle and caring. Whispering comfort. Were she given to superstition, she would think it her parents.

She thought of Ma'ma the eve of Adara's Delta Presentation, the night they were all ripped from her. Eyes closed, she tried to blot out that terrible night, but the images dancing along the walls of that wretched Symmachian chamber returned with unwanted, unrelenting fervor. Imprinted upon her mind, memories that did not belong to her but to Darius.

She smoothed her hands over where his child grew. It did not seem real. The budding babe already strained the buttons of her bliaut. It would not be long before her body would betray the secret.

"Your guards are lacking." Myles loomed behind her.

Though she had anticipated Myles might show up, Kersei still flinched at his deep, rumbling voice, but she kept her gaze on the ruins. He was why she ordered Thorolf and Belak to stay with the horses. They protested but yielded when she vowed to stay in view. "They are clearly not your equal."

"What do you here, my lady? 'Tis not safe."

Aware he remained just out of sight of the two aerios, she resisted the urge to turn and inadvertently alert her guards to his presence. "I owe you thanks."

He grunted.

"You saved my life a sabbaton past."

Silence settled between them, and she dared not ask what she longed to know. Yet it leapt from her tongue. "How did you survive?" Now she did turn to the overlarge man. "Were you in league with them?"

His gaze darkened to match his wiry beard. "Nay." He was a mountain of turmoil, struggling in his own grief and anger. "What of you—are you?"

The question should offend, but too much had happened to be so easily affronted. "Nay, but I fear I cannot say as much for my uncle." She mournfully recalled taking aim at Uncle Rufio as he slipped expertly away on that accursed ship. "The night of the explosion, he was hurrying down that side passage"— she let her gaze linger on its distant location—"and I thought it curious he would hide in tunnels while his niece was bound to a prince. I called after him, but he did not slow. Down we went, around one corner, then another until . . ." She could still smell the ship's fuel. Feel the shock of finding that metal contraption glowering in the dark.

The crunch of rock beneath Myles's boot drew her back to the present.

"He had a ship in the cave and forced me aboard. When we took off . . . I know not what happened, only that I awoke much later, alone."

"Alone? Where did he go? You mean you flew that . . . skyship?"

"I did not." She did her best to temper that terrible memory. "When I came to, the ship was adrift and I was pinned to the metal floor by a shard." She ran a hand over her thigh where it had pierced her leg. "How my uncle and his man escaped I know not, but he left me there. Mayhap he thought me dead." Her throat constricted. "Mayhap he did not care."

"It pains you."

Hot tears freed themselves against her will. "Aye—he was my uncle!" She wiped the tears, realizing he was too close. "Back," she hissed. "You will be seen."

His thick beard concealed the smile that teased the edges of his eyes. "Why come here, Princessa, when you have—"

"I have nothing!" Feeling childish for the rushed hatred, she toyed with the edges of her long sleeves. "Everything I love was torn from me." She squinted against the sun and told herself not to think of Marco.

"Except the prince."

"Feign not, Myles. You know my heart and stubborn will."

"The iron of the machitis," he said. "Aye, you have a good measure of it."

"So you can imagine my thoughts toward Darius. A sparring partner, even a friend, but never . . ." She pressed her lips together, unwilling to speak against him. Against the father of her babe. Again her hand rested there. When silence squirmed between them, she found his gaze upon her hand. She let it fall away.

Shrewd eyes the color of a darkening sky considered her speculatively. "What know you of Darius, Princessa?"

She frowned, noticing he now referred to Darius by his first name. "He is my bound, the heir presumptive, a prince by blood, albeit a petulant and conniving one." She meant to make them laugh, but it only rubbed the ache raw.

Myles continued his appraisal. "Do you not find it interesting that he survived when none of his family or yours did?"

Defensiveness rose through her. "He says he left the solar where my parents met with the iereas and saw me slip into the passage. Though he gave pursuit, he was too late to avoid the blast. He has scars across his back from the explosion. The iereas recovered him."

"Iereas." Myles sniffed, his gaze rising northward across the plains. Toward Kardia. Something twitched in the scar on his right cheek. His mouth was grimly set.

"What ails you?"

Those sea-colored eyes found hers again. "Would you want to know if it concerned the father of the child you carry?"

Her breath caught and she stepped back, glanced to the guards, blessedly still unaware of her guest. "How—"

"A guess now confirmed." With a cock of his head, he smirked. "Come. I would show you something, if you are willing to see it, no matter the price."

His ominous words rooted her to the ground. Had there not been enough dark truths haunting the past? Aye, and it was time to enter the light. "Show me."

"When the walls were intact and the rooms filled with chatter—you knew Stratios Hall well, aye?" He picked his way around the stones and debris.

"It was my home. I could walk it blind—and did, sneaking about many a night."

He turned his palm up to her. "Take my hand and close your eyes."

After another glance to the regia, who were distracted with a dog, Kersei chose to trust and placed her hand in his. He guided her a few paces, steering slightly to the right.

Kersei easily planted every step, though the ground was uneven. Sometimes, he told her to climb around a stone. She scooted over it and felt the edge. Lowered her legs, appreciating the balance his grip offered.

"Where are we now?" he asked.

"The great hall," she said as he helped her. "To our right, the great stone hearth."

"Care—"

Her omnirs caught on something and held her fast. She stumbled. Her shin cracked against stone. She grimaced in pain.

"Only a scratch," he said.

She had to smile at that. True to form, Aerios Myles. In training, he put up with little and gave plenty.

He continued on and started right. "And now?"

Discombobulated at the stinging in her shin, she refocused her thoughts. They should be . . . "The foyer, I think." She pointed slightly left. "The grand stairs there, the kitchens and servant quarters beyond." Eyes still closed, she turned and imagined the hall. Paneled walls. Enormous paintings. Chandelier. "The hidden passage was just past the gilded reflecting glass." How many times had she stolen a glimpse of her reflection before entering a feast? "Flowers— Ma'ma always had flowers on the table beneath the mirror."

"Open your eyes."

Kersei did, blinking against the brightness of the day. Where in her mind's eye she saw the gilded glass, now an enormous slab of rock greeted her. It pained to see her home so fallen, so defeated. She looked to him, ready to proceed.

But Myles just stood there, watching.

What . . .? What had she missed? Darius. He asked about Darius. Who had said he came down this passage. She turned to it, visually tracing the massive boulder. A thought began to form in her mind, one she refused. One that had her climbing over the giant rock to the other side, peering down where stone met stone. She glanced around. Stared at the ground. There would be no blood—likely rains had washed away what was once visible.

Yet . . .

Surely there was an explanation. She made another revolution, searching the stones. Maybe she was confused. A little off . . . The stone was too large, too flat, too crammed against the floor. She lifted her gaze.

Myles watched, aggrieved. "You said he was pulled from the passage near the mirror."

Heart thundering, she saw the problem that hovered amid shadows with a thick, terrible implication. "'Tis not possible." Silently, she begged him to say she was wrong. That . . . that she had miscalculated. Misheard Darius. Anything!

"These stones remain where they fell." Myles stuffed his thick hands on his belt. "Even with ten men, we could not move them."

"You . . . accuse," she whispered, unable to speak the words. "Perhaps he wasn't . . . in this . . . location." She realized Darius would have been crushed flat. "He was injured," she said, grasping for an explanation, "and mayhap the inaccuracy was simply a mistake." Yes, that made sense, did it not? "A blow to the head and he could have forgotten." How then did she have his memories in her mind?

Myles watched, silence his answer.

It could not be. Her stomach protested. A wave of nausea rolled through her. She may not have wanted to bind, she may hate how high-handed he had been, but at his heart, at the core of who he was . . .

No! She would not believe this!

"I fear for your safety, Princessa." Myles's deep voice rumbled in the afternoon. "Be he true or traitor—"

"Never again voice those words to me!" she hissed, abruptly facing him. "That is your prince you speak of, and he would *never* do anything to harm this kingdom or his people."

Discerning eyes considered her for a long moment. "What if he thought *this* was in the best interest of the realm?"

"*This?*" she balked, indignation writhing. "This—the slaying of his father? Of Zarek's most loyal man and that man's wife? Of hundreds of regia, aerios, and machitis between the two provinces?" Heat rose through her, and with it, bile from her stomach. "The man you trained with, the man who commands the armies—you think him so corrupt as to slaughter those not in line with his views?"

"Nay," Myles said gravely, "but I do think there are those who use him and his power."

Kersei scoffed, turning away with an empty laugh. A great hollowing of her hope began that moment, a hope that Darius was not the blackguard he seemed to be. That one day she would again find the friend she knew long ago. "Now you suggest him too weak to know when those in his circle would manipulate." And were they—were the Symmachians in his circle now? She hated the doubts. Hated how unreasonably accurate it all seemed.

Seek peace where it may be found. Father had always said that, but what was she to do when those around her only sought war?

"Princessa?" Thorolf called from the other side of the ruins.

"It is hard to hear," Myles said, quieting his voice.

"No." Kersei stared up at the castle where Darius no doubt negotiated with one politician or another. "No, you cannot possibly understand . . ."

"I will trouble you no more."

Though tempted to call after him, Kersei denied him that. The accusations against Darius were unfounded! He may be many things, but a traitor, a murderer? Never!

PROKOPIOS, KALONICA, DROSERO

"You must return to Kardia."

"No." Marco turned to the lone window of the solar as if he could turn his back on Bazyli's words. Going north meant being stuffed in that stone coffin with scents that'd drive him to ruin. "I have not yet seen Trachys or Shau'li lands."

"It is not safe." Bazyli emphasized his words with a demonstrative thrust of his fist. "With the presence of the Hirakyns, the danger this far south should be plain. There is much turmoil."

"Agreed," Ixion said. "Kardia needs you there and Kalonica needs her medora—now more than ever."

Marco sat on the settee and steepled his hands as he struggled for a solution. "Not yet. The Moidian relocation was an unexpected delay, but the journey to visit the other entolis will not be put off without causing offense."

"If you ever make it," Bazyli argued. "Right up to the gates of Prokopios were you pursued by the blue raiders! They are plaguing our lands. We need you in Kardia to address the issue from the capital. A show of might."

"A show of might is not fancy suits and luxurious accommodations! A show of might is an army and a rallying call," Marco gritted out, resenting their attempt to force him back to that stench of a castle. "That can be made from anywhere."

"If you continue, we may very well be putting another Tyrannous in the ground!"

"He is right," Ixion said.

Marco moved to the window, his breathing as troubled as his thoughts. "I cannot go back." The wound was deep. The reality all too present. *She* would be there.

"What hand has been dealt you is cruel at best," Ixion said calmly, "but there is more, my liege. There is more to your purpose on this planet than her."

Marco closed his eyes, ashamed, angry.

"I am not one to pander," Bazyli said, "especially not after my own father was murdered on another planet while we yet sought answers about your father's murder." Nostrils flared beneath gray-blue eyes. "So do not expect niceties from me when it is clear in abundance that much is at stake." He huffed. "You are being petulant about Kersei and insolent about your role as medora, and no longer will I abide it."

The words yanked Marco around, his head pounding in tune with his pulse. "You dare—"

"Aye," Bazyli said with a sharp nod, "I do, because it yet seems you need a voice of reason. Ixion goes too soft on you, though I cannot understand it when he is the man to sever heads with no more than a grunt. This land *needs you*—and it must be done from the throne because ever has it been that the medora rules from Kardia. From there, the people watch for hope. From there, you choose a kyria, beget an heir. We cannot risk losing you, especially not with that mark on your arm that so visibly ties you to the future of Drosero."

"Again, my brother speaks true," Ixion said with a somber scent. "I have placated you when I have never done it with another. As two elders of your realm, it is within our right to insist on . . . more. More leadership. More maturity. More medora, less Marco."

Tasting the bile that rose in his throat, Marco shifted. The wound in his chest, the one with Kersei's name on it, was weeping and raw.

How could he make them understand? It was a burden only the Brethren could comprehend. Yet he must try lest he dishonor his people. "When Vaqar first received the gift of heightened sense, he and his men called it a curse, and aye it is so," he said miserably. "I smell now your anger, your frustration, your . . . disgust with me." He swallowed. "I know it well. You say Ixion has been temperate, but his irritation these many weeks has stung my nostrils. The Hirakyns are holding something back, and I will not trust them. I say these things to show you what it is like to be a Kynigos, to smell *everything*. From within these very walls, though I do not seek it, I can smell Kersei. And there, just beyond the door, Isaura lingers in the hall."

Ixion started at that, then stalked to the door.

"Nay," Marco said, pinching the bridge of his nose. "She has fled." He moved to the fireplace and stood there for a few seconds to gather his thoughts. "I smell them—him. On her—Kersei." He ran his hands over his head and down his neck. "And you would ask me to return and live with that daily." He stuffed his hands on his belt. "I will go mad, and . . . mayhap there *will* be another Tyrannous in the ground, but whether it would be him from my murderous rage or me from pitching myself off the cliffs . . ."

"The prince and princessa must be relocated," Bazyli insisted. "As heir presumptive, he can assume conservatorship over any estate owned by the crown. It is your right as medora to insist he resettle elsewhere."

Would Darius not love that? Being driven from the only home he'd known by the brother he had never known. "He'd never forgive me," Marco said quietly. "And I want Kersei and the babe protected."

"Babe?" Bazyli looked between them.

Now he must explain another way in which he ached. "At the Temple, the Lady gave me a . . . gift to discern the adunatos of those I encounter."

"The light," Ixion supplied.

Marco nodded, twisting the ring on his little finger that bore the Kalonican aetos. "When I said good-bye to Kersei at the Temple that morning, I saw the *Orasí*, the light of purity in her, but I also saw a smaller, fainter light." Ache twisted and tightened his gut. "A babe—a boy."

"Blood and boil. The prince did not waste time," Bazyli whispered. "Does she know?"

"They were my parting words to her."

"And the prince?"

A shrug this time. "I would not know."

"Nay," Ixion said. "Darius must be ignorant or the anticipatory birth decree would have been sent to the elders, as required by law."

"Take a kyria," Bazyli suggested again. "There are a number of eligible women, including my own sis—"

"No!" Marco snapped. "No."

"It is the best remedy, and perhaps exactly what is needed to reset your focus," Bazyli said, his mouth tight, "because what I see here is not the same man I met on Cenon. The same man who fought my brother with ruthless precision."

He was right—Marco was not the same man.

"Mayhap . . ." Bazyli's words were slow in coming this time, as if he mulled them even as he spoke. Would he betray what happened in the hall with Isaura, though he had sworn not to speak of it?

Anger sprouted through Marco and took root, hardening into resolve. "I will find a home apart from them." There would be no distance great enough to shield his receptors. "But I will not take a bound. Speak of it again, and I will look for a new First and consider a realignment of power among the entolis." They had crossed a line ordering him to bed a woman he could not love. "Begin preparations to depart."

Hope leapt into Ixion's gaze. "When do we leave?"

Marco glowered over his shoulder. "When I say."

23

"He must be made to bind." Bazyli pressed a fisted hand into the opposite palm. "He is distracted from his duties as medora."

Ixion strode to the aerios encampment to meet with Bazyli's brothers, who were among the machitis come to provide protection for Marco. Yesterday, they had failed to convince Marco to bind. "You heard him—he will not have it. And who are we to force him to take one?" He snorted. "He may not have the machinations of his father, but Marco is his own man, sharp and shrewd. Stubborn."

Squinting, Bazyli stopped outside the command tent and pivoted to him. His hair beads clacked when he looked to the city, then back to Ixion. "I came upon him in the passage two nights past—Isaura in his arms."

Heat spiked into Ixion's chest. "Isaura."

"He insisted it was naught—that he only sought to offer her solace."

"Solace!" Ixion raged. "What does she need solace over?" His anger stepped aside and allowed him to see the truth. His conscience pricked. "Her mother and sister."

"Regardless, his intimacy with her is enough to press him."

Understanding rocked Ixion. "You ask me to put my daughter where I would not wish any woman."

"As kyria of the Five Lands?" Bazyli nearly laughed. "All her needs met in ways you never could?"

"I meant with the way he broods over Kersei, I would never believe he sought anything from Isaura other than to comfort her. It was just his misguided foreign—"

"Misguided or not, it *is* a means." Bazyli lifted his brows in emphasis. "As her father, you have every right to demand he honor her."

Blood and boil! Ixion stomped into the tent, irritated with this conversation and the thought of forcing Isaura . . . He snorted, and his anger bottomed out. With the looks she had been giving Marco, it would not require *forcing* her . . .

"It was a good idea," Bazyli persisted with a bit of sarcasm, "until your daughter became involved."

"What daughter?"

Ixion glanced to Galen, standing by a small camp table, and silenced Bazyli with a glare.

"Think on it," Bazyli insisted. "You will see my words have merit." Then he turned to his brother. "How go the preparations to break camp?"

"Good," Galen said, eyeing them. "This night, we will sleep beneath the stars and set out at first light."

"What route?" Ixion asked, more than glad to change the subject.

"Scouts found the Irukandji trail coming from the west, so we head east to Trachys."

"Tricky that." Ixion scratched his beard as they considered a map. "If we are pushed too far east, we will be cut off from Throne Road. Lampros River is too swollen from recent rains and storms to cross. That would force us to hire a ship and sail north from Trachys."

"Against the tide and during storm season." Bazyli gave a grim nod. "Dangerous."

"Unless we manage to cross the river here," Galen suggested, pointing at the narrowing of the river between Trachys and Stratios.

"Graveyard Trench?" Ixion balked. "You want your medora to swim the channel?"

"I want him to reach Kardia—alive." Galen glanced at his brother. "We are too close to the Irukandji here, as evidenced by the raiders we routed—"

"I think you have that backward," came a gravelly voice.

The Hirakyn Crey stood just inside the tent, yet leaned toward his kind, who remained outside.

"You test our graces, entering uninvited and unannounced," Ixion growled. How long had they been near? Long enough to overhear talk of Marco? He stared the man down, needing to put him in his place, make him to understand he was no longer in friendly territory.

Crey held his ground. "If I might suggest—crossing the river is unnecessary, even west of Throne Road. There is a pass—"

"How know you our lands?" Galen barked, charging at him. "Have you been on Kalonican soil long enough to spy the routes to Kardia?"

The Hirakyn moved forward—not a lot, but enough to meet Galen's challenge. "Pup, I wager your elders are wishing you hadn't just informed a potential enemy spy how to reach Kardia in secret and lay siege to your precious medora."

So mayhap he had not heard what was said about Marco.

Ixion palmed the hilt of his long blade. "Hirakyn, have you purpose here?"

"To aid, Mavridis." Crey's dark eyes flashed. "Nothing else, despite being in possession of precious knowledge." He grinned at the two elders. "You are both of great reputation among our people, as was Xylander, though he is no more."

"Had you a hand in that? Is that why you come—to see which entoli to attack next?" Galen demanded. "To set your men against Prokopios and Xanthus? We will stop you, Scorcher. You will not make it past the—"

"In earnest," Crey said with a snicker, helping himself to a chunk of cheese from a sideboard, "I would restrain this pup and teach him diplomacy . . . and how *not* to convey crucial intelligence about your lands to one from enemy territory."

"So, you *are* our enemy," Galen said, triumph gleaming as he reached for his sword.

Even as steel scraped scabbard, Crey swung around, a sword appearing in his hand, and pressed the tip just below Galen's jaw, forcing his chin up. Lightning fast, the other Scorchers closed up on their leader, forming a protective barrier, their own blades aimed outward.

Bazyli jerked, dagger unsheathed and at his side, ready. He had the experience and the cold resolve that Ixion himself felt. If Crey killed Galen, he would not leave this tent alive. Nor his companions this camp.

"Aye, pup," Crey said, his voice leathery and scratchy, "look up to the man who could have slit your throat and left you where you lay before you drew steel." He edged nearer, elbow bending as he kept the sword in place. "I may be a Hirakyn, but my loyalty is to peace. Not a kingdom. To what is best for our world, for the greater good."

"Does that include slaying an innocent boy?" Ixion asked in a flat tone.

Crey's gaze had not left Galen's. "Slaying?" He huffed, his nose all but pressed to Galen's cheek. "Nay, but does he again challenge my honor, our blades will cross." He shifted, his sword raked upward, and he stepped back.

Galen hissed and clapped a hand over his jaw, which now had a trickle of blood.

"Understand me," Crey said, his men standing down, but their hands remained on hilts, eyes monitoring their surroundings in a posture of relaxed confidence that said they did not fear death. "My loyalty is to myself and those I find trustworthy. I have one mission—to ensure the people stay safe to live their lives as they will, in peace." He jutted his jaw at them. "I believe your elder, Xylander, said to seek peace where it would be found. That is what I seek. My journeys have brought me here with purpose—the hope of encountering this new medora, Marco, to see if he is of the same mettle as his father."

"He is." Ixion searched Crey's face, concerned again that perhaps the Hirakyn had heard Bazyli mention Marco as medora. He needed to divert the man. "Already I have seen him handle situations with aplomb I never saw in his father, Zarek. He is young, has much to learn, but he is what Kalonica needs."

"I hope so," Crey breathed, "because it is not simply Kalonica that needs him. I believe all of Drosero does. There is much happening of which you Upwinders are not aware."

"As in?" Galen now held cloth to his cut.

Crey cocked his head. "Sorry, lad, but I would save that for your medora. Unless he is here," he said, pausing for much longer than necessary. "I continue north and would ask that you grant us not only safe passage, but to ride with you." He arched his eyebrow to Bazyli and Ixion. "What say you, Elders?"

The man had amusement and audacity that Ixion liked, but concealed behind his mischievousness lurked a lethal, cunning warrior. Whether that would be used against Kalonica or for them . . . "Have you understanding of how raiders operate?"

A shadow spirited across the man's eyes. "My men and I would not be here had we not learned how to track them, anticipate them, and exploit their weaknesses."

"What weaknesses?" Bazyli was ready to dirty his hands, where his father had been weary of battle.

Crey smirked. "Have we an agreement?"

Ixion glanced at Bazyli, then the Scorcher. "You will ride with me." He held the man's gaze for several long seconds. "At all times."

"Is it my good looks or my charm that makes you want me at your side, Stalker?"

Grief was no respecter of persons or age.

Isaura clasped the hand of the now-resting Kita, whose babe had come into the world blue and still, crushed in the wagon fall. She had cried and grieved the otherwise perfect baby boy, and Isaura mourned with her as they buried him outside the city walls in a pauper's grave. Now as Kita slept, Isaura sent Mnason hobbling off—his ankle sprained in the tumble off the destrier days past—with his friends.

In the relative quiet of the curtained shelter, Isaura found herself thinking of the words she'd heard Bazyli utter behind that closed door two nights since. *My liege.* From the upper level, Isaura had watched Dusan storm out of the solar, shoulders rolled back, neck craned forward. He looked so forbidding, so different from that moment in the gallery when they'd been close, his arm around her. His clean, crisp scent . . . His deep resonating voice that vibrated down her spine as he consoled her . . .

"That smile," Kita said softly as she shifted, "it is for Dusan?"

How did her friend always know? "You should rest!"

"I have—for too long, I think." Kita sat up in the bed and leaned against the brick courtyard wall that was part of her shelter. "Cheer a grieving woman, Isa. Tell me what happened."

"That is unfair," Isaura said. But she took a moment to gather her thoughts. "There is a portrait hall in the elder's home." Though Kita was one of the rare few who knew her connection to Mavridis, Isaura still felt strange speaking openly about their connection. "Including paintings of his mother and grandfather . . ."

"*Your* family."

Isaura winced—*her* family had been Ma'ma and Laseria. "The paintings just . . . it made me realize I would never have a home like that or belong in such a place."

Kita sipped water. "What do these portraits have to do with Dusan?"

Her friend was persistent. "I was overwhelmed, feeling so alone and sad since Laseria . . . Tears overcame me." She bunched her shoulders. "He was there."

"Dusan comforted you." Kita smiled, then touched her hand. "I am glad *someone* comforted you—there have been many griefs in your short days." She gave her a sly glance. "But I daresay you are besotted."

Heat filled Isaura's cheeks. She rose and busied herself tidying the tiny space. "Perhaps, but he has not spoken to me since. It is better he does not."

"Why?"

"He is too great a man, too respected. Even Mavridis defers to him, and I have never seen him defer to anyone, though I imagine he did so with Medora Zarek." That thought niggled at her again . . .

My liege.

Isaura stilled, the words echoing in her head.

Deferred to him.

She straightened, her hands halfway through the motion of folding a cloth, thinking. Could it be . . .?

"You should talk to Mavridis," Kita said.

Pulled from that unbelievable thought, Isaura looked at her friend. "About what?"

"You and Dusan."

She nearly choked, and hoped no one heard that. "As said, it will not happen. Speak it not again, Kita."

"Why? You are clearly—"

"Because!" She traced the embroidered daisies on her blue gown. "I would not lose those moments he talks to me. He is kind and does not treat me . . ."

"Like Delirious Deliontress's daughter."

Isaura nodded. "Strange thing is, I told him about her, how people saw her . . . me . . ."

"And he is still your friend."

"I am not sure it is true to say 'friend,' but unlike most, he has not fled." She rubbed her temples. "Perhaps because he feels responsible for her death, which he is not." She glanced at Kita and saw the weariness, the pain. "Oh, Kita! I am going on about this frivolity when you—"

"No!" Kita lowered her legs off the cot. "No, I want to hear of Dusan. It is happiness where there has been little." She stood and washed her face then stilled, leaning on the basin, back to Isaura. "I do not know what I am to do or where I am to go."

Isaura pulled her into a hug. "I fear the same things."

Stepping back, Kita took Isaura's hands in hers. "We shall be as sisters now, in pain and in a new life."

"Agreed," Isaura said with a laugh. "I suddenly find I can face—"

"Isaura!" boomed a deep voice beyond the curtained room.

She jumped, guilt wrapping swiftly around her like a sodden blanket. Mavridis. What was wrong? She stepped out and found him striding down the line of canvas walls that sectioned off rooms for the Moidians. By the Flames, he looked angry. What now?

His gaze connected with hers and sharpened. "What do you here?"

"I was visiting Kita." She motioned into the small space.

Expression shifting, Mavridis looked to her friend and nodded. "Kita." Addressing her in the familiar . . . "My condolences about the babe, that we did not anticipate the trouble that caused your loss."

Isaura blinked, surprised that Mavridis would know of such a small thing—well, not small for the people, but as elder . . .

Her friend flushed. "Thank you, Elder Mavridis. I am grateful for the protection you have provided—you and the Stalkers."

Curious at his softening and her friend's stammering, Isaura glanced between them.

"It is my duty." His gaze darted around her shelter. "Have you family here for you and the boy?"

"I—no, my family is near Stratios. I had hoped after the babe . . ." Kita's mouth tightened but she rallied. "I will find a way to journey north with some caravan or wagon to reach my parents."

He angled in, his intensity changing to . . . vulnerability. "When we ride to Kardia, I would not have Isaura travel alone with Stalkers and machitis. Would you consider being her companion for the journey?" He shifted in the doorway. "I can promise provision and assistance if you are able to make the ride. We can arrange for a carriage for the three of you."

Excitement rushed through Isaura.

"I . . ." Kita looked at her, face flushed. "I would be glad to be of use."

Crouched on the crossbeams of the commons within the covered arena, Marco scouted the area to match the nefarious scent with its owner. He felt intrusive, hovering above the exhausted, bedraggled Moidians. He'd picked up the roiling efflux shortly after sunrise, tracked it amid the confusion of scents that was this city, finally landed here. He drew in a long breath, distracted to realize *she* was here, too—her Signature steeped in sadness, yet not drowned by it. Which reminded him of their encounter in the gallery, her attraction, his . . . temptation. Bazyli's warning.

Forcing himself to concentrate, Marco flared his receptors, caught a hint, and leapt off the building. Nearly missed the first ledge, his mind still too much on the willowy beauty.

Focus. Coming to rest on a roof, he finally matched scent to person. The hooded man slipped into a tent, so Marco waited. His thoughts drifted to that calming Signature.

She was here, somewhere in the commons.

As if responding to Marco's thoughts, Ixion stormed into the tent city-within-a-city and went straight for Isaura, who emerged from one of the linen-partitioned rooms two aisles away from Marco's quarry.

The hooded man shot from the tent, yanking Marco's attention back to the matter at hand. Rank, shrill terror assaulted his receptors.

Marco leapt at a steel pole attached to the wall and slid down it. Hopped to the ground as a man jumped out of his way. "Mavridis!" He called for the Stalker's support as he sprinted after the intruder, fearing the man had killed someone. Though the blur of white tents proved disorienting and confusing, he let the scent lead. Pursued it around one, down past two more, then left.

The man slapped open a tent flap, spotted Marco, and bolted.

Recognition hit—no, it could not . . .

Aye, it was.

He broke into a sprint, wishing these tents were buildings so he could tic-tac higher, gain the advantage. He plunged into the open, scanning the road and city for his quarry.

Feet thumped behind him, filling the courtyard with the familiar efflux of his First. "What is it?"

"Trouble—I've been tracking him for the last two oras."

Screams erupted again from the main area, along with panicked scents. Had he gone back in?

"He's in the commons?" Ixion started back toward the arena.

"No." Marco squinted against the sun as he probed the square. "He's here, in the market. Wearing a brown hood." A splotch of the earthy color flickered between two tan draping canopies. "There!" He sprinted after the man, darting down an alley, then a cobbled road, the area darkening due to the building heights.

A whistle creased the air as Mavridis summoned his Stalkers for the hunt.

The quarry had taken cover, but his stench was close.

Marco tucked his chin and called, "You do not want to die tired." He closed his eyes and angled his head to better catch the scent. More Signatures rose around him—Stalkers—but he isolated the stinging one.

"You are Kynigos." The man's voice echoed on the high brick walls enclosing the alley. "You have no jurisdiction here."

"I can't tell where the voice is coming from," Hushak muttered.

"Mavridis!" came the quick, urgent voice of another Stalker. "He killed Ven'tac. Slit his throat."

That explained the screams from the commons—discovery of the body. They had to catch this man before he killed again. Though the scent climbed the walls, it was localized to one area, and Marco trained his mind to quiet, to isolate it . . .

Ixion indicated to a stack of crates on the far right.

Marco shook his head and pointed to an alcove. Desperation surged through the air, elevating a maliciousness. Viciousness. Their prey was lethal and would not care if more spilled blood was the only way to escape.

Hushak and Ixion started past Marco, but he stopped them and eyed the iron downspout attached to the wall. He shifted back a couple of steps and launched himself. Toed the wall and vaulted up. Caught the pipe, which groaned at the assault of his weight. Brick scratched his knuckles as he swung himself in an arc, driving his knee into the alcove.

As he released the pipe, Marco sighted the darkness. Saw the man, his weapon trained not on an assailant from above but the skittering shadows of Ixion and the Stalkers on the ground. He must've heard or felt something because he snapped up his gaze. Surprise lit his face as Marco nailed him in the nose. His head bounced back. Groaning, he crumpled in a heap.

Marco landed and lurched at the man, driving a knee into his back to keep him still. He patted him down for weapons and found something in the coat pocket. Knew that shape. He lifted it and stood, aiming the newfound pulse pistol at the blue-marked body.

"Dead?" Mavridis asked.

"Not yet." Marco flipped down the man's hood.

"Irukandji!"

"Princessa!" Ypiretis's apprentice skidded into the solar, panting—wrangling around aerios and Thorolf, who slowed him. "They've brought him!"

"Let him pass." Kersei tucked the parchment she'd been writing on into the leather folio and rose from the chair. The plans had waited these many months; they would hold for a few more oras. "What is it, Duncan?"

"Not what—*who!* Myles, my lady." He heaved a breath, shaking his shaggy mop of hair. "He's fighting them, and he's a right mean one. The aerios said you ordered his arrest."

"It was an invitation," she growled, hurrying from the solar to the grand staircase. Even as she toed the first step, shouts came from the bailey. Aerios and regia sprinted across the foyer toward the front doors. Then came Hadrien and Caio, clomping in step with their prince regent.

Oh no.

Darius would be livid.

A loud crack ricocheted through the open door that let sunlight streak over the gleaming marble.

"No." Kersei launched herself down the last few steps. Outside, she saw naught but a thick, fevered throng of men and horses and aerios.

"I beg you, my prince." Ypiretis's voice strained over the crowd. "Please—"

"Stand aside, iereas," Darius growled. "This is a matter for—"

"Stratios Hall came down, and yet he lives," someone shouted. "The traitor should hang!"

Kersei shoved through the muscled, sweaty bodies. "I fear not!" Only then did she gain the attention of the aerios, who shifted to let her pass. "If he is a traitor simply because he survived the attack on Stratios Hall"—her breath heaved with adrenaline, for she felt Darius glower at her for usurping his authority here—"then we must also arrest me and the prince."

"You were kidnapped by those spacecrawlers," Kaveh grumbled.

"I thank you for understanding my position during those disastrous times," Kersei said, "but that would still leave your prince in question, and since I know well that you would not speak such an accusation against him, neither can we, in good conscience, label this aerios as such." She finally looked at the man of whom she spoke and drew in a sharp breath at his swollen eye and bloodied lip. "Who dared set upon a man I invited into my home?" Though she glanced around for the assailant, she knew none would come forward.

Darius shouldered up to her, his back to the men. "What do you, Princessa? This man has been wanted—"

"This man," she spoke loud and clear, "has protected me on two occasions, when the regia and aerios our prince gave charge of protecting me failed to do so."

Emotions vied for dominance in the weathered, scarred face of Myles, whose hands were restrained. Forced to his knees, he kept his tumultuous brown eyes fixed on the stone. His expression reminded her of dark storm clouds ready to throw lightning bolts.

"He is my guest, invited to Kardia at my request." She focused on him again. "Release him."

Regia Hadrien and Caio looked to Darius, whose face had reddened and his fists clenched.

"Do we not owe him our gratitude for keeping me safe when others did not, my prince?" She kept her voice sugary.

Lips thinned, Darius let several dreadful seconds hang between them. "You heard the princessa," he said.

Freed of the shackles, Myles stood stiffly, his gaze never venturing past Kersei or Darius. It pained her to see so fierce a man cowering.

Nay, this was not cowering. Then what? Regardless what played behind those eyes, Myles must be removed from this bailey so that tensions might settle, including her own.

"Aerios Myles, would you attend me, please?" When he hesitated, she silently begged him not to argue or deny her.

With each breath he took, his spine straightened, his ferocity returned. "Aye, Princessa."

She started back inside with a stinging awareness of what she had done, how furious Darius must be. Yet, she would not be dissuaded as she noted the steps that came behind. Not heavy ones as would be expected of someone Myles's size, but light, decisive steps.

Once well within the foyer, she glanced over her shoulder and saw his expression. Not anger or frustration, nor gratitude . . . "Have I erred, Aerios

Myles?" she asked quietly, eyeing the door where the movement of the regia and aerios interrupted sunlight.

He again hesitated. "I know not, Princessa, to what end you have brought me here. When they forced me into shackles and the cart—"

"That should never have happened, and I will be sure they—"

"No. Leave it." His brown eyes pierced. "I beg you."

She swallowed, then nodded as Darius's athletic form filled the door. "Come, we will talk in the solar where it is quieter." She climbed the steps with him at her side, and somehow felt the rightness of having him here. At the top, she touched his shoulder. "Myles—"

He jerked, as if her touch sparked through him. Staggering, he blinked but said nothing, looking bewildered.

Unsure what transpired, Kersei drew back her hand and headed into the solar.

"I attended Medora Zarek on occasion and in this room mostly," he said as they entered. "It is strange not to find him waiting."

"I am sure the prince feels the same." Kersei motioned to a chair. "Please."

"I'm not fit to sit on these chairs, Princessa. I was working when they set upon me."

She smiled and remained on her feet, though her lower back ached. "I would offer an apology, Aerios Myles. The manner of your . . . arrival here was, unwittingly, my fault. I instructed them to bring you in whatever way required, but I never intended what they did. I only meant for them to not accept no for an answer." She sighed and touched her brow. "You are an aerios, trained and proven. After our last meeting, it would be unrealistic of me to expect you to come willingly, but I beg your mercy for the ill treatment." She motioned to the red rings on his wrists.

"If you knew I did not want to come, why am I here?"

Kersei turned away, hating the nagging doubt he had planted in her head on the ruins of Stratios. "You said I was in danger, that you feared for me." She faced him again, this time with a weak smile. "What better way to ensure I am safe?"

Though his lips did not speak, his expression and posture did.

Quiet resignation fell over her. "I see in your stance that you are not pleased with my . . . presumption to gain your protection."

"There are things I must be about, Princessa. I cannot—"

"Please." She hurried to him and touched his arm.

Sucking in a breath, Myles drew up sharp again. Frowned at her fingers on his arm.

Kersei released him, concerned. "I beg your mercy. There is nothing untoward meant by my touch. Only urgency." Was it truly so easy to rattle this fierce aerios? If so, was this a mistake? No, conviction beat in her breast. Told her it was necessary. "Myles, I beseech you—promise me the protection of your sword."

He stared hard. "This is about Darius," he whispered.

She swallowed. Refused to acknowledge what he spoke, words that terrified and haunted, yet her hesitation now spoke for her as well. "Do I have your sword?"

Determination carved hard, deep rivulets along the sides of his mouth. "Aye, you have my sword."

"Good," she breathed, then realized how that likely sounded. "I thank you. There is a room on the second level that is yours. I will call Ypiretis to show you—"

"You expect me to stay here?"

Kersei whirled, the room canting as she did. She touched her brow.

"Easy, Princessa," he said, catching her by the shoulders.

She rolled her eyes. "I am no damsel in distress, or have you forgotten that day I unseated you?"

"If you want my sword, never speak of that again." There was almost a smile in the mountain-of-a-man's face.

"Agreed. Let me show you the room." She started for the door, which flung open and struck her. Kersei yelped, stumbling away, cupping her face.

"Kersei!" Darius rushed to her. "What happened?" His glower turned against Myles. "Speak! What have you done?"

Kersei jerked from his hold and put a couple of steps between them. "*You* injured me—knocking me with the door you thrust open."

With indignation and maybe a tinge of remorse, which only lengthened the glower in his expression, Darius closed the door. "What say you to being alone with this . . . man?"

"I am alone with my chosen regia as I have been with Ypiretis and Thorolf. Would you flay their honor so freely?"

"They are different," he snarled. "They are aerios. Ypiretis an iereas. This man—"

"Is an aerios, a rank bestowed upon him by Medora Zarek, your father." Her heart thundered, hating this game. Afraid of where this might lead. "Do I recall correctly, Myles, that you were also a training master?"

Myles had gone very still, his expression dark as he stared at the prince. "Aye, my lady."

Had his use of 'my lady' been a deliberate attempt to reveal his loyalty?

"And you vanished after Stratios Hall collapsed," Darius barked. "How do you answer for that?"

"Darius, please. This will not—"

"I will answer," Myles said, "but only because I know this will dog my steps. Even do I answer, it may yet haunt me." He paused, his jaw muscle working. "When the explosion occurred, I was outside on the terratza. The force of the blast threw me backward into a column." He shifted and lifted the length of hair he'd queued back, revealing a scar across his head. "Left me reminders. One on my leg as well."

Darius considered him, and when no more story came, he frowned. "That explains what happened in the blast, but not after."

"I was taken to a healer. Stitched. My leg splinted."

"Are there others?" Darius asked, his question bordering on quiet, piqued. "Others who survived?"

Myles glanced to Kersei.

"Look not to her when your prince inquires of you!" Darius ordered.

Fists opened then closed. "Since both of us survived, as well as the princessa, then it is possible that *others* made it out alive." Myles's words were shrewd and pointed.

"Did you not say he saved you two times? When I did not?" Darius challenged. "In front of all aerios and regia—you tell them I failed you."

"Never have I spoken such words!"

"But you did—"

"When?" she balked.

"When you tell all that this man saved you—and they are left wondering where I was when your life was endangered!"

Understanding dawned as to how things could be construed. "Surely not . . ."

He jerked back to the aerios. "How is it you were close enough to save my bound when neither the regia nor I were?"

Myles had gone red as well. "A fortnight past, the princessa was without guard in the Great Black, the Stratios tavern. Unsavory folk accosted her and I pursued."

A tremor wormed through Kersei. That was not the truth of it. *She* had followed him.

"And the second time?" Darius insisted.

"I am uncertain of which time she means," Myles said.

"Then there are more?"

"Make this not an issue, Darius," Kersei said, her breathing shallow.

Uncertainty flickered through his brow as he considered them before finally removing himself to the window.

Though stubbornness demanded she not, Kersei went to him. Touched his back. "Darius, in earnest—there is naught between myself and Myles save duty of an aerios to his princessa. I would have him here because this is where he belongs."

"You humiliated me in the bailey," he said quietly.

It grated that he would chastise her when he had been petulant and arrogant. Yet she must rise above petty things that were so determined to wedge between them. "I see that now. It was not my intent, but I apologize."

He placed a hand against the glass. "That I had so utterly failed to protect you . . . to let you know I am here for you . . . that you seek out another man . . ." He shifted and looked down into her eyes. "What will it take for you to believe I love you? That what I do is out of a bound's need to protect what is his—because he loves her?"

An ache blossomed in her breast and swept down into her womb. "I do know you love me." *In the only way you know how.*

Yet . . . was it enough?

It would have to be, especially with the babe on the way. The words nearly danced off her lips, the need to tell him that all would be well, that they had a child to unite them. Perhaps she should bridge that chasm . . .

Not yet. Not until she determined if Myles's accusation held truth. Not until she learned whether or not her family had been betrayed by Darius.

PROKOPIOS, KALONICA, DROSERO

"No!" Marco barked. "The Irukandji are here in the city and they are smarter and more shrewd than before—I could not smell the nidor of the Ladies' curse on him! I swear to you, this is no time for me to flee north like a coward when the danger is *here!*"

"But you said it was time to—"

"I said *prepare* to set out to Lampros City."

"Now is *exactly* the time to leave, especially if you are unable to detect them," Ixion all but growled. "We will not have your blood so soon on our heads."

"You said prepare—we are prepared." Bazyli palmed the table and looked up through blond brows. "Let us break camp and depart now."

"The battle is nigh upon us," an aerios said, "but it would be wiser to make the stand from Kardia."

"What stand? Who are you that you would instruct me?" Marco demanded.

The man dipped his head. "Theilig of House Vereil, sire."

Bazyli almost smiled. "Commander of Kalonican armies—your armies." The words were quiet, so no one outside the tent heard them. "He led the aerios down with me."

Marco hesitated, sizing up the man who commanded the armies under Darius. The commander was younger than expected, but clearly seasoned. Rough-edged yet . . . not. "Well met, Theilig. But the fact remains—there will be nothing left if we depart now! Are we to leave the Moidians and Prokopians to their deaths?"

"Stalkers and aerios are more ready than you to defend this land," Ixion gritted out. "We have been at this a long time and will not so easily surrender or succumb."

"How many times have the savages been inside these walls?" Marco challenged. "Right among your women and children?"

"*Look,*" Ixion roared, his voice like the howl of a rhinnock, "to the truth of what we speak. You have heard the grumblings of the Moidians—they have given up hope that their medora cares, but that is because they have no face to the crown set upon his head. Lead as a medora should! Stop hiding—" His First dropped his gaze and words, but he could not hide his rank frustration or disgust.

At the lack of deference and hefty chastisement, Marco drew up, the scents around him flooding his receptors, and he saw in Ixion regret for the way he'd spoken, though he felt the words justified.

Awareness grew of what they played at, what their words minced but never spoke whole. He glanced at the others—Bazyli, Galen, Theilig, Edvian . . . Agreement in their subterfuge. It stung. "I see." Afraid to speak lest that diabolus which prowled his gut spring free, he clenched his jaw.

Curse the reek, he did not belong here. He was unworthy of a role he so clearly could not fulfill. Aye, he'd said to return to Kardia, and now they wanted him to take the fastest route to the one place he could not handle . . . Stricken by their betrayal, by the truth that he stood alone in this world, he took two steps back, seared by the cold silence of the men and their scents. Of what they thought but dared not speak because he was their medora.

With a sharp nod, Marco stalked to the tent opening amid the waft of their disappointment. He had to buy himself time for his own preparations—mental ones. "We leave in three days." Striding into the open, he felt his pride, his honor, lay on the floor in that tent. Though he knew he'd failed them, he searched for an answer. A way to be free of the storm that besieged him.

He heard the steps and smelled the nerves of the aerios who obeyed Mavridis's order to stay with him. But Marco did not want protection. Did not want this role or this accursed planet. He ached to return to the life where he belonged, where he excelled, where he was looked up to and respected. Where he could be . . . himself.

But who was that? Who was he deep down? Not Dusan. Definitely not medora. And torturously, not even Kynigos.

I am lost.

"It was too good to last," Isaura murmured as she took one last glance at the mansion, just visible beyond the city wall as dawn pushed back night's heavy veil. Dinner the last two eves had been strained, Dusan absent with no explanation from anyone.

"Mnason, stay close!" Kita called after her son, who limped to where the sea of green-and-white aerios were loading horses as well. She gave Isaura a rueful smile. "Already missing the fine comforts?"

Isaura wrinkled her nose. "Aye, and I'm not entirely sure why Mavridis would have me continue on with him to the capital. He has no home there, and neither do I." It would not feel so lonely were Laseria still alive.

Kita eyed her. "'Tis a good thing, is it not, that he wants you to stay with him."

A horse nearby whinnied, and she turned to it, smoothing a hand along its side. Over the broad back she saw someone coming their way.

Dusan stormed toward the horses, unaware of her presence. She was glad, for the sight of him knocked the breath from her lungs—it had been days since they last spoke. Brow furrowed, head down, he seemed enraged. What had so angered him?

He went to his Black and motioned away the two machitis provisioning his horse. Jaw set tight, he focused on his task. The mark across his nose seemed to draw shadows that did not exist. With a grunt, he tested straps. A sack fell from his saddlebag. He uttered something she could not hear, but it took little imagination to think he spoke words unsuited for gentler ears. Hands on the gear he'd secured to the Black, he hung his head.

Isaura eased around the destrier, careful not to startle horse or man.

"Leave me," he said, his tone firm and . . . weary.

She retrieved his sack and extended it to him. "You dropped thi—"

"Leave me!" Dusan snatched the pack from her. His gaze seared.

Startled, Isaura flinched back, and the sack fell between them. She heard metal clatter against a rock and roll toward her. It thumped against her boot.

Again, she bent to it, stilling as her fingers closed around the object, her mind refusing to make the connection to what she held.

A circlet. *Crown.*

Breath stolen by the realization, she assembled the many clues that had littered the weeks they traveled together. The way Mavridis deferred to him, tasked others to protect him, to provision his horse . . . how he spoke with authority . . . A bubble of a laugh climbed her throat—when Bazyli had said "my liege," he had not addressed her father, but Dusan. Now with this, the pieces finally formed a whole picture.

She brought her gaze to his. "You're . . ."

He shifted closer and took the circlet. "Speak it not, Isaura."

"You're med—"

"I beg—"

"I knew you were a great man," she breathed with a smile.

A pained expression rippled through his handsome features as he lowered his head. "I wish that were true." He tucked the circlet in a pouch and returned it to his saddlebag.

She could scarce think as ramifications flooded her. How she'd spoken to him. Played children's games. Fawned over him. The heat of embarrassment climbed her neck into her face. "By the Ladies . . ."

"Have you not things to do?" he groused, preparing his Black with crisp, precise movements that rustled his curly black hair. But this was not anger alone. The desperation, the frustration seemed as thick and abrasive as that wool blanket he now secured.

She drew him back around, battling with the truth that she touched the medora. Her fingers curled away on their own. "I know not what has angered you—"

"Leave it."

Curiosity got the better of her. "Why do you hide who you are?"

"It's better this way."

"Is it?"

His gaze slammed into hers, his eyes sharp, piercing. "Yes."

"And *this* is better—you angry, frustrated, and . . .?" She glanced around, aware of the others avoiding him. There was something terribly amiss that stirred an ache she could neither understand nor leave alone. Again, she touched his arm. "Dusan."

"Marco," he bit out, pulling from her touch. "I am *Marco* Dusan."

"Medora Marco." Saying it somehow made it real, yet . . . "I know him not. But I am familiar with Dusan, a very good man who—"

"Who has failed at every corner. Who has made a mockery of the role his dead father left untended these many months." He grabbed the reins to the destrier. "If I am great, then it is as a great failure."

VOLANTE STATION, ORBITING SYMMACHIA

This was where she belonged—in the cockpit with nothing but stars for company. Eija knew every nuance of her corvette, every rattle and instrument indicator, and the *Prevenire* was based off a 'vette's system. The rings appeared on her screen, and she adjusted her pitch and verified her flight vector path. She had no idea how Patron had pulled it off, but she'd not only avoided expulsion, she'd been immediately assigned to Alpha team. Not for the first time did she wonder exactly how her patron had so much knowledge and power. Regardless . . . Eija landed her dream assignment.

"*Malika* One coming around for target practice," she said via comms.

"Copy that, *Malika* One. The target is yours."

Even as she increased velocity, Eija felt the prick of her PICC-line and the icy liquid slip into her veins to protect her against the inertia. It was a dry run. One she'd practiced hundreds of times in the simulator on the ground. This practice run in orbit over Symmachia would create a more realistic experience, closer to what actual launch from the *Chryzanthe* would feel like. Being in orbit without gravity altered the game, and she reveled in the freedom, letting irritation slide away.

Diggins said she was staying on, but only if she gravved down and stopped being a show-off. But if she didn't raise her scores, she'd have no home or hope. And that could not happen. A shudder traced her spine that wasn't entirely the PICC-line's fault.

Problem was, it wasn't dramatics that had her failing the sims. It was instinct.

Which was failing her—literally.

So, she'd played the game. Done what they said was right. Shelved that insipid instinct that had her looking the moron to everyone else assigned to Alpha. Graduating from sims, they'd now entered secondary training, taking runs at concentric rings in orbit, matching the velocity and trajectory set by . . . someone. Which was wrong. But hey, if she wanted out of Kedalion, so be it.

Straight ahead, three concentric rings hung in the blanket of space, the only visible part the lights that blinked at her as if winking, like it, too, knew this wouldn't work in real life. *But hey, let them think it does. We can all die later.*

Right. The farthest ring was the smallest and the reason HyPE needed the best pilots—it was just big enough to catch and thrust the 'vette into the created slipstream.

Up here in practice, there wouldn't be a slipstream. The last ring wouldn't even catch the ship. She just had to clear it without tagging the sides. "Point one," she annotated her velocity into her comms, which both recorded it and transmitted it to Command.

Stretching her torso, she eyed her readout . . . the rings . . . "Point two."

At three, she hit the first ring. Exhilaration zipped through her. In the real jump, there'd be a lot more reaction between her ship and the first ring, which should vault her toward the second in a contract-and-release maneuver. "Point three."

She watched her flight vector and that stinging awareness hit her again. Her thumb hovered over the stick, ready to alter course. *No. Game not lame. Game not lame.* Diggins told her that—to play the game so she wouldn't be lamed—grounded. "Point three mark six." Her 'vette sailed through the third ring.

And bam. If this had been the launch, the ship would've been pitched into the slipstream created by the *Chryzanthe.* "Third ring cleared," she reported.

"Good," came the gravelly voice of their gunnery sergeant. "Do it again."

And she did. Over and over, never once nicking a ring, until it was time to RTB. The thought of going back, dealing with the snark and glares from the rest of Alpha, who'd completed their runs earlier this week, nudged Eija to fly out a little farther than necessary. Anything to enjoy the quiet, the peace and exhilaration of the 'vette beneath her, the controls responding, instinct—well, what she was allowed to follow. Nobody telling her she was doing it wrong.

The PICC-line withdrew, and she took its cue to return to the station. Once docked, she unstrapped. Boots gravved, she removed her helmet and made her way off the *Malika.* In the causeway, she stowed the helmet, then unzipped the thick pressure suit.

"Hey, slick flying out there."

Eija glanced over her shoulder to Reef, who clomped toward her. "Thanks." She extracted herself from the pressure suit, feeling weird when he stepped in to assist, holding it behind her as she climbed out of the legs. "Almost didn't want to come back."

He grinned as he stowed the suit. "Exhilarating, isn't it?"

"Never gets old, and it's better than . . ." Eija let her words fall away when she saw Bashari and Gola round the juncture.

"You didn't push the 'vette." Ah, there was his chastisement.

"No need," she said. "Velocity isn't going to matter here since the rings aren't going to hyperaccelerate us. The practice rings are tubes with lights."

"But if you don't get into the habit of pushing it—"

"Pushing it only strains systems. And in this situation, it doesn't prepare me for anything. Current limitations on velocity and flight vector prohibit us from reaching the .875 sweet spot we'll need to hit the third ring on launch. Can't reach that on our own. The purpose of this exercise, as we were instructed, was to focus on a smooth trajectory through the rings." She lifted her jaw. "I accomplished that. Without error."

Reef's expression shifted. "So, you haven't changed."

Mentally, she pulled up straight at his words. *Play the game,* Diggins warned. "Changed who I am?" She sniffed. "No, and—"

"I need to know you aren't blowing air—"

"I'll do what needs to be done when it needs to be done."

Reef shouldered into her. "Remember who I am, the orbs I wear—that it's my duty to protect this team, so if I have a question, I'll ask it."

Her heart thrashed in her chest, knowing she bordered on insubordination for speaking to him like this, but she would not be questioned when she'd played their game and gone against her conscience to do so. She managed a nod.

"They told me to watch you," he said. "At the slightest hint of trouble, I'm required to report it."

She eyed him, wary, scared. The last thing she needed was for Patron to get wind of more trouble—especially since she'd been the perfect Shepherd since that encounter in the barracks. "I didn't do anything wrong."

His brown gaze held hers for a long time, considering, probing.

Did he want her gone? She'd thought him an ally. Was she wrong?

"I know," he finally said. "But if they gave me that order—they could've given it to the others, too. Be careful, Eija. They're watching."

A hollow note crackled into his awareness and pulled his attention to the plains. Marco could see neither person nor structure across the flat land. What was he detecting?

The advance north toward Kardia moved faster with only aerios and Stalkers than it had with the Moidians. For three days they pressed hard for the northwestern edge of Trachys. On this, the third afternoon, darkening clouds filled the sky, forcing them to break early.

Kersei's Signature seemed unfairly strong, growing more so as he drew nearer with each hour. Watching the clouds, Marco grew tense as humidity thickened scents and made his head ache. *How am I to focus when there is such agony?*

A burgeoning sense of trouble drifted on the heavy air, seeming to tumble with the swelling clouds. What it was, he could not say, but it left him on edge. A low, mournful sound like a horn billowed through the humidity, sending a chill across Marco's shoulders. He eyed the small band of rhinnocks traveling with them.

Crey emerged from among them and walked toward Marco. "The rhinnocks sense it, too. Something is amiss, yeh?"

Nodding, Marco scanned the valley again. Though no specific threat appeared, he sensed . . . *something* prickling the hairs on the back of his neck. To his right, Bazyli and Ixion were laughing and chatting over their meal, seemingly oblivious to the threat stalking them. The men had spoken little to him—and Marco did not make an effort to speak. It was wrong, of course. He had mentally chastised himself many times, but his mood had grown more foul with each meter they gained on Kardia. He eyed the green-clad aerios sitting outside their tents, ready to seek shelter when the rains fell. While they had set their tents in a circle around him, and another around that to protect him, he yet felt the outsider.

"Are they scary to ride, your beasts?" came a young voice, drawing Marco's attention to the two women among their troupe and the young boy.

"Eat your honey cake, Mnason," Kita said, tapping his bread wrapped in waxy leaves.

"But I want to hear about the rhinnocks," the boy complained.

"Little Warrior, they are gentle lambs," Crey said with a smile as he lowered himself to a log outside his shelter. "You should ride with me on the morrow."

Mnason hopped onto his knees, excited, and looked to his mom. "Can I?"

Kita pointed to the food. "No, I think not. Eat." Her gaze darted to the grizzled Hirakyn, uncertainty swamping her scent.

"I am sure he means well," Isaura added softly.

"See?" Mnason insisted. "Isa says it's okay!"

"What harm, yeh?" Crey grinned. "If your mother is concerned for safety, she could have a ride first to make sure—"

"No," Kita said quickly. "It is a kind offer, but I am still healing from the attack."

More likely the babe she lost, Marco thought.

"Then you." Crey grinned at Isaura. "You could show the boy it's safe."

"That would be inappropriate," grumbled Bazyli from the inner circle, his blue eyes blazing. "You will not touch the girl."

Isaura's embarrassment reared.

"Easy," Marco murmured as the voice of reason. "He may have been out of line, but we invited him into our circle. Let us not dishonor him or ourselves."

Ixion lifted his jaw and considered him. "Aye, eat in peace then check the tents. Make sure the women and boy have what they need to bed down. Once the rains pass, we must make up time since the journey is yet long."

"And filled with danger," Crey tossed in, then shrugged. "If our rhinnocks are any indication."

The herd grazed on vegetation that grew more lush the farther north they traveled. A low moaning seemed louder now and lent an eerie feel to the stormy night.

Edvian, the brawnier regia who'd come with Bazyli, grunted. "They have done that since we set out from Prokopios. What is that noise?"

"Their call," one of Crey's men, Kakuzo, spoke from the side. "They trill the air to warn other herds not to draw near."

Crey nodded. "They have almost impenetrable scales that serve them well in the deserts and fire gorges, make good boots"—he pointed to Marco's—"and armor, but they are sensitive, intuitive beasts."

"They are known and sought on many worlds," Marco noted. He lifted a water skin and sipped. And for the thousandth time wished for his waterpack from his scout, filled with filtered, nutrient-boosted water.

"Then it is good Drosero maintains its technology nonproliferation pact, or the herds may well be hunted to extinction by those seeking to profit off their hides," Hushak said, and most around the circle grunted or nodded their assent.

Except the Hirakyns. Crey tucked his chin and said nothing.

"We do not need skycrawlers telling us how to live and grow as a society," Galen asserted. "We are a strong and thriving people. Making advances and adhering to our codes. Let them in, and it will be annihilated."

Marco roughed a hand down the back of his neck. It was a shortsighted view, albeit a popular one. Why was it wrong to seek the aid of a culture that could help them grow? He thought again of clean, filtered water. Advanced medical care. Lifesaving skills and methods not in use here because there was no technology to support them. Granted, a world forced into technology before its time would very likely devolve and decay rapidly, just as a first-year at the Citadel would never accept a Decree because he was not prepared for the responsibility.

The archaic values, the patriarchal systems—while good and honorable— had those things blinded Drosero to what was coming? No. Kynig had technology, yet even the Brethren with their enhanced abilities hadn't anticipated what hit them. The Symmachians, the murders, the kidnappings, that creature . . .

Skin crawling, Marco stowed his pack in the tent, then started for the open valley. He caught wind of Edvian and Kaveh following. He turned. "Remain here. I walk but a short distance for solitude. Do not plague me with your scents."

Though they complied, irritation pulsed.

He moved a little faster than necessary, picking his way past the lowing rhinnocks so that at least the bestial scents interrupted the din of the aerios. He longed for a higher vantage, but there were no ridges or outcroppings, so he aimed for a large boulder. Warm air flicked his hair, which needled his face. Interesting—warm on a cool night.

Progenitor.

Why he thought of that name from the Lady, he had no idea. Maybe it was the odd scent or the stench of rhinnocks.

. . . your enemies relentless . . .

They were that. Even Roman had warned him Symmachians were looking for him. Xisya, that wretched, foul creature excelled at pain and misery.

A sprite of a scent darted up behind him.

Marco pivoted and latched onto an arm wielding a weapon.

A tiny yelp burst from Mnason. The weapon—a stick—wavered in front of large brown eyes that swelled with fright—just like the boy's scent. Then he wilted with a groan of frustration. "How *can* you do it?"

Marco motioned him away. "Go on with you." He could not fault the boy—in fact, he must admire him. Long ago that was him, determined to prove he could do what others said he couldn't. But tonight, Marco needed quiet.

Once more, he turned back to the trouble weighting his mood. The Irukandji were essentially invading Kalonica, peppering it with fear and death. Somehow, they had pulse weapons, which indicated they were in bed with Symmachia. Despite the Droseran-Tertian Accord, technology *had* come to Drosero. Was that the intent—to dismantle the accord? To what end? Why were they so fixated on this backwater planet? Why could they not leave Droserans to their primitive world?

Though Marco missed traveling among worlds and the ease of technology, Drosero seemed to call to him. Hint that what he'd looked for in the stars would be found here. Yet everything he encountered argued that. He'd never felt more lost.

Ahead pranced Mnason's notoriously mischievous scent. Somehow he'd circled around. Determined little pup—menace. No doubt he intended another sneak attack. Having no friends to play with, the boy must be bored.

An unexpected urge hit Marco . . . He shifted out of sight and crouched by the rock. From his hiding spot, he homed in on Mnason's scent, which morphed into confusion, then determination. The boy's steps were fast and light. He rounded the great rock.

"Augh!" Marco lunged and caught the boy, hoisting him off the ground and into the air. He caught and rolled him over his knee, pinning him, and dug his fingers into his side.

Writhing beneath the tickling and shriek-laughing, Mnason tried to extricate himself. "Stop. *Stop!*"

Marco held him fast, next targeting a spot behind the knees that left the boy kicking and begging for mercy. A sharp amused scent struck. He looked up.

Isaura stood nearby, laughing.

The distraction gave Mnason the chance to escape, and he tore off laughing, yelping, clearly expecting to be chased.

Feeling foolish, Marco stood and swiped a hand over his mouth. "Can I have your word?"

"About what this time?" She crossed her arms. "That you, a grown man, knows how to play games and laugh like a child? Where is the harm in that?"

As he dusted off his pants, Marco sighed. "Plenty. Especially when there is much pain and heartache in the realm." He ran a hand through his now disheveled hair as he started walking.

"Laughter is not only good but needed. Besides, where there are people, there will always be pain and heartache," she said softly.

"A rather dark outlook."

"Only if you end it there." Isaura plucked a blade of the tall grass and played with it as they paused near a crumbling stone wall that protected a dilapidated empty farmhouse. "I would not trade loving and knowing people simply because hurt or sorrow will come. In truth, those only strengthen the experience of having known and loved."

Surprised at her wisdom, he eyed her, then leaned against the wall to pick brambles from his pants. "That is profound, especially considering all you have lost."

"And had I not loved my ma'ma and Laseria, who would grieve them? I am better for having been a part of their lives, no matter how short."

Marco knew she wasn't lying—her efflux told him so—but he had trouble reconciling how she could feel that way.

The wind grabbed her hair and whipped it about. Her skirts flapped hard beneath the beating gusts.

Marco directed her around the side of the ruined house to find protection from the wind. Thunder rumbled the ground. Lightning crackled and split the night.

Isaura jumped but then laughed, inhaling deeply of the misty air. "I love storms," she said. "It is as if all this tension that has built up frees itself. The rain comes and washes everything anew."

"Storms also ravage lives and homes."

A serene smile touched her lips. "But then . . . the darkness fades, the sun comes out, and there's a new beginning." She tilted her head.

"Do you see everything so . . ."

"Positively?"

Naïvely.

Thorny vines growing up the wall snaked out in the increasing wind and snagged her hair, holding fast. Isaura yelped, jerking back.

Marco angled to the side, caught the ensnared strands near her throat. "Sorry." It must hurt, but pry as he might, the branch proved insistent. "I can't . . ."

"Cut it."

"No—"

"It's just a few strands," she said. "I would rather that than be stuck in the storm."

Marco could hear rain pelting the earth in the distance. He refused to cut her pretty hair, though. Shifting closer, he squinted at the tangle, located the right cane, and snapped it off.

"Aha!" Isaura shifted away with a laugh, her hands going to the spot—then yipped and shook her finger, which she then pressed the tip to her mouth.

He saw then the thorn and motioned her closer. "There's a piece stuck in your hair."

She moved toward him, turning her head. "You should have just cut it."

"And have my blade so close to your throat? Too dangerous."

"Aye," she said, wrinkling her nose. "Mayhap you are right. Far too dangerous. After all, were you a greater man, you would have experience to prevent you from harming me with such a task."

Amused that she sought to provoke him, Marco arched an eyebrow. "You think me inexperienced?" Her hair was soft in his hands as he plucked out the bramble. The wind taunted him, tossing her blonde strands into his face.

She caught her lower lip between her teeth, smothering a smile. "Since I am unharmed and now freed of the deadly vine," she said, her left eye narrowing slightly, "mayhap not completely inexperienced." Her words had merriment. Mocking.

"Now who is the menace?"

At that she laughed. It was hard to reconcile the mischievous side of a woman who'd been through so much, offered so much wisdom borne of experience. Desert wisdom just as Ixion had his desert justice.

Green eyes struck his, and she swiped a hand to control the loose strands getting in their eyes. Her scent was drenched with spiced attraction. "Your mark . . ."

Words so softly spoken shouldn't have the power to awaken thunder, but that is what happened in his chest.

Stand down, he warned himself. There'd been lecture enough from Bazyli.

"The one on your arm," she clarified, tucking her long hair behind her ear as she glanced at his right forearm. "May I see it?"

Reticence clawed, the brand somehow a tether between him and Kersei. Their link. What brought them together. Showing it to Isaura seemed . . . wrong.

"I beg your mercy," she whispered, shaking her head. "I should not have asked."

When she started to leave, he caught her hand. "Wait." Why he did it, he couldn't say, but Marco drew up his sleeve to reveal the glowing brand, the blue surprisingly bright against the dark night.

She held his arm and glanced at him, as if to ask permission—those green eyes lit anew with the purest light that streaked straight down to his adunatos. He'd seen it in the gallery hall, and it'd startled him then, too. He nodded.

He swallowed as she lightly traced the arcs and whirls, his heart like a rhinnock on a rampage.

For some reason, her eyes went glossy.

Grief lanced his receptors, coiling about his chest and heart. Marco shifted at the unexpected dolor. "What is it? What's wrong?"

Her hand went to her throat—no, not her throat but a leather cord around her neck. She drew it from beneath her bliaut. Held it and whatever sacred secret it represented close. "I have never shown this to anyone. I . . ." She wet her lips, then seemed ready to speak again, but no words came. Finally she rotated her wrist and lifted her fingers, revealing a pendant.

The wan light prevented him from seeing it clearly. "May I?"

A small, almost imperceptible nod.

He took it and leaned closer to see—

Marco sucked in a breath. Straightened, he stared in disbelief. "The brand." How could she have the *Trópos tis Fotiás*, the Way of the Flame, on an amulet? It was a brand tied to their prophecy, his and Kersei's—both halves etched into this piece. A prophecy handed down by the Ladies of Basilikas centuries ago. "I don't understand." It was impossible to explain to her its significance, what this mark had done to his life and Kersei's. The irrevocable tie.

Her gaze darted over his face, her nerves rank in her efflux. "Neither do I."

"But that's my brand from the Holy Order of Iereania—the Lady Herself. Do you know what it means?"

She shrugged and shook her head, tucking the necklace away.

"How is it you have it on your amulet?" His pulse thrashed against his ribs. "It was between me and—" Kersei, though he protected that truth. "The iereas said it was rare and largely unknown. It's impossible for you . . . *How?*"

"I know not," she said with another shrug. "When I was ten, I started having dreams of this pattern, and in them, it showed up in rivers, valleys, the desert, stars. Carved on a tree, a stone, a swirl in the water, a hut . . . a man's arm."

"What man?"

Her eyes slowly returned with wariness and uncertainty. "I never saw his face, but his name was Progenitor."

Feeling as if he'd been punched, Marco jerked. Stepped back. "What did you say?"

"Pro—"

"No. Stop." *This can't be* . . . He turned away, dragging a hand down the back of his neck. Then pivoted back, stared at her.

"Long ago, Ma'ma said I would know what it meant when I found the man."

Why would she be dreaming about it? How? Could she be tied to it? Impossible. The brand was complete, the prophecy awakened, two lives connected—his and Kersei's. Yet here was this sweet, naïve, beautiful woman with the same mark.

Ypiretis. He would know the answer. Suddenly, Marco wanted to make for Kardia.

"Are you angry?" she asked quietly.

"No." He mentally shook himself. "Surprised. Confused. I only have half the brand. The other half . . ." He swallowed. "It's connected to a prophecy." He glanced at her and moved to the half wall. "It doesn't make sense why you'd have the brand. She and I were two halves of a whole."

Isaura lifted her chin. "Kersei."

He twisted to her, detecting rawness. Defeat. "She bears the other half. We thought it meant we belonged together, but she's bound to my brother." Strange how the silence that fell seemed to be louder than the building storm. Even more peculiar was his regret, sensing the distance that sprang between them just then.

"Then I am not the only one who has borne much loss." Soft and sweet were her words against his receptors, a menthol of healing and hope.

"You bear it with more grace." He glanced up at the moons as they fought to push their light past the thick clouds. What did this mean? Why did he feel more lost than ever?

As the first drops of rain reached them, Isaura lifted his hand and turned it over. Her unexpected touch and gesture shifted his attention to hers, unsure her purpose.

"Right here." Intention in her words, she raised his palm. "What you do with hurt, with grief, is not determined by whatever happened or whoever perpetrated it against you. They do not have that power unless you give it to them. The decision is in your hand." Compassion shrouded the air. "It does not seem you are a man who easily allows another to control his actions. Tonight, let the rain wash it away, Dusan. You are stronger than this wrong done you, better than it, and with a far greater purpose. I've known that since I first saw you in

Moidia." Something strange spurted into her scent—a reticent awareness. She placed his hand back on the stone. "It is easy to forget you are . . . my medora." She stepped back, her efflux rank with deference.

"No." Marco reached for her, missed her arm, and caught her waist. "Please—not you."

Uncertainty glanced off her expression, and she stilled with an explosion of longing.

It cautioned him to step off, but . . . not yet. "Ever have you spoken straight and true to me. Please do not . . ." His eyes met hers as the moons finally peeked through a gap, their glow caressing her face. "I would have friendship, not deference." Though he felt the curve of her waist and knew he should move away, he couldn't. He wanted this . . . grounding.

Her hand rested on his upper arm. "I never believed my ma'ma when she spoke of the symbol, because it seemed too impossible that the strange arcs could mean anything, let alone appear outside my dreams. She said I would find its meaning," she whispered, her eyes molten and the seconds drawn out. "Now I have, but I do not know its significance." Her warm Signature blanketed and lured him closer. Invited him in.

"It's bewildering," Marco agreed, his voice husky. Marveling at her. The thought proved heady and warned he should remove himself. Yet . . . He tilted her chin up, gaze dropping to her lips. Angled his head—

"Anyone seen Dusan?" called a not-so-distant voice.

Drawing in a sharp breath, Isaura turned away.

Marco glanced back and spotted Crey coming around a rhinnock. His scent was filled with amusement—clearly, he'd seen what transpired between Marco and Isaura.

Without a word, she walked quickly back toward camp.

"You disagree," Marco said, deliberate in his attempt to distract the man. "About technology coming to Drosero."

Crey hesitated, glanced after Isaura, then shrugged. "Not really."

Anak'ing, Marco drew in a slow breath and found deceit. "You are sure?"

The man's scent grew confrontational. "Mayhap we should discuss the girl." He smirked, their shoulders nearly touching as they stared each other down. "She is clearly open to your advances, yet you don't—well, mostly."

"The storm comes. Let's return to camp." Marco moved around the man.

Crey followed. "I would understand you, *Kynigos*."

"To what end?"

"To know the man I pledge my life to."

Marco stopped short and pivoted, squinting around the downpour that now came in abrupt sheets. "Kynigos hunt alone—no need for a pledged sergius." He turned again.

"You are the reason I am north of the border." Crey cleared his throat and gave a reverent nod. "Medora Marco."

Unsteady at having his true name spoken openly, Marco squared his shoulders. "This from a man who betrays his own kin and swears fealty to a foreign ruler."

"I am banished, shunned from Hirakys through no fault of my own." The scent coating those words confirmed his honesty—for the most part. There was some discordance there. "A grave wrong was done me, and in that, we have much in common."

Aye, having Kersei ripped from him on Iereania could be called that. But even now, Isaura's words haunted him—as well as that near kiss. What had he been thinking?—and he glanced at his hands, where the power over those wounds rested.

"If I again set foot in Hirakys, I will be put to the sword."

All true. Marco stepped closer, deliberately shrinking the gap between them, pressing into the man's face, searching for a way to make skin contact. To know this man's adunatos. "You speak smooth words, but there's something you withhold, Hirakyn. Until you come clean, there can be no alliance between us."

"Then you *are* Medora Marco."

Blinking as the rain heaved its bounty on them, Marco offered his hand. The Hirakyn didn't hesitate to accept the acknowledgement. Though a tinge of pale blue hung in his eyes, it was . . . blurry. Vague. What did that mean? "And you are no simple Hirakyn or Qicien."

"Then what am I?"

"Someone with few options," Marco said, "making you one of the most dangerous men I know."

"Is that your way of flirting with me?"

Marco nearly smirked at the man's levity, but a scent pushed through his distraction with the Hirakyn and drew his gaze over the storm-darkened plain to the deep woods bordering the northern half of the valley. From the rustling leaves whispered an ominous threat. "Come, we'll talk more of this, but I think danger may be at our heels."

"They will have neared Trachys by now," Darius said as they finished their meal in their apartment.

Fork in midair, speared with potato, Kersei glanced at him. His hair was longer than normal and wavy. His blue eyes pierced with challenge. "I beg the Ladies to watch over them."

"They are aerios," Darius grumbled as he took a sip of wine to wash down his last bite. "They need not the Ladies for protection—that is their job."

"It was the duty of the Ladies—"

"I cannot believe you still cling to those stories."

Bristling, Kersei let her mind travel a road avoided these long months—back to the *Macedon*, to what Captain Baric had said: . . . *of Nicea, a Lady of Basilikas* . . .

"Kersei?"

She blinked.

"You look ill," he said, setting down his utensil.

"I . . ." She bolstered herself. "I recalled something the captain said during my captivity on the ship when he accused me of murdering my family." She gave him a pursed smile and lifted the water glass. "So, aye, it makes me ill to remember it."

His expression softened. "I am truly sorry for what happened to you."

"Then you believe me?"

"Of course." His brow rippled in confusion. "Why would I not?"

She shrugged. "Many do not, and the Stratios who remain question why I am alive and my family dead—their families dead." She did her best not to eye Myles, who had posed that very question to her.

"You do not talk of what happened up there."

Dark memories leapt at her. "It is best forgotten." She tore off bread from the loaf, which suddenly seemed more palatable than the heavily spiced meat.

Darius reached over and covered her hand with his then also tore a chunk from the loaf sitting between them. "You have night terrors," he persisted. "Is

Captain Baric behind them? Did he . . . take liberties—"

"No!" Strangely uncomfortable speaking of this, Kersei felt even more awkward since they were not alone. "He . . . tried." The swell and burn of tears over that horrible time on the metal flower broke over her anew, the torment of months aboard the *Macedon* suddenly anvil-heavy in her chest.

But something severed her tenuous encounter with the memories—how had Darius known the captain's name? Never had she mentioned it. Her heart hitched, trapping Kersei's breath in her throat.

"What did he do to you?"

"Nothing," she said, her voice cracking, noting Myles shift his stance from ease to readiness.

"Why do you look to him?" Darius demanded. "*I* am your bound."

"I look to no one—only to escape speaking of what happened to me."

"Not even Marco?"

"Oh, Darius," she whimpered, shaking her head, weary of his jealousy. "I beg you—cease this challenge." A whisper of a flutter erupted in her belly, so quick and so light she thought it merely the food. But she stilled, realizing . . .

I feel him. I feel my son! Tears bubbled up, for in that moment the babe became real. Beautiful. "Marco is not here. You are, and I am bound to you. And I—"

"You are right." Darius lowered his eyes, his shoulders with them. "In earnest, I do try. However . . ."

Well she could imagine what it must have been like for him to come upon Marco and her in that room on Iereania, hugging and talking of binding. "I know."

"Come, let us retire to the solar. I leave within the ora with Elek for Trachys." He stood and offered his hand to her. "We hope to persuade Marco to host a Council of Elders while he is yet there."

"Why would he object?"

"He likes things on his own terms and Trachys is Elek's territory."

She could not argue. Marco enjoyed being in control.

Kersei forced a smile, her thoughts anxious for rest but also wrestling how he had known that name. She was ready to leave the confrontations behind. Would he? She was weary of it, and as the babe grew, so did her need to abandon that terrific grief and loss. Accepting his gesture, she allowed him to lead her.

They turned down the hall, and her hand rested on her belly, marveling at the curving beneath her palm. She should tell Darius. Soon.

He nudged open the door to their private quarters, and the servant who had lit the fire exited the side door. Darius shrugged out of his dinner jacket, tossed it onto a chair, and loosened his cravat. "My father tried to dissuade me from taking you as my bound. He said you were too wild."

"And you would not be deterred."

He moved to the side table and poured from a decanter, all ease and confidence. "I knew I loved you," he said as if it were the only possible reply. "My feelings revealed themselves at the Winter Solstice Celebration when you came out."

Kersei lifted her eyebrows, disbelieving. "I was but four and ten!" She joined him at the serving table.

"Aye," Darius said, his voice soft. He lifted the glass toward her, asking if she wanted one, but she declined—for the babe—and chose instead the peppermint tea.

"After being forced to dance with all the primping and preening daughters of every notable noble, I was ready to abandon the ball. That's when I heard shouting in the bailey and found you sparring the grand duke's son—"

"I gave him a solid knot on the head for his remark about me in that dress!"

Darius laughed. "I also recall the grand duchess hauling you before my father-medora and the entirety of the ballroom." He took a sip and shook his head. "When he asked what defense you had, you said—"

"'A sword, my medora.'" She laughed. "I would not give anyone the pleasure of begging mercy when that overstuffed lout deserved punishment and humiliation, not me." She set the tea on the table, then retrieved her favorite pillow—lower back pain had been her constant bane these last weeks.

"My father laughed for days." Darius caught her hand as she started past him.

"Mine was so angry with me. And my mother!"

"I determined then I would one day set petition." His expression sobered as he lifted her hand to his lips and kissed it.

As she stared into his blue eyes, the flutter came again. Only, this time, it wasn't the babe. What then? Attraction? It seemed impossible.

She must release what could not be. Vow to leave it behind. Darius—just as intense as Marco, but in another way. Handsome as his brother, even with the scars on his face and neck—which somehow made him appear a rogue. Where Marco was dangerous, raw, Darius was practiced and composed, the politician to his brother's warrior.

"Is that why you changed?" she asked. "One day you were my sparring partner, the next . . ."

"Yes," he said, entwining their fingers. "We were in the training yard when I told my father I wanted to set petition. He nearly put me on my backside. Said if I wanted to take anyone as a bound, I had better get serious about my duties as prince. That day, he arranged my training with the Xanthus, then Elek, and the Plisiázon."

Dumbstruck at his story, Kersei took in his features, trying to gauge the legitimacy of his words. Eyes so earnest and clear. "That's why you left me." Her heart gave a start at those words and their truth. "I was furious with you." Long had she said it was over losing the one sparring partner who would not hold back, but admittedly, she had missed his friendship, his banter. Challenges.

His smile was gentle. "It was because of your anger that I dared hope you cared more than you spoke."

Unsettled to understand that she *had* cared about him as more than a friend, she could not tear her gaze away. Then she had been too blind to see it. Too focused on her own wants. "Your father would have been very proud of you, Darius." Where those words had come from, she knew not—only that they were true.

Surprise widened his eyes.

No . . . no, his pupils were enlarging as he took her in. Studied her. That pervasive tension between them since Iereania seemed to lessen. Her stomach squeezed, but she did not look away . . .

Again, he lifted her hand to his lips. Eyes on her, he rotated her arm and pressed a kiss to her inner wrist, causing an eruption of nervous jellies in her stomach. Then he laid her arm across his shoulder and drew her closer. Cupped her face. "It is too much to believe that you are mine," he whispered, his gaze falling to her mouth.

Kersei's breath caught, intention clear in his gaze. How strange that she had not stiffened at the kiss she still felt on her wrist. Or at his touch and proximity—no fear. Only . . . anticipation. *What is this?*

His lips dusted hers, then his hand came to her waist. Seriousness washed through his handsome features, yet he did not pursue more. Why? What was he waiting for?

Permission. The thought stilled her.

It surprised that though Kersei could not bring herself to search out his kiss, neither did she dread it. With a whisper of a smile, she angled her head, and he met her halfway.

This kiss was firmer, stronger. His hand sliding to the small of her back, he deepened the kiss. Exhilaration wove through Kersei as she unlocked the door of her heart to his love.

NORTHWEST OF PROKOPIOS, KALONICA, DROSERO

Marco shook the rain off his duster and ducked into the tent. He set it on the ground and sat, accepting a satchel of dried meats. He took some and passed it on, only then noticing Isaura in the corner. Why was she not in the carriage, where it was dry?

Ixion was already moving toward her, urging her to leave.

"Mnason is asleep on one bench and Kita on the other," she explained. "There is no room for me there."

"Why are you following Dusan through the night?" Bazyli growled at the Hirakyn, a razor-edge in his words. "To ambush him?"

As if bred from air, five Stalkers melted from the shadows and circled them. Their scents were fierce, protective.

"Why would I save your king's life in Prokopios only to kill him later and much farther from my home?" Crey snorted, shaking his head. "I would be a fool with no escape."

"Just moments past, you claimed you had no home," Marco pointed out.

The Hirakyn growled. "You have no time for madness. The Irukandji hunt you."

"Why?" Marco asked, recalling Roman had said as much, too, but how did this Hirakyn know as well? "What do they seek? I am but one man."

Crey wiped his hands and took a gulp from a waterskin. "I know not why you are so important to them, but their interest is not their own. Offworlders have—"

"Offworlders?" Marco leaned in. On a planet without spacefaring ships and technology, there should be no reference to *offworlders*. "What offworlders? How do you know this?"

"It is only a guess," Crey said, but he was a bad liar with a rank stench. "Tell me—what route will you take to Kardia? The Medora Road or—"

"What concern is that of yours?" Bazyli bit out.

"I seek to help you."

"Help us? In our own lands?"

"Our course is direct," Marco said, tearing off some jerky, seeing no reason to hide their path.

Ixion followed his lead. "We make for the Altas Silvas."

Disapproval rippled through Crey's dark features. "Is there any way I could dissuade you? We ride for Throne Road. Let us remain together and you will have added protection."

"Throne Road would add a full rise to our journey," Bazyli grumbled.

"Why do you hesitate?" Marco asked, eyeing the Hirakyn leader.

"Nothing I can prove."

"Yet you have concern."

"Aye," Crey said, tossing a stick onto the small fire before them. "You smelled them out there, right? You said there was trouble."

"I did not smell them," Marco said, tilting his head, recalling the strangeness in the air that could not be justified or explained. "You think they will attack there?"

"They have attacked everywhere else, have they not?" Crey said with a snigger that seemed to loosen a knot of tension that had grown in the now-humid, musty tent.

"You negate your own point," Marco noted wryly.

"Aye, but in the woods, you will be cut off from help—trapped. We cannot be there to assist, and as I said—you are why I'm here."

"Why can't you travel there?"

Bazyli bristled. "Think we will allow you to wander our realm unchecked? The deal was you will not leave our side."

"The road is too narrow and crooked for the rhinnocks," Crey explained. "Make for Trachys, and I can stay with you. The beasts and their protection are reason enough to reconsider, aye?"

"Too much delay," Ixion muttered. "Yet, he is right—the Altas Silvas is too narrow for rhinnocks. There are places where even we will be pressed to get the carriage through."

"Agreed—Trachys is too costly a time diversion," Marco said, the rain slapping the tent harder now.

"Costly would be holding course and not seeking protection," Crey insisted. "They are out there, I assure you."

"I detect no savages here. I will trust the gift given me." Yet . . . what was that strangeness in the air?

Crey all but growled. "Do that and you will not live another day." He looked to Ixion but cocked his head at Marco. "Is he always as difficult as a new rhinnock calf?"

"Give care how you speak—"

"Of your medora? Aye, I will," he grumbled with a gleam in his eye, "but a difficult, thick-skulled bounty hunter?" He shrugged. "I care not how I speak to such a dog."

"Have you a will to cut your life short, Scorcher?" Ixion demanded, the Stalkers shifting, expressions darkening.

"I have a will to live," Crey said, his lips curled, "and to see this one reach Kardia so there is hope for this accursed planet. Someone to lead a war against the Irukandji, who have climbed into bed with Symmachia." His disgust and frustration were so intense, they thumped against Marco's receptors.

"I appreciate your concern, Crey of Greyedge," Marco said, "but even you see the need that I reach Kardia urgently. You take the Throne Road and meet us in Kardia as soon as you can." He raised a hand to still Ixion's objection. "I'll give you a writ of passage."

"So it is true," Kakuzo muttered. "You are . . . him, the medora."

The aerios and regia shifted, their gazes locking onto Marco, who stared down the formidable Hirakyn.

Crey cracked a rueful grin and nodded. "Very well. If we reach Kardia and you have yet to arrive, I will know you have perished in the woods." He chuckled darkly then offered Marco a cordi and took one for himself. "Since you are new to ruling, I advise you speak with King Vorn. He has swiftly rallied a kingdom on the verge of collapse. The people nearly ousted him, but he turned it and them around."

"You sound enamored," Bazyli grunted.

"I know when to respect a ruler, even an enemy."

"Enemy," Marco mused, wondering how many in this tent he saw as enemies.

"Not per se, but neither is Vorn a friend. He is fierce and ruthless."

"He is called the Errant," Kakuzo said, "because he so sharply deviated from the practices of his father, who pandered and placated the people. The kingdom was in ruin because he did not want to offend the people with taxes."

"The Errant is also said to have taken a Lady to wife," Ikku offered with a lecherous smile.

"A Lady?" Theilig laughed and shook his head. "They are myth!"

The irreverent laughter and rejection of the Ladies' existence struck a hard chord in Marco, coiling his fist. He thought of the Lady who'd spoken to him and Kersei, set their feet on this path of war that would find them whether or not they sought it.

"You disagree, my liege?" Bazyli said, his tone and efflux even—not challenging, but inviting. He wanted Marco to share his experience.

"On Iereania, did you not say a Lady spoke to you?" Mavridis supplied.

"Only spoke?" Ikku barked a laugh, others joining in the mockery. "They are said to lure men to their beds for far more than speech!"

Anger rose through Marco and he pinned Ikku with a glower. "Give care the words you speak."

"So, one did speak to you?" Ikku's words had mockery but also intense curiosity.

Marco held the man's gaze, forcing himself to calm. "Aye." He then looked to Isaura seated in a corner nearby, a blanket around her shoulders, and thought of her amulet. A new thought filtered into his mind—had a Lady given her the dreams?

Theilig furrowed his brow. "If . . . assuming you're . . ." He cleared his throat. "I beg your mercy, I do not doubt your word, but by legend told, they are gone from this world since the Great Falling. They have not been seen for centuries."

Marco bit into a cordi, watching the commander all puffed up and regal in his greens. "Do you breathe, aerios?"

Hesitating, Theilig was experienced enough not to look around in disbelief at the question of what was likely seen as yet another absurdity. He held his medora's gaze, but his hesitation was plain even as he answered. "I would well hope, sire."

"And do you see that breath?"

Theilig gave a faint smile. "Only in winter."

Clever. "The point," Marco said, "is to not assume something does not exist simply because you cannot set eye on it."

On a normal day the intoxicating scents of a forest would enthrall Marco, but as they rode into the embrace of the thickly treed vegetation, the Hirakyns long gone, something—not the normal dolors of trouble or danger—grated. He couldn't pinpoint what, and that alone frustrated and made him open wide his receptors.

Marco strained in the dim light to see ahead. The road had changed from hardpacked dirt to a more earthy and rutted path—but even that seemed short, for the darkness grew complete mere meters ahead. What warmth had been found in the predawn morning after the storm surrendered to the loamy power of the forest.

Ixion rode beside the carriage transporting the women and the child. He angled closer, where the young boy hung out the window. "Keep a weather eye on the forest and its floor, Mnason. There are species here you will find nowhere else on Drosero."

Innocent eyes widened as the boy leaned farther out. "Can I ride with you to see them?"

"Maybe a walk instead," came Isaura's soft voice, even as the carriage door opened. She hopped out, landing softly, not having given the driver a chance to slow. Mnason and Kita followed suit.

"It's creepy-dark," Mnason said with a nervous laugh as he gripped his mother's hand.

Bazyli let his destrier fall back toward them a bit. "The ancient name given this place is *Sirlar Mabadi*, the Sanctuary of Secrets. It is said that when one enters, he knows not what will happen to his secrets—whether the trees allow him to keep them or drag them out of him."

"Willing or unwilling," Ixion added, his tone grim as he passed beneath the arch of swaying branches. "One way or another, they will pry them from the deepest parts of a man and leave him irrevocably altered."

"What does that mean?" Mnason asked, his voice tremoring with fear.

"You're frightening the boy," Marco said.

"Him?" Hushak chortled. "Half these men wet their pants at the thought of entering these woods."

"Beg off," Kaveh grumbled. "We fear nothing here save that I can smell you more."

"Aye," Marco agreed. "All of you." Entering here—aye, there had been unease, but also an overwhelming sense that urged him to slow, to stop, to savor. He slipped to the ground and drew the Black aside as the others continued past. The squishy mossy undergrowth closed around the toe of his boots with a splurch that made him smile. He let his gaze track over the towering trees, the vines that draped branches. This . . . this was holy, sacred.

Ixion's face shone in the light of a touchstone as he rounded back. "You well?"

Marco nodded.

Overhead, the first rays of dawn fought to thrust shards of light down at him, but the trees stood defiant, guarding their territory. The creak and groan of rubbing branches murmured softly, as if the trees held council to determine if Marco and his companions were friend or foe. Despite the soft banter coming from ahead, he also detected the steadily rising alertness of the men as they moved deeper into the shrouded mystery of the forest. Their disquiet and sharper pungency of unease interfered with his anak'ing. Kynigos most often hunted in packed cities and villages, but rarely—never in his experience—a forest this rich and dense.

Shadows danced as if wraiths of the trees, the faithful guardians, and Marco recalled many a lesson at the Citadel about not trusting what his eyes could or could not see. He closed them and centered himself, allowing the overwhelming dominance of vegetation to waft over his senses. At his shin, he felt the teasing distraction of a fern with its lemony tang. Then there was the damp undergrowth and rotting decay of the thickly padded forest floor.

Inhaling, he let the reek of the city and desert wash out of his receptors. A smile curved into Marco as unease fell away and he savored every delectable, unusual scent. Somewhere to the east, he caught the cool scent of water—clear and clean, inviting. Wrapped in the titter of leaves and the rustle of critters, he felt a part of this place. Yet entirely the intruder. Still, he couldn't help himself—Marco touched the nearby machi tree, feeling its rough bark but also the soft carpet of moss on its trunk.

Beside him came the familiar fragrance of lavender and white oak. Isaura was near. Also near was a creature of some kind eating a nut.

And there it was again—that oddness—smacking Marco out of his inventory of this amazing place. He opened his eyes and found that the leaves and fronds seemed to pull back the curtain of darkness for him—he could see much clearer now. Felt guided and invited.

"You are smiling," she said softly and took a step closer.

"Is that so rare?"

She snickered. "For you, aye."

He shook his head and started walking, realizing he'd allowed too much distance between him and the rest of the line. "I've never been in a forest—in all my hunts, all my years . . . nothing like this." His flicked his gaze across the shadows, searching.

Isaura looked up and around, her aromatic pleasure entwining with his awe. "Having lived in a desert, I, too, can appreciate this beauty. It is . . . unparalleled."

Marco nodded, homing in more on the oddness to the air.

"Last night, when you returned after talking with the Hirakyn"—she gave a small yelp as a fox scurried across their path, then let out a nervous laugh—"you seemed much changed. Upset even."

He recalled returning to the camp and being stuffed in the tent with a dozen others as the rains pelted the canvas and thickened the air. It was natural she would assume his mood was about the Hirakyn. Mayhap it had been, in a way, but the greater concern was what even now started to rankle: the odd scent.

But those things weren't what kept him from answering now. It was remembering where his thoughts had gone last night, what he had almost done. How even now, her presence, her Signature, seemed to comfort.

"What is illuminated in your sight will be your measure and burden . . ." The Lady's words came to him from that moment outside Prokopios when Isaura seemed lit by the sun in the dead of night. What did that mean? And her amulet—

"Have I angered you?"

"What? No! Why—" Something splatted his face. Then several more dollops hit his shoulders and head.

Isaura drew in a breath and then let it out with a laugh as some landed on her. "It's pollen—*glowing* pollen!"

Marco wiped a hand over his face and found a smear of turquoise on his palm. He looked up and saw a twisting vine with large golden blooms dangling over the path, spitting its spores on unsuspecting travelers. He used his sleeve to clean his face.

"If we remain beneath the bough, this may well be a lost cause." She moved out from the plant's reach and bent, using the hem of her dress to clean up. The gentle glow of touchstones and the bioluminescent plants emphasized her tawny complexion.

"Why did you think I was angry?"

"You have been very quiet since . . ."

Since he'd nearly kissed her. He started walking again. "Forgive me. I am not angry, merely . . . distracted." Marco didn't want her believing he held any ill will toward her, though he held plenty toward himself. Had they not been interrupted, he may very well have taken that kiss. Wouldn't Bazyli love that?

Isaura nodded. Her gaze hit something to his left, then bounced right. A spurt of nerves—fear—spiraled out.

Marco shifted nearer, glanced in the direction she had. "What did you see?"

"I . . ." She shook her head. "I thought . . ." She sniffed. "Shadows, I suppose."

But even as she said it, Marco locked onto an area—the scent was there, yet wasn't. He paused, glancing around, taking in the towering trunks that shot up into the canopy. Dawn was attempting to force its presence past the leaves . . . twinkling darts of light pierced the void.

Void. Yes . . . *void*.

While he'd felt the sacredness of the woods before, now he felt . . . stillness, menace . . . threat. The absence of scent in those patches of black—no animal scents, no fluttering wings or scampering feet. It was as if the vegetation, too, held its breath. No, worse—it withdrew.

They were not alone.

Marco touched the small of her back and whispered into her ear, "Find Kita and Mnason—get in the carriage."

"Then, there *was* something?"

"Do it. Now." Gently, he urged her toward the lumbering black box, unwilling to hurry and alert whoever prowled the forest that he detected them. That prickling at his nape worsened as Ixion turned to him. Marco cursed himself for not yet learning the Stalkers whistles.

Isaura hurried ahead, softly calling to Kita and Mnason and waving them to the carriage.

Anak'ing, Marco eased off the path and stood beside a tree. Though he thought to close his eyes, he dared not. Something was wrong.

Behind him came Ixion. "What—"

"They're here," Marco said, unsure how he knew it was the Irukandji, yet . . . he did.

Ixion let out a warbling whistle, and almost instantly, Stalkers spirited back to him.

Thunk!

The nearby tree rattled with the heavy impact of a dagger. He flinched aside but yanked free the blade. Marco rolled around a cluster of trees, grabbed a branch, and hauled himself up. He felt Ixion's surprise even as he hurried forward. From a branch, he leapt up and across to another tree, hearing arrows whistling just below, one skimming his leg. He grimaced but kept moving higher until he was hidden among dense branches. Peering down, he probed the shadows and trees, using the scant light of the touchstones and glowing plants.

His heart thudded when he spotted nearly two dozen blue raiders. Their marks blended well into the Altas Silvas—too well. They must have smudged them with dirt. But how and why hadn't he anak'd their presence? That many should've overpowered his receptors before he even set foot in this sacred domain.

Sounds of battle erupted below. Two aerios near the front were already engaged in hand-to-hand with several raiders. Feral screams streaked through the foliage.

Marco sighted the half dozen closing in on the carriage—did they think he was in there? Why else would they focus on it? He searched for another thick branch nearby that'd put him closer, then leapt out and caught rough bark. He swung and launched out to the thicker branch.

Even as he aligned his body, fire seared his shoulder and neck. He jerked. Missed the limb. Plummeting, he felt the scraggly fingers of branches as they tried to catch him, scratching his face, arms, and back. He did an aerial, breaking his fall just before his boots thumped on the carpet of forest litter.

Weight slammed into him from behind. Pitched him to the ground. Rancid breath seared his nostrils. He swung his arm back and caught the raider's waist. Flipped him and their positions. The man was rabid, his movements frenetic and unpredictable. Wild yellow eyes glowered with a feral viciousness that bespoke his thirst for blood. Somehow, he produced a weapon—a pulse pistol.

Heart jammed, Marco clamped a vise around the raider's wrist, forbidding him from singeing a hole through Marco's head. He punched to render him unconscious, but the searing pain in his shoulder weakened him. Made the gun waver. A blast shot off, the heat wake trailing Marco's cheek. He cringed away.

The raider seized the mistake. Hit Marco, sending him flying backward.

He careened into a tree. Breath ejected from his lungs. Though aching, Marco rolled out of it and onto his feet, snapping to the raider. Saw him take aim again. The feral eyes gloating and manic.

The moment powered down to a terrifyingly slow pace. He saw the raider's finger press the trigger. Saw blue erupt from the muzzle at the same time gold whizzed across the marked throat. Marco dove for cover before he could sort out what that was. He came up on a knee and glanced back. Blood gushed as the raider dropped, gaping, unaware of what force had ended his life and fed his blood as a peace offering to the woods.

Marco staggered around just in time to see Isaura whirling behind a tree, a smudge of golden grace and fire. An arrow thumped into the bark that protected her, rattling not only the trunk, but his heart.

Having snatched the raider's pulse pistol, Marco sprinted toward her, but detected a rancid scent from the right. He ducked in time to avoid a fist. Shouldering into the attacker, he drove a hard uppercut into the blue-marked jaw, sending his opponent spinning away, disoriented so much he stumbled onto all fours. And curse it all if the savage didn't look directly at Isaura's hiding spot. He lunged toward her.

"No!" Fury vaulted Marco at the raider. He leapt and toed a tree, using it to launch into air—he drew back his fist—and collided with the raider, coldcocking him. A sickening crunch signaled the man's death. Marco landed and went to a knee to regain his balance.

Isaura gasped, snatching his gaze to hers—no, behind him.

A threat shoved him into a dive. He came up in a fighting stance, dagger in hand. "Get to the carriage!" he growled to her as he sighted the raider.

Hushak sprinted at the raider. With the same lethal precision as his Plisiázon leader, he did an aerial over the raider and delivered the creature of his head. Even as his boots slid on the ground, the Stalker faced another raider charging him and waited . . . letting the raider expend his energy.

Isaura rushed at Marco with her now-bloodied moon discs.

"Why aren't you in the carriage?" He anak'd around them—spotted an aerios dead next to a raider, evidence of a hard fight carved into both bodies. Another aerios straight ahead was losing his battle against two raiders.

Marco lifted the pulse pistol, took aim, and fired at the stronger of the

Irukandji. A hole lasered through the raider's chest and his shriek died with him. Though the aerios turned his attention on the remaining raider, he was badly wounded. His leg buckled. The angle and the trees prevented Marco from shooting that one.

Isaura whirled and flung a disc. It sliced through the raider and thudded into a tree behind him. The raider fell. "I was still needed," she said to Marco, exultant.

Ahead, he saw another skirmish between a regia and raider. He rushed up behind the raider and fired the pistol—but too late. The sword had found its mark. Both men collapsed.

Ripping off his coat, Marco dropped beside the aerios. Placed the coat against the wound, blood pulsing warm beneath his hands. Even as he felt the man's life slipping away, so did the sounds of battle. He glanced up for help, but Ixion and Bazyli were assessing wounds, dispatching Irukandji who had not yet succumbed. Forlorn, Isaura trudged through the foliage back to the carriage, where Kita and Mnason emerged from behind a thick tangle of ferns and shrubs.

The aerios at Marco's feet wheezed his last breath, and Marco slumped. Drew up a knee and rested his elbow on it. He wiped his forehead with the back of his hand.

Ixion had been right—the Sanctuary of Secrets had torn secrets from many men this morning. A shaft of light stabbed through the dense greenery, the decaying undergrowth adding the lives of warriors to its coffers. Absorbing the thrashing of men, the forest once more returned to its quiet, powerful repose.

The Altas Silvas was no place to tend wounded or do surgery, and Isaura was glad to be free of the darkness that yet hung in the forest.

Many were wounded and several lost in the melee with the Irukandji. Mavridis sent Hushak charging east to get help from Trachys, while the aerios loaded the dead into a wagon and the wounded into the carriage so they could exit the woods and set up a triage area. The intersecting road toward Trachys was not long—not even an ora and they broke out of the forest on its eastern edge. Mist lay heavily over the hilly terrain, the gray stonework of Trachys faint in the distance.

"Two stations," Mavridis instructed. "Hushak, divided the injured into those needing surgery and those needing stitches."

Even as tents went up and men were sorted into groups, Isaura spotted a small cart bearing two men, one grizzled and white-bearded, the other just barely old enough to be called a man.

They emerged from the chest-high grain field, and the older waved at her. "I am Keril. Saw your rider dart out of the woods half an ora past, then saw you lot emerge bedraggled. Guessing you need a pharmakeia."

Isaura hesitated, glancing at Mavridis and Dusan.

"That's quite a timely observation," Dusan muttered as he joined them.

"You are not from around these parts," Keril responded, eyeing Dusan speculatively. "This is not the first time someone was attacked in those woods and won't be the last. I live not far from here, retired from serving the elder nigh on ten years." He nodded, looking around. "So, can you use my help?"

"Please." Mavridis motioned to the tent and flicked a hand toward an aerios nearby. "See the pharmakeia has what he needs."

Keril climbed down from his cart and went to the back, where he donned a leather apron. "My apprentice will attend me in surgery. I assume the aerios can assist with binding wounds and prioritizing patients—not too petty a thing for their time, I hope."

"We are glad to help our warriors," Theilig asserted.

Keril bobbed his head, then his gaze connected with Isaura. "You ever stitched flesh?"

Squeamish at the thought, Isaura looked to the waiting wounded. Beyond the tent, two cookpots gurgled, boiling water sending spirals of steam into the predawn morning. Help was clearly needed. "No, but I am capable. Not skilled though."

"Don't need a royal seamstress to knit two sides of flesh." He motioned behind her. "And the other one?"

Isaura glanced to Kita sitting with Mnason, both very rattled. "If she is needed, I am sure she can."

"I will help," Kita said, standing, but her legs swayed.

The pharmakeia shook his head. "You ain't got it in you." He tapped Isaura's shoulder. "Well, let's start with you, see where we get."

He turned to the aerios Mavridis had assigned him. "Your name?"

The dark-complected aerios snapped to attention. "Cetus of House—"

"Cetus will do," Keril groused, waving at him. "Line up the wounded outside and rate them from most critical to lesser. The girl"—he swung to her again—"your name, child?"

"Isaura."

Keril gave another bob of his head. "Cetus, send the minor wounds to her for stitching." At the basin, he immersed his hands and arms as his protégé poured a sanitizing liquor over them. He looked at her again and frowned. "You waiting on something?"

"I . . . no." Isaura went to the basin and washed, then entered the tent where the first aerios—a regia—waited, sans tunic. Once she got over the subtle tension and vibration of the thread tugging through the skin, she worked quickly. The next ora was spent whittling down the line, stitching injuries as the men bandaged each other.

"How go the surgeries?" she asked Cetus, cleaning her hands after tending the last aerios.

"Not well. They need another pharmakeia—Malkias died waiting for surgery," Cetus said grimly. "How do you fare?"

Considering the others and their wounds, Isaura had no complaint. "Tired." With a sigh, she brushed loose strands from her face. "Very tired."

"I mean that cut on your cheek," Cetus said. "Need me to stitch it?"

Isaura touched the swollen cut that had given her a dull headache, but it did not feel deep. "No." There was still work to be done. "I will see if I can aid Keril—after a quick bite."

She grabbed a cup of water and a chunk of bread to replenish herself, gazing over the camp as she ate. The sight made her heart ache. They were all so tired and weary. Those accursed raiders! Never had she been given to bitterness, but it tempted her this day. These were good men and did not deserve the brutality wrought against them.

"Isaura!"

She whirled and found Cetus waving her over. Skirts lifted, she hurried to the tent, but hesitated when she heard sharp words from within. A man barked that he was not in need of a pharmakeia. Another told him to keep still before he did more injury.

After washing her hands again, she slipped through the curtained area. She lifted her eyebrows to Shobi, letting him know she had heard the argument. Then she saw her patient, who sat with his head down. Her heart skipped a beat. "Dusan," she breathed.

He jerked to her, his expression morphing from that brooding scowl to surprise, then back to irritation. "I do not—"

"My liege—please. Stay," Shobi insisted, then addressed Isaura. "Mavridis insisted that the cut on his shoulder be tended."

"I do not need you to speak for me," Dusan growled.

"I speak to the girl to relay the orders of her elder."

"She has a name!" Dusan seemed of the mind to argue over everything.

"Indeed!" Isaura snapped, silencing them. "If you both keep shouting, all of Trachys will know as well." She eyed his tunic with an indelible hole, the edges blackened. Red flesh peeked through, angry and sweltering. "Dusan— in the chair." Once he complied—with more than a little grunt of protest— she moved closer to assess the wound and saw the fabric had *melted* to his skin. "By the Ladies . . ." This had to hurt. She had tended so many patients, and while those wounds had bothered her, this . . . this felt worse. Deeper. "Shobi, bring fermented cordi for him."

"Nay," Dusan countered, coming out of the chair. "I never drink it fermented."

"Please." She touched his good shoulder and, with gentle pressure, guided him back down. "You will want it. Trust me."

Blue eyes so pale in the dim light of the shady tent locked onto hers, unflinching. His jaw muscle jounced. "Fine."

He sounded uncharacteristically petulant, which almost made her smile. Until she realized what must happen next. The embarrassment of it made her turn away. She straightened already orderly instruments as she spoke words she would rather have died than allow to cross her lips. "You will need to remove your tunic."

Why did it have to be Isaura? "This is absurd. I do not need tending."

Her scent was bemused but also embarrassed. "Then you prefer infection and blood poisoning to go with your foul mood?"

That she spoke so boldly . . . Marco flicked his gaze to her.

Long blonde hair hung in a plait that seemed to capture sunlight from the open tent flap and fling it off, as if she were too good for even light.

"I'm fine," he groused.

"That you are not," she countered.

At her contradiction, he again looked at her sharply. She appeared unusually tall as she arranged the instruments on a serving table. The leather ties of her apron seemed to emphasize her small waist and the curve of her hips.

He didn't mean to notice that. Shoving his gaze back to the ground, Marco cleared his throat. He knew better than to ignore an injury like this, but did it have to be *her*? Wincing as the burned fabric tore from the wound, he shrugged out of the tunic. Without it, he felt naked.

No, he did not need that thought in his head.

Isaura set three metal instruments on a smaller table near the stool, and her gaze grazed his chest, then she turned for more tools. "The wound is already weeping."

He fisted a hand. "It was a pulse pistol."

"A what?"

"A Symmachian weapon," he growled, "which is a problem."

"How would raiders come by such devices?" Isaura sat on the stool at his side, the air awash with her Signature, so calming and again that sense of coming home. She shrugged her plait over her shoulder as she leaned in to work.

He spotted the red line on her cheek. "You're cut."

"Mm, just a scratch." She used the back of her hand to nudge loose strands from her face. Dirt and a dark smudge on her temple said she'd done that several times in the last few hours. He recalled the way she'd fought at his side with those discs, all elegance and determination. "It would lead one to believe our quiet world is not as it seems."

What? Oh. Right—the raiders. "They were waiting for us—knew our route."

She lifted a bowl with a cloth soaking in a strong-smelling liquid. "This will sting."

He clenched his teeth. "It's not my first injury." As she bent forward with the drenched wad, Marco got slapped with a heady scent—a mixture of a floral aroma and . . . sage. Embarrassment. Attraction. Stretching his neck, he angled his head away, told himself to focus on the attack. "They weren't just hiding from us, they were *waiting*—lured us right into their trap."

Isaura's touch was gentle as she debrided the wound, which seared from the alcohol. "It was terrifying, but you were a sight to watch."

"You should speak," he teased. "Even after I ordered you to the carriage—"

"I know you meant it for my safety, but I had to retrieve my discs. Still, it was little compared to you . . ."

Marco looked at her—those green eyes wide with admiration, which saturated her Signature and bathed his receptors. He should respond. Speak.

Color suffused her cheeks, brightening the golden hue of her complexion. "I recall seeing you in action in Moidia, but what you did in the trees . . ."

Marco glanced at his hands, feeling embarrassed, yet proud. Then angry. "That's how I got this wound—they shot me while I was trying to reach you—I mean, the carriage."

More of that admiration and pleasure sifted the air as she worked.

"They were intent on slaughter." He recalled the scent of rage and vengeance. "You did good work with those discs."

A flush rose in her cheeks again, made all the more alluring with the backdrop of golden hair, sprigs loose around her face. Hands moving deftly, her touch gentle but confident, she shifted, focused on dabbing his wound. Again, she used the back of her hand to push hair from her face, a move so simple yet captivating.

Talk, idiot! "H-How long have you been tending wounded?"

"Before today, only here and there. I learned enough to tend injuries, but . . . it was not a profession I sought."

"Because of your mother."

Isaura inclined her head in a shrug. Pain sharpened her efflux, green eyes flicking to his, and an efflux of rose washed over him. Quickly, she withdrew her gaze.

Marco forced himself to keep talking, pretend he didn't know the scent that now blanketed him. "You're good at it." From petulant to stupid in the space of a few seconds. He was setting new records. "You don't like healing?"

"I like that people heal," she conceded, "but I would rather there not be wounds, nor that I should have to dress them." She sighed, no anger or irritation in her scent.

"You would have peace."

"Would not we all?" She straightened away from her work and turned to the tray, where she ground herbs for a poultice. "Some say, 'seek strength where it may be found,' but is it not stronger to seek peace—as Elder Xylander often said? If we seek peace, therein lies our strength."

She'd been through much in her years. Her words held an innocence, not borne of naïveté but of having seen too much pain. Yet if the prophecy of the Lady was true—and he believed it was—there would be little peace in the coming days.

"You disagree?" She cocked her head as she again turned back with a clean, saturated cloth and patted his shoulder with it.

"Nay," he said heavily, "but I fear peace is not my purpose here."

"I think perhaps you confuse my words regarding peace with passive frailty," she whispered, her breath dancing over his chest and up his neck.

"I . . ." Marco swallowed, ignored the way his gut clenched. Watched her tend his injury, her expression slightly stern as she bent nearer to apply a poultice of strangely minty herbs with a fragrance that was warm and inviting. It wrapped around him, powerful yet demur.

No, that wasn't the herbs. That was her. *She* was the fragrance infesting his senses. A tantalizing aroma that drew him in. Those green eyes wide and lips tinged coral.

Only when she dropped her gaze did he realize he'd been staring. She'd said something a moment ago. Something he should've responded to. Instead, his body responded to her Signature, shut down his brain, and stirred desire.

"I . . ." Isaura shifted. "I . . . I need to get a bandage and linen." When she moved away, her scent remained, infesting him like the poultice she'd applied. Saturating . . . healing . . . "So, you think the Symmachians are here?" Her voice was strange—she felt it, too. The . . . thing happening between them that he was apparently powerless to extricate himself from.

Marco told himself to leave. Before he did something he'd regret.

I am a grown man. I can handle this.

Besides, this path could not be. Because of Kersei. Because of his vow . . . Made because of a vision. But mayhap that'd been but a dream borne of wanton degradation. After all, Kersei was lost to him.

Wait—she'd asked a question again. He mentally shook himself. "Likely," he managed, gruffly. Roughed a hand over his face. What was happening to him?

Isaura returned and bent toward him, her plait sliding over her shoulder again as she hunched to apply the first bandage laced with more poultice. The salve was cool, yet somehow made his skin burn, fanning an ache he was desperate to appease. As she secured the first length, her touch was gentle—teasing, soft . . .

Mercies, he did not want it to end.

Her hands paused, gaze rising and falling like the churning of the Kalonican Sea during a storm. "I . . . You need . . ." Her efflux was potent, demanding.

Demanding his attention. Pulling him in. "I . . . can't . . ." he said, voice thick. He dared not move. Could not. Knew one twitch and she would be in his arms. He'd take the kiss waiting on her lips.

"The cotton goes around . . ." She spoke so softly, her words almost weren't there. "Lift your arms." Her instruction sounded as heavy as his thoughts, leaden with what they both fought to wrangle into submission.

Somehow he obeyed. As she wrapped the cotton around his chest, her fingers grazing his flesh proved electrifying. Eyes never meeting his, she reached behind him. Teasing touches as she secured the bandage around his chest, then up over his shoulder—forcing her to lean over him, which landed her soft plait against his pectoral and abdomen. Closing his eyes was pointless—her Signature alone was an abundance of torment.

He had not detected a bouquet like this since . . . Kersei. And yet this was different . . . piquant. It tested him like no other.

The luxury of her touch enlivened things in him he hadn't thought possible. Things he knew he shouldn't enjoy, yet he longed for more. He would see her eyes, see that what writhed in him—this forbidden yearning—swarmed in her as well. But seeing it in her eyes would only deepen his.

No, stop. Bazyli would enter.

Marco stood. Held her out at arm's length.

With a nervous smile, she finished the last wrap. "Almost done."

He intended to move her away but grew frustrated that she wouldn't meet his gaze. He had to know, some urgency demanded it . . .

Isaura slowed as she fastened off the binding. Her hand slid from the bandage to his chest and did not deprive him of the connection nor create proper distance between them.

Please . . . He cupped her face, urging his gaze to hers.

And then she granted his wish—her eyes rose ever so slowly. Something sparked in him as they met his.

Marco captured the kiss he needed and ignited a fire in his gut greater than any he'd known. It was perfect. *She* was perfect, melting into him with a soft moan. He crushed her against himself, and the kiss deepened on its own. Drowned him to the cares of the world. Bathed him in peace and exultation of the pure.

A roar came from behind.

Marco spun, disoriented, moving Isaura behind him to protect her as he faced the vicious assault of frankincense, a pungent odor that slammed aside passion. His shame came to the fore when he saw the face, all rage and fury. Heard Isaura's gasp.

Ixion.

"Unhand her!" Ixion unsheathed his sword, instinct and outrage blurring against the oath he had sworn to the man who had just stolen the virtue of his daughter. Never had he anticipated finding them such. He grunted through several hard breaths, gaze locked on the ground, refusing to look at the half-naked man embracing his daughter. "Isaura. Out."

Her pale green dress shifted from behind Marco. "Mavridis—"

"*Out!*" he bellowed, then took deep, gulping breaths. "I will deal with you later."

Marco had the gall to step forward. "Ixion—"

"No!" Incensed, he angled the sword to the man's throat, which yanked a strangled cry from Isaura.

Marco drew up short, his expression pinched, his bandaged chest rising and falling unevenly as he lifted his hands. "Easy . . ."

Shouts came from the camp and hastened heavy boots inside as Isaura fled in tears.

"*Never*," Ixion growled, "did I imagine . . ." He could scarce look upon the man who was their medora and had taken liberties with a woman not his own. "I trusted you, and *this* is what you do?"

Expression tight, Marco leaned away from the blade.

"Ho-ah!" Bazyli stopped inside the tent, palms out as he glanced between them. "What goes here, Mavridis?"

"You," Ixion snarled at Marco, "who speaks of honor, who . . ."

"Ixion, lower your sword!" The command came from a new voice—one he had not expected. Despite his willingness to run Marco through, he started when his eyes confirmed what his ears heard. "Prince Darius." He gritted his teeth, knowing what distanced the brothers of the royal family. Knowing how this would aggravate the strained relationship.

Blood and boil, he cared not. "I beg your mercy, my prince, but I cannot sheath my blade. This . . . *man* and I have something to settle."

"You threaten your medora," Darius said evenly, stepping forward and placing a gloved hand on the blade as he came between Marco and the tip. "I, of all men here, well understand your anger, but do this and your life is forfeit."

Ixion heaved a breath, noting for the first time how, though Marco kept his chin up, everything about him sagged. Sweat and blood caked his long hair to his face, which bore scratches as well. He'd incurred that shoulder wound in defense of his men.

"Medora Marco, perhaps you should dress," Darius said, nudging Ixion's blade away as he faced his brother. "Are you badly injured?"

Glowering, Marco snatched his tunic but said nothing. He threaded his hands through it and tugged it down, with more than a little grimace of pain. Then his gaze fell on Ixion, and he stared for several long ticks before he backstepped and departed.

Nostrils flaring, Ixion sheathed his sword. Roughed a hand over his beard and face as he turned to leave as well. Shaken at his own ferocity, yet unwilling to release this offense. Had he been wrong about Marco, to think him honorable?

"Mavridis," Darius called. "I would have a word with you."

Were he any other man, Ixion might ignore the insistence, but since he was prince of the realm . . . He slowed and angled back. "Grant mercy, my prince, I must take an accounting of my men before we can chat."

Darius's gaze darkened, confidence in his every step until they stood toe to toe. "You draw your blade on the medora of Kalonica, threaten his life with it, and think I want to *chat*?" In the prince's gaze sparked a warning filled with all the authority he owned. "Forget you who I am? Who you are? Well it has been known that you do not like me, but I do not ask for your affection or permission." He narrowed his eyes. "We will talk." He lifted his brows and cocked his head to the side. "Now."

Properly chastised, Ixion forced his thrashing pulse to calm. Tightened his jaw. Gave the only answer he could. "As you will, my prince." He looked at Hushak. "Go to Isaura. She is not to be alone."

Hushak inclined his head, clearly suspecting what had transpired.

Darius stepped back, his sandy-blond hair tussled in the morning air. "Bazyli, if you please." They removed themselves to the far side of the makeshift camp, weaving among the cookfires that had begun to spring up with the sinking of the sun. "What happened?" he asked, his tone much different, almost . . . friendly. "Long have I known of you, Mavridis, and never would I have guessed to find you nearly running your medora through.

What offense brought this about?"

Though Ixion could scarce think past the fury of finding a shirtless Marco hungrily kissing Isaura, no space between their bodies, he quickly understood the damage he could do to his medora. The prince standing before him, demanding to be informed of events, was the same man who had taken away Marco's first love. For Ixion to tell him that Marco touched Isaura's virtue— the prince would love that, would he not? Make sport or use of it.

Though Marco had breached Ixion's trust this night, he would not turn on him. "None, my prince," he lied. "A misunderstanding."

"Misunderstanding," Darius snorted. "I think I misunderstand you."

Ixion set his jaw, glancing at Bazyli, who had the same determined, focused expression.

"Ah." Darius slowly lifted his head. "You fear betraying him."

"I will not speak against him."

"But you would run him through." When Ixion did not respond, Darius shifted to Bazyli. "Will you help me understand?"

"To speak," Bazyli said, his voice gravelly, "would require I betray *two* men to whom I have given an oath of loyalty."

The image was seared into Ixion's mind: Isaura in Marco's arms, her hands on his bare back, that kiss . . . nothing chaste there. Not solace this time. Ixion had begun to suspect their feelings—certainly hers—but Marco's brooding over Kersei seemed too determined and persistent. What was this then? He did not—could not—believe Marco so dishonorable.

"Ixion," Darius said, his pretense of friendship gone, "I would remind you of our laws. A threat against the crown is a threat against Kalonica. You drew sword against our medora, and that is an act of treason. If you do not name the offense . . ."

"You know me better than to—"

"I nearly cut my hand trying to divert your sword!"

Ixion withdrew his gaze and argument.

"You force me, Ixion. I have no recourse." Darius stood there for several silent seconds, then shifted. "I will ask one last time. Will you speak of what you clearly know?"

Silence held fast among them. Darius addressed a nearby aerios. "You?"

The aerios shifted awkwardly.

"No, Cetus," Bazyli growled.

"Stand down, Elder Sebastiano," Darius said, holding a hand to the elder. "He is aerios. They answer to me and to the crown. None else." He nodded to the green-cloaked aerios. "What say you?"

"It was the girl," Cetus said quietly, displeasure apparent in his glower.

The prince started. "What girl?"

"Cetus, I vow you will regret this," Ixion snarled.

The aerios eased back but continued on. "Mavridis is her guardian. Marco was kissing her."

"Forget you whom you speak of—your medora!"

Cetus flinched and fell silent.

Darius lifted his head, his gaze raking Ixion. "This is true—my brother with the girl?"

Refusing to answer was the only recourse.

"Guardian . . ." Darius nodded. "Aye, well would it explain your anger." His gaze then narrowed. "Or does it? For a ward, why so much anger and a willingness to do injury not just to Marco but to yourself and the Prokopians? There is no justification that I can find for your actions. According to our laws, unless you can otherwise defend your actions, there is but one punishment for threatening the life of the medora: execution. So, speak—plainly. Are you the girl's guardian?"

Ixion considered the younger royal. "Aye."

Darius nodded with a grim smile. "Good."

And Ixion knew he had handed the prince exactly what he'd wanted.

VOLANTE STATION, ORBITING SYMMACHIA

During rec time, Eija used the zero-g room to float the gauntlet, exercising her ability to maneuver her body and objects without gravity. It was a good mental workout but also required a lot of core strength. Hair wet with sweat, she finished the fourth attempt with her best time yet.

"Now with interference and competitors," a voice barked into the space.

Eija rotated and caught sight of Bashari, Gola, and Reef floating upward.

"You and Jadon against me and Gola," Bashari said, his straight black hair standing up at all angles. "Ready?"

No, she wasn't. Eija didn't want company, let alone competition. Thankfully, she spotted Milek Aoki. "There's your fourth," she said. "I have—"

"He can't," Gola said with a snigger. "He nicked the rings, so he has to repeat the sims tonight. Figure out how to fly straighter."

"I did it on purpose," Milek called from where his boots were still gravved to the deck. "Tried to show nicking won't ruin the rings."

"Yeah, but it took a chunk out of your billion-tassol corvette," Reef growled. "They should ground you."

Milek snorted. "Not happening. Besides—what about Zac? She was slow enough to let a rhinnock catch up."

"Slow is smooth, smooth is fast." Eija shrugged.

"She's not the one who tagged every ring," Reef said, defending her, which was weird.

Eija saw Shad enter the room and glance up. "Ah, now there's competition for you, Bashari, and a partner for you, Sergeant." She scissored her legs to move away, but Reef snagged her hand.

"I already have a partner," he said, a spark in his brown eyes. His buzz cut was tight and high, like his ego. It was bad enough he was their team leader, but why did he have to be so . . . perfect?

Eija watched her friend on the deck flee back out the door.

"Oops," Reef teased. "Guess that leaves you and me. C'mon. Show me what you've got, Malika One." He hit the buzzer, starting the clock on the course. "Go!"

The first task was to maneuver a crate into a net and secure it. With Reef being Eidolon, their team had an advantage. They anchored it, and he grinned as he punched the timer, which then released the second challenge—liquids. Red-dyed water bubbles floated into the void of the room.

Eija rotated off the wall, aiming toward the ceiling, where she detached an empty water bottle. She moved slowly and deliberately, knowing that once in motion, she wouldn't have anything to stop her, except her partner. As long as he was close.

"The bulkhead," Reef noted.

Eija looked up and groaned. Three droplets were spreading apart and moving toward the ceiling. She scissored her legs and swam for the two closest to the electronics panel and tilted the bottle to catch the first.

A solid thump against her back—Gola's aggressive interference—made her miss, sending her colliding into Bashari.

He cursed—loudly. "Scuz you, Zacdari! That was a foul!"

Glaring at him, she heard the system log a penalty.

Team Two Penalty, the system droned.

Bashari cursed at Gola for the move that cost them a point.

That droplet burst against the panel, so Eija negotiated the space to catch the last bubble. She had too much momentum in the zero-g to stop and catch the last one, so she opened her mouth and swallowed it. The rules didn't exactly allow for drinking the droplets, but they also didn't specifically exclude it.

Reef sailed over to the buzzer, punching it and moving them to the final obstacle. He corkscrewed to her with a lopsided grin and clapped hands. "Nice."

Suddenly, Eija's stomach twisted. Last test was to gear up in less than thirty seconds and link into a fake oxygen line. But you had to put on your own gear, then dress your "unconscious" partner. The thought of dressing up Reef Jadon sent her heart into a spin.

"I have more experience," Reef said, "so I'll dress you."

Yeah, not happening. "I need more practice, so—"

"Not during the gauntlet." Reef's competition ferocity startled her. The guy was usually playful, flirtatious.

He hooked her arm, and together they maneuvered to the wall where the suits were stowed. She gripped a handrail and watched as he stuffed himself into the suit as if it were a second skin. He winked as he secured the neck latches, nodding in the direction of Gola and Bashari, who had just hit their buzzer for the third round.

Reef lifted his helmet and locked it into place. He unhooked her suit and motioned for her to let go.

Swallowing her pride, Eija released the rail and floated, going limp.

Jitters scampered over her skin as his fingers grazed her stomach to catch her waistband and draw her close. He used a tether to anchor her to the wall, so he could work her legs into the pressure suit. It took everything in her power not to think about him touching her, his hands moving along her legs to work the suit up to her hips, then disconnecting the tether. He pulled it past her waist.

His gaze hit hers, and those brown eyes looked abashed. Or maybe not. He was suddenly focused and guided her drifting arms into the sleeves. She cringed at the way her thermal shirt was bunching up to her elbows as he tugged the pressure suit over her shoulders. He worked deftly, but more than once his gaze bounced to hers. Was that a flush she saw?

Each touch was a movement that nudged her toward a section of bulkhead that stuck out. She wanted to prevent an impact, but that would disqualify her, so she braced.

The air beside her swirled and she saw too late that Gola was floating dangerously close as she geared Bashari. Their eyes connected and Gola's narrowed. She adjusted Bashari, knocking him into Team One.

Eija's head rammed into the corner of the bulkhead. Pain ricocheted across her temple. Red bubbled in the air.

"Gola!" Reef barked. "Back off!" He hesitated for a fraction, assessing her injury.

"Hurry," Eija said, itching more than ever to beat Gola.

He slid the helmet on her head, and blood from the gash she'd incurred bubbled around her face. Even as he snapped the helmet into place and oxygen flowed, the buzzer sounded, signaling they'd finished. Apparently, he'd hit it with his foot.

Reef grinned at her and patted her helmet. "See? We make a great team."

Gola growled. "You got in the way, Zacdari!" She flung Bashari's helmet at her.

"Like you did with round two!" Eija said. "And you swung Bashari into me."

"Can't help if it you're clumsy. Maybe you should quit while you're behind."

"Grav down," Reef said, his voice low. "It was a fair course."

Eija removed the helmet and suit, then made her way back to the deck. She clicked her grav boots and felt the connection pull her spine down. Touching the gash, she knew she'd have to seal it, so she headed back to quarters.

She rounded the juncture and hesitated at Shad coming toward her. "Hey."

The girl straightened. "What happened to your head?"

"Gola."

Shad groaned as they entered quarters. "Again?"

"I have no idea what her problem is." Eija grabbed her med kit and sat on the bunk, fishing out the tube of liquid stitches.

Shad took the tube and sterile wipes to tend Eija. "Don't you?"

"What? Because of the sims? I fixed that!"

"Besides that . . ." Shad cleaned the wound, making it sting. "And besides being better at everything, and pretty much . . . well, prettier . . ."

"Please." Eija rolled her eyes. "I—"

"Keep still," Shad snipped. "Don't argue with me. I may not be as physically capable as the rest of you, but I'm observant, and I've *observed* Jadon is soft on you. And the way you ran that course? Brilliant. I saw the way he was hovering over you."

"He was my partner—and my sergeant, remember. He hovers because he's still afraid I'm going to get everyone killed."

"We all know you're one of the best out there, when you focus."

"So you think I was crazy, too."

"I think you made some choices that were unconventional and didn't work. You took a risk that backfired. But once we're out there, those mistakes aren't just about your scores. It's the rest of us—all of us."

"I know," Eija said miserably. "I've . . . I haven't listened to the . . . instinct since."

"Guess that meeting with Lieutenant Diggins did you some good."

Good for whom? Every time she complied with their rules, she felt a piece of herself die. What scared her was not getting kicked off—Diggins assured Eija that her slot was secure. She was terrified of being out there in the slipstream, an unfathomable distance from home and making the mistake.

"It's a good thing they put me in Engineering. I can't screw that up."

"Well, you could." Shad tapped Eija's shoulder to let her know she was done. "But why would you?" She motioned to the bunk. "What's that?"

Eija glanced to her pillow and saw something peeking from beneath it. She slid out an envelope and turned it over. "I have no idea."

The dinner bell sounded through the station.

"We'd better get washed up."

"Yeah," Eija said, noting her friend head toward the sink. She tore open the envelope.

Toilsome is the road pocked with hardship and loneliness. To be thrust so fully into a purpose we do not understand may, at times, leave us bereft. Trust that the way will be made plain, that your purpose within this program is not only right but imperative. Important.

When we first met, you asked why I'd chosen you. First—it wasn't I who chose you. This is much bigger than us both. But that very thing within you that has seemed to steer you wrong is the reason you were chosen. It is the beacon that will light the way to truth. Do not doubt it or yourself.

We will speak soon, but until then, give them what they need to see. Sometimes, those with small minds have the hardest roads. Let them think you subdued and corrected. Let them think they have the power. For when the time is right, they will see the truth and the light. Until then . . . believe. —Patron

Shame shoved Marco into the sinking sun. He strode past the aerios and Stalkers. Well beyond camp, he fell into a lope then an all-out sprint. He ran hard and straight, not caring where he went as long as he *went*. Battered by disgust, he scaled a wall. Vaulted up over the edge and found a foot-wide path on the other side. He ran, sighted a building, and leapt into the air, onto a roof.

Anger pitched him across one building after another. A tall spire rose ahead, and he felt it calling. Challenging. The distance was too far for him to make. Still, he sailed into the air. Felt grief and gravity snatching at him. He'd taken advantage of Isaura, violated his vow to the vision.

He sagged, hating himself. Willing the heights to take him. End this.

Rock and plaster rushed him.

Self-preservation forced Marco to grab a windowsill. His body slammed against the building, knocking out his breath. His shoulder screamed. He felt a fresh trickle of blood from the wound Isaura had tended. Sucking in a hard breath, he dangled there, losing the will to hang on. To pull himself up.

She was so sweet, so willing.

Face pressed to his bicep, he berated himself for his weakness. Tasting her innocence. With a strangled cry, he firmed his hold. Drew himself up and searched for the next hold. Hiked his body and swung upward. Caught the iron bars of another window. Mortar groaned beneath his actions—like his conscience—but he dragged himself over the ledge onto the roof. Cradling his shoulder, he rolled to his back and stared up at the bright blue sky. Fought off the torrent assailing him.

Isaura's efflux wafted across the distance and throttled him with her grief.

Ashamed of himself, he hooked an arm over his eyes as he choked back his self-loathing. Nausea threatened to toss his food back up his throat. Add to the humiliation that Darius arrived with the regia just in time to insert himself into this confrontation with Ixion. Oh, how his First hated him—with every right.

Marco sat up and roughed his hands over his face as if he could slough off his guilt. He glanced at the gray structures surrounding him, the people bustling below. Surprise struck him hard. He'd scaled his way into Trachys. To his left, across rooftops, he caught sight of the Kalonican Sea. He hadn't detected it earlier because he was too absorbed in his own thoughts. As he'd been when he kissed Isaura. If he'd been in possession of his faculties, he would've sensed Ixion's approach.

Marco rolled off the ledge. Dropping, he caught a pole jutting from the building. He swung around it and vaulted over the wall and saw too late the thatched roof on which he'd land. His foot shot through, and he barely caught himself. Struggled to pull free. Suddenly, the wood released, and he fell backward. Flipped into the open and plummeted, face first, toward the ground.

Hay broke his fall. Marco lay there, deflated. Defeated. No matter how far he went, how hard he pushed himself, he couldn't escape . . . himself. He pushed onto his knees, palms planted against the prickly hay. A strangled sob fought its way free. How could he have violated the vow to Kersei? Given up on that vision of his future with her?

He slammed his fists into the hay. Did it again. And again, growling his fury. He hit it again. This time, his knuckles found hard ground. Felt the retaliation of pain radiate through his hand and wrist. He slumped, hanging his head. "Lady, have mercy!" He had wronged Isaura, dishonored her. Himself. His role as medora. Kersei . . .

How long, Progenitor? How long will you mourn what cannot be?

But the vision! The one he'd had on the cliffs that granted hope, provided a means to get back on his feet.

And what if it is many years?

The thought pummeled him, but he shook it off. Focused on mending what he'd broken. He must go back, beg Ixion's mercy. Vow to live chaste and focused on Kalonica.

Yet . . . how could he face Isaura?

Sweet, beautiful Isaura. So different from Kersei right down to her golden hair and green eyes. Wisdom, gentility, strength borne from hard upbringing. Those discs she used with a fierce elegance . . . Her lighthearted laughter rooted in a lifetime of challenge and heartache.

He would only add to it.

Go north to Kardia. The scent of Darius on Kersei would drive him crazy, but at least he wouldn't cause more injury to an innocent, a woman he cared about.

Resolved, he pushed back on his haunches and stood. Turned and started for the camp. The walk gave him enough time to get his head and plan sorted. He'd beg Ixion's mercy. Well and true, he may lose the man as his First, and he didn't want that, but this was for the best. Isaura was strong and would understand; she was beautiful and would have many suitors vying for her hand.

They'd be friends—as they were now. Strangely, he hoped she would continue to call him Dusan in that guileless manner of hers. That was what was attractive about her—her innocence. The warmth and gentleness of her touch on his back, skin to skin, flared through him. Her soft moan . . . her sweet willingness . . .

Marco stretched his neck again and walked faster. Aye, that kiss made him lose his good sense, but so did the way she wielded those discs, stood tall when she disagreed, confronted wrongs done to others. Still, he'd crossed a line. Failed. Too often.

Why did you choose me? he balked to the Lady who had stood before him and warned the days ahead would be cruel and filled with heartache. Was this the great jest of the Heavenlies?

And Darius! Curse the reek! Why did he have to be here to witness this humiliation? It pained him. Angered him.

The nicker of horses drew his gaze across the field. Camp had already been broken, and they were making for the city, toward him. By the time he reached the hardpacked road, he was met by Blacks bearing Darius and Kaveh, who held Vahor's reins. "Since you were not around for the discussion, the elders and I agreed it wise to make for Trachys so the wounded can rest and . . . things be dealt with."

Ignoring the insinuation, Marco vaulted up onto his destrier. He angled around to check the line—in truth, the carriage, which was worse for wear but lumbering along surrounded by aerios. Ixion had positioned himself at the window, and when their gazes met, his scowl was hot enough to burn.

Duly chastised, Marco turned toward the city with Darius at his side as they made for Trachys. Not until the contingent reached the city walls did Ixion join Marco and Darius at the front. Once inside the city, they were welcomed home by Elek and his wife, Eldress Faula.

"Welcome, Medora Marco," the elder said with a grand gesture. "Trachys welcomes you and Prince Darius to our city. It is a pleasure to have you here."

Shoulder stiff and aching, Marco nodded, going through formalities when all he wanted was solitude for a few more hours. Days. Weeks. Months. The rest of his life would do, too. "Thank you, Elder. The prince and I are grateful for the refuge you provide."

"We have an apartment and sergii ready to attend you, Your Majesty. I would introduce—"

"Elek," Ixion said tersely, interrupting the introductions of the half dozen courtiers waiting in the grand hall. "Our medora has been attacked and is in need of rest. Introductions can wait, I believe, until we sup this eve. If you would be so kind to show his majesty to his apartment?"

Nearly bald save for white tufts over his ears, Elek reddened. "Of course. I beg your mercy." He inclined his head, taking Marco in. "I pray your injuries are not grave, sire."

"I yet stand." Marco walked with Elek and two regia up the grand staircase. They turned to the left and moved through a set of gilt doors.

"This wing will be yours for as long as you are in residence," Elek said, as a sergius slipped from the double doors on the right of the hall. He led them into a large solar where the sun gleamed through tall, narrow windows. Fire blazed in the hearth hugged by a settee and chair. On his right were a table and chairs—a place for breaking a fast. Beyond the solar, through double doors, was a large canopied bed, fireplace, and a sitting area nestled into a bay window that overlooked the ocean. Another door led to a bathroom.

"I hope this meets with your approval, sire." Elek inclined his head.

"More than—this apartment is grand. Thank you for your generosity."

"Sergii have prepared the bath and aired out the room," Elek said. "Please avail yourself of the lavatory. Also, I am told you travel without a wardrobe, so my steward, Royce, is already securing fresh clothes for you."

Marco felt the state of himself, the blood and sweat, the hole in his tunic. "Again, I am grateful."

For a moment, Elek looked as if to say something, but then wagged a smile and headed to the door, where Edvian and Kaveh waited.

"My men—where can they refresh?" he called after the elder.

"They have already been shown their rooms, down the hall, and my own guards will supplement yours until they return."

"No need," Kaveh said. "We will take turns with the aerios."

Elek gave a nod to Marco. "Until this evening."

The door closed, and Marco gave the room another once-over, then headed to the lavatory. He undressed, removed the bandaging around his chest, and climbed into the steaming tub, letting the heated water massage away his aches. After cleaning around his shoulder wound as best he could, he emerged and found a gray doublet, black shirt, and black pants. Not a perfect fit, but close enough. Dressed, he poured himself some water and sat in front of the fire, thinking. Wondering how Isaura fared. Was she being cared for? Was she angry with him?

A knock came at the door, and he stood as Edvian—bathed and in a clean white-and-green regia uniform—stepped in. "An iereas, my liege, to see you."

Marco frowned. What need had he—

The priest rounded the corner.

"Ypiretis!" He laughed and moved to embrace the aged man. "How goes it with you?"

"Well, well." Ypiretis nodded, but something was amiss in his scent.

Marco had given the iereas the task of watching over Kersei, but the man was here. "How does she fare?"

"Quite well, sire." Ypiretis's smile faltered and he shuffled as he seemed to cast about for courage. "I, uh . . . would you join me in the library?"

Marco studied him, processed the scent, then sighed. "They sent you to retrieve me."

Ypiretis faltered. "They would speak with you."

As he expected. His violation of Isaura could not go unaddressed. "Then let us go."

Even as they reached the library, he caught the anger and resentment. The aerios were quiet and deliberately distracted as he strode past them and entered the large room filled with many chairs and walls lined with books.

Bazyli, Darius, and Ixion came to their feet. At least they still afforded him that decorum.

He set his gaze on Ixion. "I would—"

"Your Majesty." Effectively silencing him, Ixion stood and produced a parchment. Beleaguered gray eyes considered it, then he extended it.

Warily, Marco glanced at the others, who watched with regret yet challenge. "What is this?" He took the parchment, unnerved by the dolor and the way Darius studied him.

Marco finally glanced down. Frowned at the official seal of House Tyrannous. The royal house—*his* house. "I don't understand."

There was a hard set to Ixion's jaw, a dark glint that pinked the scar bisecting his brow. "'Tis a petition." He moved closer, skewering him with a determined glare.

"Petition." Though Marco said the word, his brain refused its admittance into his understanding. Then it came in a rush.

A petition. Set petition. A marriage contract.

Stunned, he felt his gut roil and tighten. How could they ask this of him, knowing where his love lay? Knowing the heartache . . .

"No . . ." The word was but a breath, his throat thickened by the rawness of what they suggested. Grief waxed hot across his conscience, and he tucked his chin. Met Ixion's glare and struggled for a breath that did not sear.

Anger surged—at himself for the violation, at them for forcing him down this path. He felt cornered. Pulse thundering, he swallowed. Stepped to the Stalker and, with a ragged fall of his chest, whispered, "I beg of you—do not ask this of me."

A storm surged through Ixion's shadowed eyes. *"Ask?"* he hissed, leaning in. "It is *demanded* of you!"

Marco startled at the tenor and scents peppering the room.

"Where is this honor you hold in so high a regard? What is the character of the man who sits on the throne and rules Kalonica?" With each accusation, Ixion inched nearer, his lip curling. "Who is the son of Zarek? Does he steal innocence and virtue without thought to repercussions or those involved? Is *that* the man who is medora and would seek to lord other men?"

"You question my honor when you won't claim the daughter born to you?" Immediately, Marco regretted his angry words, which were selfish, seeking to turn the guilt and attention from himself.

"This is true?" Darius moved forward, glancing at the Stalker. "She is your daughter?"

Ixion gave a curt nod. "Ward or daughter—regardless, his actions toward her demand an answer."

Darius hesitated, then inclined his head. "True enough."

Powerless, Marco struggled not to rage. Felt the assault of those accusations. Fought for air—any air, searing or not. Yet . . . they were right. His actions had consequences, irrevocable repercussions. Aggrieved, he dropped his gaze to the crinkling paper. It signified so much, but not what these men expected. It was death. A death sentence not for him, but for Isaura. He could never love her as she deserved . . .

What have I done?

"I would speak with my brother alone," Darius said firmly.

Ixion stormed past him without a word, and the others filed out behind him.

Marco hung his head. Long, painful minutes passed as he stared at the parchment. Wrestled past his rejection of the petition to acceptance of its meaning and inevitability. There was no way around it without leaving Isaura shamed and ruined. She had already endured so much . . .

He sensed Darius at his side.

"Do you resist because of Kersei?"

Marco rounded. "You would force this because of your hatred of me. Because I have loved Kersei."

"I would do it," Darius ground out, "because it is the law of the realm you rule. A medora cannot simply sit on the throne and represent laws without adhering to them."

"But this"—he snapped it between them—"would give you pleasure."

Tyrannous blues glittered back. "Aye. Greatly. I think it wise for you to be focused on your *own* marriage and bound."

He wouldn't give Darius the pleasure of rising to his bait. Anger volleyed back and forth with annoyance. "The system here is archaic. It needs to be reformed."

"Why? To suit your lust for a woman you cannot have?"

Marco grabbed Darius's lapel and yanked him forward—just as a side door opened and Ypiretis faltered between the jambs. Awareness flared through Marco of his poised fist, ready to strike Darius. The fight gusted out of him. Releasing his brother, he turned away. "I can't . . ." He pinched the bridge of his nose. "I cannot do this . . ."

"Then you do not care for her?"

Marco clenched his jaw. "I will not speak with you about this."

"From what I hear, you were engaged in quite a kiss—shirtless, even!" He cocked his head. "Or do you go around kissing every fair maiden?"

"*Don't* mock me," Marco growled, sick to his stomach. "I have ever only . . ." He tossed down the parchment and palmed the war table, desperate for an escape.

"Only this girl and Kersei?"

"Get out!"

Darius's face rippled with anger. He pivoted and stalked out.

There was no argument to be had—by the archaic laws, Marco had violated Isaura, and he must set it to right. But how could he marry her when he barely knew what he felt for her? At least he could admit that—he *did* feel . . . something.

"Sire?"

Ypiretis. He was still in the room.

"I cannot do this," Marco said with a groan.

"May I speak candidly?" The iereas sounded calm, reasonable.

Miserable, Marco dropped into a chair and bent forward, head cradled in his hands.

"I know on Iereania you thought to make Kersei your own," Ypiretis said, his voice unusually flat. "That was not how things ended."

Killing an iereas would probably get him executed.

"It has been nigh on four months since then. From what is told me, you have developed a solid affection toward this girl, Isaura."

Marco punched to his feet and paced, running a hand down the back of his neck.

"Sometimes, we do not get what we want, and when something good and true does come along, we are blind to that . . . treasure." Ypiretis waited for Marco to look at him. "You are aggrieved over your conduct with her, and that tells me it was not borne of a dissolute manner. What I know of you *is* bred in honor—you are, after all, a Tyrannous and a Kynigos."

Marco eyed the former iereas. "I know not what I feel for her . . . only that . . . it overtakes me." He shook his head, morose. "But how can I, so soon after losing Kersei, even consider taking another as my bound? As said—it has only been four months!"

Earnest in countenance, Ypiretis smiled. "Love is not constrained to a fixed timeline under which it grows. Why can you not consider that this affection between you and Isaura might be something different but . . . wonderful?"

Marco could think of only one way to make the man understand. "When I returned to Kardia—bereft and brokenhearted—I had a vision of myself standing on the cliffs of Kardia with Kersei at my side." He shifted sideways. "She was mine—my bound, pregnant with my child. And they would ask me to throw away that promise of the Lady? How can I?"

Ypiretis considered him for several long seconds. "If I am to be honest, the vision alarms me, as does the importance you give it. It seems to indicate your brother's demise." Leveling a long look at Marco, he continued, "But, since he is alive, since Kersei carries *his* child—"

"What if he dropped dead tomorrow?" Marco hated himself as soon as he said it. "Morbid, but we don't know how our days are numbered."

"Oh, Marco. How long will you make life difficult?"

He tasted defeat in those words and refused them.

"Perhaps Kersei would have been good for you, but have you considered that Isaura *is* best?"

"A convenient suggestion," he scoffed.

"Yet no less potentially true. What if you reject this petition—which I must add would unequivocally tarnish your name, as well as the crown, and bring dishonor to Kardia, your father's name, and even this lovely young woman—and as a result, miss out on the best designed for you by the Ladies?"

"You work hard to convince me." Marco pushed the parchment across the table. "Kersei felt forced into marriage, and I will not do that to Isaura."

"Neither do I want her forced into binding with you, which—unless you can see what you're feeling for her—would make her feel like an obligation."

Marco turned away, cringing at the words that had too much truth. "Are you here because they sent you to convince me?"

"I am here because I felt the Ladies tell me to come."

He eyed the older, shorter man, who had shed the white robe of the Iereans, feeling they had lost their way. "I don't know what to do."

"I think you do," Ypiretis said quietly, then angled his head. "Do you care for her?"

"Darius asked me that." Rubbing his scratched and scabbed knuckles, Marco could almost hear her laughter. Remembered the way she'd tried to touch him without his knowing. The way she'd teased him, saying he wasn't experienced. That magnificent skill with those discs . . .

Truth scaled his arguments. "I would not have kissed her had I not," he confessed, surprised at how true that was. "She has slipped past my perimeter and stolen into my heart. I know not how deep." He sighed. "Yet, she is there." He knew what had to be done—to honor her. "But it has only been four months."

Another excuse.

If he had behaved more admirably, he would have had time to sort things and court her properly. With a start, he realized—he would've done just that. Their kiss . . . fast-tracked the process. "Bring them in."

There was nothing for it. He must honor the law and Isaura. Himself.

Ixion stalked in, looking ready for a fight. Bazyli and Darius joined him.

"I will sign it." Marco felt as if he'd just jumped off a cliff. "On one condition."

"This is ridiculous." Nervously, Isaura smoothed a hand down the soft green silk gown she had been forced into. Not two oras past they arrived in Trachys and were invited—*insisted* was more the truth of it—to a small dinner with Trachan nobles. After a luxurious bath, she was attended by sergii who dressed her in the rich, elegant gown. Pearl buttons gathered the sheer lace duster to her waist and bodice, but it hung loose down the skirt. She gripped Ma'ma's amulet at her throat, needing a connection to her simple past.

Kita's head shook. "A year's wages, that! You are absolutely stunning."

"Absolutely exhausted is more like. I would remain here and res—"

A rap on the door startled them both. Finally, Mavridis had returned to escort her.

Maritza, the sergius, hurried to answer the door. "She is ready!" Gasping, she suddenly curtsied. "Your Majesty."

Stomach squeezing, Isaura drew straight when his gaze connected with hers. Nothing had been said between them since Mavridis discovered them kissing, and Dusan's dark expression was not helping her nerves.

A shadow deepened around his eyes. "I would speak with Lady Isaura." He stepped back, indicating across the hall. "If you please."

Hesitantly, she complied, feeling all the more ridiculous in the finery. Her shoes were loud in the quiet marble hall she traversed, following him to a much more lavish room with a place to sit and break a fast, a seating group near the fire, multiple doors along the far wall that led to other rooms. A whole apartment!

Dusan stepped in behind her and closed the door.

They were alone. In his chambers. This was . . . inappropriate.

"Please, have a seat."

She settled on a settee near the fire and folded her hands in her lap.

Dusan stalked to a desk, picked up something and hesitated, staring at it. Finally, he turned and faced her. Something played cruelly in his features, clearly tormenting him as he stood over her. Without word or preamble, he extended the parchment to her.

Uncertain what this was about, Isaura accepted it. "Is something amiss?"

"That is for you to tell me." He lowered himself to the chair and perched on the edge. "I swore to them the only way that"—he nodded at what she held—"would be valid was upon your agreement."

"My agreement?" she said with an airy, nervous laugh, palms sweating. "With what?"

He looked so conflicted. "It's a petition, Isaura." His blue irises were so earnest, worried. "For us."

"Kalonica?" Her heart thumped, knowing he meant something different, but her mind refused the truth.

As his gaze lingered, he reached across the space between them and touched her hand. And that's when she knew he indeed meant more. Far *more*. More connected. More intimate. She unfurled the petition and read:

> *Tyrannous Achilus, so likened Marco Dusan, First of His Name, Medora of Kalonica and her territories, son of Tyrannous Zarek and his bound, Athina, hereby sets petition for the hand of Isaura Mavridis, daughter of Ixion and Deliontress. By witness of Prince Darius and Elder Bazyli Sebastiano, the petition is accepted. Henceforth she is likened Tyrannous Isaura, bound of Medora Marco I and Kyria of Kalonica and her territories.*

She covered her mouth as tears spilled free. "It is impossible."

"I assure you it is not," he said. "I told them this isn't valid unless you accept it."

"Oh, Ladies," she whispered. "I cannot . . . it cannot . . ." Her name there. Her name on the petition *he* set. This was a significant moment. A wonderful one. She should feel elation or thrill. Instead, as she looked at Dusan, she saw only sadness, which made *her* sad.

It dawned on her that Dusan would never do this of his own will. "They forced you to do this because of the kiss."

He lowered his gaze.

"Ah." So, he did not want her. This was simply what the law required. What Mavridis required. Tears blurred her vision, and she blinked them furiously away as she stood and moved from the heat of the fire. "Mavridis did this—put his name with mine to press his right to demand you set petition." She eyed him. "Do I speak true?"

Dusan hung his head. "Insisted on it. Measures are in place to make you his legal heir."

She could not help but laugh, yet the sadness rushed in again. What should be a happy moment, left her stricken. Blood and boil, it was more than a dream come true to bind with this man she held in the highest regard, but . . . it was not right. Not for him.

"I sense your grief." He rose and joined her. "It is valid only if you agree."

Strangely calm words pushed out of her mouth. "I do not agree." The words firmed in her heart. "You do not want this or me." She saw him twitch, so slight an affirmation but there all the same. "I would rather die than have you look at me with regret for the rest of my days." She handed it back. "I am honored by your effort to save my reputation, but—"

"You mistake me, Isaura." Dusan tossed aside the petition, his expression wrought.

Hope struggled to rise on feeble legs. "Then this petition is set by your own hand and will?"

He blinked. Hesitated. Again.

"As thought." She lifted her shoulders and strength. "Do not fear for me, Dusan. I am used to ridicule and would not have you resent me forever over a small indiscretion."

His lips quirked beneath somber eyes. "You speak brave words you do not feel."

Her heart beat hard in her chest. "Now you name me liar?"

"No," he said gently, then sighed. "Forgive me. I wound where I only sought to mend a wrong."

"A wrong—nay. Only a . . . mistake." She could not look into his eyes, so she rested her gaze on his vest, recalling the moment they'd shared. Her heart broke that it would be their only kiss.

"No." He scooted closer, placed a finger under her chin and urged it up.

Isaura resisted peering at his pale eyes—it would hurt too much.

"I cannot call it a mistake," he said.

Those words forced her to look at him, and hope firmed on those weak, feeble legs. Yet, she dared not take the thread he dangled. "Do not trifle with me, Dusan. Please." This was hard enough as it was.

"I would be forthright, but I ask that you hear all my words before you respond."

Her frenetic pulse set the pace her feet should take. "I will hear your words."

"Thank you." He took a breath. "What has arisen between us, I cannot explain. Aye—I did fight it. What I had with Kersei . . ." He shook his head, his gaze skidding past her to the fireplace again. "All my years I have lived by a Code that kept me from dishonoring myself, and it ordered my actions at the Temple with Kersei, but I was . . . bereft. Your father and I left Iereania at once, and on the cliffs of Kardia I had a vision in which Kersei and I were bound with three sons and she yet carried another child."

Painfully cruel words confused her more and made his love for the princessa palpable. "I—"

"Please," Dusan said quietly, "you promised to listen."

"It is hard to hear your love for her."

"And equally hard to speak it for fear of wounding you, but it must be said, because I don't want secrets between us." He ran a hand through his hair and huffed. "That vision gave me hope, helped me keep going after I felt all the world had died on Iereania when Darius appeared out of the blue, alive and, according to the laws of Drosero, rightfully married to Kersei."

"I am aware of your . . . loss."

"Your amulet"—he nodded to the cord around her neck—"has made me realize that, though Kersei and I share two halves of one brand, the meaning and power of what it represents is not limited to two people. It allowed me to consider my feelings for you, which are true. And strong." The shadows lingered still.

"That makes you sad?"

"No," he said quickly, with a faint smile. "What I have started by kissing you, by setting that petition, makes me sad. Because of what it would mean for you, for your . . . future."

Understanding then dawned. "If that vision is Lady-birthed and true, then in order for you to be with her . . ."

"The vision almost certainly implies your death," he said quietly, his brow furrowed. "It would mean a loss I cannot bear. I lost her. I cannot lose you as well, Isaura."

Breathless at those words, she pushed around them to his meaning: death—it meant she would die if they did this. "I do not fear death, Dusan." She never had. "But I do fear living alone and unloved."

"Well said." And more true than he wanted to admit. He didn't want either of them to be alone and unloved—or for her to die.

"Do you recall what I said on the plain about new beginnings?"

He knew where she was leading.

"It is in your hand, Dusan. *I* am in your hands, and I confess, that scares me, because you cling so fiercely to this vision."

Marco huffed, saw how it hurt her. Recalled what Ypiretis said in the war room. "A friend who is an iereas said something earlier that resonated—that when we don't get what we want, sometimes we get something different." He hoped he did not butcher this. "Sometimes that turns out to be . . . better."

Isaura's eyes were wide, hopeful—yet scared.

The petition was set—that was over, done. He had a delicate flower in his hands now and must not crush it. "I have been too focused on what I didn't have to see what I *did* have, what was right in front of me—you."

She drew in a breath and looked down, her chin trembling as she restrained tears.

He thought of their journey. "These last weeks we've traveled together, *your* scent is the one I noticed. The one that made me smile, somehow calmed me." He shook his head. Why hadn't he seen it before? "Isaura, *you* are the only way I've been able to let go of what could not be."

"Dusan . . ." She seemed to plead with him, as if she did not believe his words or that he truly meant them. Tears slipped free, her efflux replete with nervous, tenuous hope.

"Kynigos do not bind because our entire focus must be on the hunt. Gifted by Vaqar, our commitment to the Citadel and hunt is a foundation, a grounding. To love a woman shifts that focus from the Brethren. She becomes the grounding, the foundation." The words were true, but he'd never understood how powerful that change felt. "*You* are now my grounding, Isaura." Cupping her face, he kissed her tears away and whispered, "I didn't just find better . . . I found *best*, my kyria."

Isaura's eyes widened and she gasped beneath something unseen. Her spine arched, pushing up. She froze, shock etched into her face.

Only then did Marco feel the roar of the flame in his brand, see the brightening beneath his sleeve. What on earth . . .? In her eyes he saw the *Orasi* grow to the measure of a supernova, which he felt in his veins—not painful, just powerful. Somehow, as he named her his kyria, what was in him had transferred to her.

The *Trópos tis Fotiás* in the hand-carved amulet suddenly glowed against the hollow of her throat. Isaura reached a trembling hand toward it. She was still rigid against him, a tear slipping free.

"Isaura?" When she did not respond, he looked to the door. "Isaura!"

Her trapped breath gusted against his neck as she slumped into his chest. A tremulous sob shook her as she clung to him.

Marco tightened her in his hold. Cupped the back of her head. "Are you okay?"

"You aren't the one who found *best*," she whispered. "I did."

What Isaura saw in the frozen moment of white-hot fire as Dusan held her she would never speak. It was as if lightning had struck the desert sands of her life and turned them into a beautiful, fragile piece of glass. It would break eventually, but for now . . . there was beauty. And Dusan. She would treasure both.

"What is it?" Mavridis bolted through the door and glowered at them.

"Nothing. I am well." She could never voice what she saw, what happened. Well, not all of it. "I think . . ." She looked at Dusan, who seemed just as shaken. "I think I saw . . . Her."

Understanding ricocheted through his face. "Eleftheria."

"I take it this irreverent pup made things right," Mavridis said.

Annoyed that he would speak so poorly of Dusan, Isaura nodded. "Apparently, I now have a new surname"—she took much pleasure seeing Mavridis wince—"and a bound."

"Good." Mavridis produced a box and thrust it onto the table between them. "Elek is the treasurer of Kalonica and had this in the vault. It will be useful."

Dusan's consternation turned from her to the box. "What is it?"

"Rings," Mavridis announced as he flicked it open. "They belonged to your mother, Kyria Athina, and so it is natural they are Isaura's now. One should do well for her wedding ring."

"What?" Breath stolen, Isaura blanched, seeing how it annoyed Dusan. Yet she could not hide her reaction to the five gorgeous rings nestled in green velvet, all different gems and styles.

Dusan's expression tightened and he glowered at Mavridis.

"Also," unrepentant Mavridis went on, "Elek is pleased to host the small but official ceremony to seal your binding this night at dinner."

"*What?*" Marco balked. His gaze hit hers, then flashed away. He swallowed.

Isaura tried to withdraw from the situation, knowing Mavridis pushed too hard here.

"Isaura," Dusan spoke, his gaze still locked on her father, "he is right— they are yours." His gaze fell to the jewelry. He touched one with a pale blue oval sapphire encircled by diamonds. "I remember this one . . . she wore it often."

"It's beautiful," she whispered, touching his back, wanting him to know she was his ally and did not appreciate Mavridis's interference.

"Pick one. You can have whatever you want. If none of these work, you can have—"

"The blue one," she said. "In honor of your mother." Also, because it reminded her of his eyes.

Dusan plucked out the sapphire ring and slid it on her finger. It nearly covered the entire length from knuckle to knuckle.

"The hall is full and the guests waiting."

Now Dusan seemed ready to erupt.

"I do not think . . ." She struggled around a jagged breath. "Please, Mavridis—"

"Fine," Dusan said. "At least there will be no question or argument about your validity as my kyria. It will also settle once and for all that you *are* spoken for. We'll make sure Hushak hears."

That he attempted humor lightened the dread that had begun to pile on Isaura. "You do jealous very well."

"Never have I been known to share."

With more than a little tension still thrumming between Mavridis and Dusan, they made their way downstairs. For Isaura, it was strange seeing guards, aerios, and regia bow—to her as well as Dusan.

As they approached the hall, the doors swung inward as if on their own, and a caller announced their arrival, "Medora Marco and Lady Isaura."

Guests rose as Dusan led her across the room to the front dais and head table. Embarrassment flooded her as she stood before the people. She felt keenly the shocked looks and heard the tittering voices—all aimed at her, who she was, why the medora seated her at his side.

Dusan turned to her and lifted an eyebrow.

"This can wait," she whispered, "until you are—"

"Having second thoughts?" He smiled, but it did not reach his eyes.

"No," she said firmly.

With a cockeyed nod, he faced the guests. "If you would please endure a moment longer before we sup." Dusan took her hand and drew her forward, to his side. "This evening, I set petition for the hand of Isaura, firstborn of Elder Mavridis, who greedily accepted."

Laughter and murmurs filtered around the room then a quick applause.

Isaura noticed Mavridis now looked annoyed. Served him right for pressing all this formality before Dusan was ready.

"Thank the Ancient, Isaura also accepted," Dusan said with a chuckle, which the crowd mimicked, "and I would now ask Ypiretis, an old friend and iereas to oversee this ceremony here with you as our witnesses."

Another applause went up as Dusan led her to the side, where they were officially bound. Her stomach swam with nerves, shocked that Dusan would do this so publicly, unabashedly. It was a simple ceremony, the tethering band encircling their hands, symbolic of their lives being tethered from this point on. She stared at his large calloused hand holding hers, the gorgeous pale blue sapphire gleaming in the torchlight.

"By the Ladies and Vaqar," Ypiretis pronounced, "you are hereby and forever one."

Never had Marco felt as awkward or nervous as he did in closing the door to his—*their*—apartments after an extravagant meal and dessert reception. He knew now to not trust Mavridis past how far he could throw him. Sergii had helped Isaura change into a dressing gown, then left them alone.

After removing his dinner jacket, cravat, and vest, he lifted a steaming jug of cordi to her. "Would you like some?"

She shifted, her hands moving awkwardly from her waist to her sides and back again. "I . . . I do not think I could."

Nerves. Exactly why he wanted the heady drink. Yet, as he lifted his mug, the waft of citrus and spices nearly turned his stomach. Ugh. He set the mug down.

"I would have you know . . ." Isaura came forward a few paces but used the armchair as a barrier, resting her hands on its spine. "I am aware that Mavridis pressed us into what happened this eve. We do not have to . . ." She glanced aside, then back. "You need not . . ." She looked down.

Her nerves buffeted against his frustration with Ixion's highhanded maneuvering. "Your efflux—"

"My what?"

"It's the scent a person puts off, paired with their Signature." Marco roughed hand over his face, too aware of what hung in hers. "Yours has become as familiar as my own. I can read it as one might read the books on the shelves." He stood beside her. "Mavridis . . . pushed for what transpired, yes. But no man can bend my will."

She glanced down, tracing the smooth wood of the chair. "It is not fair," she whispered.

"What's that?"

"That you can so fully know my feelings, but I cannot know yours." Those green eyes came to him.

Though a thought came to him—things were happening too fast—Marco eased in and traced her lips with his own, sending a jolt through his heart.

"Know it, Isaura." He caught her mouth again. When he felt her hand on his chest, he homed in on her efflux as the kiss deepened. Still a lot of anxiety . . .

Or was that his?

A harsh rap at the door jarred them apart, spiking the room with her alarm. "It's okay," he said huskily. Though they were bound, he checked himself as Isaura hurried out of sight, a blush crimson on her fair face.

Too soon, Marco. It's too soon.

The rap persisted. He whipped open the door with more irritation than intended.

Theilig snapped his head down in respect. "Begging your mercies, sire. You should come. They've captured a raider!"

"I . . ." Marco eyed the bedchamber. He shouldn't leave her on their wedding night, but . . . mayhap this was better, smarter.

"Commander Theilig, he's awake!" shouted an aerios from the end of the hall. "Hurry!"

When Theilig looked to him expectantly, Marco grabbed his doublet and went with him. "Where was he taken?"

"The Altas Silvas," Theilig explained as they stalked away from the apartments. "He was wounded from the attack. We brought him in—oh, and the Hirakyns finally showed up again."

"Good." Ignoring his conscience about leaving Isaura, Marco hustled down the spiraling stone stairs into the dungeon. "Has the raider said anything?"

Theilig hurried ahead, hand on his sword hilt as he went. "No, sire. He was still half out of it when I left to find you."

They rounded the final bend, delivering them to an iron gate with two guards. The men snapped to attention. "Sire!" They made way for him to enter.

Marco traversed a half dozen more steps, the scents acrid and roiling. He found himself in a long, narrow room where the Irukandji raider lay on a table with gaping wounds, which were being tended by a less-than-gentle pharmakeia. Ixion, Elek, Bazyli, Darius, and a handful of aerios stood around the perimeter.

"Should he be secured?" Marco asked.

"He's too weak," the pharmakeia said. "Won't be going anywhere, and even if he tried, there are enough blades to end him."

The raider's yellow eyes locked on Marco. "They're coming for you, hunter. Once you are gone, we will be free. We will be rich!"

The naïveté of his claims pushed Marco forward, anak'ing. He slowed, realizing he detected no scent. Unsettled, he remembered how Commander Deken had hidden his scent on the passenger transport when he came for Kersei, ambushing them because Marco could not anak him. Was that why he'd struggled to pinpoint the raiders in the forest? Why there was a void instead of a Signature? Was it Symmachia's doing?

Mayhap alone each raider's scent was infinitesimal, but together, the myriad scents had created a vague emptiness that confused his receptors. Hidden but not completely.

"What have you learned?" He glanced at his First, still irritated with him, then he noticed the Hirakyns. "Crey."

"Hunter."

Marco scanned the others. "Where is Ikku?"

Crey's expression hardened. "Shadowsedge."

"So far?" How could the man have traveled to the other side of the continent?

"It is a euphemism for the underworld," Ixion said. "He's dead."

Though Marco frowned, Crey merely shrugged, so he turned his attention to greater matter. "What have you learned from the raider?"

"We have gleaned little," Ixion said. "He was unconscious until a few moments ago—then he went wild with fury, so the pharmakeia gave him a muscle relaxant."

Marco moved nearer, staring down at the strange face. Olive complexion, black hair shorn close, and blue whorls snaking beneath his skin as if some diabolus wanted free. "Why do you seek me, raider? Why were you sent to find me?" He dared the man to name Symmachia.

"For Hirakys." The man leered and cackled. "It's why they got rid of the Grey meat and put another in his seat."

"Grey meat?" Marco glanced to Crey for understanding.

"Kederac," Crey said.

"The rex who named his heir," Ixion reminded them of what they'd been told by the Hirakyns not long ago.

"He's been replaced," Crey growled.

"You said they would co-rule." Marco considered the burly Hirakyn. "What happened?"

The cold edge of Crey's glare told Marco there was much to this story. "Wh—"

"We must *bleed* them!" the raider shrieked, his voice eerily like that of the alien on the *Macedon*. "Both the Uplanders and the Progenitor—so we are free from the fire of Her marks and touch."

Marco drew up, disbelieving the name that snuck into the dungeon with a surprising punch to his gut. "Who told you about the Progenitor?"

The raider hissed beneath the pressure of the pharmakeia's tending, done without benefit of herbs or liquors. "Theon. He trained us."

Thick-chested Kakuzo stalked to the table and sneered down at the tortured man. "He told you what you need to do?"

The raider's scent went wild with panic. Fear—terror.

"Beg off," Ixion hissed at the Hirakyn. "We will do the talking."

Theilig frowned. "What is the Progenitor?"

"Me," Marco said. "A Lady named me that on Iereania. It's tied to the prophecy of my brand." Though he did not understand the connection.

"Wait." Bazyli came off the wall where he'd been watching and pointed to Crey. "Your people know he is medora?"

The question sounded like an accusation, and Crey gave him an apathetic look. "They know a Kynigos is medora, so his sigil is a dead giveaway."

"If they are looking for him, then they could think he's in Kardia. Kersei!" Darius barked, his panic saturating the damp air.

"Seek peace, Prince." Ixion's efflux was strong with irritation. "Theon has known Marco is medora since Iereania. He had weeks to attack with him in Kardia and did not."

"Aye," Marco said with a huff. "So why did he wait?"

"Good question," Ixion said, "'Tis clear not only does he know you are no longer in Kardia, but perhaps he is aware you are here."

"Which would be why Ikku is dead," Crey offered. "But he may not have acted alone."

Marco's skin crawled with the implication. "We have a spy." An acrid scent erupted, snapping his gaze to the raider on the table. "Hold him!" He pivoted too late.

Steel glinted beneath torchlight as it arced up and slit the pharmakeia's throat, the arm wielding it swinging around as the nimble raider launched from the table—all in one fluid move—and sprang at Marco.

Rather than jerk away, Marco threw himself forward, using momentum in his favor, and struck the blue-marked neck. Swiped at the leg to upend him, but the nimble raider hopped away. Shrieking, he arched his spine—a blade sliding through his chest, his heart, silencing him.

Extracting his bloody sword, Crey lifted his jaw, daring anyone to challenge his kill.

As the Irukandji fell limp at his boots, Marco stepped back.

Shouts rang as the aerios converged on Crey, demanding he drop his sword, while Bazyli and Ixion shuffled Marco aside to protect him. Kakuzo was shoved away by Theilig and Cetus, who were less than gentle, pinning him to the wall.

Marco rifled through the scents, struggling to understand why. Why had the raider attacked? He'd been content to have his tale told, but then . . . His gaze found Kakuzo and his all-too-pleased expression. What was that about? And a strange scent hit him.

"Take the medora abovestairs, and be sure he's well-guarded," Ixion ordered Theilig.

"What? No," Marco argued. "I—"

"Please," Darius said quietly. "It is best until we are sure things are safe."

Conceding, Marco glowered at Mavridis again, then started from the dungeon with Darius and the aerios. Even as he walked the cold, damp halls, that strange, acrid scent punched at him again.

They gained the main floor of the palace and made for the apartments. He was about to round the corner when, for the third time, he caught that stench. Which of the men with him was panicked, worried?

Eyes closed to distraction, Marco pivoted and let the scent guide, followed his receptors as they narrowed in on one target. He careened into the person and slammed him against the wall. Opened his eyes, stunned to find blue eyes bulging. "Darius."

"What do you?" His brother's voice trembled.

"*You*? You are the collaborator?"

"What? No!"

"I can smell it on you—panic, worry, *fear*!"

"For Kersei," Darius cried, incredulous. "Knowing they razed Moidia, attacked you, I want to be sure Kersei is safe."

Could that be the reason his Signature was so rank? Marco hesitated. Wondered. He released him and eased off. "You would have cause to be concerned with the babe," he thought out loud.

"What babe?"

The question, his brother's frown stilled Marco. Had Kersei not told him? "I . . . I misspoke." He must cover his error. "I assumed you had, you know . . ."

Darius's eyes widened. "Our intimacy is no concern of yours! Perhaps you should give attention to your kyria." He still looked perturbed. "What know you of a baby?" His tone eerily quiet, his scent . . . roiling. "Did Kersei tell you she was with child?"

In that, Marco could plead innocence. "How would she tell me? I have not been in Kardia in months." A sergius approached with a tray of steaming mugs—the scent reaching Marco long before the sergius. He seized a cup and took a sip, allowing the warmth to slide down his throat, the taste and familiarity soothing.

"Then why mention it?" Darius persisted.

"After the way you"—it took everything in Marco to keep his tone level—"*claimed* her on Iereania, it presumes a child would be on the way."

"How do you know what happened on Iereania?"

"Because I *smelled* you on her. Your rank pleasure infested those halls."

Darius drew up, surprise in his features and dolor, along with a hefty measure of guilt. "Did you smell the babe on her, too?"

Misery coddled Marco. "I misspoke. That is all." He couldn't understand why Kersei would not tell Darius, but it wasn't his concern.

His brother narrowed his eyes. "No, you never do that. You are too meticulous, too methodical. And like you said, you *smell* it. The way you did in the forest—the aerios speak of it. So, it is not a stretch that you could smell a babe—"

"I did not smell a babe!"

"But you know she's pregnant."

Marco lowered his head and sighed. "Leave it, Darius."

"Leave it?" his brother balked. "She carries my child and doesn't tell me? She goes out all manner of times with other men—it may not even be my child!"

Marco threw a punch and stood over his stunned, bleeding brother. "She is the *best* thing that has happened to you! Do not malign her name because you are not man enough to earn her love!"

Touching his split cheek, Darius looked wild. "I will never be good enough for her, but I have vowed to be the best I can. For her. Just as you should with Isaura. Go to her."

"I will not force myself upon her as you did with Kersei."

"*Forced* myself?" Darius scoffed. "Is that what you think of me? That I . . . raped her?"

"You were embroiled in jealousy and fear that she would reject you."

Darius laughed. "I dare you, brother, ask her. *Ask* if that's what I did." Embarrassment now doused him as he straightened his coat. "I will forgive this humiliation for I know the stress you are under."

"I do not need your forgiveness." Marco was done with Darius. Would be removed from him. "Kersei is not in danger."

Irritation darkened Darius's brow.

"But it is wise for you to return to her." Mind flicking back to the raider,

Marco knew the hour of war was breathing down his neck. He turned and, leaving Darius in the hall, headed to the war library.

"Sire," Theilig hurried after him. "Your chambers are this—"

"I must do research, Theilig." Closed in the war library, he worked well past dawn and on into the afternoon in painstaking digging through ancient scrolls and books.

Sergii brought food that went cold on its tray, and still Marco sought answers. Even when his eyes blurred, he kept reading until, at some point, he woke with his cheek pressed to a velum document, dimly aware the day had passed, and cursed himself for the wasted time. He straightened. Resumed his research . . . and lost another day.

Rubbing his eyes, Marco leaned over the long table that spanned the great library of the Trachan palace. Leagues south was the shore of another great power—Jherako, which consumed the entire southeastern coastline of the continent, as well as the peninsula that jutted out into the Vantharq Ocean and toward Ironesse Island. He recalled Crey encouraging him to seek out the king there.

Across the room, the door opened and Darius stepped in, sconce light dousing his brown hair and swollen cheek.

So a night hadn't been enough to rub off his irritation. "Why have you not returned to Kardia?" Marco tried to keep his tone civil.

Darius pointed to the windows, where wind tossed dirt and leaves against the glass. "A storm is coming. When it passes, I'll depart."

The storm—any storm, really—reminded him of the night of his Reclaiming by the master hunter. But this night, he had other concerns.

Darius crossed the room. "We need to talk."

"Is that not what we're doing?"

"About your mistrust of me."

Ah. That. "It was a mistake. The scents—"

"I am your *brother*, but I do not know you, nor you me." Darius stood at the war table strewn with ledgers and papers. "Two times in as many days you have made 'mistakes' that give grave cause for concern."

Two days? Marco squinted at the clock on the mantel, surprised to find the time. He glanced at the windows—sunlight. Palms on the table, he stared at the map without seeing it, his thoughts ricocheting off his little brother challenging him. It grated. "You make no mistakes?"

"Oh, I do." Darius eased nearer, his thigh bumping the table. "Yet I speak of injury done to the reputation and character of those under your influence. You physically assaulted me in front of others and made an accusation of treason. Although I well understand your disdain of me, I *am* the crown prince and heir presumptive. Such a suggestion that I collaborate with the enemy does injury to my character and House Tyrannous. Then there is the matter of your bound."

"No," Marco growled, straightening. "If you are bent on arguing, do it, but Isaura is not your concern. Leave her out of this."

"As my kyria," Darius said, arching his brow in emphasis, "she is most definitely my concern—and that of every aerios in this land. When word reaches our ears of her pain and injury, we are bound by oath to act."

"What pain?"

Darius shook his head. "Are you not the hunter? Tell me what you smell."

Marco glanced down, unwilling to admit he'd ignored many a scent from her as he wrestled with his own . . . fears, misgivings. Yet her hurt and sadness reached him, chastised him. He hung his head. It was one thing to have passion when she was in his arms, but another to . . . love her. The latter he struggled to reconcile.

"When were you last in the chamber abovestairs with her?"

He jerked up. "As you said the other night—our intimacy is none of your concern."

"How have you missed it? Have you even listened to the talk among the sergii? Well, your regia and aerios have—'tis said you have not even lain with her. That you left her alone on your binding night—"

"I was called to the dungeon!"

"—and spent the last two evenings here with"—Darius flicked the papers on the table with his fingers—"maps and war."

Marco detected the uncomfortable nerves of Theilig and Cetus near the door. "Leave us," he demanded of them, gaze locked on his brother, who stood resolute. When the door closed, he struggled to hold his temper in check. "I will not speak with you about this. I have not gone to her because war is at our door. No other reason. Understood?"

Darius seemed ready to argue again, but the door opened, and in walked Mavridis.

Muttering an oath, Marco let his gaze fall again on the maps and bent his iron thoughts toward political machinations. "What know you of King Vorn?"

Though irritation peaked again, it slowly abated.

"I've met the Errant," Darius mumbled. "He's strident and determined to drag his kingdom back from the destruction of his father's complacency, even if it means overturning every nobleman or business."

Lips pursed, Marco moved to the windows. If he could just breathe for a moment . . . He stared out across the Kalonican Sea in the direction of Jherako. Moonslight danced on night-blackened waters.

"If you mean to start a war with him, I advise against it," Ixion said. "Jherako has a strong army, well-fed and well-paid. My Stalkers have had tense encounters with his patrols along the border."

"What are his views on the Droseran-Tertian Accord?"

Darius sniffed. "He is . . . not fond of it, though I do not think he would renege on it. However, the Errant will do what he feels is best for Jherako, even if it means his own death. He is no one to be trifled with."

Do not trifle with me, Dusan.

Isaura's words haunted him, but he shouldered them away.

"Why do you ask?" Ixion finally asked.

"Something I detect in the air." Marco squinted as he sought the fetor once more. Strange that he did not need to step onto the balcony to catch the scent. "I think mayhap a visit to Jherako is in order."

Darius shifted. "I am not as sure." His voice was shaky, his Signature unsettled.

What was this? Marco considered his brother, the red knot below his right eye. *He's nervous.* "What do you fear, brother?"

Darius lowered his head. "In earnest? I fear Medora Marco does not know policy or the people well enough to engage in a battle of wits with the Errant, who is one of the shrewdest men I have encountered."

For now, Marco would ignore the obvious slight against him. "Kalonica has war at her doorstep—and in her skies," he said, returning to the table. "I wouldn't have her decimated because we're afraid to broach new boundaries or alliances." He picked up a marker to gaze unhindered at the southern border on the map. "I don't need to know policy to engage in an invigorating battle of wits with a shrewd man."

"I only meant—"

Silencing Darius with a hand, he thought of the Altas Silvas attack. "Do you think Vorn is aware of the Irukandji raids?"

Ixion arched an eyebrow. "If he is not, then he is ill-informed."

"And an ill-informed king is a dead one," Darius said.

"So he knows." Marco tossed aside the marker. "Then all the more reason to visit Vorn." And rout that scent in the air.

Words do not a man make. They had been bound two evenings ago, and since their binding night when regia pulled him from the apartment, Dusan had spent no time with her. Long ago she had learned the pain of hope, but since he set petition, put a ring on her finger, and went through the trouble of a binding ceremony . . .

Isaura sighed. Hope was a dangerous thing. This hurt keenly.

Though this morning there had been fresh tears when she again wakened alone in a cold room, she dried them. Bathed. She donned a clean gown and broke her fast. Then she curled up in the large chair with a book. In earnest, she tried to delve into the words, but his kisses, which he said were evidence of his feelings, invaded her thoughts. The strength in his hands as he held her . . . What had she done wrong?

The door opened and a brisk gust of air ushered Dusan into the room. He stopped short as she shoved to her feet and wiped her tears.

"I beg your mercy . . ." Isaura was not sure why she apologized. So convinced had she been that she could be strong and insist he explain his absence, but now all she desired was that very absence.

"We are leaving." He moved to the dressing room.

So she would get her wish—one she suddenly did not want. "When?"

"At once. Elek is even now ordering a ship to take us south to Jherako."

"A ship." Could she mask her hurt from him? "So far . . ." Not just out of the city but the country! She fingered the spine of the book.

Two sergii carried in portmanteaus and went to the wardrobe.

"Light fabrics," he said to the sergii. "It'll boil your blood down there."

Jherako was very near the lands where she had grown up. "The south is not *that* hot," Isaura countered. It was hot, but not the way he made it sound. Mayhap she should leave him to his packing. She replaced the book and turned to go. Yet . . .

She whirled back to him, fisted her hands. "I would know what I have done that you would avoid—shun me."

Stilled, Dusan furrowed his brow, shock and anger plain. "What?"

She forced herself to speak before she lost the nerve. "I . . . we *are* bound, yet these two days you have not returned to me or . . ." She shook off the thought. "Now you rush off to Jherako."

"Give us a moment." Dusan flicked his hand to the sergii in what seemed irritation, and they fled.

Embarrassed, Isaura wished to go with them, but . . . "I had thought to know you, as you urged. The other day, you were quite . . . convincing. Yet, I have spent these days alone. Do you regret it, Dusan? Do you regret me?"

"I have no regret, especially not you." He set aside a small leather case and moved to her, held her shoulders. "*We* go to Jherako. You and I. To meet Vorn."

Searching his eyes for truth, she stood stiff in his hold. "Do you jest?"

"I go as medora, *with* my kyria."

"Me? I am to go as well?"

Dusan smirked. "Aye. A storm is building in the west, so we leave at once." He nodded. "Maritza has orders to pack whatever you need." Then he hesitated. "Are you okay with guiding her?"

Still stunned, Isaura swallowed, drawing herself up. "I am." She went to her own chamber, where she and Maritza laid gowns, necessities, and unmentionables in the portmanteau, then she rejoined Dusan. Mavridis, aerios, and regia led them to a waiting carriage, which ferried them to the docks. There they boarded a ship bearing the royal standard.

It was all so strange, so . . . awkward.

On the deck, which already swayed and surged on the irritated waves of the Kalonican Sea, a short, barrel-chested man met them. "Medora Marco, I welcome you aboard the *Basilikas*. I am Captain Jurgard and will see to your safety on this journey." He gave a curt bow. "If you will come this way, we can settle you both in the captain's quarters."

Even as she followed them belowdecks, Isaura felt her stomach somersault over the movement of the ship.

KRS *BASILIKAS*, KALONICAN SEA

Marco held the bucket for Isaura several times in the first hour as she emptied her stomach. The ship's pharmakeia brought herbs and wine, which now had his kyria laid out on the bed, trembling from dry heaves. He felt terrible, for his treatment of her in Trachys and that she suffered seasickness.

After a deckhand cleaned the sick and exchanged the pail, Isaura collapsed wearily on the bed. "It is unfair that you are not affected by the tumult."

"A ship of the sea or the air . . ." From the chair, he shrugged. "Not much different than my scout." He watched her drift into an exhausted sleep before surrendering himself to the greedy claws. The discomfort of sleeping upright was no match for his encompassing weariness. He awakened to the first light of a clear day shining through the cabin windows.

A knock followed by the click of the latch brought him up straight, bleary-eyed as Ixion stepped in.

Glancing to the bed, his First closed the door. "How does she?"

"Resting," Marco answered quietly, going to the bowl and pitcher to dispel his own drowsiness. "Has she ever been on a boat?"

"Not much water in the desert," Ixion said.

Having freshened himself, Marco turned. "Let's go topside." Abovedeck, they stood at the rail and once more caught the acrid scent rifling the wind. He set aside what transpired between them in Trachys, the petition, the ceremony . . .

"I have a suspicion," Marco said quietly, moving to the bow and acknowledging Captain Jurgard with a nod.

"Of?" Ixion asked, eyeing him.

"I am not wholly convinced Vorn has abided the Droseran-Tertian Accord."

"You think he harbors Symmachians?"

Marco shook his head. "No, more subtle. I think he's bringing technology to Jherako. Specifically, aircraft."

"*Aircraft?*" Ixion balked. "When they have no electric lights or technology?"

"Yet fuel hangs in the air—more than a little, too."

"You are sure?"

"I have lived with it most of my life—it's a distinct fetor." Salty air swept his face, and he breathed it in. "I detected it months past when we first entered the Outlands, but it was so out of context, I shrugged it off, then Roman showed up and I thought the fetor was his ship. But here on the water, it is stronger, so I suspect Vorn is the culprit."

"I know many seek the technological advancement of Drosero, but I do not. Weapons might eradicate the Irukandji, aye, but I fear the decline of our civilization."

"Agreed."

Ixion considered him. "To what end have you have brought Isaura?"

Though he thought to tell Ixion that she was no longer his concern, Marco wouldn't be petty. "She is my kyria—recall, I set petition and was induced to hold ceremony in Trachys. So, why would I not?"

"Because south is far from the fortress security of Kardia that you and Darius sought for Kersei. Because a foreign court is treacherous ground for a woman who grew up among common outcasts and has yet to feel a crown on her head."

Nodding, Marco sighed. "True, but she is wise, perceptive, and I have heard Vorn has taken a Lady to wife."

Ixion bobbed his head, eyeing the sparkling seas. "But Isaura is not trained as a spy."

"Nor would I have her be," Marco said. "One thing I admire about Isaura is her ability to process her environment, use her wits, and guard her tongue when necessary. If anything is to be learned of the Jherakan queen, I believe Isaura will be the one to find it."

"Let us hope her seasickness passes before we dock."

LAMPROS CITY, KARDIA, DROSERO

There was no more hiding the heir she carried. Kersei tried to loosen the stays, but the reflecting glass showed the absurdity of that. When a knock sounded, she did her best and reclaimed her chair.

Myles entered with a deferential nod. "The prince is back, my lady."

Only four days of peace then? Kersei glided toward the south-facing windows. The view overlooked the Lampros River and swalti fields where she had long ago sparred with Darius. He was returned, and she knew what she must do, but her courage squirmed. She must tell him. So, she would. This day. The resolve was sudden and startling, but . . . right.

Myles's large frame shadowed her as she left her apartments to meet Darius in the foyer. "You will tell him?"

Kersei gaped up at him. "How—"

He lifted a thick shoulder in a shrug. "Your countenance is much changed."

"Boils," she muttered, disbelieving how easily he read her. "Think you others . . . are aware?"

"Many suspect." He gave her a sidelong glance. "Why have you not told him?"

"Because," Kersei said, slowing to a stop at the bottom of the stairs, "this was one thing that I *could* control."

"You're a Dragoumis," Myles said, disappointment tingeing his words. "I know only by choice do you find yourself in this situation."

"I beg your pardon?"

He raised his hands. "Mercy, Princessa. I only meant that you are strong, and had you definitively been against the binding, against . . ." He motioned to her belly. "This would not have happened. But you are not Faa'Cris."

Now more confusion. "What does that mean?" A commotion in the bailey turned her toward the main doors, anticipating Darius's imminent appearance.

"Strong does not mean you defy tradition. Strong means you are resilient when tradition does not grant your every whim."

"*Whim?*" she balked. "You do vex me this day, aerios."

Myles tucked his head with a sheepish look. "Perhaps I should have said 'wish.'"

"Mm, indeed."

Light exploded not twenty feet away, then was eclipsed by forms passing through the bright doorway. Darius entered, talking rapidly with Echion and Maur until his gaze hit hers. He hesitated, held a hand to his regia, who broke away, and then his gaze fell to her stomach.

No. It could not be. That was her imagination.

Kersei noticed his cheek was swollen and darkening his left eye. She hurried to him. "Your face! What happened?"

He caught her hand, roughly, then relaxed. "I am well." He met Myles's gaze with a nod. "We should talk." With her hand in the crook of his arm, he led her to the stairs. "Our medora is gone to Jherako."

"Jherako?" Kersei climbed the steps with him. "To what end?"

"He was intent." Darius pressed her fingers to his cool lips.

Kersei could not help but recall her last evening with Darius before he'd ridden out to join Marco. It had been . . . nice. "I am glad you are returned." She smiled up at him, but his jaw was set, lips thinned as they gained the upper level. "Did he give no explanation for visiting one of our enemies?"

"Vorn is not an enemy," Darius countered as he reached the solar.

"Perhaps," she said quietly, "yet neither is he an ally."

"Which is something I have been working to turn around." When they cleared the jamb, he held a hand to Myles. "I would be alone with the princessa."

Myles's gaze shifted from Darius to Kersei, then back before finally acquiescing. He pivoted and put his back to the entrance.

Darius closed the doors and pulled her into his arms. Kissed her. Still cradling her, he gazed down at her. "You will be pleased to hear Marco is well . . . and has taken a kyria."

"I—" Kersei jolted and her smile vanished as his last words registered. "What?" She felt sick, a hand going to her stomach—which she quickly altered. "A kyria." Sounding natural was impossible. "So soon? Who?" It had been a little more than four months since Iereania.

His cheek twitched. "Isaura, daughter of Mavridis."

"He has a daughter?" Kersei faltered, a funny taste in her mouth.

"It seems she lived in Moidia, though I do not understand the circumstances completely. Irukandji razed the town, so Marco and Mavridis aided the villagers in the treacherous journey to Prokopios." He seemed entirely too casual and attentive. "He and our new kyria apparently had weeks of travel together to become acquainted. A sabbaton past, there was some . . . impropriety between her and Marco, so Mavridis demanded he set petition."

"Impropriety!" Kersei breathed a laugh. "That is not Marco. He lives by the Codes—by honor." And yet, she knew his impropriety with her.

"Bazyli gave witness and seconded Mavridis's demand."

"Two elders . . . so he made her kyria," Kersei murmured.

Darius nodded, his expression wary. "Medora Marco and Kyria Isaura should be reaching the shores of Jherako even now in the hopes of forming an alliance."

Kyria. *That would have been my title . . .*

"After my brother left me this reminder," he said, touching his cheek, "I asked him why he mentioned something." His shoulders squared and his light-brown hair glittered in the sun that pushed past the windows. He fell silent, and though she was curious to know what Marco said, an ominous feeling weighted the air. The halo around him seemed a bit. . . orange. Strange.

He narrowed his eyes. "Do you carry my heir, Kersei?"

Heat streaked down her neck, shoulders, and spine, snatching her breath. Deflating, she looked to the rug. "Yes." She brought her gaze back to him just in time to see his hurt. "It is too late to be believed, but it was my intent to tell you this day."

"I wonder," he said, his chest moving raggedly, "why you would keep this from me, yet so eagerly share it with Marco!"

"I—"

"It is *my* child!" His shout seemed to rattle the glass. "Do I not have the right to know?"

"Yes, of course," she said, tears springing free. "You have it wrong—I did not tell him." She trembled, feeling once more the flutter of their child. "Marco told me."

Darius scowled at her. "What say you?"

"I know not how," she rushed on, "but before he left the Temple, he . . . he knew I had already conceived. It was impossible for him to know, yet he was certain." She cried, remembering that moment, his grief, her tears. "He said I carried his brother's son."

Darius faltered. "Son." Then he scowled. "How can he know?"

"The *Orasi*—High Sight. Ypiretis said that since the prophecy in the High Temple, Marco can divine a person's adunatos when he looks into their eyes."

Regarding her with speculation, Darius stood without moving for several long seconds. "A son."

Kersei let herself smile. "So he says." Her hand landed on her abdomen, and this time she did not move it. "The royal physician has confirmed the pregnancy."

Ferocity bled into his blue eyes. "I will have him relieved of his duties."

"No! You must not! I beseeched him for time to—"

"He is required by law to inform the House at once of a pregnancy. Since you are . . ." His gaze flickered. "Iereania was four months past."

She nodded, feeling the arc of her womb. "I beg your mercy. Do not punish him for kindness done for me."

"Kindness!" But his expression softened. A shaky smile was followed by an equally tremulous laugh. "A child—my child. *Our* child!" He strode toward her, beaming. "Why did you . . ." He lifted his jaw. "No, I know the answer and deserved it."

Surprise lit through Kersei, unsure how to respond to his acceptance of her withholding the news.

He laughed and hugged her tight. Then let out a louder laugh—an exult. Putting her at arm's length, he looked down at her belly. "Do you think he has it right—a son?"

It was strange talking openly, and it overwhelmed. "I know not. Does it matter?"

He sobered. "No. No, it does not." Again, he hugged her. Cupped her head as he held her close and kissed her temple. "This baby brings hope and a new beginning."

VANTHARQ OCEAN, JHERAKO, DROSERO

A sleek ship darted across the waters toward them.

"They move fast," Theilig commented, his powerful build casting shadows on those around him.

"Aye, too fast," Ixion muttered.

Marco again caught the fetor of fuel. "It has an engine."

"Weigh anchor and prepare to be boarded!" a shout carried on the wind. "Or you will be fired upon!"

"You should go below, my lord." Ixion urged Marco back toward the berth below.

Marco anak'd the incoming scents, sorting them from the sea and the crew. "No," he insisted. "There is no threat. Run up the Tyrannous banner."

"They are Jherakans on an impossible ship," Theilig said, hand on his hilt. "They *are* the threat."

"If they have engines, I assure you that sword will be no match against other technology they likely have," Marco said. "Theilig, go below to the kyria and tell her to prepare herself. Captain, my banner, please."

Jurgard did as instructed.

Marco watched as the winged aetos climbed the mast, flapping in the wind. Even as it reached its highest height, there came a shift on the air. He smiled, watching the men on the other ship point to the banner.

"Even they are not foolish enough to fire upon the ship of a royal house," Ixion said as the fast craft pulled alongside.

The bosun ordered the ladder lowered, and Marco straightened the green embroidered doublet, waiting for the Jherakans. Four men came aboard, their uniforms practical yet a striking black and gold.

"I am Captain Ba'moori of the king's fleet. What do you in Jherakan waters?" The light-haired officer stood with all the authority afforded him as the commander.

"Is this how you address a king?" Ixion demanded. "With disrespect and—"

"We have one king," Ba'moori said flatly, "and he is in residence at the moment. There was no request received or approved to allow a Kalonican ship in our waters. By law, we have every right to sink this ship."

"No request was sent," Marco said, stepping forward, "because our mission was unscheduled, and this trip hastened to avoid disruption of our mission. We beg the deference of King Vorn for our breach of protocol, but it is imperative we speak with him."

Ba'moori cast a speculative glance to Marco. "You are Kynigos."

"If you are aware of the Brethren, you are surely aware the medora in Kardia numbers among them. I am he, Marco Dusan, medora of Kalonica." He caught Isaura's Signature as she stepped from belowdecks, resplendent in her green gown, royal sash with its brooch, and a tiara. His heart might have skipped a beat.

The Jherakan took him in, his scent rank with disbelief and more than a little readiness to protect his country and people. "The medora is said to have a brand . . ."

Marco unbuttoned his cuff, rolled up his sleeve, and extended his forearm.

When the Jherakans saw the glowing arcs and lines, they muttered curses and stepped back.

Ba'moori gave a curt nod. "We will escort you to King Vorn."

Entering the palace brought a sense of chill and emptiness, so Marco kept his head high and receptors open. Though he detected no threat or direct sign of deception, he searched for the deviance. There was something missing from the opulent palace. No sense of belonging, of identity. Of home.

Appearing regal in spite of her seasickness ordeal, Isaura slowed and angled closer to him. An unconscious move Marco liked, because it meant she already looked to him for security. Her green eyes fastened onto his, and though her expression remained unchanged, her efflux flung concern at him.

A tall, lanky man strode toward them, the point of a phalanx with a pair of guards two steps behind and two women positioned between the guards. "Medora Marco," the jovial man said, "welcome to my home!" He nodded to Isaura, his gaze lingering. "And your lovely queen—Forgelight is honored by your beauty."

"Thank you, King Vorn." Marco's hackles rose, noticing how the man gawked at Isaura. "We extend apologies for entering Jherakan waters without permission."

Vorn's eyes sparkled. "I am sure you had a good reason, and I would hear it—in time." He clasped his hands, then stepped aside. "This is Aliria, my queen. She would see yours to her chambers abovestairs, so that we might converse unhindered."

Queen Aliria sauntered forward with her lady's maid, but she was not what Marco expected for Vorn's consort, what with her exotic allure and sensual moves. Not what would be expected from a queen or a Lady. Then again, mayhap the reason she sat on the throne was to adorn Vorn's arm and make other women jealous.

Isaura glanced at him with uncertainty that matched his own.

"Oh, come," Vorn said with a guffaw. "I know you are newly bound, but surely she can do without you for a few hours."

Annoyed at the implication, Marco placed a hand at Isaura's back. "Forgive us—seasickness robbed my kyria of her strength, and she fears she may be poor company." He shifted in front of her marginally. "Mayhap later."

"I have remedies for that." Aliria glided forward and took Isaura's hand and led her to the stairs.

The scent . . . That woman's scent was . . . wrong. Controlling. Shrewd . . . diversionary.

Marco took in the marble floors and walls that were void of portraits or tapestries. "This is an unusual palace." He made deliberate eye contact with Ixion and lifted his eyebrows the slightest, indicating the stairway. Isaura reached the top and the queen peered down with a smug look. She tugged Isaura's arm.

The scents coalesced at once, and conviction pulsed. This scenario was wrong. Isaura was being led away—and that couldn't happen.

Alarmed and angry, Marco sprinted at the wall beneath the overlook. Tic-tacked the corner amid shouts and singing swords. A laser beam ate a chunk of plaster as he grabbed the balustrade and hiked himself up. He hopped onto the upper level and leapt in front of Isaura, protecting her, a dagger produced from his leg holster.

Boots thudded toward them.

"What is this, Medora Marco?" Vorn stood on the lower level with a pulse pistol aimed at Ixion, who held a sword to the Jherakan's throat.

"You are not Vorn, and this is not Aliria," Marco said. "I will not allow my kyria to be separated from me." He drew in a rough breath. "I had no intention to harm you, but you have made it clear the same cannot be said of you."

Doors swung open from a room that was richly ornamented with tapestries and gilt furniture. A dark-haired, -bearded man stood there, clapping. "Bravo, Marco. Well done." He strolled forward with his hands behind his back. Not much older than Marco, he was powerfully built beneath a shirt spliced open with no buttons. "What gave them away?"

Anger bubbled through Marco as he felt Isaura's touch at his back. "Are these the games you exert upon your guests, Vorn?"

"I must!" the burly king said. "A cutter entered Jherakan waters without invitation or permission. It is told me that this ship bears the banner of Tyrannous, and only one man may sail under that banner—the king himself. Of a northern country that has not quite been my enemy, yet has also not done much to gain my favor. And here, I am told the king has a queen. 'What is this?' I asked my chief advisor. 'The new king has no wife.'" Vorn's thick hair was queued down his back. He circled Isaura. "So, you see why I had to know if you were truly who you claimed to be. Am I to let any fool into my home who asserts to be a king, even if he has a vision of a beauty with him?"

Isaura's efflux flushed with embarrassment as she drew in closer to Marco. Which made him glad, considering the strange spiral of jealousy that coiled through him.

"And is your man to kill mine or not? I grow bored of their standoff. They look quite ready to end each other."

Marco glanced to the lower level where Ixion and Theilig held swords on Jherakans. He gave them a nod, indicating them to stand down.

"Good. Come," Vorn said, slapping an arm around Marco. "Tell me how you knew this was a ruse." He started back into the lavish hall.

"I heard there was more brawn to the Jherakan king than this man had. Any king entertaining another would want as much pomp and circumstance as possible to impress, so to be brought in through a back entrance spoke false. Last, there was the woman." Marco slid a look to the woman they claimed was Aliria. "Forgive me, but you walk more like a chatelaine than a queen. However, it was not until you pulled Isaura's arm that I knew you were no queen—for a Lady would never drag another noble anywhere."

"Yes," Vorn said, his gaze narrowed as he closed the distance between them. "But what else was there, Marco, with your nose so marked and your life so . . . unusual? Was it Captain Tarac's nerves that betrayed him?"

"No," Marco said, considering the king's man. "In truth, he was masterful at the game he played. But there was a discordance among scents. Where nobles would have confidence and perhaps even arrogance, there was only a stiff . . . display. Too much control, restraint."

"Brilliant." Vorn shook his head, dark eyes pinched with admiration that also saturated his scent. "Just brilliant." He inclined his head in respect. "*I* am Vaanvorn Thundred, fourth of his name and ruler of Jherako and Ironesse. You are much welcome in Forgelight and Jherako, Marco." Shifting back, he motioned to a stunning woman who glided forward in a cream gown and pearl tiara. "And *this* is my queen, Aliria—who does not walk like a chatelaine." His boisterous laugh rattled the cavernous space.

Air sucked from his chest, Marco stared at the woman with dark hair and violet eyes. She was so beautiful and elegant. But there was something far more compelling about her. Something familiar . . . dangerous. "This is what I expected of your queen." He flinched at the sharp pang of jealousy from Isaura. He inclined his head. "It is an honor, Queen Aliria."

She extended her hand to him. "An honor for me as well, Marco."

Their fingers touched. Light exploded and wreathed the two of them in an aura through which he glimpsed what his mind would not believe—wings and armor on the woman before him. A thousand voices sang in Marco's mind, banishing all else from his thoughts.

"The Trópos tis Fotiás *prophecy*," she said with a note of surprise, awe spearing a voice that rang with the clarity of the Heavenlies. "*You are Touched.*"

He started. "*What is this?*"

"*Lifespeech,*" she explained. "*Your mother was a Lady.*"

"*No.*"

"*She* was," Aliria insisted. "*We will talk.*"

When she released his hand, Marco stumbled backward, his mouth dry. He glanced at the others, expecting the need to explain what happened. But this moment, outside the shocked light, felt . . . cold and empty.

Somehow, he gathered his wits and reached for Isaura, needing her touch, her presence. "I would introduce you both to my kyria, Isaura, recently bound to me and not yet presented before our Council."

"That new, eh?" Vorn laughed. "Is that why she scowled as you greeted my Aliria?" He bellowed a laugh, and an acute sense of embarrassment filled the air from every corner—including Marco's.

He would need to remedy the inadvertent rift with Isaura, explain what happened. Yet how could he explain what he did not understand?

"Come," Vorn said, motioning them toward tables. "We will eat and talk. I have arranged a feast of welcome."

He heard Isaura groan quietly and turned to her. "You okay?"

"If not seasickness, then nerves," she muttered, taking his arm as she eyed the spread. "Mayhap some bread . . ."

Guards and guests quickly filled the room to crowded. Revelry carried for several hours as they chatted about families and Marco's journey to the throne, which intrigued both king and queen. Though Marco did his best to talk, he grew more curious about the fetor of fuel. More curious about whatever it was that Vorn hid beyond the ships with engines and the pulse pistol in his personal guard's hand. There was a subtle undercurrent of giddiness, which seemed contrary for a king dubbed the Errant.

At length they left the table and moved to a library, where drinks and pastries were served. Itching to go to the windows and sniff out that fuel, Marco forced himself to remain with the others. He noticed Isaura on a settee, rubbing her neck, and went to her. "Please tell me you are bored as I am."

She smiled faintly. "A little, perhaps." But her smile vanished as a sad scent coiled around him. Hurt. Jealousy.

He needed to explain. "I want—"

"Your Majesty," Ixion said as he approached. He indicated to the side. "The king would like to speak with you in private."

Marco glanced at doors already guarded by Jherakans, then to Isaura, detecting more sadness. "I would have you—"

"Go," she said softly, touching his hand. "He is why you are here. Not me." Another smile with no joy behind it. "I will be well."

"Would you like Theilig to find you some privacy?"

"No," she said. "We are here for diplomatic purposes. I am not as fragile as I might appear."

"I think you are as iron. There is no fragility in you."

"Oh," she whispered somberly, "I would not be so sure."

"Kyria Isaura," came the melodic, accented voice of the queen, who drew near and inclined her head gracefully. "Would you join me?"

"It is incredible that I am invited by a queen," Isaura whispered to him as she rose.

He stood and planted a kiss on her cheek that seemed as natural as breathing. "*By* a queen? You *are* a queen."

Once she was with Aliria, separated from the crowds and pressure, he followed Ixion to the next room. The door shut behind him, and Marco flung out his receptors, but found nothing more than curiosity from the king sitting in a richly appointed chair.

"They will party and I will learn." Vorn lit a thick cigar and puffed on it. "Out there, we must play to the whims and decorum. In here, we shed our crowns and speak as men. Agreed?"

"Heartily." Marco looked out the window shadowed by heavy drapes. He could still see the lighthouse on Ironesse, as well as the *Basilikas* anchored in the choppy waters.

Amid a haze of smoke, Vorn joined him. "What is the real reason you have come south, Marco?"

There was an edge to the king, yet this was not what Marco had expected. "Why are you called the Errant?"

Vorn sniffed. "It was the worst name they could conjure to describe the sweeping changes I made. The rich and nobles hated me—*blamed* me for my brother's death. Said I killed him to take the throne."

"Did you?"

His scent sharpened with his gaze. "No," he groused, honest in his reply.

"We were not the best of friends, but never would I wish harm on my own kin. Tamuro drank himself to death over insecurity and fear. He was a good man but not a sagacious one, and he was well aware of how he lacked."

"And you are not one to placate or praise where it is not warranted."

"To what end?" Vorn balked. "I tell him he is great, and he is eaten alive by the savages who rule the houses and clans of Jherako, not to mention our enemies. Truth stings a little when first applied, but lies and pandering bludgeon a person to death." He stepped onto the small terrace that overlooked the ocean. "Unlike my brother, I defied every charge my father handed down on his deathbed."

What must it have been like to know the father one followed to the throne? Marco's only memories were those of a six-year-old boy. "I am told Jherako was crumbling before you came to power."

"Rotting from within." Vorn stared out across the waters. "My father started his reign with vigor and won hearts and minds—as well as the Avrolis princess, my mother. In the end, he grew fat and complacent." Disdain colored the king's voice. "Sought to placate rather than rule. It drove our economy into the dirt, and I refuse to let that continue at my hand. They do not have to like or thank me. The end result—growth of the economy and the strengthening of Jherako as a continental power—does that well enough."

In other words, he would do whatever was necessary to protect his kingdom and its people. "Is that why you violated the Droseran-Tertian Accord?"

The words had their intended effect—Vorn jerked straight, his shoulders warning he'd be quite a man to contend with. "That's a dangerous thing to say to a king in whose house you and your wife sit." Like a rhinnock sizing up its prey, he stared, as if waiting for Marco to backpedal.

"As you said, truth stings only a little when first applied."

The hint of a smile pinched Vorn's left eye. "What makes you think I violated it?"

"The fuel. I can smell it. Have since I set foot on Drosero, but I couldn't discern its source and even outright denied what it was to my own mind because this is a non-technology planet." Marco smirked. "Or is supposed to be. But the pungent fetor of fuel is especially strong upwind of Ironesse."

"Waves of Providence," Vorn muttered with veneration. "I told him you would know." He lifted the cigar. "Tarac said this would stifle your nose."

"While it annoys my receptors, it does not affect my abilities." The things people did to trick a Kynigos never failed to amuse. "Your violation might've been overlooked, shrugged off with one or two ships—you could lie, say they were recovered from downed wreckage, but . . ." Marco appreciated the air trilling with a delicious mix of sea spray and fuel. By Vaqar, he missed flying. "How many ships?"

"If that nose is so great, you tell me."

"Testing me again." Marco was not ruffled by the game. He liked this man, though mayhap he shouldn't—a formidable man willing to violate an accord that more than a dozen state officials signed . . . "A lot." He drew in a long, tasting breath and let the ether deliver the answer to his receptors. The fetor was strong yet muted—and clearly not visible. "Fifty, at least."

Irritation plucked at the large man as he considered the waters, the island. "Why do you ask about the ships? Have you come to haul me before the Continental Alliance? Do you think this gives you right to invade or attack?"

Marco resented the accusations. "And this is your speaking as men," he muttered before setting aside the more petty feelings to focus on the biggest matter. "Our little planet is drawing a lot of attention. Symmachia wants not only this planet but my brethren, and I don't want to see the day when they succeed." Time to be frank. "If you are in bed with them, then before you stands an enemy."

"I am in bed with no one." He shrugged and laughed wickedly. "Well, not at this moment, but I have a satisfying queen . . ."

"I will not tolerate Symmachia on this soil," Marco warned. "Their plans for Drosero are unknown, nor does their interest make sense when you consider this planet is without technology and offers no known natural resource to exploit. Symmachia has infected every other planet in the quadrants, and I am determined to ensure they do not get this one, though I hear they are digging their boots into your neighbor."

"Why?" The question held curiosity but something else, too . . . Protectiveness. "You were not raised here, so why do you care what happens to Drosero? They place a crown on your head and suddenly Droserans matter to you?"

Rather than let the words grate, Marco chose the relevant narrative. "Instead of trading barbs, let's focus on facts. Symmachia is obsessed with this planet—our planet—and I've seen their dark deeds for myself, experienced them." His temper sparked. "I was born here and, while I lived offworld for two decades, I'm here now and a ruler. One could say that living among the people has deadened you to their plight. If you would rather take issue with where I gained my training rather than what it tells me, you are not the man I need to have this discussion with."

Vorn grunted, his efflux trilling his dislike of Marco's challenge. "And if I *am* in bed with them?"

"I will stop you."

"And if I'm not?"

"All the better, especially considering you have ships. You likely acquired them elsewhere since, gauging by the acridness of the spent fuel, I wager you didn't barter your soul or kingdom with Symmachia."

Another flare of surprise. "How could you know that?"

"Fuels have their unique scents," he said with a shrug. "To stand our ground, ships could be helpful. Useful. Possibly a deciding factor in whether Drosero remains an independent planet or gets absorbed into Tascan authority."

Vorn nodded slowly, then more earnestly as he looked toward Ironesse. "Sixty." He indicated the island. "I have sixty ships in the caves that span miles underground, so extensive some say they reach Shadowsedge, the rumored sacred home of the Faa'Cris."

Excitement sparked. "Show me."

Finally! After a couple of weeks on *Volante*, Alpha was finally boarding the corvette to make the days-long journey to the *Chryzanthe*. Since the obstacle course competition, tensions between Eija and the others had only worsened, but she kept to her own and did what was expected. Which felt a lot like having her entire body gravved down instead of just her boots.

She strode down the umbilical with her gear and spotted Shad ahead with Reef. Things had been weird to say the least since the competition. Eija deliberately slowed and quieted her steps, not wanting to draw his attention, but he turned and nodded, hanging back as Shad climbed through the hatch. "Ready?"

"I can't believe it's finally time."

"Same." After an awkward silence, he motioned her ahead of him. "Ladies first."

"Then you should definitely go first." She wanted to slap herself right then.

With a smile, he entered the transport scout. She climbed aboard, stowed her ruck, and slipped into the seat beside Shad, who—as always—offered her a welcoming smile.

"Aw man," Bashari grumbled as he strode up from the rear bay door with Gola. "I was hoping you slept through your alarm, Zacdari."

Ignoring them, Eija secured her five-point harness.

"Voids," Gola said as she swung around him. "I still can't figure out how you got on Alpha. I'm really concerned for our safety." She turned to Reef and pressed against him. "Aren't you, Sergeant? What if she gets us all killed?"

"Stow your gear, Tildarian," Reef bit out, "and get locked in."

"It's scuzzing real, now that we're headed out there," Bashari said. "Maybe we need to file a complaint. Who do we talk to?"

"You talk to me, slaggers," Gunnery Sergeant Crafter barked as he stepped inside. "Now buckle up, and get ready for the ride of your life."

"Maybe she slept with someone, and that's why nobody can get rid of her," Milek muttered, piling humiliation on top of her confusion and guilt.

Crafter popped the corporal upside his head. "Silence that slag or you're yanked and tanked!" His razor-sharp gaze narrowed in on Milek, then each member of the team. "Clear?"

When nobody answered he literally growled at them. "Strap in and let's get some atmo beneath us."

The trip out was made in relative quiet, meaning silence. Eija had made peace with their rejection. After her mistakes, they had the right to be concerned. Strange how words in a letter from Patron had given her strength she didn't have. So, she did her best to keep to herself and Shad. Cramped into quarters for the two-day trip to the *Chryzanthe*, the team traveled without agitating each other, though she hated the stacked-like-discs bunks.

Reef let out a low whistle. "Check that," he called over his shoulder.

Behind the others, Eija peered through the long, narrow portal at the still-distant station. Something deep in her stirred as she got her first glimpse of the *Chryzanthe*. She'd expected it to look like a monstrosity, but the sunlight that reached around Sicane gave a warm luster to its length.

The section farthest from the planet was that infamous "metal flower." Attached to its center was a long, narrow tube—though it appeared as one piece, she knew from her simulations that it comprised three separate sections, and once powered up, they expanded and contracted via the power generated by the "flower." Around that narrow tube were the three concentric rings—that was the center they had trained so vigorously to target.

It was incredible to have seen this in their simulations and studied its intricacies for the last several months, experimented with it in the sims. It was another thing to approach it and discover how enormous it was. Feel the power it would exert over their lives. Quite simply, the *Chryzanthe* was beautiful . . . terrifyingly beautiful.

FORGELIGHT, JHERAKO, DROSERO

"Your queen is a charming, intelligent woman."

Returning to their rooms, Marco found Queen Aliria hesitating at the entrance to the royal wing. "Thank you. I quite agree."

"She tells me you have only made her your queen in the last week, yet I can see she is devout already."

Warmed by her words, Marco faced Queen Aliria. "I do not deserve her."

"Did you not bear the touch of the Great Lady, I would agree, but it is she who should be honored." Aliria's expression brightened as she tilted her head and came to him. "However, I daresay men *should* feel that way toward their wives. Yet I sense a lingering ache that hangs between you and your queen."

He glanced down, too much discernment in her violet gaze. "The fault is mine."

"Aye, I believe it is." Forlorn, she seemed to somehow steady him with those eyes. "You grieve the loss of the princessa yet not the deaths of our father or brother?"

"Our father?"

She frowned and gave him a look that said he'd misheard. "Your father."

"Right. Of course." Marco shook his head, but her earlier words stung as if she'd taken a whip to his conscience. "I knew little of my father and Silvanus before returning to Drosero."

Black hair coiled around her olive face. "I pity you the days ahead, Marco, but do not lose heart."

"What—"

"Your family will protect you. Good eve." She ducked her head and slipped into the royal wing, guards sifting from the shadows to follow.

Shaking off the chill that came with what she'd said, Marco turned. Glanced at Theilig and Cetus but then chose to speak with Ixion first. He redirected to the room opposite and rapped on the door. A barked "enter" came from within and he stepped inside.

Ixion knelt on the floor. Weapons arrayed around him, he glared up through a furrowed white brow. "When you were with the king, they refused me entrance."

Marco considered the swords, daggers, shivs . . . "And you were selecting the best weapon with which to enter?"

"Selecting? I would use every one!"

With a laugh, Marco moved to a chair and sat down, roughing a hand over his face. "He confirmed the ships—sixty of them. Likely scout class. Later, we'll go to the caves where they're berthed. I want you to go as well, if you would."

"I insist."

Marco nodded. "We need to feel him out about Hirakys. I asked, and he deftly avoided answering."

"Not surprising—a king rarely reveals all his cards," Ixion said. "He is likely to have better intelligence, since their borders overlap."

"Agreed," Marco said. "We go after tenth bell. For now, I rest."

Ixion hesitated, then nodded. "Of course."

That protective scent rifled the air, and Marco did his best not to think about the father who wanted to protect his daughter and her honor. Yet again. So strange to live by the Codes his whole life and never have it questioned. Months on this rock, and they'd only doubted him.

"Good rest." He left, and without a word to the aerios, entered his apartments, keenly aware of Isaura within. Hesitating just inside the door, he took in the layout.

A long narrow sitting and dining area huddled alongside a large fireplace. Double doors opened onto another room where a white bed stood wrapped in curtains. And there upon the coverlet, Isaura lay on her back curled slightly into the middle. Her golden hair spilled over the pillow. She didn't stir at his approach.

Even now his neck and back raged at him for having slept in the chair aboard the *Basilikas*. Marco ached to take to the bed as well but feared waking her or making things awkward. Still, she was his bound. And he would lie down.

Removing his doublet and shoes, he eyed the bed, then her. When she still did not stir, he stretched out on his back, quietly ensured he hadn't disturbed her, and closed his eyes.

Isaura shifted in her sleep, turning onto her side. Facing him. It was unfair to study her while she slept, but it kept him in check and would prevent her from feeling awkward. Her hair slid over her shoulder as she nestled in. Her nose was straight and had a nice shape, which he could easily say for the rest of her as well.

Memories of kissing her assaulted him, and he wanted to do it again. They were bound—it was reasonable for them to be intimate. Yet it was one thing to think a person handsome or beautiful, to enjoy their company. Quite another to welcome intimacy. She knew of his love for Kersei, which . . .

He marveled. It was now eclipsed . . . by Isaura.

Incredible. How had that happened? It was good, aye—since they were bound and he needed to surrender all else to nurture their relationship. Propped up, he watched her. Studied her, glad for the chance to do so unabashed. The length of golden hair on the pillow taunted him mercilessly until he finally lifted it and rubbed the silky strands between his fingers. He raised it to his nose and inhaled—still smelled of sea salt . . . and mayhap a little sick.

Yet, she seemed recovered. Her skin had its golden hue back. With his eyes he traced her cheek and jaw, landing again on those pink lips. He told himself to leave her be. Let her rest. Tonight could be a long night, and they would both suffer without proper—

"What think you of the king?" Sleepy green eyes held his.

His heart jolted, seeing her so casual in his bed. So relaxed. "He's . . . interesting."

A lazy smile danced across her lips as hooded lids fluttered from sleep. "It seems a trend here."

"Does it?" He noticed she wore but a shift, which didn't help his thoughts stay neutral.

"Mm," she said with a yawn. "The queen asked a lot of questions about you and your family." A trail of concern slipped out with her words, along with another tinge.

Jealousy. Interesting. "Did she?"

Her efflux stiffened. "I kept expecting she would divert to a point, but the more I answered, the more she inquired."

"She found me interesting?" He nodded, well aware of the irritation as he played into her jealousies. "Mayhap I should talk to her more. See what arouses this interest."

"I would not encourage it." She shifted onto her back, deliberately putting distance between them and removing that lustrous gaze from him.

"Would you not? Why?"

She shot him a scathing look.

Marco laughed. "Be at peace, Isaura. I only jest."

"You may well think with your good looks you can bring down a kingdom—"

"You think I have good looks?"

She flushed. "You have entirely missed my point."

"I think not." He dropped back and stared up at the ceiling, feigning a pout. "I think you only seek to keep me to yourself. A scandalous prospect, considering the situation we're in."

She jerked upright and glared down at him. "My feelings for you have no influence over you."

Marco sat up and leaned in, their faces a whisper apart. "So you have feelings for me?"

Isaura swallowed, her indignation sliding away as she stared back. Her breath rose and fell raggedly. "You know I do." Her gaze dipped to his lips, then his eyes. "How can you not?" Color rose through her face, glorious but likely embarrassing for her. "What of you, Dusan? Have you feelings for me?"

"I set petition. Was that not plain enough?"

Hesitation guarded her green eyes for several seconds as she considered him, her gaze darting over his face, and he stilled beneath her assessment. "No, it was not," she whispered. "There was the . . . impropriety that forced us into this."

"No," he said, cupping her face. "I wouldn't have allowed the petition had there not been feelings. I told you, no man can bend my will, Isaura." They needed to get past this, yet he feared rushing it and harming their budding, fragile relationship. "But you, fair woman . . ."

Uncertainty fidgeted in her eyes as she considered him again. "Do not mock me, Dusan. It was hard enough seeing the way you reacted to Aliria. I do not need your ridicule as well."

"What?"

"You were so stricken by her beauty you did not release her hand for ten whole seconds!"

"You counted?" Marco smarted, not realizing that much time had lapsed.

Anger flared through her pretty face.

"There is a reason—"

"Aye, you are a man bound to a woman you did not want—"

"Easy," he growled. "It is one thing to be angry, but you do injury to—"

"As you do to me."

"Isa." Using the name her sister had called her felt soft and affectionate, right. He scooted closer. "Hear me. When I greeted the queen, something happened."

"Aye, we were all witness."

"No—it's more. Recall the story I told of Iereania, when the prophecy was fulfilled and the Lady came to me?"

Wariness crowded her beauty.

"The same happened when I touched Aliria, only it wasn't the Lady of Basilikas who spoke to me but Aliria. Time stood still. Light erupted around us. Her voice, as loud and clear as if I stood in a cistern, echoed in my head."

Her gaze darted more fervently over his face. "You are in earnest? This is not—"

"It was very real. Surreal. I have come to realize that is to be expected with this brand," he said, lifting his arm, then traced her jaw and chin. "I have no feelings for Aliria. Not like that or what I have for you. And never would I *ever* seek another man's wife. So, I beg you—please stop saying I don't want you." He knuckled her jaw, tracing her lower lip.

She drew in breath, those coral lips parting. "You do?" Hope and thrill spirited from her. "You did not return, so I thought . . ." Her eyes did a dance between his chest—avoidance—and his eyes—longing.

Out of her came a powerful efflux that made Marco powerless. He angled in, set his lips to hers. Let the kiss linger, softly, gently until that slight tinge of fear faded.

Surprise leapt and excitement darted through her as she met his gaze once more then welcomed his kiss. He fell deep into the beauty of what the Ancient created between them. She lay back on the bed, one arm arced over her head, welcoming, a sign of her surrender. Her lips were brightened by kisses and cheeks flushed with passion. The ribbon that tied the top of her shift closed rested against her throat. Teased him.

He caught the end. Watched her and probed her efflux as he drew it loose. Her lips parted, expectation and nerves fraying her scent. And yet, it was enticing and alluring. He tugged off his shirt and hesitated, offering her one last chance to say no. And he determined that would be okay, too.

Isaura touched his face, his stubble. Slid her hand into his hair and around his neck. As she drew him down for another kiss, he tugged on the ribbon. Settled against her, Marco accepted she was willing. And so was he. Her fingers trailed his shoulder and her elation his receptors as he kissed the hollow of her throat.

Thud! Thud!

Her skin was warm and soft—

Thud-thud! Thud!

Marco lifted his head, disoriented.

Several more thuds.

Someone was at the door. "Bleeding fires of Hieropolis." He muttered the oath as he slid to the edge of the bed and grabbed his shirt. "If someone is not dying, I will change that."

Catching sight of her bemused but nervous smile as she covered herself, he threaded his hands through his shirt and blew out a long, slow breath, trying to tame the passion that roared through his veins. He stalked out of the bedchamber, turned and drew the doors closed, taking Isaura in once more, her Signature still lingering on him.

Cursed interruption.

Thud-thud!

"Enough!" Marco strode to the door. He ran a hand through his hair then yanked on the handle. "What—"

About to pound the door again, Tarac stilled. Took in Marco's appearance—

likely disheveled—and then grinned. "King Vorn said to come now if you want to see the caves."

"Now? But he—"

"Changed his mind. However, I can tell him you are"—his eyebrow arched as he slid a look into their apartments—"otherwise engaged."

"I'll be there." Marco started to close the door, then realized he was missing information. "Where do we meet?"

"A little hard to think after being pulled from a lover's arms, yes?"

"Where and when?" Marco demanded.

"Where you first entered," Tarac said calmly. "Now."

Annoyed, Marco closed the door and punched it. Huffed through his frustration, then returned to the bedchamber.

Isaura had secured that ribbon again. Her hair was smooth but not neat.

Cursing Vorn, he grabbed his boots and doublet. "I must go."

Another rap at the door.

"Coming!" he shouted before sitting to stuff on his boots, then he stood and fastened the doublet. He went to where Isaura stood near the large hearth, and she worked his cravat as if it were the most natural thing in the world. He tucked away strands that had come loose during their moment, and she ran her fingers over his hair. His mouth was on hers again, feeling the soft curves beneath the thin robe. He kissed her earlobe. "I would finish—"

Another more urgent rap came at the door.

Marco groaned. "A minute," he called over his shoulder. When he peered down at her again and found a smile, he tipped her chin up, tracing her lower lip. "I detect no regret . . ."

Nervous but also still caught in the embrace of desire, she gave a quick shake of her head. "You?"

Relief loosed the tightness in his gut. "Only that we were interrupted." He bent and kissed her, savoring that soft pliability. He smirked when he detected her own annoyance and wondered . . . "Wait up for me?"

A smile played at her lips, which she then chewed as she gave a shy nod.

That insipid rap came again—more a pound this time.

"Soon, my kyria." He kissed her temple and started for the door. When he stepped out, Marco drew up sharp to find his First there.

Ixion's gaze flicked into the apartment. His brows rose almost imperceptibly.

Marco pushed past him into the hall. "We are late."

Under the cover of night, Marco and Ixion were led down to the shoreline with King Vorn and his guards to— "A scout!" Exhilaration rushed through him that not only were they going to be airborne, but it was the same class ship as the Kynigos scout he used. Marco grinned at Ixion as they boarded and ran his hand along the hull, which pitched him back to his early days as a hunter when he first experienced the thrill of piloting an aircraft. Man, he loved flying.

Kynigos scouts were outfitted to support a hunter on long trips across the stars as they tracked quarry from one planet to another. This scout was standard, stripped down with no medical bay, simple net seats and harnesses, no crash couches for hard g's. Admittedly, it left him disappointed, and yet . . . it felt like coming home.

They made their way to the upper foredeck, and he stopped short when he saw the queen settling into the ship with a rueful smile. Was he supposed to bring Isaura, too?

"Do you not like my ship?" Vorn challenged, a strange glint in his eyes. "You seem disappointed."

"My Kynigos scout was retrofitted with a light-weapons system, quarters, shower, and a medbay—designed to be all I needed for my hunts. I miss it," he said with a shrug. "Therein lies my disappointment." After shooting the queen another uncertain look, recalling her words and that strange encounter at her touch, he planted himself on a seat.

Vorn backhanded Tarac's gut with a boisterous laugh. "He is more sad to leave his ship than his queen."

Sensing Ixion's admonishment in the air as well, Marco shifted uncomfortably. "I knew my ship better and longer than I knew most men."

That didn't help. Vorn laughed more, and Ixion's admonishment turned to near scorn.

For security reasons, Marco was not allowed in the cockpit, nor would he be allowed to see where or how they accessed the underground facility where the remaining ships were hidden. Vorn trusted him enough to show him the ships, but not how to get to them.

"I hope you have better armaments than I see here." He nodded to the defensive system console. Only short-range capability. Nothing large. Enough to defend itself, but no more. As they lifted off, the king seemed untroubled that this craft was, at best, lacking. Was this what the rest of the fleet was like?

The scout angled steeply and dove straight down.

Thrilling! Marco braced, mentally tracking when they would impact the water. The collision never came. Instead, the descent continued for several seconds—a cave, perhaps?—then the scout pulled up sharply and leveled off. Soon, the craft settled on terra firma.

As Vorn and his queen disembarked, Marco's receptors were saturated with humidity, compliments of the ocean surrounding them. It was, he supposed, the wet version of space, and he found it no less exhilarating. Of course, there was the thick-as-pudding fetor of fuel.

He turned to disembark and found Ixion still sitting, pinching the bridge of his nose with one hand. Theilig wasn't doing well by the green pallor to his dark complexion. Marco grinned. "Take a minute to get your land legs."

"You're enjoying this," Ixion grumbled.

"Immensely." Marco grabbed the rails to the lower deck, slid down as he had on his scout, and strode off the ship. He paused and eyed the hewn stone walls—definitely a cave. The ground was dry, but dampness clung to every surface, including his skin. The space around this landing site had been too small to hold more than a scout or two.

Vorn started up a sloping, stepped path to a steel and glass structure atop. "This is the command center," he said as he ducked inside.

A half dozen people with ear comms manned consoles and pervaded the hub with a din of chatter between technicians and, apparently, pilots. Marco eyed the blackened glass lining the right wall. Were the pilots and ships beyond that?

"This is my trade partner." Vorn planted a hand on the shoulder of a tall, lanky man.

Marco started when he saw the face. "Smirlet."

Shock crested the man's expression, which then darkened. "If I'd known you were bringing this Kynigos, I wouldn't have sent the scout," Jubbah Smirlet growled.

"Watch how you speak to the king," Tarac warned as Vorn's scent sparked with amusement.

Of all the people to work with the king . . . "I webbed Smirlet and delivered him over for justice less than a cycle ago," Marco said.

"What justice?" Smirlet demanded. "You then killed my wife!"

Rancid, the stench of fury and vengeance boiled the air, and Marco lifted a hand. "Of that I am not guilty. She was attacked by Symmachians."

"Had I been there to defend her, she would not have died! But you turned me in."

"I regret the loss of your wife—she was a friend to someone who is now dear to me—but your anger should be aimed at yourself for smuggling fruit. You had warrants—"

"I wasn't smuggling *fruit*," Smirlet hissed. "This!" He motioned around them. "*This* is what they were trying to prevent me from doing. The fruit stand was a way to meet clients." He cocked his head toward the king. "Like Vorn." He swallowed, then gave him a sidelong glance. "What friend?"

"A young woman stranded on Cenon and hunted by Symmachia," Marco explained. "Baytu helped secure her safety. That woman is now princessa of the kingdom that is Vorn's nearest ally."

"Ally," Vorn said with an amused grunt. "We shall see." Then he squinted at Marco. "Princess Kersei, yes? I heard of that offworld business. Nasty."

"Indeed, which is why I am all the more curious about this venture. Your city has no electricity, no means of supporting and maintaining corvettes, yet you say there are sixty here." Since the cave was replete with the scent of fuel, the words were but a challenge to see the ships. Appease Marco's curiosity.

"*Say*?" Vorn balked, feigning to strike Marco. "You grate, Kynigos." Eyes aglow, he punched a button. "There! There are the ships."

Marco glanced over his shoulder and felt a spear of excitement as the black glass cleared, revealing— "Curse the reek . . ." he murmured in awe. Moving to the reinforced window, he gripped the ledge, staring into a scene his eyes could scarce accept.

For what seemed leagues down a sweeping passage that was no higher than the vantage of this command deck, small crafts were being serviced by crews. Not just scouts or corvetttes, but dozens of— "Interceptors!" he said with a tremulous laugh. Light, fast-attack crafts whose primary purpose was to reach and destroy bombers before they could launch their payload.

A wide, tall passage fanned out to one side, farther than Marco could see, and had been transformed into a flight training area. Which was smart—they were maneuvering in a tight, confined space. Training here would make their instincts stronger aboveground and when slipping in and around bigger ships.

Yet, the thing that struck him most— "There is no end." Again, he took in the interceptors, which looked new and well equipped. "Impossible . . ."

"That is often said of Shadowsedge," Vorn said.

Marco frowned at him. "That's in the Outlands. Why—"

"It's wherever the Ladies bleeding want it to be," Vorn said with a snort. "But the jagged mountains just beyond the fire gorges are said to have entrances to their city, though no one knows the way, and these caves are rumored to reach the southern side of that ancient city. However, those I've sent to verify this have never returned." He spared him a speculative glance. "Do you know of the Ladies?"

"Too well." Though he didn't understand why the king asked about that while showing off his fleet, Marco tugged back his sleeve and revealed his brand—the best evidence he had of knowing the Ladies.

Tarac took a step back. "He's Touched," he breathed. "Get him out of here!"

"Wait," Vorn said, stepping closer. "Explain this."

"Your superstitions are at play again, Tarac," came Aliria's melodic voice. "Marco's brand *is* a Touch of the Ladies, but not punishment like those of the Irukandji. This is the *Trópos tis Fotiás*—the Way of the Flame. I told you he was important," she crooned to Vorn.

"What is it?" Tarac asked.

Aliria smiled. "Only one of the oldest, most sacred prophecies among the Faa'Cris."

Marco stilled, gaping into her strange eyes. "I didn't know that." He knew little of the prophecy or what he was supposed to be doing—or not doing.

"Do not worry," Aliria said, casting him a look over her shoulder. "You are already doing it."

Marco started to hear his thoughts on her tongue. "Who are you?"

"She's my queen," Vorn said, his tone dangerous and his scent . . .

Alarmed. Intriguing. "Why did you ask about the Ladies?" Marco asked, diverting the conversation but not his receptors. These two hid something.

"Because," Vorn said, "it was the Ladies who told me to travel to Cenon and meet Jubbah. It was the Ladies who guided me to this tunnel system."

"Not directly, of course, Achilus," Aliria said with a laugh. "Vorn felt inspired by the Faa'Cris, but then, he has been long obsessed with them."

Something in her voice, the way she used his birth name, flung Marco back in time. To the halls of Kardia. To the night of his Reclaiming. His mother was crying, reaching out to him, speaking his name. "You . . ." Aliria sounded strangely similar. Like his mother. Yet . . . not.

Why had the queen used that name? Strange that she knew it—but not impossible. The question and Aliria were distracting. He turned his attention back to the king. "Why show me this, Vorn?" He once more studied the expansive flight program thrumming below a city unaware.

"Aliria believed you would be an ally." Vorn planted his hands on the wide ledge and stared at his fleet. "By comparison, it's small."

"Aye." Marco knew the Symmachian fleet had more ships than this awaiting repairs in its shipyard. "Yet the only hope this planet has for defense against Symmachia."

"My thoughts exactly. When the accord was struck, my father argued against restricting ourselves, limiting our advancement." Vorn's hazel eyes followed the nearest interceptor as its canopy closed and the pilot guided her from the bay into the training passage. "I saw the truth in what he spoke. Knew if we didn't at least try to match their might, we'd never have a boiling chance."

Marco agreed. "I don't know if I can convince Kalonica to change, but it needs to be done." He was more convinced than ever of that. "I believe some, if not most of the elders"—his gaze slid to Ixion's reflection in the glass—"would at least listen."

"Hirakys is as good as an enemy." Vorn's breath bloomed over the cold window. "The Irukandji are spilling from there like rats being driven by a flood, and we have reports that the Hirakyn true heir was turned out because of his sentiments against Symmachia. They put someone on that throne who is not the blood heir."

"How do you know this?"

Vorn slid him a sly smile. "Jherako may be small compared to Kalonica, but my spies are effective. We had one infiltrate the Hirakyn palace and learn that Symmachians have supplanted the crown via Iereans, who controlled the last king and convinced him to overlook his own son for a weaker, more pliable heir. Then they forced the rex to abdicate now instead of in seven years. With the help of my operative, the true heir escaped and is now hunted to prevent his truth from being told."

"I have of late come to know a Hirakyn and his three men. They were on Kalonican lands tracking raiders. He saved my life."

Vorn straightened. "What was his name? Where is he? Can you bring him?"

The flurry of questions unsettled Marco, but he was not sure why.

"The Hirakyn," Vorn said. "Was his name Crey?"

Marco started.

"It was. He thinks of him as a friend," Aliria said, her violet gaze reading

Marco with one of those amused smiles.

Vorn clapped. "Ladies be praised! Ironic, is it not, that the spurned heir connects with the lost heir of Kalonica." His gaze went distant, his eyes seeming to flick through some memory or piece of information. With intent, he shared a look with his captain, who chewed the inside of his lip, then arched his eyebrow and nodded.

"You should tell him," Tarac said. "He needs to know."

Marco frowned at the silent communication between the two. "Know what?"

Vorn shook his head. "I like you and would not be your enemy . . ."

"I see little chance of that."

"Pull it up on the glass." Vorn stared at the window that once again grew black, then filled with a grainy image. "Our spies in Hirakys caught this on video about a month ago."

With a swipe, Tarac activated a video. "This is just inside Vysien, near the capital."

Onscreen, two men walked through the capital city.

"Technology," Marco muttered, watching as whoever had the camera moved closer then into a building. "Technology on a non-tech planet. They used this openly?"

"Button camera—smaller than the thickness of my finger." Vorn grinned. "Thanks to Smirlet for this, a bonus for our large purchase."

Marco focused on the dim setting the spy had entered. "Too dark and grainy. Can you—"

Tarac tapped the upper right corner and the image zoomed. Clarified. He pointed at a young, corded man with the bearing of a rooster. "That is Rex Theule of Hirakys."

As he studied the group standing at the back of what seemed to be an office or government building, Marco felt his gut drop then tighten with a blast of disgust. "That Ierean high lord colluded with the Symmachian captain and an alien creature Xisya who tortured not only Princessa Kersei, but me." It should be no surprise really that they were ingratiating themselves on Drosero with Kalonica's enemies. As Vorn said, manipulating the weak and pliable. But then Marco started. Jerked forward, staring at the image on the screen. "No," he breathed. It couldn't be . . . "Zoom that!"

Tarac complied.

What Marco hadn't expected, what made him sick and furious . . . There was no denying it now. Blue eyes. Sandy hair. That pompous, arrogant . . . "Darius."

"Welcome to the *Chryzanthe*, Shepherds." Captain Baric's voice echoed in the shuttle bay where they'd docked.

Eija's excitement overrode the weird vibration running down her spine as the captain inspected their line. She steeled herself and stared straight ahead—out the shielded bay opening that afforded a brilliant but terrifying view of the monstrous metal chrysanthemum that had given this station its name.

"Once shown to your quarters, remain there. You will not wander the station. Any person found doing so will be immediately expelled from HyPE. Am I clear?"

"Yes, sir!" their simultaneous answer rang out.

"Gunny, they're all yours for now." Baric stalked toward a hatch and stepped through.

Crafter motioned them to follow, led them around the station, and paused outside a series of doors, each marked with a Shepherd's name. "All right, slaggers, stow your gear, then back out here. Drills start at 0400, so you'll bed down after that. Go, move!"

The quarters were more like hotel rooms. Way more sophisticated and luxurious than any accommodations Eija ever had. She tossed her ruck on the bed and returned to the hall. Gunny then escorted them to an industrial-looking dining hall where food was downed in record time. Twenty minutes later, they were back in their bunkrooms.

Eija stared at her room—a small couch and table, a kitchenette, private bath with sonic shower, and a real bed—not a bunk or a cot. Hugging a pillow, she wandered to the window. The black void of space was stingy with light and generous with its dark emptiness. Yet, somehow, Eija felt at home. She climbed into the bed and opted not to shield the window, falling asleep to the lullaby of the quadrants.

Reveille summoned Eija from a dead sleep. She leapt from bed and donned her PT uniform. In the corridor, she stood at attention, hands fisted at her sides, chin up, sensing the others doing the same.

"Shepherds!" Gunny barked from Eija's right as he stormed down the passage. "Twenty laps around the station, then weights in the gym. You have one hour. Then shower and hit the mess. By first bell, be in the briefing room. Clear?"

Sir, yes, sir!" Eija shouted knowing anything less than a loud, clear response would have them pounding the ground and eating industrial-grade carpet.

"Then move!" Crafter bellowed, striding back past her.

Eija went through the regimen, appreciating the wake-up call to her brain and the blood pumping in her veins. She had always been fit and trim, so she made good time with the workout, then hit the sonic shower. Then she donned her uniform. A snappy tunic spliced in half with the upper a deep blue and the lower a soft gray. Black slacks and boots with grav anchors pulled it all together. Hair plaited away from her face to look clean and professional, she headed to the galley. It took her all of ten minutes to eat the protein-laden breakfast, ignoring the glower from Gola, who wore the wine-colored tunic of an officer—like Reef, who was already heading out the door that whispered closed behind him.

"Now," hissed a voice as Eija returned her empty tray to the recycler for sanitizing, "if you forget your place, just look at your uniform." Gola shoved past her, tossed the tray into the bin, and strode out.

It was wasted energy to give in to Gola's baiting, but the thought of spending weeks cooped up in the *Prevenire* with her slowed Eija as she entered the briefing room.

Arcing the lectern, four rows of seats, each with its own arc-shaped desk, accommodated twenty Shepherds. Twenty? There were only a half dozen Shepherds and stations on the *Prevenire*.

Eija planted herself in the middle row, middle seat, and tried to ignore the fact that Gola was chatting up Reef, no doubt forming some alliance of "officers" and "crew." Why it rankled, Eija couldn't say, so she reached for the data channeler docked at her seat.

"Touch nothing!" Gunny charged in and went to the lectern. He looked to the door. "Late! Aoki, two laps around the station, then park it."

Halfway through the door, Aoki started to sag—which made Eija cringe, knowing his punishment would get doubled—then pulled himself upright, turned, and started jogging.

Gunny gripped the lectern. "Okay, let's get started. Activate the channeler at your station. Log in and verify your information. It'll lead you through." He nodded. "Go."

Eija tapped the channeler, and it came to life. It first showed her name and SMID number, then asked for her confirmation on her historical background.

> HOMEWORLD: NAPE
> NEXT OF KIN: NONE
> EMERGENCY CONTACT: NONE
> HAIR COLOR: BROWN
> EYE COLOR: GREEN
> HEIGHT: 1.60 METERS
> BLOOD TYPE: AT+
> ALLERGIES: NKA

Then there were, of course, the more invasive items, like the evaluation of her psychological state upon entering the Academy, her flight scores, her entire HyPE record, which would haunt her until the end of time. She couldn't fight who she was, and it was all there in blue and green on a screen.

"'Bout time you returned, Aoki. Get your flight card filled out," Gunny grumbled as Milek strode in, out of breath, and plopped into a seat beside Bashari. The gunny ran his disapproving gaze over them until it hit on Eija. "You done?"

"Yessir."

He checked his own docked channeler. "We need a contact name and—"

"My family's all dead."

"Regs won't allow interstellar travel without that intel."

"I'll be her emergency contact," Reef offered.

"Negative," Gunny countered. "Can't be someone on the same mission or team."

"Sorry, sir," Eija reiterated. "I don't have—"

"Skip it," growled Captain Baric as he joined them.

Gunny frowned at that. "Sir? But—"

"Sign off," the captain insisted. "It won't matter anyway."

Now the gunny scowled—and so did Eija. What did that mean, it wouldn't matter?

"Get on with it, Crafter," Baric ordered.

Face like stone, the gunny flexed his jaw and tapped the channeler. "Moving on. Next you'll see your assigned duty station on the *Prevenire*, as well as your training regimen for the week."

Eija checked her designation: ZACDARI, EIJA X, LANCE CORPORAL, 1E2H.

The X indicated she didn't have a middle name. She didn't know what the other designations meant.

"As you've likely noticed," Gunny said with a nod, "there have been some rank upgrades for the purpose of this mission alone. You'll refer to me now as 'Chief,' since we couldn't have one of you slaggers outranking me. Due to his top placement in the program, Jadon now holds the rank of Warrant Officer and is your executive officer on the *Prev*, second only to me. Any situation arises—go to him. If he can't resolve it, he'll bring it to me."

"What're these numbers, sir?" Bashari asked, nodding to his data.

"Hold your jets, Ashan." Gunny—the chief—indicated a vidscreen looming above him. "Stat cards have a four alpha-numeric designation. The first digit is the primary role that you'll serve as for the duration of the mission. Should you become injured or incapacitated to the extent you cannot carry out your duty, a secondary will assume that position, but be clear that this means you've put a strain on your fellow crewmembers." Another screen flashed over his head. "These are the duty stations and their designated numbers from your card. Match 'em up."

With a moan, Eija noted her primary was Engineering. Why? She hated Engineering! But, to her surprise, they had assigned her as secondary pilot.

"Pilot!" Bashari lifted his hands in victory. "Who's second?"

No way would Eija fess up.

"I got medical," Shad said quietly. No surprise there for the combat medic.

"I'm third in command," Gola announced, raising a gloating eyebrow at Eija. "Thanks for failing so miserably."

Bashari and Aoki crowed and high-fived.

"Enough!" Baric shouldered behind the lectern as the side door to the briefing room whisked open, drawing their attention.

Eija nearly leapt out of her chair. A tangle of limbs and she-knew-not-what came through the door. A chill scraped her spine as she took in the . . . *thing* standing there. She heard Gola gasp and Milek mutter, as did the others.

What was it? But even as she wondered, it struck Eija—this was the alien whose knowledge had birthed the HyPE program. Its thin, elongated body and legs gave it a strange gait. All-too-perceptive eyes in the narrow head were . . . weird. Wrong. Translucent-pink skin hung on its frame, seemingly gray in some places, as if the skin had lost pigment. At its midsection, a belt held lengths of sheer material—it wasn't a waist, as the torso seemed solid, inflexible—that draped over legs that bent back like a bird's. The creature's appearance, though odd, wasn't any worse than other alien species encountered in the quadrants, yet Eija's stomach churned.

This was no curious-looking animal. This was a sentient being.

"Shepherds," Baric said as the alien gained his side. "This is Xisya, the Khatriza entirely responsible for the knowledge that has made this program possible."

Xisya turned her strange eyes on them. "It issssssss a great pleassssssure to meet you allllll." The timbre of her voice sounded like the scream of metal on metal.

Eija hunched, as if she could protect her ears and stomach from that awful noise. Teeth clenched, she noticed the others doing the same. Shad was crying.

"Asssss you heeear," Xisya continued, "my larynx makes ssssound differently than yoourssssss."

"To aid instruction," Baric said, "quicken progress, each of you will receive a uni-com implant to translate her native tongue. I assure you it is far less painful."

A universal communicator? She glanced at Reef—as an Eidolon, he'd have been the first to use one of those, but he looked just as surprised that the technology had been perfected.

"You have one, sir?" Reef asked, still braced, though Xisya wasn't speaking.

"I do." He looked at Xisya, and though there was no dialogue, the captain bobbed his head. "She would have you know her story to understand the importance of HyPE. Why your mission is crucial. Three years ago, the *Invictus* was on routine patrol on the southern edge of Kedalion when they discovered her small craft adrift. Xisya was malnourished and injured. She had been jettisoned from the science and exploration vessel, the *Ash'ta'Ni*, which had been viciously attacked in their own system by a race called the Draegis. These brutal warriors are relentless in their slaughter of other races and will spare no one." The screen sprang to life. "She escaped with this to prove her story and plead for help."

The video had no sound but was no less ominous. The classroom went eerily silent as security feeds from the *Ash'ta'Ni* unmasked the evil swarming the ship. Enormous black beings moved unhindered against the less powerful creatures. Xisya's kind snapped like twigs beneath the large, powerfully built, and much taller creatures whose faces looked like charred remains. No— more like lava as it hardened. Four molten eyes were mere vertical lines in the slab of black. Shoulders twice as broad as humans' bore armor that spread down to their chests and along segmented arms. Despite their massive bulk, they moved easily and fast. Advancing through the corridor, they rotated their limbs, and a wide amber glow rippled out. Struck the Khatriza, who collapsed in a withering, smoking mess.

"Are they even human?" Milek asked, his voice thick with disgust.

"No, that's the point, slagger," Chief said. "They're not."

Baric glowered. "They're beings without conscience."

"Sir?" Reef sounded disbelieving. "What are *we* supposed to do against those things?"

"Nothing," Baric said. "Your only purpose is to take the *Prevenire* to Kuru System. Once there, you'll connect with Khatriza ships to download your data. With that, they and their advanced technology will establish a hyperbridge between our systems. Tascan Command is even now readying warships and supplies to send through to aid the Khatriza and save them from extinction."

It seemed . . . too good. Too simple. Especially when staring Lavabeasts in the slitted face. If the Khatriza had the level of technology to establish a hypergate, what could Symmachia's fleet—vastly underdeveloped by comparison—do to help?

"The Draegis have nearly wiped out the Khatriza, which is why they sent a last-hope ship for help. I trust this demonstration will help you overcome reactions and disrespect to an intelligent, peaceful race." He lifted his jaw. "Any questions?"

Uh, yeah. Dozens. Asking them, however, would not only draw attention to her but would earn the ire of the captain, who was so wholly convinced of their mission. So why wasn't Eija? She should be more excited? Great. Now she was second-guessing herself.

Excitement or not, she just wanted out of the quadrants.

"Okay," the chief said, stepping back to the lectern. "Head over to the simpods in the lab and get to work. Jadon, you're up first for uni-coms. Go with Xisya."

"Yes, sir." Reef undocked his channeler, the screen compacting to two inches square, and attached it to his uniform. His gaze hit Eija's, and he flicked up an eyebrow, as if to say he wasn't sure about this either, but what could he do? They weren't going to say no and get shredded.

"Move, people!" Chief barked.

On their feet, the Shepherds left the briefing room. Eija glanced after Reef, who trailed the slow-moving Khatriza down the corridor to the medlab.

"This is scuzzed," Milek whispered to Bashari as they headed to the lab.

"Her voice is extraordinary." Shad came alongside Eija and bumped her shoulder. "But man, it made my head spin."

"Extraordinary?" Eija balked as they entered the lab with its half dozen simpods. "It's like shards of glass in my mind."

"And it's so ugly." Milek shuddered.

"Shut up," Gola bit back, snapping her channeler into the simpod. "That *female* is amazing—she survived so much to get help for her people. She's a hero."

"An ugly hero with a painful voice," Bashari summarized as he climbed into a pod.

"What do you think?" Gola asked Eija, her expression far too smug.

The last thing Eija wanted was to be ambushed in a conversation with *her*.

"Always afraid to take a stand, huh?" Gola taunted. "Just can't commit."

"She can commit," taunted Milek. "But she'll change her mind at the last minute."

I'll never change my mind about you.

Silence draped the fog-drenched woods as Darius rode deeper, a sense of foreboding raising the hairs on the back of his neck. Knowing Marco and the aerios had been attacked on the southern edge of these same woods unsettled him, even riding with Hadrien. His heart thudded each time a branch snapped or popped beneath his Black's hooves.

They followed the trail that wound along the river toward Stratios, a now-sad, beaten stretch of land that once held the most formidable of Kalonica's leaders and people. Mist snaking through the thick trees felt ominously like the spirits of the dead.

Darius had set out later than preferred, unwilling to leave Kersei during dinner and arouse her curiosity. Once she retired to the bedchamber, he said business would keep him late. The lie so convicted him that he almost confessed his true reason for not joining her immediately. Too many lies and half-truths had escaped his lips since he reclaimed her on Iereania. The first ones had come far too easily. He had been convinced he was doing it for her good, for Kalonica.

Deceit. Vain deceit.

As the fog thickened, snaking around the trees, Darius straightened on his mount. Moonslight stabbed through the branches and unveiled the ruins of Stratios far below. He recalled the night he set petition there. The night so many died—Father, Silvanus, Iason, Kersei's family—in Stratios Hall.

Where I should have died as well.

He urged his Black on, leaving the ruins and guilt. Had he died, Marco would have bound with Kersei and ruled with her at his side. It might have been simpler that way. Perhaps even better. Yet the thought repulsed Darius. He reveled that she carried his child. That his heir grew in her womb was more incredible than he'd imagined.

"We are here, sire," Hadrien said, his quiet words loud in the dark eve.

With reticence, Darius looked to the cave meeting place. He slowly slid his gaze around, wondering how many eyes watched this time. Never were they truly alone and every encounter risked Kersei and the Kalonicans, if he did not . . .

"Those scars will be the least of your agonies."

Turning back to the cave, he felt the ridged skin of his scars rub against his cravat. He dismounted and led his Black out of sight, then descended into the shallow cave. As he did, light flared from a touchstone, illuminating the white-and-red robe of the unnaturally tall iereas who held Darius's leash.

"You're late," snarled Theon.

Darius found delicious, rebellious pleasure in the iereas's irritation.

"The times are set," a deeper voice warned as a dark-blue uniform emerged from the shadows, "with deliberate care to conceal our presence and yours."

"You care not a whit for my welfare," Darius spat. Of course, Baric would have the gall to send his lackey. "Where's the captain?"

"Busy," Theon sniffed. "Mr. Cleve speaks for him."

"You're right," Cleve said, cold as the space from which he had come. "Our concern isn't for some puffed-up prince but for this planet."

"To what end?" Darius asked every time why they sought control of Drosero.

"Don't worry about that." Theon tipped his chin up.

"This is my home and people! I would have answers!"

"We bought you," Theon said, peering down his long nose at Darius, "your soul, and your cooperation by returning the girl to you. That was the agreement made in these very woods a year past. We protect her, you cooperate."

"And I have," Darius barked.

Theon's laugh was menacing. "Have what? Bedded the girl? Gotten a child on her? Lived in your luxurious palace, unaffected by the slaughter you aided?"

"Never did you say what you intended. Only that change—"

"Guilt hangs from your neck, Prince. Do not cry now when you have everything you wanted and regret the price." The iereas turned, the illumined stone casting deep shadows over his sallow face. "Have you given thought to those lives, Darius?" He looked at Cleve. "What was the fatality count again?"

They taunted him as always. And every time, he felt himself die a little more.

"Three hundred twenty-two," Cleve said in a bored manner.

"Ah, yes." Theon tilted his head down again. "How do you sleep each night, knowing you were complicit in the deaths of three hundred people—your people?" He tsked and shook his head. "No, Prince, you have done nothing but save your own hide and bed that pretty wife of yours."

Cleve's gaze hardened. "Now it's time to pay."

Darius glanced between the men and saw something he had not noticed before—darkness, wickedness. Dread returned, roiling through his gut as, outside the cave, Hadrien's boots scratched. He would have this over with. He shifted forward, angry that they were here. That they were calling in his debt. "What do you want?"

"There is a band of rebels rising from the ashes of Stratios," Theon said. "They need to be squashed, and that starts with their rogue of a leader. He must be silenced."

"Silenced? I will not kill anyone!"

Cleve sneered. "Oh, I think you will. Because this man has your wife's ear. What will she think when she learns what you've done? How you killed her father, mother, and sisters? Your own father! What will she think of her child's father then?"

"I wouldn't be surprised if she wanted to throw herself off those cliffs," Theon crooned. "It would be a quick death compared to dying for the rest of her life, knowing she is married to the man responsible for murdering her family and people!"

They sought to rile him so he would agree to kill. But who was the person they targeted? A large, powerful shape filled his mind. "Myles." How could they know Myles now lodged at Kardia? "I will not kill one of the best aerios Kardia has ever had. I don't care—"

Cleve slammed Darius backward, pinning him against the cave wall. "You think you have a choice? Do it or your pretty wife will know pain unlike anything—"

Machitis training rose to the fore. Darius shoved his hands up between the man's arms and swiped his foot at the same time.

Startled, Cleve stumbled back. He rolled his shoulders and shook his head. Growling, he surged forward.

Darius sidestepped. Landed a blow in the captain's gut. He heard the *oof* as he felt an impact to his own side. The blinding agony of the knife-hand strike dropped Darius to his knees. Another blow nailed his jaw. Pitched him backward. Pain rocketed through his skull as it impacted on the stone wall.

"Know your place, Prince," Cleve growled through ragged breaths.

"You think much of yourself," Theon said. "You will never be free of us.

We own you, Darius." He moved in closer, his cloak emanating that spiced fragrance of the iereas. "Concern yourself with finding the rogue and putting him to the blade."

FORGELIGHT, JHERAKO, DROSERO

Darius had betrayed them and would pay—with his life, if necessary.

After leaving Ironesse, they returned to the palace and parted ways with Vorn and his entourage.

"The prince is complicit." Ixion spat the words. "I knew him petulant, but *this*?" He stopped as they gained the upper level. "Think you this is true? You believe it?"

Marco raked a hand through his hair, shaking his head. "I know not what to think but we have long wondered how Darius survived. The story he gave Kersei . . ." He wrestled with the part of him that wanted his brother to be corrupt, to justify punishing him . . .

"Give careful thought to this. Already there is bad blood between you two—if we lay the charges without evidence . . ."

"There *is* ev—" Marco snapped his mouth shut, realizing they could not use that video without compromising what Vorn was building here. "Augh!" He threw a punch into the air. "What if he was involved in the Stratios attack? It would mean he killed our father!"

"Tread carefully with that accusation," Ixion warned. "If you are convinced, we must speak to the Council of Elders."

"Bazyli," Marco said with a nod. "I trust his counsel."

Ixion gave him a rueful look.

"What?"

His first shook his head. "You choose the man who is most hard on you."

"You mean, outside of yourself?"

Ixion gave him a wry smile. "That was understood."

"If this is true . . ." Marco's thoughts darkened. "I could . . ." He narrowed his eyes. "He is responsible for the death of Kersei's family."

"Slow down," Ixion said. "We saw him with the Ierean and the Symmachian—"

"Who *are* responsible for the attack. Who are colluding with the alien that put me in that horrific contraption and yet kill the Brethren."

"I am not fond of Darius, but I cannot believe him so wholly lost or so wholly polluted. There must be an explanation—"

"For killing an entire clan?"

Ixion seemed tormented. "What if they hold something over him?"

"He had a *choice*." Marco knew he was being too hard on his brother and sagged. Made himself think through what they could have that— "Kersei. They saved her to control him."

With a heavy exhale, Ixion gave a slow nod. "It would be . . . effective." He clapped Marco's arm. "We have a long journey on the morrow back to Trachys. I shall leave you for now. It will give us time to think and for you to cool."

Marco arched an eyebrow.

"I know that temper too well. It mirrors my own." Ixion jutted his jaw. "Rest and think. We will talk in the morning."

"Good eve." Weighted with anger, Marco stalked to the room. He nodded to Cetus as he entered, his thoughts darkly focused on how to punish Darius. How could his brother do this—kill their father. Kersei's family . . .

"What's wrong?" Isaura glided across the floor on bare feet, her hair unbound. Concern traced her gentle features. "What is it? What happened?"

He tried to shove aside the dark cloud that had come to roost over his head. "How do you know something happened?"

"That scowl."

"I always scowl."

"No, you *brood*. There's a difference." She touched his shoulder and peered into his eyes. "What is it? I thought to see you much delighted after the ships. Were they not there?"

Removing the cravat, he dropped onto the settee and stared into the dying embers of the fire.

"Were there ships?"

"Yes, they were there," he said, making himself divert his thoughts. "And glorious! Interceptors—a fighter-class ship that's better, faster than a corvette. Can take on bigger craft. The latest and greatest."

"So what disturbs you?"

Marco huffed. "Vorn uses offworld technology . . . With it . . . There are images of . . ." Augh! Why did the words stick in his throat?

"Of what?" She joined him on the settee and tucked her feet beneath her.

Mayhap it would be better when he . . .

What? Had proof? It already exists.

Talked to Darius.

To what end? He is guilty and clearly has no remorse!

He leaned back and stared up, eyes tracing but not seeing the murals on the ceiling. Somehow, his rage was bottoming out as he thought through the ramifications of Darius's actions. Of how it would crush Kersei. Shame everyone.

Darius would have to be punished.

What would that look like?

He was just starting to know his little brother. Had gained a modicum of respect for him, begun to think perhaps they did not have to be enemies.

"Dusan?" Her touch was light on his arm. "This? This is brooding."

A smirk tugged at his foul mood, and he rolled his head to look at her. "Ixion suggested I take time to think things through before I speak more." He roughed a hand over his face. "I think that wise."

Hurt coiled around her like those golden strands. "You bear so many burdens, and you may have forgotten—but I am your kyria, so it is my responsibility to help you."

Marco touched the locks draped across her shoulder. He did not want to draw her into this tangled burden. Nobody should have to bear it, but he would for the realm, for Kersei, so he turned his attention and hers. "I wish you could've seen the shipyard."

She chewed the inside of her lip, argument lingering in her expression. "I . . . cannot imagine." Her efflux was rank with hurt, yet she valiantly nudged it away and accepted his avoidance. "But I do so love the way your face glows even now."

He smirked, amazed at how she altered her course and attitude. "I am grateful for you."

Never had anyone been grateful for her. His words were powerful, silencing her objections. Long ago had she learned that when a person needed solitude to work through their thoughts, it was best to let them have it. Thus, she decided to say goodnight and leave him to sort whatever it was needing sorting.

She leaned over to kiss his cheek.

Dusan, however, turned, and her kiss landed on his mouth.

"Oh," she breathed, surprised. Embarrassed. "I will leave you to your thoughts."

He caught her waist. "You bid me goodnight?"

She searched his features for the meaning behind those words. It seemed there was surprise. "I . . . you seemed to want time alone."

His lips drew to the side and he did not argue.

Accepting his answer, Isaura stood. "Good eve." He had said to wait for him, and all these hours she anticipated his return, her belly a bowl of butterflies as she thought of what might happen. But he walked in distracted and irritated.

In the bedchamber, she turned down the oil lamp, shed her robe, and slid beneath the covers. She turned to the window, mostly to hide her disappointment. In time, she must believe, things between them would settle into a routine. He would accept her. Sure, he said he was grateful for her—but that was because she had not challenged or pestered him. Survival meant not making a pest of herself. All those years skirting Ma'ma's fits. Doing all she could to simply be overlooked. She had not imagined her life with Dusan would be the same, but she could do it.

How desperately she did not want to be overlooked by him.

Tears fell on her pillow, but she had also long ago mastered silent crying and letting herself fall asleep as she tried to empty the grief from her chest. Dreams flickered into her thoughts—her dancing around a fire whose flames resembled the mark on Dusan's arm. The fire became a pyre and she stepped back, stricken to see her ma'ma atop it with someone else. Confusion over the change drew her closer, her heart screaming not to draw back the burial cloth covering the form—for now, there was only one as she reached for the cloth.

No, don't look. Leave.

But she couldn't leave. They had come so far. She must see.

The cloth flapped as she ripped it off, and it billowed away. There, she saw him—Dusan. Now, however, he was no longer on the pyre, but in a large wooden chair . . . dead. Fires leapt and danced around him.

To her horror, she realized he was not yet dead. His eyes, nearly silver against the flames, touched hers as roaring shadows dove in to devour him.

"No!" Her own shout ringing in her ears, Isaura jerked up and awake, breathing raggedly.

Dusan appeared beside her in the bed. Touched her shoulder. "Isau—"

With a strangle cry that he was very much alive, she gripped his shirt and sagged against him. "Oh, Dusan!" Sobbing, she could not speak of it.

His arms came around her shoulders, and they lay back against the pillows. "Easy." He quietly cupped her head to his chest, where she clung. "Just a dream. It was just a bad dream."

"It was so real," she said through her tears. She pressed farther into his shoulder. "I could not bear it if something happened to you."

Dusan tightened his hold.

After a time—she knew not how long—the tears shuddered to a stop. Embarrassment rushed over her, making her very aware of their situation— being abed, in each other's arms. She told herself not to notice how his chest was sculpted and his abdomen tight. There was no softness about this man, and in his arms she'd truly felt safe and protected. "I also . . . I dreamed my mother was burning on a pyre."

"Likely the impact of seeing Moidia razed and your mother fall to her death."

"Ma'ma did not fall," Isaura said. "She jumped."

Dusan stilled, then rubbed her back. "I hoped you had not seen that."

His voice rumbled in his chest, where her ear rested. She lifted her head and looked up at him, resting her chin on her hand, which felt the thump of his heart. "Why?"

"It was horrific," he said, brushing her hair back. "I would not will that on any person, let alone her daughter."

"You are very kind to me."

He kissed her forehead. "Is that what woke you? Seeing her—"

"No," she sniffled. "The pyre became this large wooden chair with a giant aetos seeming to soar from the top of it, and you were there . . ."

"That sounds like the throne at Kardia."

She felt the color drain from her face. "A great shadow tried to devour you."

"Hey." He slid an arm around her waist, rotated their positions, and laid her back against the mattress. "It's going to be okay." Again he smoothed her hair. "Trust me?"

"Always." Yet disconcerted, she looked into his blue eyes. "How could I dream of something I've never seen?"

"Likely to tell me I will live long and sit on the throne until I die of natural causes. Sounds quite dull."

"It sounds wonderful," she corrected, brushing back the unruly curls from his face. The dream had been so dark, vivid . . . "I would very much like that—for us to live a very long time together."

Dusan caught her hand and kissed her palm, sending darts of exhilaration through her stomach.

"You are trying to distract me."

"Did you know," he said with a smirk, "that the Lady gifted me with what they call *Orasí*—High Sight?"

Her stomach squeezed at the huskiness of his words.

"When I look into a person's eyes and touch them"—his fingertips traced her cheek and lips—"their adunatos reveals itself to me. I can see what they're made of."

"And what am I made of?" Isaura swallowed as he lowered himself. She wanted to resent the distraction, but . . .

"Purity." His mouth caressed her ear then trailed down her neck, sending shivers into her spine.

Isaura slid her arms around him and held on, anxious for those visions from the dream to be gone.

His kisses returned to her ear and jaw—once more claiming her mouth. Suddenly, an urgency rose in his kisses, in his touch that enlivened her. Dashed away the fears that held her hostage. Ready for what she had once dreaded but now welcomed as he made her his kyria.

Chief Warrant Officer Crafter wasn't kidding about running the sims backward and forward until memorized. After an hour in the simpods, Eija spent the rest of the first day going through emergency procedure modules on her in-room system. In addition, they had new sims related to each of their assigned specialties. For Eija, that meant mind-numbing hours going over engine schematics, functions, and maintenance.

Today her online training module focused on the effects of long-term space travel on the body and mind. The program had over fifty levels, each one successively harder and requiring more creativity. Challenged by the increasing difficulty, she persisted. Even levels she passed—if her score was not in the upper ten, she ran it again until mastered. She blamed the lower scores on distraction, curiosity over the implant. What it'd feel like. How it'd differ from the PICC-line.

When the chow bell sounded through the facility, Eija stretched out the kinks in her shoulders, then headed to the galley, her gaze instantly tracking for Reef. Who was hunched shoulder to shoulder with Gola, whispering.

Annoyed, Eija retrieved her partitioned tray.

"Apparently, they're too good for us now," Bashari said. "Got the implant, so they think they're superior."

"We're all getting one," Milek muttered, digging into his protein stack.

"Maybe it messed with their brains," Bashari said, much louder this time.

Eija chose an empty table, unwilling to join in their general cruelty. Friend or foe, those two mocked everyone.

"For your information," Gola preened at them, "the implant is fine. No side effects." She lifted her hair, showing her PICC port, its circumference a little red but otherwise normal.

"Wait!" Bashari leapt up, his face contorted. "Did you—oh slag, Gola. This . . ." He turned to Milek. "It's not just me, is it? You see this right?"

Milek frowned as he pushed to his feet. "I do . . ."

Eija rolled her eyes and focused on her chow. They were jerking Gola's O_2

line, and by her whiter-than-normal complexion, she was buying it.

"What?" Gola shifted to Reef. "What is it? Is there really anything?"

He snorted. "If you haven't figured them out by now, it's going to be a long jump."

"Jerks!" She lasered Milek and Bashari, who were laughing hysterically and high-fiving.

"Did it hurt?" Shad asked as she stood at their table with her tray. "I tossed my cookies when I got my PICC-line, and it ended up infected, too. Turns out the port was damaged and had to be remov—"

"Oversharing, Shad," Gola sneered.

Case in point—the cruelty they injected on the quiet combat medic who asked a simple question and wanted to be relatable.

Finishing her food, Eija didn't have that problem—the cruelty or the need to be relatable. She just had to get out of the quadrants. This jump would be irritating with the five of them and their quirks, their arrogance. She stuffed the protein stack between bread, wrapped it in a napkin, and left.

"Eija, hold up!"

She glanced back, surprised to find Reef jogging toward her with a tart in hand.

"You missed your cue."

She frowned. "What cue?"

"The one to save me, get me out of there." Reef grinned as he picked the crust from his tart. "I was trying to make eye contact, and you totally scuzzed me."

"If your intent was to ditch them, you're failing."

"What?"

She arched her eyebrow toward the passage's industrial-grade carpet littered with crumbs from his tart.

"Slag," he grunted. "Chief will make me eat them off the deck."

Eija laughed. "Probably." Rounding the first section, the sim lab came into view. She wasn't really ready to face the simulator again, so she slowed, fully expecting Reef to bail. There might be a small part of her that hoped he wouldn't. Small. Infinitesimal.

He whipped around in front of her and walked backward, facing her. "So. Hack it up."

She frowned, trying not to laugh as he walk-tripped. "What?"

"Why'd you walk out of the galley? Just shred me like that?"

Her laugh was jittery this time. After all, she wasn't exactly going to admit she felt like the veritable fifth—sixth—wheel, or that she didn't expect him to want anything to do with her. "I needed some quiet."

"Right," he said with a snort, "because being in our quarters or simpods all day isn't quiet."

"I have no desire to be where I'm not wanted."

"Ah, but see—you forgot about me. Again. *I* wanted you there. Remember, 'Bail me out'?"

"You don't need my help. If you left, they'd follow you."

"Exactly! That's why I need you—to get rid of them. They'd follow me right out an airlock."

"That's one way to get some quiet." As soon as she said it, Eija realized how it sounded. "I mean—space is quiet. Not that . . ."

He sniffed. "I got it. Don't have to explain."

They walked in silence for a while. That awkward, weird silence that made her wonder if she'd missed something. What did he want? But he continued on, and they'd nearly made the full circuit, the galley coming up on their right again, when she stopped. "What're you doing?"

"Thought that was pretty obvious." He motioned to the deck. "Walking."

"I mean—why aren't you in the galley with Gola?" That sounded way more jealous than she'd intended. "And the others."

"Because I'm with you." He clicked his tongue. "I mean, this isn't rocket science, Ei. I thought you would've figured that much out."

She breathed another laugh and shook her head. "So you got the implant?"

His hand went to his neck. "Strange, but not as bad as I'd expected."

"And you can understand . . . her?"

"Surprisingly. It's not that the sickening screech goes away completely, but at least I wasn't wanting to blow chunks every time she talked." He shook his head as they again neared quarters. "I just . . ."

She glanced at him, waiting for him to finish, but he didn't. "What?"

He huffed. "We had the PICC-line for the jump couches and hard g's, so . . . why did"—he visibly convulsed—"that *thing* have to dig in my head?"

"What do you mean? Was it so strange to have her put it in?"

"Uh, yeah." His brown eyes were wide. "She literally put some . . . appendage into the port."

"*What?*"

He shuddered. "I felt . . . violated." He seemed disconcerted, concerned.

Was he yanking her O_2 line? Though Reef was a gregarious smart aleck, he wasn't a jerk like Bashari or Milek. And he was definitely better looking.

"You're afraid?"

"No." The bark betrayed his lie. "I mean . . . not really. I guess." He shrugged. "Dunno. Maybe it was just me being so freaked about some transparent-skinned, screeching-voice alien touching where I couldn't see." Now he looked sheepish, running a hand over the port again. "You know, maybe it wasn't really her head or finger or . . . whatever. She probably used a standard Tascan probe like when they installed our PICC-lines. That'd make more sense. Right?"

The sincerity of his question gave her pause. She shrugged. "Sure." One thing she'd always admired about Reef was his confidence, which he was seriously lacking right now. Somehow it made her feel bad, yet she was glad she wasn't the only one with misgivings. "You're not one to lie or let your imagination run wild."

His gaze drifted to the metal flower through the windows, a few yards from the lab. "It's all unknown territory. I guess something is bound to be weird or off." He bumped her shoulder. "Well, besides you."

The taunt pierced her protective barrier and struck dangerously close to her heart. Eija couldn't say why it hurt so much, but it reminded her she was alone on this mission.

"Oh, hey." He touched her shoulder. "Wait, I said that wrong. I didn't mean—"

"No." She gave him a tight smile, conjured from the depths of personal experience in salvaging awkward situations, and waved him off. "It's good. I get it."

"No, I—"

"What're you two doing?" Chief stormed toward them, anger in his brow and warning in his tense posture. "Get back to quarters and start studying!"

"It's chow time," Reef said with a nervous laugh.

"Negative," Chief growled. "That ended ten minutes ago."

Eija glanced at the channeler docked to her sleeve and started. "Djell."

"Exactly, Corporal, now hustle it up, and if I ever catch you two sneaking off for some galoching, I'll have you jettisoned faster than you can suck O_2!" His intense glare seemed more vicious than normal. "Clear, slaggers?"

Drawing in a sharp breath at the insinuation that they were making out, Eija pulled back and felt flames scorching her face. "Of course, sir."

Reef had a smile tugging the corners of his lips.

"Go! Now!" Chief bellowed.

Eija could not move fast enough, desperate to put distance not only between her and the chief—she wanted his respect, not his remonstration—but also from Reef, who seemed to enjoy her embarrassment.

Cutting in front of him to her quarters, she scowled. "How can you laugh?"

"Because it's ridiculous." He backed toward his quarters. "Fly smart. And no cheating by looking over my shoulder."

Rolling her eyes, Eija shoved into her simpod and spun as the door shut. Cheating? Her scores were higher than his! Of course he didn't remember, because she'd screwed up with those last-minute spurts of defiance. No wonder Reef thought he was better, so much that *galoching* with her would be ridiculous.

Why did she care? He was one of *them*. She was not. Resolve hardened and stuffed her in the chair, determined to do her best. Be the best.

Her quarters bell chimed.

Figuring it was Jadon, she ignored it. But it rang again. With a growl, she punched the open button. When the door whispered back, she snapped, "What?"

The large, muscular frame of their chief filled the hatch.

Eija jolted. "Sir!"

"Time for your uni-com. Let's go." He thumbed her into the passage.

"Right." Eija did as told, numbly walking to the lab. After pressing a code into the datapad on the wall, he palmed it. Double doors snapped back, and a blast of cold, sanitized air smacked her. Faltering, she felt . . . a weird wave of coolness slosh through her stomach and tickle her neck.

Chief nudged her inside and straightened when he spotted the captain. "Sir, Zacdari's here for implant."

Captain Baric slid a look over Eija as he shifted toward Xisya and said something to her. Quiet dialogue ensued, she guessed through Baric's implant. But then the captain glanced at them and pointed to a steel table. "Strap her in."

Chief faltered. "Strap her . . .?"

The captain glowered but said nothing, expecting his orders to be obeyed.

"None of the others—"

"Do it!" the captain snapped, returning his attention to the Khatriza and nodding.

None of the others had been strapped? Is that what he was going to say? Reef sure hadn't mentioned that. She looked to the chief, hoping he'd say this was a bad joke. They were just trying to freak her out.

Job well done. Congrats.

"C'mon." Chief hooked her arm and led her to the table. "Up here."

"Seriously?" Eija's stomach squirmed as she palmed the cold steel and hopped onto it. "Nobody else had to do this?"

"You'll be fine." Who was Chief trying to reassure—her or himself? "Lie back."

She swallowed, the hard surface digging into her hips as she aligned herself with the circular head support that left her neck and shoulders available. Why did they need to strap her down when they were just going to enhance her PICC-line?

Chief cranked the hand restraints. Cuffs tight, cold steel bit into her wrists. He moved to her feet, and Eija felt near panic cinch her nerves. Then he returned to her shoulder, reaching over and grabbing something in her periphery. He slipped a metal brace over her forehead. As soon as it snapped into place, a tremor rattled through the table. A flat surface descended from the ceiling.

"I don't understand . . ." Eija widened her eyes. She drew in a breath and tensed as it pressed her body from neck to feet—like a steel sandwich. Tight. But not *completely* suffocating.

"Easy," Chief said, his brown eyes holding hers. "Like zero-g suits, right?"

Appreciating his encouragement, she gave him a small nod. "Just . . . harder. Heavier."

"Crafter, you can go now."

"Sir." The chief glanced down at her, hesitating as if he wanted to say something. Then with a sharp nod, he left.

Gaze on the ceiling, Eija tried to steady her nerves. Force herself to relax. Reef and Gola had gone through this without complication. "Just like zero-g," she murmured.

A mechanism clicked, rattling the steel. Vibrations wormed down her spine, and Eija felt the table canting and grabbed the edges. The left side dipped down. She groped for something to hold onto but her fingers found no traction. She whimpered as the entire table rotated so that she faced the floor.

The room thrummed with a silence that made her reconsider being a part of this mission.

Black grav boots clomped closer on her left. Captain Baric. Though tempted to wonder why a battlecruiser captain was here, she guessed he needed to oversee the alien's every move. After all, what Marine in their right mind would trust an alien entity so entirely?

On the right came those spindly legs of Xisya. Though she wore a garment that resembled a skirt, it wasn't a whole swath of material—instead, it had many slits that allowed the ostrich-like legs to bend backward. It was creepy. Surreal.

Panic struck Eija with an urgent, frantic need to get out of here. To flee.

"Please," she said, her voice hoarse. She cleared her throat to repeat the plea. "Let me out." Something icy swept the hair from her neck, followed by a pinch of pain. She sucked in a breath and tried to talk, but her mouth wouldn't comply. Her eyes wouldn't move. Wouldn't close.

What's going on? Wait! Stop!

"She's under," the captain said.

No. No, I'm not.

"Begiiiiiinn," came Xisya's trilling voice.

I'm not unconscious! I'm not unconscious, Eija tried to scream, warn them. She couldn't move or talk, but she could hear everything.

"Her vitals are running high," the captain noted.

No djell! Because I'm awake!

No response.

A nearby metal table caught the reflection of Xisya, who lifted a long cylindrical object over Eija's body, then lowered it . . . down . . . down . . .

Pain spiked. Cold. Hot. Excruciating. She screamed—internally. Nothing came out of her mouth. Her eyes wouldn't move. Tears blurred, and she tried not to watch the reflection, but her eyes were uncooperative.

"This shhhhouuuullld work," Xisya said.

"Are you sure? If she is what you say—"

"This will neutralize any threat she could pose but also enhance what is needed for the Sentinel's beacon," Xisya said, the trilling gone.

Threat? What threat?

Chaotic, bloody images scored Eija's mind. Orange lasers severing people. The collective scream of a dying city. Smoldering ruins. A massive mound rose from the center of a crimson city with strange domelike structures. Dark skies bled red as ships fell from the sky. An army of large, thick-chested Lavabeasts descended on a village, slaughtering every form of life. Vicious. Cruel. They reveled in their kills.

Suddenly, one turned toward her with decisiveness. As if he knew she was watching from across the universe. Knew she had intruded. Witnessed his murder of innocents.

He lifted a crescent-shaped weapon and lunged at her with lightning speed.

Noooo! Terror gripped Eija. The world yanked her into the black fold of that terrible creature.

The curse of being a hunter. Marco stood at the balcony door, anak'ing a scent that had drawn him from the warmth of Isaura's comforting presence. Terror hung on the winds of the city and had yanked him from a sound sleep.

Trouble comes.

Or did it merely follow him? Symmachians sought him, Irukandji hunted him. His brother hated him. He glanced to the bed where Isaura still lay curled on her side, facing away from him, the soft curve of her hip reminding him of last night.

Sunlight glittered off her golden hair spilling across the pillows. It had been soft and fragrant against his face as they had loved. Why he had fought his feelings for her, he could not fathom. True, he'd feared hurting her, forcing her will in this, but the way she loved him last night promised she had no reticence. And once he had accepted that, believed that, there had been none on his part as well.

Though he couldn't account for Kersei and that vision, this . . . this was right. Mayhap—as Ypiretis had suggested—better. *Best.*

It surprised him how much Isaura filled the emptiness within him. He'd made sure she was legitimatized as Mavridis's heir, because he knew what it meant to her. She'd wear the crown of the land, and all would know she was his kyria.

Marco slipped back into bed beside her, choosing to enjoy this moment for as long as he could have it. He kissed her neck and relaxed against her body, the fit so right, so perfect. "I love you." The words embedded themselves—and her—in his adunatos.

Isaura glanced back lazily.

"Did I wake you?" he whispered.

She rolled onto her back, her expression dreamy. "It is the best way to be awakened." The violet light in her irises was so bright, so—

Marco stilled, disappointed. Only one. There was only one light in her eyes. Not two.

"What is it?" she asked.

It didn't matter. "Nothing." His chest tightened that she did not carry his child.

"Are you sure?" Her sleepiness fell away as she held the coverlet modestly. "You seem changed of a sudden."

"Distracted by your beauty." He kissed her, deliberately pushing away the tinge of sadness, and fell once more into the passion of his bound, his wife. His Isaura.

After a quick bath and shave, he afforded her privacy to be tended by a lady's maid. He moved into the late-morning light on the balcony and eyed the island, his mind heavy with thoughts of the armaments Drosero had not yet welcomed but would need in the coming days. And of his brother's betrayal.

The trouble that wakened him came again and would no longer be ignored. It was filling the palace, and with it came alarm.

"My lord!" Ixion burst through the doors to the apartment.

Marco strode into the living room. "What trouble?"

In a split-second assessment, Ixion's gaze flashed over Marco, who had yet to don his jerkin—then the bedchamber, and back, probably realizing there was no distance left between the man before him and his daughter. He cleared his throat. "There are skirmishes in the city—Irukandji. Vorn fears they are come for you. He even now readies an Interceptor to return us to Trachys."

"Why not Kardia?" Marco grabbed a jerkin and put it on.

"Logistics and visibility prohibit it. Vorn fears the ship being seen. There is an alcove off the coast of Trachys that will conceal our approach. Kardia is high cliffs and little beachhead, not to mention the Kalonican Sea has strong headwinds."

For now, Vorn's secret must be protected. "When do we depart?"

"Even now," Ixion said. "I was sent to bring you both to the south terrace."

Radiant in a light blue gown that so perfectly hugged curves he now well knew, Isaura emerged, plaits bound at her nape. She fastened buttons on a long cloak, a tremor in her hands and her efflux jittery. Likely over being discovered by her father after their lovemaking. "Where are we going?" Her voice was a little high, piqued, nervous.

"Raiders are here," Marco said, "We depart at once to return to Trachys."

"I will pack," she said, turning to the bedchamber.

"They will come after us." Ixion started for the door.

Marco gave her a conspiratorial smile. "If you are ready . . ."

"I am."

He moved in and stole a kiss, which fanned her happiness against his receptors. He liked it. Liked that she smiled, that he put it there. Though she still only had one *Orasi* light in her eyes, he must be realistic that pregnancies rarely resulted from the first time. It was probably for the better. Because, though he'd told Isaura her dream was just a bad dream, he hadn't told her he'd had the same dream about his death.

TRACHYS, KALONICA, DROSERO

The trip on the airship subjected Isaura to a vicious wave of nausea, but it was far shorter and more endurable than their day-long journey on the *Basilikas*. They landed nearly a kilometer from Trachys and were left to hike the beach and hills to reach the fortified city. All the while, Isaura marveled at what had transpired between her and Dusan, how the distance had vanished. His whispered confession of love did much for her, as did the moment he'd scaled the staircase in Vorn's castle to protect her.

Within the ora, they were back inside the mansion making their way toward the apartments Elder Elek designated for them. Regia moved ahead and checked the room before they entered.

Kita emerged through a nearby door.

Isaura hurried to her friend and hugged her. "How are you?"

"Rested." Kita glanced at Dusan and Mavridis. "Restless. Glad you are returned, so I will have someone to talk to."

Dusan came to her and touched Isaura's arm. "We must council. I trust you are in good company now."

"Yes, of course," Isaura said.

He kissed her cheek. "I'll return as soon as I can." With that, he strode away with Mavridis and Theilig.

"What is this?" Kita whispered excitedly, taking her hand and leading her into the apartments.

Though Isaura tried to hide her embarrassment, she knew her blush betrayed her.

"I am happy for you, Isa." Kita hugged her again. "It is clear much has changed between you and the medora."

"Mm." Isaura talked with her friend for a few oras, but she eyed the bed, her thoughts catapulting back to Dusan last night.

"You are tired," Kita guessed wrongly. "Go, rest. I'll wake you when sup is served."

Not wanting to argue, still feeling awkward, she eased onto the bed. "Did I not get sick from the ship, I would argue, but it drained me overmuch." Even as she lay back, she felt the exhaustion she had not recognized before rush in to claim her.

When she woke, light filtered through the windows. She saw Kita moving around the chamber, setting a table with food and a carafe. "You are changed."

"Aye, and you sleep like a log."

Yawning as she sat up, she noticed the coverlet on the other side was rumpled. Had Dusan come in?

"I tried to wake you last eve, but you wouldn't stir."

"Last eve?" She looked to the window and found morning light. "I slept through the night?"

"Aye," Kita said with a laugh and motioned to the table. "Ready to break your fast?"

Incredible that she had slept so much! Well, she had thrown up for most of one day, slept fitfully for a few hours, then got thrust into politicking at Forgelight. And then, of course, their lovemaking had not afford much rest . . .

Famished, Isaura dressed and ate, listening to Kita speak of how thrilled Mnason was to have aerios to watch and mimic. It made her ache for her sister, who would probably have been scampering around the city with him, ferreting out every cranny and crevice.

"There is a pretty garden on the north side," Kita said quietly, her discerning gaze taking in Isaura's grief. "Perhaps a visit would cheer you."

"I should like to see it."

After Kita helped Isaura dress and arranged her hair, Cetus escorted them down the passage. An aerios trotted up the grand staircase, pausing when he saw them.

He inclined his head to Isaura. "Begging your mercy, Majesty, but word is sent for your lady's maid. Seems her son is in need of a pharmakeia."

"Again?" Kita groaned. "What bone has he broken this time?" She turned to Isaura. "I beg your mercy about the garden."

"Go. See to Mnason. Cetus can deliver me safely to the garden." As her friend hurried away, Isaura paused at the bottom of the stairs, glancing around.

"Is something wrong, Majesty?" Cetus asked.

Majesty. She nearly laughed—she had been called many things in her life, but never that. "I confess, I do not know the way. Kita mentioned a side garden . . ."

The burly warrior motioned left. "This way, Majesty." He guided her around to the rear hall with arched windows on the left and portraits on the right.

Admittedly, it was hard not to gawk at the lavish accommodations, considering the near-squalor she had experienced in Moidia. Ma'ma had done her best with her limited resources and abilities. And how Isaura missed Laseria. What would the two of them have said of her and Dusan being bound?

Cetus flicked open a door onto a terratza. Just beyond the stones and long pool, a large green lawn invited her to its lushness. Beyond it, shrubs and small trees clustered under towering oaks.

Breath stolen at the vibrant colors, she touched her throat. Smiled as she left the cool shelter of the hall. Due to the height of the palace, shadows draped the courtyard. Aching for the sun's warmth, she strode toward the grass. Moidia was hard rock, dust, and dirt. Here she found the fragrant beauty of so many flowers she could not put name to them all. Ma'ma would love these for their medicinal purposes—and Dusan for their scents.

"All flora and fauna have purpose, Isaura. Learn them. Know them."

Could she just admire and appreciate them? Like the soft waxy bloom of the flower she cupped now? Or that one with its thin, delicate petals? Even the scalara bush with its razor-sharp thorns had its own beauty.

The sun rose high as she wandered the grounds, content to simply be in the quiet company of these unfamiliar yet inviting plants. Cetus remained a respectable distance to afford privacy but not risk her security. Ignoring the grumble of her stomach that told her it was past time to return to the house, she admired the tendril-like branches of a flower she did not know. Its blooms seemed to whisper on the wind. Determined to hear their voice, she removed herself to the stone bench beneath the arching frame. She would pluck some blossoms and make a flower circlet for her sister.

Oh, Laseria . . . How she ached for her sister's laugh and innocence.

Skittering in the nearby shrubs made her wonder what creature trespassed on her solitude. Seeing nothing, she leaned back against the bench.

With Dusan reasonably distracted with his duties as medora—she should practice calling him by his correct title and name—and her sister and ma'ma gone . . . A pang of loneliness stole over her.

The rustling came again, this time closer.

Head bent, she glanced to the hedgerow, sure she would spot the critter if she limited her movement.

A shiny nose poked from the space between dirt and waxy leaves. Intrigued, Isaura slipped over to it and crouched. "What have we here?" With care, she pushed aside the branch but saw nothing. She moved another. Craned her head, peering through the foliage.

Then something made her stand straight—she could not voice what. Some strange quaver in the air. Like breath. A very bad breath.

"My lady?" Cetus sounded concerned as he came near.

"I . . ." She glanced at the spot again. No movement. "I . . ." She swallowed. "Nothing . . . just . . . admiring."

Branches shifted—and took her heart with them. Less than a step from her own slippered feet, a boot appeared.

Isaura stepped back, her pulse crashing into her ribs, remembering the Irukandji who'd attacked in the forest. The reports of attacks in Jherako. Had they followed her and Dusan? But it would be too soon for them to be here . . .

Then had she imagined it?

In a particularly light area of the hedgerow, a face appeared. Hard, cruel eyes latched on her. Stole her breath. Lightning fast, he reached through and grabbed her arm. Yanked her forward. The moment was painfully slow and yet terrifyingly fast—the curl of writhing marks on his arm. The lecherous breath. Dirtied fingernails clawing into her arm.

Isaura screamed and struggled, her cheek scratched by thorns and branches. Terrified, she fought to extricate herself. Wished she had her moon discs. Knew if the raiders took her, she wouldn't be found alive.

She jerked hard. Broke free. Tumbled onto her backside. She scrambled away, but the man grabbed her ankle. Isaura screamed and flung herself around, digging her fingers into the grass. Even as Cetus lunged in her direction, the raider dragged her back.

"Help!"

A blur near the palace—a form leapt over the rail, slid down the slope of the covered terrace, and dove into a roll onto the lawn. Dusan came up, sprinting, his face a fury.

Thick, corded arms hauled her free.

Dusan pulled her to himself. "Are you okay?"

Breathless with fright, she nodded.

"Cetus, get her out of here," Dusan barked, turning her toward the regia. "Ixion, on me."

"Go!" Sword drawn, Cetus hurried her toward the house.

Numb yet terrified, Isaura saw Mavridis, his expression dark and enraged, sprinting across the terratza with Theilig to join the chase.

Cetus hooked her shoulder and gave her no choice but to run to the palace.

"Shut the gate! Sound the alarm!" came shouts from the walls of the palace.

More guards appeared, converging around Isaura, hurrying her through the passages.

She allowed the guards to rush her abovestairs. Even as they reached the top, more aerios joined them, and like driftwood shoved against the shore, Isaura was delivered into her quarters. Doors slammed shut and silence fell on her.

She spun, stunned to find herself alone in the ominous quiet of the apartments, drenched in the terror of what happened. When she exhaled, her breath sounded loud. She thought of Dusan confronting the raider. Of her father on his heels. And her . . . here, alone. Tears erupted with a choked sob. Trembling, she moved to a chair and dropped heavily into it, frightened and haunted. She did not want to lose the man who had just come to love her.

Never had he seen Marco in such a rage, sprinting through the garden, scaling a perimeter garden wall as if he were a spider.

Ixion ran the eight-foot stone fence like an agile, angry cat, then vanished on the other side. He hissed an oath and stopped short, scanning the wall in search of a gate. He would beat Marco for going off into the fray without him and forgetting his realm, his rule. Locating the opening, he sprinted down the wall with Shobi and a half dozen aerios converging on him.

A soft sound carried on the wind as Ixion gripped the heavy machi-wood gate—Hushak. His whistle said he'd located and joined their medora. The staccato pulsing drew him north. Relief punched him through the gate, anxious to reach them, and he signaled his approach to his captain. He paid attention to the tracks in the dirt, the way people lingering in the street stared in a particular direction, the frantic departure of rodents from alleys.

Ixion shoved past the crowd with the aerios intent on saving their medora. He slowed, entering a narrow alley steeped in the shadows of the tall buildings and ledges that perfectly blocked the sun. Long blades in hand, he squinted into shadows so wholly different from the garden in which this chase started.

A shape moved lithely through the alley—Marco.

Ixion had seen few so unafraid to plunge into dark settings. But the medora relied on a greater resource—his nose. That this young man would use wisdom, too . . .

He did not have Marco's heightened sense, but neither was he afraid. He would do what he must to protect the young man who now sat on the throne.

Shadows shifted and released their hold on the alley's occupants. A bulky shape seemed to drink the light and draw the eye.

Ixion tensed, his grip firm on his sword. "Crey," he growled a warning into the night.

When the Hirakyn swiveled toward him, something went for the man. Agile, fast. At first, he thought to name Marco, but . . . no. Theilig!

A series of soft thumps revealed Marco bouncing from one corner to another. Across a large series of crates. Into the air. With a walloping strike, he struck Crey in the head. The man flipped around. Went to a knee, fighting off the effects of the blow. Then surged upward, a blade glinting, catching some rogue torchlight. But he startled to a stop.

Ixion rushed forward even as a twittling sound rent the air.

"No!" Marco shouted as an arrow struck the Hirakyn. "Augh!" He jerked to Crey, then back to Ixion and the others. "Fools! What have you done?"

42

"He was going to kill you!" Theilig said.

"No—he wasn't. Crey was helping me corner the raider!" After having seen an unconscious and bleeding Crey to the royal pharmakeia, Marco stormed into Elek's mansion as the sinking sun cast a vivid glare off the western windows, his mind shifting to one purpose: he must know that Isaura was well. Earlier, as he stood in the great library with the elders, negotiating, her Signature that reeked of terror assaulted him. A rage unlike any he'd known yanked him from the meeting. Onto the balcony.

"We saw you attack him," Ixion said as they took to the stairs.

"Aye—the raider had been where Crey stood not seconds before. My blows were ill-timed . . . slow."

"Which we interpreted as an attack and identification of the culprit."

A growl of frustration forced its way up Marco's throat. "He *saved* my life." His own confusion was thick and his frustration thicker still—agitation reeling. "The raider was fast and wickedly skilled in evasion." His head ached from the strain of the hunt. "Most frustrating pursuit I've ever undertaken. One second his scent was there, the next it was gone. I detected Crey's scent outside the palace walls and tracked it, thinking—at first, as you did—that he was the assailant, but something was off." He drew up and expelled a breath. "They're suppressing their scents, and that comes from the Symmachians, who found a way to conceal their scents."

"That would explain much—but why would they even need or know to do that?" Ixion gained the upper level and instructed the machitis to guard the passages. "Nobody down this hall."

"It is as Vorn said—Symmachia may not have colonized Drosero, but they have infected it." Unable to shake the feeling that dreams of his death, the words of the Lady, and this aggressive move against them were just the beginning, Marco stalked down the hall to the apartments. "What do they want with this accursed planet?" When Edvian flicked open the door to the apartment, Marco stormed in, scanning. "Isaura?"

She rose from the chair, eyes puffy, hair askew. Her relief speared the air.

"You are well?" Tasting her relief when their gazes met, Marco went to her and held her shoulders. Assessed the scratches on her face, the slight reddening around her wrist, and that swell of fury rose again through his chest.

She nodded, but her green eyes were glossy and red-rimmed.

"I will make them pay." He pulled her against his chest, and her arms tightened around his waist as if he might disappear. "It won't happen again. We return to Kardia at first light. There, you'll be protected not only by aerios but regia."

"I'm safe as long as you're here."

Yet, she hadn't been. The enemy sought to steal her out from under his nose. "I must beg your mercy a while longer—the meeting is not yet finished."

Isaura straightened, glancing at Ixion, then back to him. "Must you?"

Her tremulous wave smacked him. "For a whi—"

"Rest, my liege," Ixion said with a nod, but never quite met his gaze, his scent one of awkwardness. "What is begun here can be completed in Kardia."

Marco frowned at his First.

"With your leave, I intend to speak with Elek then the Stalkers, and we will search until the attacker is found."

"I'll go with you."

Something dark passed through the tanned face, the gray hair strangely bright under the torchlight. "No." Ixion held up a gloved hand. "It is better—"

"He attacked my bound!"

"Aye, your kyria—my kyria!" Ixion held his gaze and his scent warbled in the air—the protectiveness of a father, the rage of a warrior whose king and queen were threatened. "And you, the medora, went off through the streets without thought to your safety or the possible repercussions if you were injured, captured, or killed." He tucked his chin. "I beg your deference, my liege, but your place is here with your kyria. Safe."

"*Safe* is an illusion." Marco's words negatively affected Isaura, who stiffened, and he regretted them immediately.

Ixion's jaw muscle bounced "Let your guard do their job."

Though he was right, it took several long seconds before Marco could accept it. To adjust to the role of protected when most of his life he had been the protector. He managed a curt nod before the Stalkers and aerios left. It felt like he'd been punished for doing what he knew to do, what he was capable of doing.

Isaura sighed. "The way you sailed off that balcony and onto the grass as if it were no more than a step . . ." She shook her head.

He traced the scratch along her cheekbone, the one across her forehead, the smaller one on her jaw. "I would do more than that for you." As he stood before her, Marco recalled the darkness that had raged through his veins, thinking of her injured. Of the villain succeeding. "Had I found who attacked you . . ."

She touched his face, and though he twinged that there was still no second light in her eyes, hers was as pure as ever. She tilted her head. "What is that?"

Marco frowned. "What?"

"It's the second time you have looked at me like that in as many days. Almost like regret."

He tightened his hold. "Never."

She laced her arms around his shoulders. "Then what?"

To explain would be to injure her by mentioning Kersei, who had been so far from his thoughts this past week.

"You will not trust me?" She brushed her fingers through his hair, a very distracting and enticing act.

"It is not trust," he said. "I don't want to injure you."

A knock came at the door, and sergii entered with food trays.

"Mavridis suggested you might prefer to remain in chamber this evening," Hushak said. "Food is tested and safe." Meaning either he or Cetus had sampled it.

"Thank you," Marco said as the staff set the small table with the silver and porcelain, from which they removed serving domes. Steam escaped in a rushed spiral from the plates and spiked the air with the spicy, tangy aroma.

Once they exited, he motioned Isaura to the seat and pulled it out for her.

Her embarrassment was attractive and made him love all the more her humility, which was as much a part of her beauty as the blonde hair and green eyes. "What did you discuss with the elders?"

Marco cut into his steak. "My brother."

Isaura lifted her gaze from the food she speared on her fork.

"There is evidence he has colluded with Hirakys and the Symmachians. To what extent, I cannot be sure, but it is clearly not in the best interest of Kalonica."

Isaura ate, her scent rising and falling—first grief, then frustration, then resignation. "Was a resolve reached about Darius?"

Marco sighed heavily. "That is what we were arguing about . . ."

She considered him with a flicker of a frown. After a sip of wine, she set down the glass. "Why?"

"If charges are brought, I would be without a brother." He suddenly wanted fermented cordi.

Isaura's color drained.

"Our reintroduction to each other has been fraught from the beginning. If I hand down a writ ordering his execution, as the medora must do—deliver the vote of the Council of Elders—no matter the law and the evidence of Darius's guilt, I will look the villain." He set aside his fork and knife. "And I would never do that to Kersei."

"Because you love her still?"

Marco started, then frowned. "Because she is with child. Because he is a prince of Kalonica, and because we have war at our doors and heavens."

"But if this evidence is clear, then he betrayed his country, his people—you!"

"I know!" Hearing his voice echo in the room, Marco fisted his hands over his plate. "Forgive me." He huffed and sat back. Her scents were too confusing, and he had his own complicated thoughts to sort through, so he closed his receptors. "Let us not spoil our meal."

Once done, he excused himself and went to the desk. He drew out paper and pen, noting Isaura select a book from the shelves and situate herself near the fire. He started writing through options. Determinations of what could be done. The situation with Darius must be addressed—it was the only thing he and the elders agreed upon. Execution was out of the question, no matter what law justified or demanded it.

"It is treason—he must pay with his life," Elek had insisted.

"How—" Marco clamped his mouth, not wanting to unleash the torrent he felt about this. "How am I to order my brother's death when I have just gotten him back?"

Tenderness flared, and she set aside her book.

"No, I do not want pity!" He punched to his feet and paced the room. There had to be a way . . . "I want answers. I want Darius to have a good head on his shoulders, to not have done this to our name, to our father, to Kersei!"

Isaura seemed to withdraw into herself.

"He is going to be a father. How am I to leave that child fatherless? Then what of Kersei? What of the army?" He crumpled the paper and pitched it across the room. A part of him wondered . . . was this how . . . the vision, how Kersei was his—that Darius would be executed?

The thought appalled him. Galled.

"Dusan," she said quietly, "he has done a grave ill, but the repercussions are not on your head."

"But they are, Isaura. *They are.*" He motioned around them with a wide sweep of his arm. "The whole of this realm will say I conspired to get rid of

Darius, and even sitting in Elek's library, that's exactly how it felt, the feelings I anak'd from some in that room."

"That would not make sense, since you and I are bound," Isaura said quietly.

His gaze struck hers, realizing his careless thoughts had injured her. "Happily bound," he added. But then he motioned with his arm again. "No matter his crime, I would not see Darius executed. I never knew my father, not really, and I wouldn't wish that on any boy. He's the only family I have left." He stared into the fire and willed the answers to come to him. For the Lady to speak—just once—when he needed her to speak.

"Boy?"

He flicked a hand, unwilling to be pulled off topic. "There must be a way. I have to find it."

Arms slid around his shoulders from behind, and Isaura held onto him, the warmth of her cheek bleeding through his shirt. "You will. It angers because you care about him and do not want to lose your brother. But Darius knows he has done wrong, and a man of character will own his mistakes and accept the punishment."

"*I* cannot accept it. This land needs Darius—*he* has a keen way with politicians and has been working to solidify alliances. I've seen his reports, and without him . . ."

"Can you do anything if he is found guilty?"

"He *is* guilty." Marco was grateful for her touch that soothed, along with her lavender and white oak Signature. "It is a cruel, hard thing. He has tied my hands viciously. Yet uncertainty remains about his character—is he a good man acting under some misguided sense of right? Or is he corrupt?"

On his feet, he paced again. Could he allow Darius to keep his title? It was a birthright. He must be removed as praefectus of the armies—they couldn't trust him not to pollute the army after colluding with the enemy.

Marco smacked the wall. "Augh! I could wring his ruddy neck!" He raked a hand through his hair. "But the enemy won't win. There has been too much loss already!"

Back at his desk, he worked out solutions . . . that didn't work. Over and over. Darius must be made to feel the weight of his crime. Where was this nefarious fine line that would be punishment enough yet allow Darius to remain in place—for Kersei, for the son she carried, for Kalonica . . . for him?

Hands nearly blackened with ink and shoulders aching from hours spent over the desk, he sat back in the chair and rubbed his dry, tired eyes. When he did, a glimmer of gold caught his attention, and he looked to the bed. Isaura was in nightclothes—when had she done that?—and sat with pillows propped behind her, reading a book perched on drawn-up legs. She was uncoiling her hair, its strands catching the light of the touchstone.

Go to her.

The thought was unbidden but not unwanted. He glanced at his hands, at the piles of scribbled, scrunched paper. How long had he worked to the exclusion of her? How had he been so focused that her Signature faded—

No, it hadn't faded. It'd been there, supporting, encouraging.

She smiled at him. "Did you solve it?"

He snorted. "Hardly."

"You should rest," she said. "We have had several long days, and working on matters of this import needs a fresh mind."

Yawning, Marco couldn't argue—the solution was elusive and taunting. He used a cloth and oil to clean his hands, then rinsed them at the basin and washed his face. He closed the bedchamber door and shrugged out of his doublet, his mind entrenched in his brother's betrayal. Not just of Marco, but of Kersei—what would she think?

Boots tugged off, he dropped back against the mattress and let out a long breath. "Six months ago, I was a hunter minding his own business. Now, I am married, my brother is a traitor, the elders question my ability to lead, and there are many who think me too weak to fight for the land my father ruled."

"The elders are children caught up in their own selfish game of Capture the Keep." Isaura had an unusual bite to her words. "It was elders who forced my father to send us away. They keep to the old ways and, as such, are responsible for the fact that the princessa had no say in whether she would bind."

"Or you."

"You forget? My petition was only upon my acceptance, and I am no fool, so I agreed." Her smile was coy. "My situation has, of all fortunes, turned out best."

"You are far too generous with your praise, my lady."

"Have you seen the man I am bound to? He's quite the specimen and—"

"Specimen! Am I a lab experiment?"

"—has the most gorgeous blue eyes and, while his manners are sometimes lacking and females cluck at his heels—"

Marco barked a laugh and reached for her.

She leaned away. "I am happy to report that he is *mine*. And he will be the finest medora this land has ever seen."

With a chuckle, he dragged her laughing self to him, rolling her over. "I would like to meet this husband of yours. He sounds infinitely better than the one in your bed."

She gasped. "Speak not of Medora Marco in such a way! I will have you run out of the city!"

Laughing at her playfulness, Marco brushed her hair aside and hovered over her.

Her smile slipped, her anticipation once more thick.

Marco touched his lips to hers. "Good lady." He kissed each side of her mouth, the scratch on her chin, the one on her cheek, and the one her forehead. "I do not deserve you."

Her arms around him and the soft sounds from her throat as he kissed her welcomed him once more into the bliss of her love.

Alarm snapped Marco awake. He anak'd nearby scents, his thoughts immediately on protecting Isaura, lying on her side in front of him and sound asleep. He listened to the happenings of the castle. It was strange to share a bed with someone. Was that what had startled him awake? His receptors were drenched in Isaura's Signature and nothing nefarious.

He rested his hand along her hip and pressed his face into her hair, but even as he did, he could not shake—

Wood creaked.

Flashing open his receptors, Marco stilled. There was something . . . The hairs on the back of his neck stood straight. Just like in the woods and alley, he felt more than anak'd the presence moving closer. The threat hovering. A scent . . . hidden.

Raider!

He whipped up—right into something hard that cracked against his skull. Sprinkled his vision with darts of pain. He felt Isaura come up. Heard and sensed her sleepy confusion, then panic.

She screamed.

"No." He turned back to her but felt himself being pulled away.

Her gaze met his, their hands catching. "Isaura."

"Dusan!"

He froze at what he saw. Wait—

Crack!

A torrent of pain slammed him into darkness.

Ixion stretched out on the bed, too tired to undress, staring at the ornate bedpost. He was irritated they had spent hours searching for the attacker to no avail. Footprints and a broken gate lock, but no attacker. Crey was confined to a servant's room under guard until Ixion had time to sort the matter. He understood that Marco believed the man not a threat, but the coincidence was too great—he had been in the same area as the attacker who tried to snatch the kyria.

My daughter.

Strange the tides that moved in his life. He was proud of Isaura. Before Marco's interest in her, she had been but a girl with silly ideas and too much the image of her mother. Now, watching her with the medora . . . A force unto her own, she would sit on a throne.

Ixion had greatly underestimated her.

For her sake and everyone else's, the sooner he could get her and Marco to Kardia, the better. Events of late had been dark. He snorted, recalling the days he had thought fighting the Irukandji on the border was exhausting. Now the savages invaded Kalonica and offworlders infected and usurped. And the prince betrayed. Everything had upended—even his own blood.

A long, piercing trio of whistles seared the air, snatching Ixion from near slumber. Attack!

He shot from bed, grabbing armor and blades. Running through the halls, he secured his baldric and scanned the passages. He called after aerios. Foreboding washed through him, seeing the direction in which aerios ran. "What trouble?" He rounded the corner and slowed. Empty. No guards. "No."

He lunged the last few paces and pitched himself into the royal apartments. Three aerios swung toward him, swords drawn, expressions daunted but fierce. Four more pushed forcefully on the bedchamber door.

"What is this?" Ixion demanded, stalking across the sitting room.

"Screams," Theilig barked. "I heard the kyria scream. When I entered the apartments and inquired at the bedchamber door, there was no answer—still nothing—and the door is barred."

Ixion threw himself at the barrier. "Marco! Marco, open up!" He pounded, and when no response came, he indicated to the men to continue. "Isaura!"

The door bucked but held. Over and over, it held, the thick machi wood designed as much for protection from the cold as from an enemy.

"I know another way." One of Elek's aerios darted out of the room.

"Keep trying! Our medora is in trouble!" Ixion pointed to a machitis. "Sound the alarm through the castle. Get those bells ringing!" They tried again to break open the door, then he nodded at it. "On three!"

Theilig shouldered into it.

A heavy scrape of metal sounded on the other side, freezing them.

The door opened. The aerios had lost his color. "He's gone. The medora is gone. The kyria lies dead!"

Shock vaulted Ixion into the room. "No! Isaura!" He threw himself at the bed where she lay in naught but a shift, sagged at an odd angle, blood seeping from her temple. Every vestige of composure vanished as he sought to cover her, raging that they had been attacked in their own bed. "Kaveh, Edvian, how did they get past you?"

"They did not—no one entered," Kaveh countered.

Ixion felt at Isaura's throat for a pulse, but he could not discern hers from his own pounding pulse as he visually searched for other wounds. Then he saw the rise and fall of her chest. "She lives."

"This way," Theilig growled, holding back a tapestry. "This is how the attackers entered and left—same route the aerios came through to unbar the doors. It seems our medora was dragged out this passage. There's blood."

Isaura moaned and shifted beneath his touch.

"Thank the Ladies!"

She blinked awake, then went wild. Lunged forward. "No!"

The wildness was too familiar. Clenched his stomach. Ixion grabbed her flailing arms. "Isa—"

"Dusan!" she wailed. "They took him!"

"Easy," he said.

"No, he's gone! They shot him—took him! We must—"

"Be still, Isaura! You're injured." He hated the way his sharp words silenced her—as they had once silenced another. Grieved, he looked over his shoulder to Hushak. "Get the pharmakeia."

"I'm here," an older man answered, shouldering past the aerios. "Think I could sleep with all this noise?"

"She took a blow." Ixion moved aside for the pharmakeia. "Regia, stay with your kyria. Hushak, Shobi on me." With a nod, he hurried toward the servants' passage where an aerios lay in a pool of blood. Four more Stalkers appeared beyond the body. "Anything?"

"Only this," Axeon said, pointing to the ground. "Blood."

"On me!" Following the spots that were continuously wet and not lessening, Ixion grew concerned. If that was Marco's blood . . . was he bleeding out?

A thud came from above.

Ixion looked up, thinking through the passages, the layout of the palace.

"The great library," Hushak muttered.

"Going for the grand terratza!" Ixion hurried to the end of the hall where stone gave way to stairs and took them two at a time. They rounded the last turn and slid up against the wall as light scampered beneath the thick tapestry flapping wildly in the opening. Light shards skated through the tiny holes in the fabric. A noise vibrated the air.

Ixion's heart jarred. "Ship!" He darted to the tapestry and glanced around the opening.

A yellow beam seared toward him. Smelling of singed fibers, a hole appeared in the fabric.

With a warning to his Stalkers, he shoved into the open, sighting the armored men as he stole across the grand ballroom to the relative safety behind a large sideboard. Huffing out labored breaths, he processed what he'd seen: two armored Symmachians carrying a limp Marco up into the ship while a couple more stood guard, one on a knee, aiming a phase rifle in their direction.

Ixion peered around the sideboard. Time was slipping away. Marco had been hustled out of sight.

Axeon appeared on the far end of the tapestry, his motion a blur as he vaulted the sword, end over end, at the enemy. It thunked loudly against armor before clattering to the stones.

The Symmachian glanced down and, though he wore a helmet that covered his face, it seemed he laughed at Axeon's attempt. "You'll have to try harder than that," his mechanized voice mocked.

"Be ready," Ixion said to Hushak, then gripped his swords, shoved to his feet, and pivoted around the credenza as Hushak and Shobi rose with nocked arrows to provide protective cover.

"I wasn't trying at all," Axeon said, diving as the Symmachian fired at him. "Just wanted you looking this way."

Ixion sprinted across the room. Shoved up on a small tufted sofa. Launched himself into an aerial, crossing his arms and arcing his body over the Symmachian. The shiny domed face watched.

Light pulsed from the weapon.

His right boot landed, and with that touch, he yanked his swords in opposite directions. Sparks flew as his blades severed the air and whatever other mechanical connection the helmet had. With a strange hiss, the helmeted head rolled free.

Fire seared Ixion's arm as he turned and launched into the humid morning. Toward the rear bay door of the ship, which was closing. *No!* He dropped the swords and dove at the ship. Caught the lip of the rising bay door as it lifted from the terrace. Hauled himself up, only to see an armored boot coming at him.

With timed precision, he grabbed at the foot and jerked hard, pulling the Symmachian out with him. He dropped, realizing there was far too much air between him and the ground.

The Symmachian jerked to a stop midair, thanks to his mechanical suit, and a hoist line drew him back into the ship.

Ixion had no such fortune. He slammed hard against the terrace. Air punched from his body. Groaning, he arched his back and tried to breathe. Watched the ship disappearing.

They'd won. The Symmachians had captured Marco.

"How do you like the *Chryzanthe*, Mr. Crafter?"

Sevart "Rhinn" Crafter turned from the window and nodded at the colonel. "It's impressive. Even after two weeks aboard, I'm still seeing things I hadn't noticed."

Colonel Galt couldn't possibly know he'd been here before on a violent insertion and extraction of Kersei Dragoumis, then a second time, helping the Kynigos escape. His days with Eidolon 215 had been exciting at best and confusing at worst. Then Tigo and Jez sniffed their own CO_2, shot him, and escaped. The reminder pinched the nerve at the back of his neck.

"And are the Shepherds doing well?"

"They are, ma'am." He turned to the dining hall fancied up for this evening's gathering with the HyPE Commission, the admiralty, and the Shepherds, who looked as uncomfortable as he felt in their Class A's, brown-nosing the brass.

"You think they're ready?" she asked.

"Never know until they go." He smirked. "But I trust them enough to climb into the rocket with them and light the fuse."

She smiled—and *Void's Embrace*, he understood why Tigo once had a thing for this officer. "Good. And Zacdari? I understand there were concerns about her before leaving Symmachia."

"There were, but something yanked the kinks out of her O_2 line, because she's been straight as an arrow since. One of the best pilots I've seen. Girl's got instinct."

"Indeed she does," Galt murmured, her gaze landing on Zacdari huddled in a corner with the little medic, Shad.

"Colonel." Fleet Admiral Domitas Deken joined them. "We have to travel hundreds of thousands of kilometers to see each other," he teased.

Colonel Galt nodded to the admiral, a demure smile slipping into place. "I'm surprised you're here, Admiral. I heard the fleet was running maneuvers."

"We're always maneuvering," Deken said with a wave, then his gaze hit

Rhinn's. "You're Crafter."

"Was kind of hoping you wouldn't remember, sir."

Deken laughed—and Rhinn saw then how much Tigo looked like his father. "Bygones."

"Sorry about your son, sir."

Though largely inscrutable, the admiral couldn't steel himself that time. Emotion rippled through his strong features. "Thank you. And good job with the Shepherds. They seem like a fine team to make the first jump."

"Would've been better with Tigo at the helm, but Jadon is a Tigo in the making."

The admiral considered the young man now chatting up another admiral. "Good, glad to hear it." He nodded to Rhinn. "If you'll excuse us, I need to speak with the colonel."

With a nod, Rhinn headed to the dessert buffet. He felt a fast approach from his seven.

"Hey." Diggins sounded excited.

"Surprised they let you off the rock, what with your butter thumbnail." He eyed the shiny double gold arcs on his buddy's shoulder.

Diggs skipped the banter. "AO's been digging—he thinks there's proof our golden girl isn't from Nape."

Rhinn scowled. "Waddya mean? She's as Napian as any I've encountered."

"All two of them?"

"I still encountered them." He set a lemon bar on his plate and licked his thumb. "She checked out."

"If she entered as Napian, she didn't have to take the plague test."

"She ain't sick."

"Aren't you worried?"

"Why? She's the best, and she's got a lot of grav about her. I wouldn't want anyone else."

"There's something not right about this," Diggs muttered.

"You're just worried you'll get shot again."

"You were shot, too."

"Wasn't my first, won't be my last." He paused, considered the jump. "I have a question: why hasn't anyone asked if this is smart, opening a wormhole—"

"It's not a wormhole."

"Whatever. Science ain't my thing. Shooting and keeping my team alive is. What if we're opening a gate to the enemy? What if they jump through and—"

"And what?"

Rhinn shrugged. "Anything could happen, and you know that's true after Tigo."

With a disgusted grunt, Diggs returned to the high-ranking officers and blended right in. A talent Rhinn did not have. So he planted his backside in a chair and went to work on the dessert—real sweet pastries and delicacies. Not the protein-altered numbers they fed Alpha. He eyed the table. Maybe he should've gotten more. After all, he'd be eating rehydrated food for the foreseeable future. "Definitely need more." He aimed for the cheesecakes.

". . . not listening to me, Domitas. There have been large purchases of titanium, high-grade steel, and Kevlar."

At Galt's list of items—classic materials for station-building—Rhinn slowed in his dessert selection, training an ear on the colonel and admiral.

"Alestra, in case you forgot, we're a space command. Those are vital—"

"Yes," she hissed, no doubt trying to keep her words between them, "but you and I both know there have been no treaties put before the TSC to build. I can't even get funds to update weapons for my Marines."

"You're being absurd. Those materials are always being purchased for upgrades and repairs."

"What about four nuclear propulsion contracts?"

A pause. "How do you know about those?"

Rhinn froze—nuclear propulsion. That was needed for big hauls. They'd used that to build Volante station. Something formidable enough to transport the large pieces necessary to assemble the station.

"What matters is why these things are being bought."

"I'm not a purchasing manager, Alestra." Deken laughed, but it sounded fake. "And I'd get back to monitoring these kids going through HyPE, or Krissos might think you're trying to steal his job. You have job security with the Beta and Charlie teams. Keep it. Make it great."

"Is that a threat?"

"Don't read into this. I'm not your enemy. You've been an officer long enough to know none of us is briefed on everything."

"Why is Jair purchasing large tracts of land on Cenon?"

"Summer home?" He laughed. "How the scuz do I know—and why would I care how he spends his budget?"

"Then there's the silicone and Teflon-coated cloth."

Protective measures for a station. Rhinn was seriously bugged about this now.

As the colonel inched closer, her voice lowering, Rhinn found himself shifting nearer as well, remembering to chew and act normal as he eavesdropped.

"I may not wear orbs, Domitas, but I'm intelligent enough to know all those things point to more of those metal flowers being built. Where? Why? What is going on?"

"How would I know?"

"Do not give me that! You're admiral of the fleet."

"Yes, *fleet*. What you're suggesting would be handled through the TSC and interplanetary accords, not Symmachian Command." With each word the admiral's voice was getting colder, harder. "Get your head on straight, Colonel!"

Rhinn found himself cowering, even though he wasn't involved in that conversation.

"Then can you verify the *Damocles* and *Macedon* prepping to—"

"Void's Embrace, Alestra! What is this, an interrogation? And why do you even know about these things?"

"I have many friends and many connections."

"Maybe you should stick to your job, not worry about everyone else's."

"Admiral, Colonel, you're ruining the evening."

Slag. That was Captain Baric. Rhinn told himself to move on, stop eavesdropping. But this . . . what the colonel had found out . . . it made sense. It made a lot of sense.

Then again, it didn't.

"Captain," Deken grunted.

Galt lifted her chin in acknowledgement. "Captain Baric."

Rhinn shifted away and stood to the side, eyeballing them. Galt looked peeved at Baric and Deken, who seemed like two wolves who'd cornered their prey. He felt like he was watching a docuvid where it was about to get bloody.

"Nicely done with this, Captain," Deken said. "I've talked to several of the Shepherds. They're a bright bunch."

What was he complimenting Baric for? He hadn't trained these Sheps— that'd been Rhinn and Diggs.

"Thank you, Admiral," Baric said, stealing the glory. "It's going smoothly."

Well, that'd been anticlimactic—and surprising. He'd expected the admiral to continue in on Galt. Why hadn't he? She'd all but accused him of building more space stations—in Herakles and without authorization or treaties in place.

Rhinn was about to move closer when he spotted Jadon and Zacdari heading his way. Slag, how could he eavesdrop and talk to them at the same time? "Enjoying yourselves?" He checked the officers.

"Sure," Jadon said at the same time she said, "No."

"Well, good." Either way. "Training resumes at 0600."

"Sir." After a glance to Zacdari, Jadon huffed. Tightened his lips. "Did our timeline change?"

Rhinn frowned. "Training every day until we jump in two weeks." But something in the kid's face unsettled him. "Why?"

"I might've heard—"

"May I have your attention, please?" Hand lifted, Admiral Ahron puffed his chest, medals clinking as he shifted to verify everyone was listening. "We have wonderful news to share."

Jadon gave Rhinn a long look, then nodded toward the admiral, as if to say, "*See?*"

"The Shepherd's training and progress here on the *Chryzanthe* has exceeded our expectations and in a significantly shorter time than anticipated. Therefore, the Commission has voted unanimously to move up the launch. We make history in two days!"

Were they out of their plague-rotted minds?

Elation and terror spiraled through Eija. On the one hand, she'd finally get out of here—an answer to a thousand pleas to the Heavenlies. But on the other, they hadn't done any live practice jumps. *AKA we aren't ready.* This was the stupidest thing she'd seen the Commission do.

And yet, something in her core—right over the warm spot at the base of her sternum—said it was time. Which scared her because . . . *time for what?*

Reef slowly shook his head, apparently having the same misgivings. Bashari and Gola were giddy, and Milek looked livid. Shy Shad was petrified.

Eija swallowed, staring at the puffed-up egos and jutting jaws of the Commission. They were proud of themselves. Of course they were. They had nothing to lose. During launch, they'd be behind a poly-alloy reinforced shield while she and the others would be sitting on a megaton bomb of a corvette, retrofitted to accommodate the crew for an extended period. Extended being six weeks. That was the official time it'd take to reach Kuru System and resupply. A distance that'd normally take forty years.

As the Commission members returned to their chatter, Milek shifted to Reef. Shoulder angled down, chin tucked, he flared his nostrils. "What're they doing? This is insane. We aren't ready. We do this—we launch, we die!"

Reef raised his hand. "Let's regroup in my quarters and talk there. Not here—too many ears."

"It's *those* ears that *need* to hear!" Milek growled.

"I get it," Reef said entirely too calmly, "but what're you going to do? March over there and tell them they can't do this?"

Milek's jaw muscle jounced, anger rolling off him.

Something skittered along Eija's spine, leaving a cold, tingling awareness. Head cocked, she slid her gaze to the doors. As if responding to her attention, they opened. And in walked that creature.

Gasps whispered around the dining hall.

"You all know Xisya," Captain Baric said proudly. "I felt it important that those who have not personally met her had the chance. She is, after all, responsible for this entire project to bridge the gap between our systems and species. We owe her a tremendous debt!"

Debt? More like death.

THE SENTINEL STANDS READY. THE TIME IS COME.

At the blast of ice that came with those words, Eija cringed. She did her best not to look around. She shifted behind the others, glad to have a barrier between her and the creature that had completely and irrevocably altered her. She could hear things—*hello, Sentinel?*—and sense things. The new night terrors alone were enough to keep her mouth shut and her nerves fried.

Granted, the intensity seemed to be waning. Or maybe she was just getting used to it. Whichever, she was finally able to focus on things other than the voice that kept invading her thoughts. The only time she felt unaltered was in the simulators. In those, her brain found equilibrium. Which made exactly zed sense.

Someone came up behind her, and Eija tried to steady her nerves, anticipating their intrusion. Hating that she knew someone was there. It was disorienting.

"You've done very well."

Eija pivoted. "Patron!" It surprised that she wore a full uniform and even more surprising was the nameplate: Galt. Shock wafted through her—*Colonel* Galt.

Her touch was light against Eija's arm. Then Patron's eyes went wide.

Not liking that look, Eija stiffened. "What's wrong?"

"Did Xisya implant you?"

Eija nodded, desperately wanting to tell her patron about all the things that had happened since, but knowing if she did, Galt might pull her from the mission. That couldn't happen. She was too close to jumping out of this quadrant.

"That creature may know the truth about you now."

"That I'm from Try—"

"More than that, but don't worry." Patron gave her a nod. "Your body will nullify the effect."

What did the reactions to the PICC-line have to do with her background?

Patron Galt's left eye narrowed slightly and a weird . . . aroma wafted around her. Or maybe it was from the dessert table. "Has something happened . . . since the implant . . .?"

Eija's pulse tripped over the question. "Yes," she breathed, relieved to have it told. "I can—"

"No! Not here." Patron Galt drew herself straight. "Do not be afraid of what's happening to you. It will protect you—as will I."

"How will you protect me on the *Prevenire*?"

"Once you're on it, she won't be able to stop you."

She. The creature. Xisya. Alarm pulsed through Eija, and she felt Reef's gaze, so she glanced away. Then she remembered . . . "You promised to tell me who my parents were if I—"

"If she hasn't tried to eliminate you yet—"

"*Eliminate*? What—"

"Quiet," Galt warned. "*This* is why you were on Tryssinia, why your parents—"

"Colonel Galt!" Baric's voice snapped through the room, his commanding tone jerking several people around. "A word, please!"

"Be strong," Galt whispered as she stepped away.

"Wait, no—" Frustrated she didn't have the rest of that sentence or answers about her parents, Eija watched Patron go.

" . . . *why your parents—*" Why they what? And how had Galt known something changed in Eija since the implant? Why wouldn't she let her mention it?

"What was that about?" Reef was beside her, his gaze discreet but curious.

"Nothing," Eija muttered. What had the colonel been about to say? Why did the few words she'd spoken seem to flay open all of Eija's misgivings, which had grown each day on this satellite? She never should have listened to her mysterious Patron, but she'd been so desperate to get off that plague-riddled planet.

"Shepherds are ready to talk," Reef said, touching her elbow.

After a nod, Eija hurried toward the door, unwilling to let anyone stop her. She needed to get out. Needed air. Needed someone to tell her what the djell was going on.

"Are they out of their scuzzing minds?" Milek hissed as they started around the circular passage toward their quarters. "We go out now—"

"Not yet." Reef eyed something behind them.

Eija glanced back and flinched at the Eidolon twenty paces away. The red stripe on his epaulet marked him commander of his team. Hands at his sides, he walked casually . . .

Why would Eidolon be following them? It wasn't like they could go anywhere.

"My quarters." Reef pointed around the juncture.

"Shepherds," the Eidolon intoned from behind. He waited until they stopped and turned. "You're ordered back to your quarters for the remainder of the night."

"We just wanted a few minutes to talk about the laun—"

"Now," the Eidolon said, his words firmer. Harder.

Two more Eidolon joined the first, pulse pistols strapped to their legs. Eidolon were armed at all times. But seeing the way their hands stayed ominously close to the grips . . .

You're imagining things. Yeah, thing of it was—she'd suddenly become very good at imagining things. Like the strange lavabeasts. The icy-hot feeling. The sense of being haunted. Or the vague notion of always being watched.

"I want to talk to Chief Crafter." Reef pushed past them.

Roiling anger and defiance rushed over her, then drew back and enfolded her in . . . pain, grief. Somehow Eija knew the anger—Reef's—was followed by what he would feel—pain, grief—if he persisted. She caught his arm as the commander lifted his weapon.

Eija looked into his eyes and tried desperately to convey the urgency of what she felt hanging in the air. *Please . . . please don't . . .*

Confused irises seemed to swell as he held her gaze, but he nodded. "Right." He shook his head as if coming out of a fog.

An unsettling nausea swirled through Eija as she released him, unsure what just happened. Turning toward her quarters, she saw the Eidolon holster his weapon. Without a word, the Shepherds accessed their rooms. Doors whispered closed, and Eija was left alone with the plaguing question—why had Reef obeyed her thoughts as if he'd heard them?

Was Dusan dead? Had they killed him?

Numb, Isaura dressed in a fog, tears slipping free as Kita and Maritza attended her. Over and over, Dusan being ripped from her played in her mind. She'd felt him bolt awake and heard a crack of bones. She whirled as he reached toward her. Their fingers touched just as he was shot. His blood splattered her, and he fell limp against the coverlet. Men with black helms and armor dragged him off the bed, amid her screaming. Another man slammed something against her head. She had awakened to aerios in the bedchamber, a blazing headache, and the cruel truth that Dusan was gone.

A weight settled on her head, and Isaura snapped back to the present. She touched her brow and felt something cold and hard. What . . .?

"No," Maritza said. "Elders Mavridis and Elek insisted."

Ignoring her, Isaura removed the piece and felt relief at its absence from her still-pounding head. She stared dumbly at the golden vine with entangled gems, including a large lavender gem dangling in the center. It made little sense to wear a crown when the man who made her kyria was gone.

She would be named a usurper. "No. It's not right."

"Your Majesty, if I may?" The kindly voice belonged to an older man, one she had seen around the palace talking with Dusan.

When he did not come forward, she realized he waited for permission. She wiped her tears. "Of course." Her voice sounded raw. Like her heart.

He came before her and bowed at the waist, enabling her to see the skin tags peppering the bridge of his nose and cheeks. "My name is Ypiretis, and I am friend and advisor to Medora Marco."

"He is gone." Why she said it, she did not know. Clearly he was aware. As all were in this wretched palace of stone that did not protect the one man who dared see value in her.

"Aye, but his responsibilities are not."

Isaura scoffed. "What can be done about them? Did you not hear me? He is gone!" Tears were hot and fresh down her cheeks, and she cared not.

"I have begun poorly, my kyria."

She accepted the kerchief Kita offered and dabbed at her tears. "As have I," she conceded. "I beg your mercy." What did this man want? Could he not see she wanted to be alone? "I do not mean to be unkind, Ypiretis, but what do you need of me?"

A gentle smile creased the corners of his eyes. "It is not I who am in need of anything from you, my lady. It is the people."

Her heart stumbled at that. "The people?"

"The Council of Elders has gathered in the great hall and would speak with you."

"Have they learned something of Dusan's kidnappers?"

"No," he said softly. "They must crown his kyria and return her to Kardia, so she may be the representative of her husband in his stead."

"Husband." It was a strange word with a pleasing sound, for it conjured Dusan with his brooding eyes and rogue smirk. "Crown . . . me." She glanced at the diadem Maritza had set on her head.

"Aye, it was suggested by Elder Mavridis that perhaps I could coach you a little about the process while they prepare for your arrival."

And so, for the next two oras, he went over the guiding laws of the land, which stated that in the medora's absence, the kyria acted as representative. He reassured her that the time would be short, for all were convinced Dusan would be returned to them. But he also promised she was not alone. There would be Prince Darius—the traitor. Princessa Kersei—Dusan's first love. Mavridis— the father who denied her.

She sniffed. Never had she felt more alone than this moment. To know so great a love then have it ripped from her hands . . .

"My lady." Lifting the crown, Maritza set it once more on her head. "They wait for you." She guided Isaura to the door.

Isaura thought to ask Kita to walk with her, hold her hand, give her strength she did not have, but that would not bode well for the kyria who would now carry the weight of the crown. In this she must walk alone.

Theilig and Cetus jerked to attention. "Your Majesty."

Feeling strange at the title, Isaura stepped out. She frowned at the number of aerios in the passage. "Why are you all here?" Her throat was hoarse from crying. "Why are you not looking for him?"

Theilig seemed aggrieved. "The elders await, my lady. They can answer you."

Pulling in her frustration, she allowed the aerios to deliver her to the grand hall. When she entered, Isaura slowed at the gathered crowd. Half the size of the dinner at which she and Dusan had been bound. But still, too many.

"Isaura," someone bellowed, "Kyria of Kalonica and bound of Marco. All rise."

She stiffened as the whole room snapped to attention and bowed as she passed. *This is not right.* But it was as it needed to be—for now. Isaura took in Mavridis, Elder Sebastiano, and Elder Elek and the many others in the room. Close to twenty men. All waiting, watching.

She touched her forehead, inadvertently knocking the jewel that hung there.

"The Heart of Kardia," Mavridis said. "*You* are that heart now."

"Please. I want him back."

He inclined his head. "As do we all . . . Your Majesty."

"Your throne, my kyria," Elek called from the center of the room, where a large chair carved with an aetos waited. So like the one in her dream.

Her insides squeezed as she gained the throne. Welcoming the relief of sitting, she clasped her hands and shuddered around a breath. Felt as if that aetos were an omen over her. Fought tears for the thousandth time, thinking—*knowing* Dusan should sit here. The thought helped her focus. "What know you of Dusan's kidnapping?"

Mavridis stood at attention, not answering his daughter, but his kyria. "I gave chase to the upper level where I failed to stop *Medora Marco*"—his tone was instructive, reminding her to use his title—"from being stolen away by Symmachians on a spacecraft."

"Symmachians. Was he . . . alive?" Hope burned.

"Unconscious, I believe, Your Majesty. They would not steal him away if he were dead." His words were meant as comfort.

"Why?" She tried not to sound petulant. "Why would they take him?" She had no hope of saving him now. There was no ship here, no . . . Wait . . . A thought shot through her and pulled her straight. "Vorn."

Mavridis scowled and gave a quick, almost imperceptible shake of his head, reminding her that Vorn was part of a secret. What a terrible, perfect secret Dusan had agreed to keep, and she had nearly ruined it.

"What is it?" Elek inquired.

Mavridis's cheek twitched. "There were attacks the morning we departed Jherako, as our medora told when we met yesterday. The kyria"—his gaze was sharp, warning her to respect Dusan's promise—"was concerned it might be the same brigands."

"Ah," Elek said with a nod.

Irritated with his lie and the oath that protected the other king, Isaura huffed.

"Your grief and frustration are ours as well, my kyria," Elder Sebastiano clipped out. "I have but returned to Trachys this ora, and with your permission, we would begin an inquiry as to what happened. I suggest going through Medora Marco's possessions—"

"Why?" Mortified they would seek to pillage his things, she scowled. "Already you give up on your medora and fight over his things?"

Contrition tightened Bazyli's expression, along with something else. "I beg your mercy, my lady." There she recognized restraint and frustration. "You mistake me. I ask only because our medora had in his possession a device that enabled him to communicate with the Kynigos," he explained. "We thought to use this to contact the Brethren and seek their help. While we"—he glanced at the gathered—"lay claim to him as our medora, that affection is newly placed. The Kynigos were his family much longer and have the connections, ships, equipment, and weapons to locate and retrieve him."

Hope leapt anew, and she regretted her quick temper. "I beg your mercy for my haste and harsh words, Elder Sebastiano. Please—search his things."

After a curt bow, Bazyli and a handful of aerios left the room.

"Kyria Isaura," Mavridis said, "the Council of Elders believe it prudent to hurry you to Kardia."

Her stomach knotted at the thought of going to an unfamiliar castle, where she would be left alone while the men went about the business of rescuing Dusan and running Kalonica. She did not want to argue, but . . .

"It is a fortress, and as kyria, you will have your own regia as well as many more aerios to protect you. It was also a desire our medora expressed last eve."

"Our efforts and focus should be on Du—Mar—Medora Marco." Her own casualness about his name made Isaura realize perhaps she had not respected him as she should have. The ache reddened in her heart, knowing he was gone. Remembering him being ripped from her. He had looked at her—and for a fraction, his expression had altered—but then the blow . . .

"As they already are," Mavridis affirmed, making her blink back to the present. "As our medora's temper is known, I would not want to tempt it for not properly or adequately protecting his kyria."

"Agreed." Elek's expression was pained. "Already my house is shamed for not protecting our medora while under our roof. I plead you to hurry to safety, Kyria Isaura."

Kyria Isaura. Only because of Dusan. She looked down, wringing her hands, feeling awkward about being sent to Kardia, a place she had never been. A place and people she did not know. She knew not what to say or ask and felt strangely alone.

"Might I have a word with you alone, my kyria?" Mavridis asked.

She detested when he took that gentling tone, making her feel a child all over again. "Of course."

He looked to the others, who quickly left the room.

As the doors closed, Isaura deflated. Bent and buried her face in her hands, weeping silently. "He is gone, and I can scarce breathe for the torment." Sobs wracked her until she struggled for air. "I cannot do this, Mavridis. I am no kyria and do not want to be locked in a castle where I know no one nor have friends nor am I familiar with the city." Not to mention, she would be face to face with Kersei, the woman who had more of Dusan's heart than she could hope to have.

His touch was light on her shoulder. "As kyria, you belong in Kardia. It is also safest and would do my heart good to know you are there, protected, as we find Marco."

She felt his presence and startled to find him *kneeling* at her side. Taken aback, she waited for the reprimand.

"I am so proud of you," he whispered.

At his gentle words, she fought more tears. He could not mean them. "Do not mock me, Mavridis."

"*Father*," he said, cupping her face. "I am your father and would never mock you."

Hot, urgent tears streaked down her face. "Be not nice to me. It is too strange and sets everything to wrong." She shook her head. "I cannot do this. I am . . . a stupid girl. Nothing more. In Kardia, they will expect me to perform duties that I could not even name, let alone carry out. And Kersei—" The name alone made her recoil. "I cannot face her."

"Why?" He breathed a laugh. "You had something she never did."

Isaura frowned, wary of his words. Sensing a hidden meaning.

"I know this is indelicate of me, but you may well carry his heir—"

She drew up with a sharp breath. She had not thought of it . . . of a child . . . Her heart faltered at the prospect.

"It is a hope." He gave a grim smile. "Regardless, you have known him in a way she never will."

The words were no balm to her shattered heart. "You speak as if he will not return."

He grimaced. "We will always hope and always search, but we are up against an enormous monster in Symmachia. I have heard the Kynigos taken by them are never seen again."

Sleep was for those with quiet minds and hearts. Eija had neither. She rolled out of her bunk and stumbled over to the windows overlooking the *Chryzanthe*. Technically, that was the name of the station where she stood, and the flower-looking system was an originator.

The Sentinel, Xisya had called it. A simple name considering the sophistication of what it did.

Light flickered in the umbilical between the station and the *Prevenire*. Yawning, Eija shifted for a better view. They were loading supplies? Tonight? Maybe they wanted the practice jumps to be done with accurate payloads. She shrugged and returned to her bunk. Forced herself to sleep. Tomorrow was a big day, and she could not afford to be sleep-deprived.

Wake-up intruded at 0345 hours. Eija sat up with a groan. After her morning ritual, she climbed into her gym clothes. Two days before she'd deal with Gola's snarkiness and Bashari's smart mouth for six weeks there . . . and six back.

After morning PT, she hit the sonic shower, then breakfast, which consisted of rehydrated nutrient packs. With little preamble or ceremony, she and the others suited up and headed to the umbilical leading to the *Prevenire* for their very first launch test.

"Hey, gander it." Bashir nodded through the long, thin windows of the umbilical that straddled between the *Prev* and the station. "They're watching us."

The brass and Commission. And the creature.

Shuddering, Eija kept walking—unlike the others, who paused to gawk. She had no desire to give Xisya any more of her attention or thought.

"Did you hear?" Shad asked, coming up behind her. "Colonel Galt was found dead in her quarters this morning."

"What?" Eija stopped, heart pounding. "How?" Patron Galt was dead? Her Patron—the one responsible for getting her into the Marines and HyPE. She couldn't be! She was supposed to fill in the blanks of Eija's past. Told her not to worry—and now she was dead!

"Environmentals failed," Milek said with a snort. "Dark way to die."

"Environmentals don't fail," Eija bit back. "Not in just one room. Not without alarms going off like crazy." She looked through the umbilical window—straight into the void that was that creature's eyes. Felt a claxon sound in her head, warning this trip wasn't what they'd been told. *What are you?*

The Sentinel stands ready.

What had the voice meant? The Sentinel . . . she glanced to the flower. It was ready?

"Ei?" Reef called.

Absently, she moved in his direction, feeling the creature's gaze on the back of her skull. Feeling her thoughts in there. A jumble of them. Darkness. Heat poured around the PICC port like hot water trickling down her neck. She drew in a breath and touched it, wondering if it was bleeding. It felt warm under her fingers.

"What's wrong?" Reef asked.

"Zed." Shaking off the paranoia, she moved around him and through the hatch into the *Prevenire*. She couldn't explain what was as vague and nebulous as air—or better yet, carbon monoxide. That was how Xisya felt. Like her very presence was toxic.

"You going or what?"

At the ladder to the main deck, she glowered at Milek behind her. Rather than give him the chance pull a juvenile prank, she let him go first, then climbed up, right between Engineering and Command. Crew bunks were port and starboard, as were respective engines. More than a little curiosity piqued Eija. This was the first time the team had been aboard the *Prevenire*. They'd practiced in simulators and corvettes, but those hadn't been retrofitted for the long-distance haul.

She glanced down the port passage and spotted four doors—three to the portside bunks and the last to the storage bay, where provisions for the weeks-long trip would be stocked. Is that what they'd been doing last night? Then she browsed Command deck and the galley.

"Okay, *Prevenire*," came the resonating voice of Chief Crafter as he stomped onto the deck. "Show time. To your stations. We've got a long day ahead, and I'm ready to be bored."

"Yessir." Reef shifted past Eija—where had he come from?—to his station.

In fact, everyone went to Command. Except Eija. It seemed intentional, leaving her out in the dark. Alone. *At least I'm getting away from Tryssinia.*

She forced herself back into Engineering, the area enclosed in deceptively thin clear walls. Her prison for this history-making trip. She palmed her station chair then sat in it, relaxing against its surface. Scanning the engine displays as they came online, she felt the PICC-line connect. Coolness spread through her veins. With it came a torrent of images and a darkness unlike anything she had ever felt before.

"I don't know how you got past me," a hissing voice snaked into her mind, *"but you will not make it back."*

Eija jolted forward—and the pinch on her PICC-line made her yelp. That had been in her comms, right? And it was a joke. Had to be. She waited for someone to comment on it. The voice hadn't been masculine like before. This was female, haunting.

"Zacdari!" Chief's voice punched through the comms. "Your vitals are high. What's going on back there?"

Her mind raced, realizing nobody was going to respond to that freaky voice and threat. "Thrill of the launch, sir," she lied. After entering commands on the glowing array of instruments in front of her, she secured her harness. As systems checks were sounded off, Eija tried not to think of the voice. It was *her*, Xisya. Had to be. But . . . how? Patron had warned she would know what she was now, but that her body would nullify the effects. Of what, though?

"Engineering, report."

Eija fell into the familiar routine she'd practiced in the sims. "All systems online and functioning normally."

"Prevenire, you are cleared for departure."

"Copy that, *Chryzanthe,*" Reef responded.

"Initiating umbilical separation in three . . ." Gola's voice was smooth. ". . . two . . . one."

A definitive plunk sounded beyond the aft hatch.

"Umbilical separation complete," she reported.

"Prevenire away," Jadon said.

The ship lifted and angled to port. Engines thrummed as they accelerated away from the station. She knew the pattern by heart—they would come around in a wide arc. Once on a straight trajectory, they'd punch it and hit the originator head on. That would launch them into the slipstream, hyperaccelerating their speed and thrusting them into a trans-warp jump. Sort of like a magnetic railgun that uses extra-dimensional physics to hyperaccelerate an object from one point to another.

But this was practice, so once they hit the nose, they'd fire reverse thrusters and come about. Repeat the maneuver. Separation and launch weren't complicated, but the right trajectory and speed to nail that nose perfectly—that was the trick.

And the maneuver for coming out of the slipstream and not killing everyone on board? That was the part Eija argued with. That didn't make sense.

"Good trajectory," Chief noted as they aimed down the rings at the Sentinel.

Something buzzed her skin, pebbling it. Her hair stood on end. What the djell . . .?

"That's it," Chief said. "Nice and easy."

The gel couch cocooned her body as they hit several g's, aiming at the originator. If it weren't for the PICC-line, they'd be crushed. She eyed the displays, monitoring systems as Gola and Bashari piloted the *Prevenire*.

"That's amazing," Gola said in a breathless voice. "It's lighting up."

"That wasn't in the simulation," Shad muttered.

Eija itched to run to the Command deck and see what they were talking about.

"Focus, people," Chief said, an edge to his tone. "Rings are contracting."

"Scuz me," Reef said in awe.

Eija relaxed as the hard burn rattled her teeth and pressed painfully against her joints and body. And like an explosion—she saw the metal flower glowing. Igniting. The *Prevenire* searing through it. The crew screaming. Then darkness.

"No!" Eija breathed, her words faint. They had to stop. "No, don—" It didn't make sense. She couldn't see the Sentinel from here.

"Target locked," Reef gritted out. "Prepare to fire thrusters. Connecting in three . . . two . . . one . . . Contact."

"Fire thrust—"

"No!"

"Stop!"

Without warning, it felt like something gripped their ship. Yanked them forward. Light exploded where there shouldn't be light. A cacophony of pops crackled. Her ears ached. Her body vibrated so fast it seemed a separate thing.

The practice jump should be over. Why weren't they powering down, reversing? She glanced at her panel. Lights glowed, blurring around the array of diagnostic indicators from the extreme vibration. This wasn't right. It felt . . . *real*.

Slag, slag, slag.

Panic exploded as her vision started ghosting. No, she couldn't pass out. She had to . . . Her right hand moved over the flat panel and tapped the sequence, but the vibrations were so horrific she couldn't tell if her fingers applied enough pressure. A sequence appeared on the heads-up. The wrong one.

Djell. She tried again as ghosting auras defied her vision. This time, she got the right code. Then fought to move her left hand over a fraction, which gravity forbade. Growling, she tried to twitch her finger one inch to the switch . . .

Gravity was a beast and entirely more powerful.

Biting the mouthpiece hard, she strained, felt the switch. Another quarter inch . . . just . . . a little . . .

Success! She crooked the switch and tugged it back. A light flared. There.

As she slumped, her vision gray like a static-snow display, there was no doubt. They weren't returning to the *Chryzanthe*.

They'd jumped.

The skies cried the day the royal carriage arrived for Isaura. She watched from the apartments as it rolled through the city with its regia arrayed in their finest splendor. An impressive and formidable sight. It should have been for Dusan, but she alone would be ferried to Kardia.

She rolled the ring on her finger, watching as the procession made its way along the crowd-lined cobbled road to the palace. Somehow, it reminded her of the time she had spent with Dusan, traveling with the caravan from Moidia to Prokopios. How he had so clearly stood out. Brooding, yet confident.

Would she ever see him again?

She felt more than saw Kita beside her, watching the phalanx of warriors. "My, how impressive."

"It is better suited for Dusan." *Not the fraud who stands here.*

"And his kyria." Kita gave her a wan smile. "Come. We need to prepare you for the ride to Kardia."

Isaura wilted. "I would that I could stay here."

Kita guided her back into the room. "I know this is hard, but you must go. For him."

"It is absurd! I had his love for such a short time, and now they send me north to be kyria."

Kita squeezed her shoulders. "No matter the past, no matter how long you had his love, you did have it. He set petition—and it was clear he could not be influenced to do something he did not want to do."

"No man can bend my will."

Kita helped her into a rich green gown and overcloak with brown fur trim, then added the crown. When Isaura started to object, Kita silenced her, pointing to the window. "It is no frivolity. There are a thousand reasons to wear it, and they are lining the streets this moment to see you depart."

Despair rushed over Isaura. "I am terrified, Kita, and do not want to be alone."

She hugged her. "I would well imagine. But you do not go alone—Mavridis will be there, as will I. Think of it as going to Kardia to wait for him. To prepare for his return."

The thought made the idea bearable. How long would she wait?

"Kynigos taken by them are never seen again."

"Ready?" Kita lifted the satchels, and when Isaura reached for hers, her friend stopped her. "No, that's my job now. Yours is to be kyria." She rapped on the door and it sprang open.

"Make way for the kyria!" Theilig bellowed.

Swallowing hard, Isaura thought to shove the door closed. Hide here a while longer. But Dusan . . . she would not dishonor him. With a nod to Theilig, she stepped out, then turned—and faltered.

Aerios in their greens-and-whites lined the passage, spines straight and chins jutted. At the far end waited Elders Elek, Mavridis, and Sebastiano.

Seek strength where it may be found.

Near to trembling, she made the impossibly long walk down the line of aerios, who bowed as she passed and pivoted to fall in behind her. At the corridor that opened into the wide foyer, the three elders bowed.

Mavridis came forward and indicated to the column of aerios along the stairs. Isaura started that way, sensing her father and the other elders flanking her down to the grand foyer. The procession paused near the great doors, and the elders turned to Isaura.

"Kyria Isaura," Elek said, "regia will see you to Kardia. Be at peace, Your Majesty, for these are our best."

"Thank you for your kindness, Elder Elek," Isaura quoted the practiced lines, "for the apartments and generosity you so graciously spared Medora Marco and me during our stay. We are grateful."

"It was my honor, Your Majesty."

Isaura faced the arc of regia.

A shout brought them to attention. A brown-haired, brawny regia stepped from the line. "My kyria, I am Regia Kaveh. With your consent, the aerios and I will see you safely to Kardia."

Stomach tight at the formality, she prayed she did not make a fool of herself. Or Dusan by proxy. "Thank you, Regia Kaveh. I accept your protection and aid."

He and three more guards snapped into a square formation, then pivoted and faced now-opening doors. They left a gap, and Mavridis encouraged her into it. When she did so, they fell in with her, escorting her out into the morning sun and onto a small portico with a dozen steps down to the cobbled courtyard.

A raucous cheer arose from a throng that rattled the bailey gates beyond the gilt carriage and column of green-clad aerios.

There were so many—hundreds, maybe thousands—cheering for a girl they did not know. A girl who, a month past, would have been on the street with them. Awe swept her as she took in the people, wondered that they could accept her as their kyria when she had never been seen before.

Feeling disingenuous, she firmed her spine, raised a hand, and acknowledged the crowd—for Dusan.

Sunlight bathed her as the roar grew to deafening.

It was a relief to reach the carriage. With the lightest touch from Kaveh to steady her, she climbed in, followed by Kita and Mnason. Adjusting her skirts, Isaura stared out the small window as the door was shut tight. The carriage lurched into motion.

"I am a fraud," she murmured as they threaded the needle of the gate.

Riders remained on either side, protecting the carriage and Isaura as they hurried through the city crowded with people cheering and throwing flowers at the box.

"A normal feeling to be sure," Kita said with a smile. "But is it not amazing?" She ran her hand along the green brocade that lined the interior. "What is this?" Bent, she drew back a cloth from a basket and gaped at the cheeses and stoppered cask.

It took the better part of an ora to reach the outer gates. The streets then grew rutted and the ride more turbulent once they were on the road to Kardia. The steady clip of the carriage did little to ease her fears or chase away thoughts of Dusan, but under the influence of the repetitive motion Isaura soon fell asleep.

Thump!

Isaura started, glancing at the curtained window. A blur of fabric. Then the door wrenched open. Kita flew to her side with a yelp as a billow of fabric delivered a lithe body into the carriage.

After securing the door again, Mavridis folded himself on the bench. "Forgive my unorthodox intrusion." He smirked. "We could not stop without jeopardizing your safety, and we must speak before you enter Kardia."

"Of what?"

"When we arrive, you must remember that you are kyria. Kardia is your residence." There was an odd tone to his words. "Prince Darius is there, but recall who rules and what our medora discovered in Jherako."

"I have given much thought to that," she confessed.

"It is fine to accept his welcome, but in the medora's absence, *you* are in charge of Kardia."

Isaura blinked. "Never have I even set toe in that castle! How am I to know where I will lay my head or take my meals?"

"Anywhere you wish is the answer." Mavridis had a grim set to his mouth. "Remember it, Isaura. They are there to serve you, not you them. I know this will be a change after the life you have led, but for Marco's sake, you must step into this role with confidence."

"Which I do not feel."

"Never speak it!" Mavridis perched on the edge of the seat, elbow on his knee. "You will need to pick your own advisor and personal guard from the regia. I recommend Theilig, as Marco was impressed with him. Hadrien"—his gaze went dark—"is Darius's man."

"Theilig is commander of the army, is he not?"

"He is."

"Then it would be a demotion."

"But safer for you."

"For me?" she balked. "*Kardia* must be safe. It would be unwise to remove him from his station out of fear for me." She shook her head, confused. "Your counsel on this makes little sense. I would prefer he stay commander. Does not the realm need as little disruption as possible in light of Dusan's absence?"

"Medora Marco. You must remember to use his correct address."

"I will!" Isaura rubbed the tension knot between her eyes. "I beg your mercy. It has been . . . difficult."

"It has." He nodded again. "You have borne it well."

She sent him a wary look. "You were Marco's First, were you not?"

Frowning, he gave a slow nod.

"Could you not counsel me?"

"I fear there would be talk of my influencing you. There is already rumor that I swayed the ear of the medora and was complicit in his kidnapping."

Isaura started. "Ludicrous! Who speaks these things?"

He smirked. "Good." Yet another nod. "That is how you must address anyone who speaks such. I again admonish you to take Theilig as your personal guard."

The road changed from the steady rocking of the country roads to a cobbled one.

"We've reached the outskirts of Lampros City," he said. "I must go. Be strong, Isaura. Marco needs to you to keep his throne."

Keep his throne. That is what this all meant. Why he urged her to come north quickly. Was it in danger?

Of course it was.

He flicked open the door and scaled out as if he were made with wings, not skin. His horse came up, and he thrust himself onto the Black even as he kicked the door shut.

For the next ora they rattled through Lampros City, the streets lined with people, cheering. Soon, they clattered across a bridge that led them along a cliff road overlooking the Kalonican Sea, and she had her first glimpse of Kardia. The road to Kardia was long and twisting, each curve higher than the previous.

Isaura was in awe of it, the castle made of stone that glittered and seemed to soak in the sun. Dusan had said he was born here, yet he had only come back to it this cycle. What would it be like to grow up here, to know the halls and passages? To know no lack of clothing, food, or shelter? She sniffed, unable to imagine such a life, and yet, this *was* now her life.

"Look, my lady." Kita indicated out the window.

A thick gray wall lined the road at the top and bore sentries at the ready as they banked up the last turn. Gilt gates barred the way. A shout went out that sounded like Theilig, demanding the gate be opened in the name of the kyria.

"I'm going to be sick," Isaura murmured.

"Don't you dare," Kita chided. "I cannot get sick out of that dress in time for you to be presentable."

They clopped across a wood bridge before passing through the gate. In the yard of the bailey, they circled around to a wide staircase leading up to a terratza, which bore dozens of nobles and behind them, too many sergii to count.

The carriage jounced to a stop.

"The prince and princessa!" Kita whispered. "Oh my—isn't she grand?"

Isaura's stomach churned, finally setting eyes on the beautiful Kersei with her thick, curly black hair and wide eyes. And her belly rounding with the prince's heir. Kita was right—the princessa was all elegance, grace, and beauty. No wonder Dusan had loved her.

"Sit back," Kita hissed. "Look calm."

"I am not calm!"

"That's why I said *look* calm."

"I will faint." She glanced to the door and reached for the handle.

"No! *You* never open a door. Wait."

The moments of stillness and quiet were haunting and never-ending. Isaura smoothed her skirt as she peered through the curtain to the waiting crowd. She felt herself coiling in, wishing for Dusan. Craving his strength and courage.

The door clicked open. A gloved hand presented itself to assist.

Isaura drew in a breath and let it out as she stepped from the carriage.

48

A war drum thumped in her head. With a groan, Eija opened her eyes, fought to clear her mind. She squinted around the pain to read the diagnostic array before her, but something was strange and disorienting. Numbers weren't right. The alignment off. Shifting, she groaned again but found she couldn't move.

It all rushed back to her—they'd jumped! She snapped fully alert. Though the crushing weight of the hard-g burn was gone, there was still a formidable exertion of gravity. She hit her couch's release. Gel seeped from the tubes, freeing her. Her PICC-line retracted.

The heaviness in her head receding, Eija eased forward. She stared at the blinking lights. They meant something. *Get it together, Eij.*

Life support.

I'm alive, so yeah, working.

Engines.

Online, evidenced by the thrum in the deck.

Thrusters—fine. Sensors . . . She eyed the panels. "Yep, wor—" Hmm, a fraction off, but . . . not significant.

Okay. Communications. Eija keyed her line. "Engineering to Command." She scanned the instruments and diagnostics, glancing back at the sensor array readout. They weren't mapping.

When nobody responded, she repeated the request. "Command, this is Engineering." Why weren't they answering? Unsettled, she shrugged out of her harness. With her head pounding, pulling herself from Engineering into the main passage took a monumental effort. Because of security protocols, the door didn't open automatically, so she palmed the Command panel. "Zacdari Whiskey Tango Six Two Nine."

Shunk!

Locks disengaged, and she gravved down, pushed aside the hatch, then trudged over the lip. On the Command deck, she took in the situation. Blast shields had deployed, so the only view was the steel plating. Not a big deal, but it hadn't been part of the simulation.

All six of the crew were unconscious in their crash couches. She went to the chief as his eyes sprang open.

His head rolled toward her as he hit the release and spat out his mouthpiece. "What in the scuzzing Void . . .?"

"We jumped," Eija said, "which is stupidly obvious." She glanced to the others, debating who to rouse next. The darker side of her decided to leave Gola till last. Or never. "And we're somehow off course by a fraction." She approached Reef and nudged his shoulder. "Reef—sir."

He groaned and slowly came to. "What . . .?"

Boots gravved, Chief stood and stretched his neck to shake off the effects of the jump. After a second, he woke Gola and Shad. Milek and Bashari came around on their own. "Rise and shine, *Prev.* Seems we've had some unexpected excitement."

"What?" Gola shrieked. "We jumped? But I wasn't ready! My—my dad . . ."

"Gut it up, Gola. Your noise won't help anyone," Chief barked.

She choked back a sob and slumped against her couch, tears floating in the zero-g. If the girl hadn't been a Class-A witch, Eija might feel sorry for her.

Chief glanced at the others, who were pale and daunted. "We're buried in some serious slag." It played in dark streaks across his face and shadowed his eyes. His gaze hit Eija's. "Get back to Engineering. Recheck the numbers. Run a systems analysis to make sure being off isn't a sensor fault or something else. Find out why we're off course. What about speed and trajectory?"

"We're off course?" Reef asked, wobbling on his feet.

"Sensors might've been knocked out of alignment when we hit the originator." She shrugged. "They're off by a fraction."

"And a fraction could result in us being millions of miles off course. Jadon." Chief pointed to the nav console. "Get on that and find out what you can."

"They really made us jump?" Shad stared blankly at the communications console. "Wh-why would they do that?"

Backing toward Engineering, Eija waited for the chief to answer. The silence that hovered over the Command deck was painful. Obviously they had jumped, but they all seemed to want to hear him say it.

"Yeah, they did." Chief ran a hand over his face. "Don't know why and doesn't matter, because there's no way to find out and no way to get back—"

"You're giving up?" Bashari interrupted with a disbelieving laugh.

"—except to go forward." Chief glowered at him. "Remember, we get the return jump-point from the Sentinel on the other side. So we deal with one thing at a time. First, assess our situation." His voice was preternaturally calm, but he balled his fist. "Shad and Ashan, see if we can establish a connection with the *Chryzanthe*."

"That won't happen because we're already light-years away." Gola tapped the digital readout. "According to the display, we've been in the hyper-slipstream four hours already."

Shad whimpered.

"I can't believe they did this to us," Bashari whinged. "They need to tell us why."

Eija rolled her eyes. "If they didn't share their reasons before, they won't tell us now." Hadn't Xisya promised that Eija would never return? Was this what she meant?

Chief met her gaze and tilted his chin down. "Engineering, Zac."

"On it." She ducked through the hatch and returned to her station. She was right, though. The brass wouldn't tell them. This was exactly what Xisya wanted. And Eija had six weeks to figure out why.

After making adjustments to realign the specs with the manuals, Eija recorded the changes in her log. Then in a private one, she jotted thoughts on possible problems ahead. She'd learned long ago to cover every angle so it didn't come back and bite her in the rear.

Hours later, Bashari and Shad glided out of the Command deck, past her station, and straight into the crew lounge, which abutted Engineering. Gola, Reef, and Milek came a few minutes later.

"Zacdari." Chief stepped up behind her. "Inside." He indicated to the lounge as he moved toward it. "Let's debrief and grab some chow."

She hesitated, glancing at the diagnostic array that glowed at her fingertips.

"It's not going to radically alter course on its own," he said, his tone mocking and sarcastic, "and if it does, you're within five feet."

"Ten." Not that she'd counted. She was just irritated at being stuffed into an already crowded space.

As expected, the lounge felt like three of them climbing into a maintenance tube at once. The air seemed heavier, too. Maybe she should check the environmentals. Wasn't that how Patron died—or was killed? She skirted inside, parking herself along the bulkhead. In the corner of the back wall curved a padded couch and a small, anchored table for four.

Chief leaned against the hull and folded his thick-as-logs arms. He gave them a long perusal, his brown eyes rife with intent. "The only thing that's changed is the timeline—we started early. Nothing else changes. Not your jobs, not your responsibilities." His jaw muscle twitched as he paused to let that sink in.

The chief was handsome in a raw, I'll-crush-your-skull-if-you-defy-me kind of way, with muscles too large for his shirt and a head too big for most hatches. But he also knew his stuff. And he'd been an Eidolon, whom Eija tended to hero worship. She had mad respect for him and secretly thanked whatever bodiless entity put him on the *Prev*.

"Follow duty rosters. Half will bed down and start REM. The rest on duty. It's going to be six long weeks of boring." He planted his hands on his tac belt. "But I know this is scuzzed, so for the next five mikes, floor's open. Say what you want and get it off your chest, because after this, those feelings need to be flushed down reclamation with any other slag that stinks up the place." His gaze narrowed. "Clear?"

A series of "yessirs" filtered out.

He made a deliberate display of his timepiece. "Five mikes—go."

"I just want to know why." Reef didn't waste time or mince words. "It was all planned. Why pitch us into it? Was it my fault? Did I give the wrong specs or orders?"

"No," Chief said. "Had nothing to do with you."

"But—"

"Get your head out of your butt," the chief grunted. "This entire thing isn't about just one of us. We're here. We're alive. We do the job."

"You don't have to be a jerk about it," Gola muttered under her breath.

"Gola," Reef admonished.

"It's cool—floor's open, right?" Chief's gaze sharpened on Gola. "Pandering doesn't alter our situation or our responsibility. Me saying it nicer doesn't change a thing."

"But it can have a direct correlation to the way a crewmember performs." Eija had quavered more than once at his barking.

"I don't need you to defend me," Gola snipped.

Eija rolled her shoulder to the side, turning away from the high-strung girl. "I didn't say I agreed with you. In fact, I think you were out of line."

"He opened the floor!"

"To *concerns*, not childish name-calling," Eija huffed.

"Childish? You would know about—"

"Enough!" Chief glowered at them. "See? That! That slag needs to stop now. We have one purpose—all of us—to get to the Sentinel and deliver the information so we can get back. So, learn how to get along!"

"You mean how to murder without leaving evidence behind?"

"Zacdari!"

Properly chastised, Eija lifted her hands as a beep sounded from his vambrace.

"Thank the rings," Shad murmured, looking particularly piqued. "Can I be on the first rotation for sleep? I'm not doing so well."

Chief was still searing Eija with a glower that seemed to have been retrofitted with phasers.

She squirmed inwardly, knowing she'd crossed a line, and blamed the unusually thin air.

"That's Jadon's call."

Reef straightened in his chair. "Beta, bed down. Alpha, on deck."

"I didn't bring anything—we weren't supposed to jump," Milek said. "What do we do for supplies?"

"I have a feeling our stuff is here," Eija said quietly, recalling her inability to sleep and spotting the ship being loaded.

Curiosity pushed the team out of the lounge and to their quarters. Exclamations carried through the *Prev*, relaying that their supplies had indeed been brought on board. She kind of hated being right, but at least their belongings were here.

Eija turned to exit the lounge and collided with a solid mass.

"Never"—Chief leaned into her face—"let me hear you suggest murdering someone."

"It was a joke—"

"It's *never* a joke. Ever!" Ferocity bled through his eyes as he somehow leaned closer. "We are stuck like glue to each other. Like maggots on meat. That close. And there is no room, *no room*, for that talk, no matter the intent."

She swallowed—her pride and a gallon of adrenaline.

"Clear?"

She nodded, then quickly remembered that wasn't an acceptable response. "Yes, sir." When he eased off, she exited—and saw Gola slipping around the juncture. Sneering. Smug.

Djell. Just djelling great.

Eija clomped to her bunk room, glad Reef had given her team downtime first. Inside, she dropped against the mattress and gripped her head. How did Gola always manage to bring out her worst? Eija just had to keep her mouth shut. But no, she had to rise to the bait.

She stared up at the bulkhead. Gray, boring bulkhead. Her view for the next six weeks. She tried to sleep, but a weird hum ran through the ship, one that wasn't the engines. Or the air recyclers, so . . . She palmed the wall, feeling a thrum that seemed to have a thump to it every so often. Strange.

That was going to be seriously annoying. Arm over her eyes, she tested if she could shut it out. But there it was—*vrrrrm-thump*— over and over. No way she could sleep with that noise and this much irritation—thankyouverymuchGolaTildarian.

She went to her locker and flicked it open. "The Go Box," she muttered, pulling it from the shelf. It was disorienting to find things here that she had last seen elsewhere. One of the Academy HyPE assignments had been to take a small wooden box into the city and fill it with items that would fit in the box, sustain them for a two-month trip, and cost under two hundred credits.

She opened it, smiling. A channeler with thirty books and ten entertainment vids. A comfy thermal shirt she hadn't been able to say no to—it was orange, not exactly a uniform-code color—and . . . the necklace. She fingered it with a frown. What . . .?

Only when she lifted it did the memory reawaken. A replica of the Ladies, the deity honored on several planets in the quads, including Tryssinia.

"Hey, Z, you should get this. It'll protect you." Reef tossed it into her box.

"Nothing can save her," Gola bit out. *"She's a lost cause."*

"Neh, that's how she always looks," Milek shot back.

"You kept it."

Eija jerked, not realizing her door had opened. "It was locked! How—"

Reef shrugged as he stepped in and the door clanked shut. "XO's prerogative."

"That is not a thing."

He jutted his jaw toward the necklace. "You seriously kept it."

"Accident." Eija stowed the box in her locker and slammed the door. "What do you want? I need to bed down."

"I . . . was concerned."

She rolled her eyes. "D'you really think I'd kill her, too?"

"No, but it isn't like you to say something like that either."

"She calls our mission leader a jerk, and *I* get chewed out."

"She showed disrespect. You voiced a threat."

"Djell!" She spun away from him, but there was nowhere to go. "It wasn't a threat. It was just . . ." She deflated. A threat. Inappropriate and childish.

"She gets me so . . ."

"Yeah, that's Gola," Reef said quietly. "But you're better than that."

Surprised at his words, Eija eyed him. Tried to see past the handsome flyboy who'd flirted with every girl in the Academy, including Gola. Dark eyes, dark hair, cocky . . . and so djelling adorable it wasn't fair to the rest of guy-kind. There was no way in any quadrant that he was interested in her. So . . . what did his words mean?

"It won't happen again," she muttered.

He smirked. "I knew I could count on you."

Man. Was that all he wanted, reassurance she wouldn't sabotage the mission or kill someone? Yeah, like she thought—no interest. The sting of that realization pushed her away, and she heard his grav boots thud against the deck as he headed to the hatch. When she turned—he was there. Not at the hatch, but right in front of her.

Whoa. Had he always been this tall?

His eyes pinched with the hint of a smile. "Thanks, Ei."

She shifted but he didn't move. "D'you need my space to breathe, too?"

Softness unrecognized a second ago vanished. "You're on deck at 0300." And he was gone.

She cursed her quick tongue. The last thing she needed was Reef against her like the others.

The steps were high and many. Way too many. Exhaustion gripped at the thought of the climb looming far overhead. From this vantage the pointy tips of the Temple could be seen, its gold capturing sunlight and spinning it off in different directions.

But oh, his legs ached. "Must we, Ma'ma?"

Her soft, warm hand closed around his. "Aye, we must." He heard it—the sadness in her voice, and she smelled . . . strange. Not the roses like normal. This was . . . gross. He wrinkled his nose and rubbed it as she pulled him up the many-stepped path. Feet on fire and legs wobbling like fruited jelly, he whined. Stomped his feet. Glanced up and saw there was still just as many steps.

"Come along, A—"

"I cannot! There are too many." He stamped his foot again. "This is a trick— the Iereans just want us to think we climb."

Ma'ma lowered to a crouch, her blue gown billowing around her like mist off the sea. "Now that does not make sense, does it?" She smiled at him. "We must reach the top or we cannot get very important answers." Light glowed in her eyes, and she smelled of roses again. Rich, fragrant roses.

His arm started burning. He bit his tongue not to speak of it, but the pain— more than ever before—overwhelmed him and he screamed. It burned as if he'd fallen into the great fireplace in Father's solar. He stumbled back.

"Wait, no!" Ma'ma said, reaching for him. "Give care! The heights!"

But his arm was like a well-spent fire log, all outer ash with glowing embers still within. It started crumbling. His fingers vanishing. His palm. His wrist. He screamed and screamed, jumping up and down in agony, in terror.

"Stop—the cliff!"

And he was falling. Fast and cold into icy nothingness.

Eija jerked awake, panting hard. Staring at the wall, she shuddered around the frenetic pace of her heart. What a crazy dream! It had been so terrifyingly real that she felt compelled to examine her arm, which had seared like the boy's had, though there was no evidence of burns.

"Djell," she whispered and dropped back against the pillow. Touching the hull, she felt the steady thrum of the *Prev* racing along the jagged slipstream. After five weeks on the ship, it had grown far more agitating than expected. So had Gola. Eija found the time in her quarters alone valuable and sanity saving. The only respite was the chats she and Reef had over chow.

She lifted her hand from the hull, still surprised that only seconds of touch had numbed her fingertips. Yet through it, she detected the ominous *vrrrrm-thump-thump. Vrrrrrrm thump-thump.*

What created that odd rhythm? She pressed her palm to the wall, her imagination once more traveling the wild explanations she'd come up with, from the more probable—a part needed to be recalibrated or a sensor needed realignment—to the downright ludicrous—the ship was . . . living. And the crew, acting as bacteria, would eventually die off because the living ship would kill them.

She snorted. "You've been watching too many FicVids."

But what if that was right? Insane, but hey—they also never thought they'd be taking instructions from some alien creature on how to build a jumpgate that threw them into a hyperaccelerated slipstream to, in record time, reach another system. A new thought hit her—what if that's what Xisya really wanted, to have them bring the ship to a nest of other living ships?

Annoyed with her own conspiracy theories, Eija groaned and swam onto her back, hooking her arm over her eyes again. Best thing for her to was get up, do PT, shower, and get to work. For the millionth time in the last month. The recalibration she'd done that first day showed things were functioning as they should. Somehow they'd gotten off course by such an infinitesimal amount that it shouldn't be a problem. Navigation had realigned but it was something that required daily altering for some reason they hadn't been able to resolve. Her goal each shift was to figure out why it was doing that, and in the last five weeks, she hadn't, but hey, it was a new if artificially measured day right?

After her morning ritual, she slid into her flight suit, then stuffed on socks and grav boots.

She stilled at the subtle thrum worming through her boots and legs. Not the normal one connected to the engines, but that other one. The *vrrrm-thump.* Another mystery she would like to solve.

"Zacdari, you're late!" Chief's voice boomed through her comms implant.

Eija checked her vambrace readout—and frowned. She still had three mikes. "I—" Arguing would only get chewed out, since the chief was always right. "On my way, sir." She clomped to the door and palmed the panel.

Curiosity getting the better of her, Eija touched the wall, glanced down, tuning into that strange rhythm once more, then slid her hand along the hull, her ludicrous thoughts more fanciful imagination than anything. *What are you . . .?* She'd made the mistake once of asking the others if they knew what it was. They'd all stared at her as if she'd seen a ghost. Which exacerbated her "living ship" theory.

"D'you need a moment alone with that bulkhead?"

Eija jerked around to the chief. "Sir." Did he sound nasally, or was that her imagination?

"Late! Let's go." He thumbed back down the passage and started that way.

She swallowed her excuses. But if she didn't explain that she wasn't late . . . "Sir, no disrespect intended, but my vambrace says I have thirty-five seconds before I'm actually late." Her steps sounded heavily in the corridor.

"Then recalibrate it because you're late." He pointed to Engineering. "Weeks lost and you still haven't fixed the navigation trajectory."

"I've tried—every shift!" She clomped through the hatch to the main passage. "I really think Milek should re-verify our plotted course, because I can't figure out what's off, a sensor or the calculations. Or why it keeps resetting."

"About time," Milek growled as she moved into Engineering. His fingers flew over the console.

"That sounds like excuses, Zac," Chief bit out. "But we—" He stiffened. "Hold that thought." For a man in grav boots, he moved fast out of Engineering and into the lounge, and he looked a bit green.

She logged in and quickly scanned Milek's notes of the goings-on during his shift. "Lot of plasma turbulence and automatic course corrections."

"Yeah," Shad said, her voice soft. "It's been bumpy."

Eija glanced at the diminutive girl. "You were in your rack."

"Who could sleep with all the thunder?"

"Thunder?"

Shad shrugged. "All the groaning and popping makes me think of thunder. It's better than the truth—that it's gases bent on ripping our ship apart." She climbed up on the glowing array table and sat with the instrumentation beneath her crossed legs.

"Aren't you supposed to be at your station?" Eija frowned at the ever-increasing disparity in stats and sensor metrics.

"Jadon is running more system-wide tests, and nobody needs me in the medbay, so the chief said I could take a break."

"Must be nice," Eija muttered. "He said I was late, but I wasn't."

"But you were." Shad pointed to the digital display.

Irritated, she checked the numbers. And stilled. "That . . ." She verified her own piece. "I . . . it's off. But that's . . . it shouldn't be. It has a six-month life without recharging." She removed the timepiece and clicked it into the dot receiver on the array. It recalibrated, and she returned it to her vambrace, frowning. What was going on? Navigation was off and now her watch? Was there a sensor fault or some short in the electrical conduits?

Great. She'd have to run yet more tests.

Shad scrambled off the unit and thudded to her feet. "You . . . you okay, sir?"

Chief propped himself against the bulkhead just inside Engineering and huffed before pushing off and entering Command. "Turning the bridge over to you, Jadon."

"Understood, sir. Get some rest."

Scowling, Chief again leaned on the bulkhead, then navigated his way starboard to his office and quarters.

"He's been sick all morning," Shad said. "I was in the lounge and heard him hurling."

"Doesn't have the stomach for it," Bashari said smugly.

"He was an Eidolon," Eija growled. "He's done more zero-g time than you, as well as hard drops from high altitudes."

"He was also rated the top pilot in his class." Shad's squeaky voice sounded infatuated. "And he was hand-picked by Commander Deken for the Two-one-five. And by Admiral Krissos for HyPE."

"Whatever it is, it's not space-sickness."

"How do you know?" Bashari demanded.

"Seriously?" Eija speared him with a heated look. "We're flinging through space, off course, with faulty sensors or wiring, and you want to pick apart the chief?"

"She's right," Reef said, joining them from Command. Then his brows furrowed.

"Whatever," Bashari grumbled as he headed to the galley.

Reef jutted his jaw at Eija. "What electrical problem?"

She shrugged. "Not sure, really. I've noticed some anomalous problems with readouts." Actually, one problem—her timepiece. "Could just be faulty display or bad connectors."

"That's not a small problem," Shad noted. "That could be significant."

"Agreed," Reef said.

"I know—already running tests on the electrical system. But our priority remains sorting navigation. The .006 variance doesn't seem big, but the longer it prevails, the wider the gap between our destination and where we actually break stream."

Something twisted through Reef's expression.

"Don't worry," she said, guessing it bothered him as much as it did her. "We'll get it figured out. I am more convinced it's in our system and not the actual 'vette, but since it's been retrofitted with alien tech . . ."

"Keep me posted." Reef turned back into Command.

Eija eyed her notes. Maybe she'd create a duplicate program so she could attempt more drastic measures with no risk to the true system. Run them side by side. She'd have to wire the ship's sensors into it for accuracy.

That shouldn't be too hard, but it'd require making sure the programs didn't cross-contaminate. They couldn't afford navigational mistakes or it wouldn't matter how good of a pilot Bashari was, he'd never nail the nose on the Kuru Sentinel because they'd never make it there.

"I think he likes you."

Surprised to find Shad still there, Eija looked up. "What?"

"Jadon," she said with an endearing smile. "He likes you."

"Jadon likes himself." She recalibrated the port sensor array, which required taking them offline for a few seconds—a treacherous task, considering the *Prev* relied on them for navigation, but diverting that to the secondary backup array would compensate.

The numbers counted down to the completion of the recalibration. Twenty-four percent . . . thirty-six . . .

Vibrations wormed heavily beneath her palm, and she eyed the slick black surface.

Vvrrrrrm thump. Vrrrrrrrrrm thump.

She drew in a breath and lifted her hand, unsettled and curious. The rhythm stopped. Once again, she palmed the glass, and it resumed—strong! Faster than . . . An echo of a scream warbled in her mind.

Wait.

Eija eyed the recalibration percentage. Fifty-four.

Vrrrrrrrm-thump-thump. Vrrrrrrrrm thump-thump. Vrrrrrm thump-thump.

Concern flared through her. She'd never felt the pulse beat this fast. Was it somehow connected to the array?

But it was offline.

So . . . what? A living ship—*which is stupid*—but what if it was . . . compensating for . . . one of its arms being cut off? "No, *that's* stupid."

"What's stupid?"

Eija drew back, glancing at Reef, who was back. "Zed." The lie was hot on her tongue and bald on her face. "There's . . ." She cleared her throat. "I'm recalibrating sensors and . . . can feel the ship responding."

Brown eyes sparkled at her. "That's normal. Any good pilot listens to his or her ship. The way it talks says whether or not it's handling a maneuver well."

"Right." A smile struggled into her face. It made sense. But this felt like . . . more.

Reef came to her side and glanced at the glassy diagnostics. "How much longer?"

She tapped the readout. "Ten seconds."

He seemed intent, concerned.

"What?"

"Zed." His face brightened. Too much. "I'm glad you're in Engineering. It's not my best field."

"It's not mine either, but I'm here." *As in, not a pilot, which* is *my best field.*

He touched her shoulder. "And I'm glad."

She considered him. The glint in those dark eyes. The smirk shadowed by stubble. "You should be grabbing rack time."

He lifted an eyebrow, apparently misconstruing her comment.

"Because you look rough."

"Wow, don't mince words, Z."

"I mean—" She rolled her eyes. "Beta's on duty now. Shad needs her station to get her work done or Chief will crawl down her throat."

Reef backstepped and saluted. "As you command."

"She's your subordinate," Bashari said, emerging from the galley with a tray of food. "Don't let her talk to you like that."

"You mean, the same way you just talked to me?" Reef clapped his shoulder. "Space those negatives, Bashari."

"Yeah, well if we end up dead in the water, it's on her."

"Navigation is on you—so why don't you fix that trajectory?" Eija bit back.

"Easy," Reef growled. "We've been in tight quarters, so let's watch the tone and dial things back. Give each other room to breathe." He nodded and then left.

Eija stared after him as he headed starboard, which seemed more appropriately titled the Alpha side, since that's where most of Alpha team had berthed. She couldn't figure him out. One second he seemed all intense and arrogant, the next . . . likeable. More than friend-likeable.

Which was insane. Reef Jadon wasn't a likeable guy—well, not true. He was *likeable*. Everyone liked him. But she shouldn't. Couldn't. He was meant for someone like Gola, and they'd have their requisite one-point-two kids. And Eija? She'd end up with the leftover point eight.

Verifying Shad had gone to her station, she pressed her hand against the panel.

"It hurts! It hurts, Ma'ma!" The shriek echoed in her brain.

Eija sucked in a breath and pulled her hand away. What was that? What were the visions? Who was the boy? Why was the pattern going faster now?

Sick of wondering about this for however many days, she decided to get answers. Okay, first—the pattern. It seemed mechanical in nature, so something within the ship or engines? Did it matter where she touched the ship?

After ensuring her tests were running and nobody else was paying attention to her, Eija took four steps to the right and pressed her hand on the wall separating Engineering from the main corridor.

Vrrrrrm thump-thump. Vrrrrrm. Thump-thump.

It didn't seem as strong as in her quarters. Hm . . . Would it get louder closer to the source? In the lounge, it seemed quieter. On the Command deck where Bashari bent over his station, she surreptitiously ran a palm over the other station.

"What're you doing?" he balked, munching something from his rehydrated food tray.

She glanced at the blast shield. "Any thought on bringing that down?"

"Nope. Too much force," he said around a mouthful of food. "Ya know— with the hyperaccelerated rate of speed. It'd crack."

She nodded, paying more attention to what she felt in the ship than to his arrogance. The pattern was here, too, but not as strong. Smiling at Shad, she moved toward her station. "How're things?" A deliberate plant of her hand startled the oxygen out of her—so strong!

"It's quiet," Shad said. "But the ship is talking to me."

Eija twitched, glancing at the girl. Did she feel it, too? "Talking to you?"

Shad nodded. "I mean, you know—a ship and her pilot, even though . . . I'm not a pilot."

"Zac, aren't you supposed to be in Engineering?" Bashari asked.

Stubbornness had long outweighed allowing anyone to force her to do anything. And Eija hadn't finished her informal experiment with the rhythm. She focused on Shad. "So, um . . ."

Shad peered up through delicate brows. "Is something wrong?"

"No." Distracted, Eija managed to squeeze a smile as she surreptitiously leaned against the bulkhead. As soon as cold metal touched her shoulder, an explosion of images assaulted her thoughts.

A strange black vine twisted around an arm, constricting, making her pulse thump against the skin. Driving winds and rain in a terrifying, storm-ridden night. A sea churning violently, slamming waves against boulders, each surge like a hammer to the temple. Falling from a great height and being crushed against the earth. A spike-like claw puncturing a chest. So many thoughts, screams, emotions, and a searing scent that made her stumble, gasp.

"Eij?"

A vise closed around her throat and squeezed . . . tighter . . . Spots sprinkled her vision.

"Eija!"

She shook hard, her vision finally snapping to blue eyes that peered into hers. Hauling in a breath sounded loud in her ears. "Reef." She clamped onto his arms, feeling like she'd just come out of a zero-g bubble and needed grounding. She steadied herself. Realized she'd used his first name. "Sir. I . . ." She anchored her mind as if with grav boots.

Wariness crept along the edges of his eyes. "You okay?"

She released him. "Yeah." Angling around him couldn't be done fast enough. "I need to check something." Through the hatch, she crossed into Engineering. Flopping into her couch didn't help the heaviness of her limbs abate. It felt like someone had altered environmentals. She glanced at the dull glow of the instrumentation, reading the information. There had to be an explanation for what the djell happened in there, why she saw all those images.

"You're supposed to be grabbing rack time," Chief grumbled as he stepped into the crew lounge two days later and went for the strong black brew in an insulated tumbler.

"In a minute. Are you feeling better?" Eija swiped through her data channeler, still trying to figure out how her measures for the navigation and trajectory kept resetting. No matter how hard she tried, she couldn't solve the electrical issue or the question about the pattern in the hull.

"If you don't get REM, you're no use to us," he said, ignoring her question.

She squinted at a log entry in the system controls . . . Her login. But . . . she'd been in the rack spinning Zs at that time. Who . . .?

"Shift change, Zacdari. You need sleep."

"I need to solve this," she snipped, then registered whom she'd just done that to. "Sorry—sir." She dropped her channeler against the table and held her head, a sick feeling in the pit of her stomach. "Sleep is pretty useless. Or rather, trying to sleep is." Honest to the rings, she was afraid to touch the bulkhead and experience that onslaught again.

"What's going on with you?" Gripping the chair across from her, he leaned heavily on it. "Jadon said you were in a trance or something the other day." His color didn't look right and there were dark circles beneath his eyes.

"He needs to mind his own business." Man, what was with her?

"His business," Chief bit out, "is this ship and its crew. *You*, Zacdari."

Chagrined, she nodded. But her nerve endings were on fire, and feeling like she was injured or sick when she wasn't sort of set her teeth on edge—which was exactly what the pulse pattern was doing to her.

"He's worried you're getting Void Sickness. Staring into space—and even I found you petting the hull."

And there it was. She could've guessed and probably should've. But admittedly, she'd begun to wonder, too, if being locked up for weeks in a ship was getting to her. What else could explain that strange pulsing?

Chief lowered into the chair, leveling his dark, probing gaze on her. "You agree."

"No!" Snapping wasn't helping her case. So she had to give him something strong. Solid. Because she sure wasn't going to tell him the ship was alive. Yeah, that'd go over well. "I was just thinking—hard." When his expression shifted, Eija knew she needed something better. "I think someone's tampering with the system." Okay, that was a massive, colossal leap with zed proof, but what else would explain the misalignment resets? *Wasn't me, so . . .*

He squinted, a storm crowding his already-fierce gaze. "That's a very serious accusation."

"Why d'you think I didn't say something?" Funny how it was okay to suggest her brain was addled by space—*meaning I could* de facto *scuz this ship and crew*—but not okay for her to suggest someone else was off their rocker, trying to sabotage the *Prevenire.* Which would permanently strand them and ultimately kill them.

His jaw muscle jounced. "Proof?"

She swiped the device and spun it to him. "Someone logged in while I was in my bunk—with my login. Every day I've found the changes I implemented to adjust our traj back on course were reverted. That's not a mistake or an anomaly. It's been changed. Manually."

Lips thinned, the chief stared at the screen. "Why?"

That weight in her gut gained a couple of kilos. "I don't know—another reason I've kept my mouth shut. There were other changes that I don't even have access to. There are only two people aboard with clearance to make changes like that—you and . . ."

"Jadon." Chief's gaze hardened, understanding the implication. "But we have a ship full of geniuses, so anyone could be hacking—assuming that's what's going on." He ran his large hand over his stubbled jaw.

He was taking this a lot better than she'd expected. Why wasn't he reading her the riot act for accusing her shipmates? And why had it been so easy to thwart him from her own strange behavior? "You already suspected . . ." Drawing in a sharp breath, she scooted up in the chair. Yanked the slack out of her spine. "You figured out someone was doing something to the ship, and *plagues*"—she gaped—"you thought it was me!" That's why he'd been riding her tail.

"I thought," he said with a growl, "you'd been acting weird. Then to have Jadon mention his concern . . ." Again, he scruffed his jaw. Leaned on the table. "Look, this just confirms . . ." He sighed, and his blue eyes locked onto hers. "The water's contaminated."

Eija started. "What?"

"I haven't been sick in the last ten years because Eidolon are put through rigors and 'roids to make our insides like steel. So for me to be sick . . . I've been running tests on the water." He gave a grim nod. "It's contaminated. I've been trying to refilter it."

"I've been feeling off, too, but I thought it was—"

"Acclimating to deep-space travel." He nodded. "Tildarian thought the same. I had Shad give her an anti-nausea cocktail."

"But you're the only one actually sick. Why?"

The chief glowered. "Haven't a clue, but I do not like where my thoughts are going." He nodded. "Reclamation of the water is going to consume system resources we didn't anticipate. Recycling water in space is incredibly inefficient anyway, so we've been losing a fraction of water since I started last week. Normally, that wouldn't be an issue, but unless we can find potable once we clear the Sentinel, we'll come up short for the return jump. And if we don't get the alignment fixed and we drop out of the slipstream—well, that's not a mistake we can afford to make." He nodded, roughing a hand over his face. "I guess I need to start watching everyone a little closer."

She'd have to be extra careful as she experimented with the hull and the pulse pattern.

"I've been reviewing security footage." He referred to the constant video feeds that recorded their trip, so when they returned, the Commission could dissect the trip and weed out any problems.

"Want to explain why you were touching all the bulkheads?"

"Not *all* of them."

He scowled.

She chewed the inside of her lip. "I want to explain, but . . . you'll think I *do* have Void Sickness."

"And not explaining is better?"

"Point taken." She drew in a breath. "It's just . . . you know how Shad says the ship talks to her?"

He gave a slow, wary nod.

Not reassuring. "Okay, well, it talks to me, too. Just . . . different." Yeah, that'd win an award at the Tascan Interplanetary Debate Tournament.

"What do you mean, diff—"

"I heard something." An unexpected pull exerted itself on her body. She drew in a breath and glanced to her right, to the wall separating the crew lounge from Engineering.

Chief drew up straight. "We've slowed."

"How?" she balked. "Reverse thrusters would have to—*djell*! That just wasted a ton of resources." Eija grabbed her channeler and clicked the dot into it as she swiped another screen.

He gave a low moan, leaning against the console.

"Chief , you look like—"

"I'm fine."

Something caught her gaze. Made her stomach plummet. "*No*," she breathed.

"What's with the fuel readout?" His large hands worked the console next to her. He cursed. "This can't be . . ."

"It is." The weight in her stomach was like an anchor. "We just dumped nearly a quarter of our fuel!" Engines were programmed to balance speed to the fuel output so they wouldn't get stranded in the slipstream. "The fuel dump forced the engines to slow to compensate—that's what I felt."

"This mission is starting to feel scuzzed."

"*Starting*?" Eija checked the other system levels to make sure they weren't dumping anything else vital—like air. "Do we have enough to get to Kuru?"

He worked frantically. "We can pull from the reserve tanks, but . . ."

That anchor in her gut now felt like an entire battle cruiser. "But that reserve was a stopgap to be sure we could get back. If we use it now . . ."

"Yeah . . ." His brow knotted. "Maybe Kuru has an acceptable source we can use or convert to refuel. If we don't get there, we won't know."

"Accessing reserves . . . Tank one is—" She strangled a cry. "It's empty! How can it not be there?" *Okay, skip battle cruiser, and let's go with planet.*

He cursed again. And again. "Someone is sabotaging us."

"You will not make it back."

Xisya's haunting threat made Eija roll over in her bunk for the thousandth time. The alien had vowed Eija wouldn't return, and now they were seeing the fruit of that. But why would Xisya hate her? Was Eija alone to blame for that focused hatred?

Knowing someone had sabotaged the *Prev* kept her awake, convinced they'd alter her environmentals and kill her in her sleep, just as had been done to Patron. Who was Xisya's puppet?

Sleep was an evasive enemy, leaving her exhausted. Then there was the insipid, ever-present nausea that was likely due to water contamination. Chief had worked at her station through the rest of her shift, and with the fuel loss and navigational problem, she started to realize why. He still thought she was responsible.

Ever since she'd encountered the torrent of that strange pattern, she couldn't quite escape the sense of hovering anger, desolation, and hopelessness. A suffocating, excruciating pain. Not just bodily pain, but a tormenting heart pain. Like an ache you could never get rid of, that drew all the mind to it, inflaming it.

And the smell!

How could she feel pain when she wasn't injured? She had to find out more, figure out the source. Maybe all her problems were connected.

Eija looked at the bulkhead again. "What are you?" Mustering courage, she reached toward the wall. Withdrew her hand, afraid of touching it, of finding that torrent again. Finally, she unfurled her fingers and let the tip of the tallest touch the cool, hard surface.

The thrum was there, but it wasn't overwhelming. She closed her eyes, probing what she sensed. It only confused her because she caught a rush of euphoria with a strong undercurrent of . . . pain. Euphoria *and* pain? And that djelling rhythm was there, too.

It's not real. It's not real. It can't *be real.*

She opened her eyes and touched another finger to the wall. Then her pinky, her pointer . . . She felt it. The rush. The anguish. She gritted her teeth. Rolled onto her side. Facing the hull, she pressed both palms to it.

Pain barreled at her with incredible force. Invaded her. Enveloping, lingering . . . begging. Powerful, so much more powerful than . . . ever before.

So much pain. A boy ripped from his mother's arms. A youth leaping from a rooftop—trying to break a fall. But . . . missing. The emptiness of open air as he plummeted. Screaming. A shout that made no sense.

The small boy again. Standing in a fountain, holding a sleeping infant. Glancing across rippling waters to two noblewomen. Men in red robes. Women in luxurious gowns. An eruption of light and agony. He nearly dropped the babe. Scrambled to firm his grip. Saw a black mark on the tiny arm. A tall, elegant, formidable woman broke from the onlookers and strode into the waters. It would be a mistake to see her as merely a woman. A disservice to think of her as simply lovely. As she knelt before the children and touched their shoulders, gone was her soft complexion. In its place, a terrifying presence and fierceness. Gown gone, replaced with pearlescent armor that sheathed her body and limbs. A brilliant helm, glittering with a living mark that roiled across the top, concealed her hair and most of her face.

Words were spoken, lost in the witnessing and apparently given only to the two children. Then the terrible, beautiful eyes turned to her.

Eija flinched against the images and removed her hands. Strange. It had seemed the woman looked straight into her soul. She lolled onto her back—and started. Heart pounding, she realized the woman was still there, towering over Eija.

Freeing her sleep harness, she sat up. Scrabbling back against the hull did no good. Screaming—her voice had no sound.

Ferocity spiked violet eyes. *"In him lies your answers, Daughter. Find him."* Urgency spiraled through words that seemed to fill the air with tiny sparking molecules.

Before it's too late.

The woman hadn't spoken the words, but they echoed no matter how hard Eija tried to shut them out. *No, it's not real. She's not real.* Who was she supposed to find? She was on a ship hurtling through a convoluted hyper-slipstream that might just kill them all. Low on fuel, environmentals skewed, water contaminated . . .

"D'you hear me?"

Yeah, she heard the hazy vision.

Someone grabbed her shoulders, shaking her. Eija blinked, focused. "Chief." She glanced at her hatch—open. "What're you doing here?"

"I commed but you didn't answer." He frowned as if she'd lost her mind.

How much had he seen? She glanced back at the wall. Where the— "Lady." She sucked in a breath. Not just a lady, but a *Lady*.

No no no. That wasn't possible. Infected Tryssinians clung to her, but not her parents. But everyone said it—Ladies were myth. Her mind shifted to the men from the vision in red robes. Iereans?

"Zacdari!"

She flinched. "Sir?" It was a weak answer. Barely audible. The best she could do.

"You look like you saw a Ghost."

Ghost. It was a joke—*he* was a Ghost, the nickname for Marine Eidolons. "Ha. Funny." Eija glanced at the wall. Just a wall. Gray, drab bulkhead. *Nothing to see here. Move along.*

"You started telling me about something yesterday, but we got interrupted." He punched the hatch panel, and the door whisked shut.

Um . . . "I did?" Yeah, this would be a great time for another interruption. She couldn't help but look at the shut door and feel locked in. Trapped. Digging in her locker, she retrieved her uniform shirt and slipped it over the thermal tank.

"The ship talking to you? Explain."

This felt confrontational. "I . . . It's nothing. Just like Shad said the ship talks to her, I guess it's the same for me." Light-years different, actually. Eija seriously doubted Shad had an armor-clad warrior-Lady giving her messages from the Void itself.

He frowned at her. "You sure that's it?"

"What, you still think I'm sabotaging things?"

Hands on his tac belt, he angled his head. "Tildarian's sick—violently so."

"You said the water was contaminated."

"I also said I recycled it."

"So, since Gola's sick, you think *I* did something." Un-djelling-believable. Lights flickered. The ship lurched.

Boom! Boom-boom-boom!

Claxons rang through the ship.

With a gentle lift that belied the clamor of the alarms, Eija started floating. Startled, she clapped her heels and gravved down her boots.

Chief thudded out of her quarters with little effort. That Eidolon training served him well. "What's going on?" he demanded as he moved toward Engineering.

Glad the interrogation had been interrupted, she clomped after him, determined to find out what had happened. In the passage, a strange wave of . . . something struck Eija from behind. Warily, she glanced over her shoulder to the port storage bay hatch. Felt an ominous chill emanating from there. Calling to her. What . . .?

"Zacdari!"

At the chief's bellow, she thudded toward Engineering. Something splatted her cheek as she rounded the juncture. She narrowly avoided a collision with a floating object. Startled, she shoved it, then it registered—a body. Floating. Blood droplets in the air . . .

She heard someone vomiting and hoped they were using a bag.

"Secure that body!" Chief's shout sailed from Command, and with it came a stinging vapor of fire retardant from the automated systems.

Eija recoiled then caught the limp leg. Milek's empty gaze struck hers. He was missing a chunk of his skull and chest. Her stomach lurched. Quickly, she turned away, fighting the bile rising in her throat.

"Help me." Complexion pale, Bashari aimed a black body bag toward Milek's legs.

Stowing her roiling stomach, she helped bag and seal Milek's body. "What happened?" she asked, feeling the shakes in her limbs, worrying over what caused this. Thinking about the sabotage she'd discussed with the chief.

"I don't know. Reef was trying to help Milek when there was an explosion." Bashari had a grim set to his jaw as they used carabiners to anchor the body bag to a steel pipe. That's when Eija saw Shad in the medbay working a nanite pod. Djell, how many were injured? Was Gola still in her quarters? There were only seven on board . . .

A tightness in her chest, she inched closer to the still-open pod. Saw the badly burned and bloodied body of— "Reef," she whispered, noting more injuries on his shoulder and right arm. With his eyes closed and his chest covered by the pod, it was impossible to tell . . . "Is he alive?"

"Yes," Reef gritted out, obviously in pain.

Relief made her smile. "Thought you were too thick-skulled to die."

His brown eyes hit hers. "You know me . . ."

"Okay, sedating you now," Shad said. "Rest, and let the nanites do their thing." With a whisper, the pod activated.

The clear shield slid over his torso and face. Dark strands of hair not burned off or melted into his skin rustled as the pod sterilized the air around him. He grimaced, then his face relaxed, eyes sliding closed.

"Artificial gravity is fixed, but I'm not activating it until we run system checks," the chief shouted from somewhere in the ship. "Zacdari—systems analysis. Now! Shad, once Jadon is stabilized, clean up this mess." He gestured to the blobs of blood and fluid Eija had tried hard to ignore.

Eija clomped from the medical bay and followed Bashari through the hatch. On the other side, she saw a gaping hole, steel jagged and scorched, in the wall between Engineering and the starboard power conduit. It hissed vapor.

"How in the Void did that happen?" Eija wondered.

"That's what I want to know." Chief came into view, brow sweaty. "Bashari, what do you know?"

"Jadon said nav was touchy," Bashari said from his station. "Then we started losing thruster power, so he and Milek went to check. Next thing I know—boom!"

At her station, Eija ran diagnostics, Bashari and the chief working as well to get systems back online and answers delivered. But every test turned out worse than the last. Stress rose and anger flared.

"There's no structural breach on the outer hull, from what I can tell," Chief said. "To know for sure, we'd have to take a look outside."

"Which isn't happening in a hyper-slipstream," Eija muttered. She huffed, nodding to the hole. "That power conduit controlled attitude and spin. Attitude is offline—Bashari's taken it manual to keep us in the slipstream. We've blown a stabilizer. Speed controls are sluggish. There's gotta be a leak somewhere."

"Somewhere?" Chief growled. "You're Engineering!"

"I'm a pilot. Engineering—"

"You're Systems Specialist because you had the highest score in Engineering."

Eija faltered. "I . . . I thought—"

"That we were punishing you?" Chief snorted. He glanced at the diagnostic panel and uttered an oath. Followed by a string of them. He pounded the glass then blew out a breath. "Shad, what's happening with Jadon?"

"Nanites are working hard to stabilize him, but . . . they're struggling."

"Aren't we scuzzing all," Chief muttered. Then he nodded to her. "Eija, get Aoki's body to storage, then—"

"Storage?" she balked.

"The drop pods are there."

Something in her did not want to see what was behind that hatch, not after the strange sensation that had rolled over her. "What about his bunk?" she suggested.

He shook his head. "Pod will preserve him till we get back, and I want to go over his quarters with a fine-toothed comb."

She stilled. He thought Milek was a saboteur?

Though he didn't lift his head, the chief hiked his eyebrows. "Get it done. We lost an engine, but thanks to the laws of physics, we'll maintain this rate of speed." He started toward the internal hull breach. "I need to look at that leak and a few other things."

Sick to her stomach, Eija unlatched the carabiner holding the body in place, gripped the drag strap, and eased it out of Engineering and into the port passage, trying not to think that this was Milek. There was no love lost between them, but she never would've wanted this for him. En route, every time his gel-packed body bumped a bulkhead, she wanted to apologize. Or hurl. Maybe both.

In the storage bay, lights flared on in response to her presence. Heart in her throat, she scanned the space as she headed to the escape pods. Accessing one, she opened it and angled the body bag in. No start-up sequence necessary. Milek didn't need vitals monitored or oxygen piped into his PICC-line. There was definitely a high level of creep happening here, but she did her best not to think. Just move. Obey orders. She pushed the hatch closed and stepped back. *Sorry, Milek.*

In light of the sabotage and still feeling that strange chill, she glanced around the bay for anything amiss. Spotted something slick in the corner, beside a few balls of floating liquid. She clomped over and crouched, frowning at the condensation on the wall panel. Sometimes that happened in areas with less environmental control. Couldn't be too serious or a sensor would've tripped.

But what if it was something more, like a coolant leak? Maybe environmentals were overcompensating, which risked them freezing up. That could burn out the system. She swiped a finger along the condensation.

Pain exploded through her skull. Shrieks and moans roiled through her head. Desperation, fear, agony, anger. She stumbled back, her spine ramming a crate. She groaned but wasn't sure if it was the cacophony that assaulted her or the pain in her back.

"Zacdari, move it!" blared through her comms.

Frantic to get away, she clomped out of the bay, working hard to make her boots move at the speed of her heart. The hatch closed with a groan. She got back to work, shaking off the terror.

For the next eighteen hours, they worked hard to get things back online and figure out what caused the explosion.

The chief managed to realign navigational controls—well, back to the wrong "normal"—then ordered everyone to the lounge for a debrief. "We need ideas on how to best conserve resources or we are seriously scuzzed."

"Ration our rations," Shad said around a yawn.

"Good. What else?"

Eija squinted at him. "If we bunk up and seal off the extra quarters, that would help. I could run diagnostics for exact numbers—"

"Do it. You and Shad together," Chief said. "Ashan, you're with me. We'll seal off Jadon's until he recovers, and Tildarian will stay where she is." He gave a sharp nod. "What else?"

"This is great, but how do we get *back*?" Bashari asked.

"Unless we survive the trip in, going back won't be a problem."

Because they'd be dead.

"But when we get to Kuru, we can ask the Khatriza for help." Shad looked around at them. "I mean, since we helped them open this gate, they'll help. We're allies. Right?"

"Sure." Chief sounded more sarcastic than serious.

"Did you find anything in his bunk?" Eija asked.

"Haven't checked yet." He roughed a hand over his stubbled jaw. "I know we're all scuzzed after everything that happened. Zacdari and Bashari— rack time. Shad and I will keep things running. We should only have two more days."

"Yeah, but does the ship?" Eija wished she'd never spoken the words. It seemed like a challenge. Especially since the Prev seemed intent on killing them.

Eija came awake. This time, it wasn't fear or pain or the rhythm. It was something she saw in her mind's eye. Something from the explosion. The hole. She got up and slid out of her sleep harness. To move faster, she skipped activating her grav boots and sailed into the corridor. She angled into the main passage and through Engineering.

Chief was working with a readout.

She sailed toward the hole, which now bore a makeshift patch.

"What're you doing, Zacdari?" he asked, his voice wary.

With ease, she removed the patch and eased herself into the conduit. Her back pressed against the top, balancing her. She flicked on her shoulder lamp and squinted at the cabling.

"What is it?" Chief demanded. "Talk or—"

She backed out of the conduit. "You said we have navigational control?"

He shrugged. "Had to do some marginal thruster firing, but we're on track."

"How?" She gravved down her boots. "The cable is sheared off."

"What?" Chief lunged at the panel.

Not waiting for his assessment, Eija went to Command and ducked beneath Reef's station, where Bashari was working. Guess he couldn't sleep either. Sleep cycles were scuzzed with the explosion and water contamination that had half their team down.

"What're you doing?" Bashari balked.

Aiming her shoulder lamp under the console, she traced the wires that snaked into the bulkhead. Something caught the beam—a sheen on the tubing. She unscrewed the wall panel and glanced inside. In the bulkhead, the tubing diverted—half went aft, the rest toward the bow.

What . . .? She angled in that direction and traced her beam along the gray wires.

Something wet struck her face.

Little balls of condensation floated among the wires. "Well, that's not good."

"What's not?" Chief rasped near her ear.

Eija started at his closeness, but shook her head. This didn't make any sense. She dragged herself clear. "I can't figure it out." Wait! She straightened, thinking, recalling . . . Then clapped her heels, freeing the magnetization, and launched into the air.

"Hold up." Chief caught her leg and drew her back.

She huffed. "I'll be right back. Just . . . let me check something."

"This isn't encouraging confidence."

Frustrated, she nodded to the bulkhead. "There's condensation building up under there. It needs to be cleaned up before something shorts out, but first, I have to find out where that cabling is going. Maybe that'll tell me why it's sweating."

He considered her, then nodded. "Go."

She sailed out of Command and swam right to Beta corridor, then thrust herself toward the storage bay. This explained why there was condensation on the panel in there, but . . . why was the cabling even coming in this direction? Both port and starboard engines were astern. So why was some of the navigation diverting up here? Even if there was some explanation, wouldn't it go in both directions—port and starboard? Yet it only went to port.

She did her best not to think of Milek watching over her shoulder from beyond the grave-pod as she unlatched crates and moved them to access the bulkhead. After grabbing a drill, she paused, eyeing the panel, which was about 1.7 meters high and less than a meter wide. There had to be a dozen bolts securing this panel. Odd. Why so many?

It was like they didn't want something escaping.

Yeah, not helping.

But still . . .

Eija went to work, removing the bolts. But with each one, she couldn't help but buy into the idea of something escaping from the bulkhead. She eased off the drill trigger and stared at the panel. *You're being stupid.*

Was she? Because there was this creepy-beautiful woman who didn't really exist telling her to locate some nefarious "him" to find her answer. Whatever that meant.

After a few more bolts were removed, she shifted and leaned against the bulkhead.

Agony washed over her, strong, powerful. That now-familiar anger, elation. Desperation.

Heart racing, she straightened, staring at the few remaining bolts. "What the djell?"

Eija glanced back to the hatch to make sure she was alone, then pulled off her glove. Pressed her palm to the access panel. As if struck by a power blaster spray of water, the virulent, violent torrential stream of feelings slammed her. She choked. Tears streamed and, though she struggled to breathe, to think around the pain, she felt the *vrrrrrp thump-thump, vrrrrrp thump-thump* through her chest.

Right here. Whatever it was . . .

Determination gripped her. She set the drill to the bolts, pocketing them one at a time. Just a few more. Finally, she clicked the drill's magnetic grip to the wall and tried to pry off the panel. But it held fast. She glanced about and spotted a manual crank. With it, she finally flung the panel free. It floated across the bay and clunked into the crates.

A curtain of cabling spanned the gap behind the opening. "What in the Void?" This shouldn't be here . . . Through the slivers of space, something moved. A bug? Her heart jolted. She redirected her shoulder lamp, only to see a bead of sweat slipping free of a wire and drifting her way.

They had some serious rewiring and insulating to do. Maybe the hyperaccelerated jump was taking a toll on the hull. Weakening it. She shifted the cabling aside to find the source of the leak.

Clear as day, she heard it. Not felt it—*heard* it.

Vrrrrp thump-thump. Vrrrrrp thump-thump.

She unclamped her shoulder lamp and slid it between the cables to the shadowy gray just beyond. A streak of black interrupted the tan-gray. But what—

It shifted.

Heart in her throat, Eija froze. All sarcastic thoughts about a living ship rushed back to her, terrifying. Telling her if she moved, it'd kill her.

Don't be stupid.

It hadn't moved. *She* moved. The cabling.

"Zacdari!"

She yelped at the chief's bark in her ear. Banged the back of her head against the bulkhead. Wincing, she closed her eyes. "Sir?" she replied through the comms.

"What's taking so long?"

"I . . . found something." When she looked back into the dark space, cabling running down the wall like veins, she had this vague, haunting notion that something had changed.

Her brain locked onto the change. She aimed the light. And screamed.

A man! There was man inside the bulkhead.

Eyes blinked silvery-gray. Over those pale irises billowed dark hair much like the cable curtain. An oxygen mask covered a mouth and nose but did not fully hide a tattoo across the bridge.

Terrified, Eija jerked back, stumbling as her boots gripped the floor. The cables slipped over her shoulder, making her skin crawl. With a shudder, she slapped them away. Held them back. Stared at him, dumbstruck.

What the plagues . . . ?

Gulping adrenaline and panic, the part of her that said to run, she stared. Her mind refused to accept what she saw.

His body seemed anchored into some kind of contraption, a harness holding him hostage. Over his head, his hands were cuffed in padded steel restraints, IVs embedded in both arms. Head lolling in the zero-g, he made no effort to lift it, as if he couldn't. Tubes ran in and out of his chest and stomach.

The lower half of his body was in some special compartment that— She gasped. That was the source of the *pattern*. She wasn't sure what it did, but she felt the thumping against her chest again. It was a wonder he could breathe with the tube running through the mask into his nostrils. Condensation pooled over the clear mask.

Wait. No, not condensation. Tears.

Her heart broke for him. "Djell," she breathed. "Hello?" She swallowed, knowing this had to hurt, had to be terrifying. "Wh-who are you? How . . .? Who did this to you?"

A slow blink seemed a great effort for him. More tears broke loose and drifted from his face.

"Zacdar—" Chief's boots thudded to a stop. "Void's Embrace!"

Eija couldn't move, the silver eyes holding her fast. "What is this? Why is he in here?"

"Slag." Shaking his head, Chief looked as stricken as she felt. He edged in nearer. "Hey, can you hear me?"

The man's eyes shuttered closed.

"This thing is killing him."

"Marco, can you hear me?" the chief repeated, but there was no answer.

"Wait! You know him?" Anger darted through her. "Did you know he was in here?"

"Voids no," the chief said, then cursed again. Loudly and repetitively. "He's a Kynigos—intergalactic bounty hunter." He roughed a hand over his face. "So *this* is what they were doing with them." He shook his head again, scanning the contraption that held the man. "Captain Baric and that creature were snatching Kynigos left and right but we had no idea why and no say. Months ago, they snatched Marco while he was hunting, took him to the *Chryzanthe*. We thought Xisya was torturing him, so we helped him escape."

"I guess they snatched him back."

"We have to get him out of here."

"I think if we free his hands . . ." On her toes, Eija reached up over the contraption to reach his restraints. A vise gripped her wrist. She sucked in a breath and froze, lowering her gaze to his face, surprised he had any level of strength.

Silvery-gray eyes held hers, exhausted but leaden. "No." His rasp behind the mask was more a forcing of air across unused vocal cords than actual words.

"Out!" the chief barked. "Let me get in there. See what's happening."

"He's got me," she said, glancing up at his vise grip. Then again stared at those eyes the color of polished silver, almost mirrorlike. They felt . . . icy. Were they natural? The border between silver and the whites of his eyes was only a thin, black line. The effect of his gaze beneath thick, dark brows and shaggy hair was powerful. Made her want to cower. Was it him she had been hearing through the hull? Feeling? His pain? How?

Instead of speculating, she remembered this was a person, a victim. And now she wanted to cry. Do anything for him. "Chief will try to help—he says he knows you. Can you let go?"

Weary eyes seemed to struggle for focus, but slowly his fingers uncoiled.

"Thanks." Rubbing her wrists, she stepped back and let the chief climb into the tight space. She tied the cables aside with extra cabling.

"Hey, Marco." The chief studied the contraption as he talked. "Remember me? I was with Tigo."

The man's fingers flicked.

"It's so cruel," Eija whispered, covering her mouth. "I can't imagine anyone doing this to another person."

"This isn't cruel," Chief gritted out. "There isn't a word for *this*." He nodded to her. "Get Shad. We'll need a nanopod once we extract him."

The fingers flicked again—but this time, he jerked his head in an awkward way.

"He wants something."

"Maybe remove the mask." Chief reached for the tube that ran from mask to wall.

The man jerked and his eyes widened, heavy with pain and exhaustion.

"Okay, okay, big guy. We'll leave it." Chief huffed.

"I have an idea." Eija snatched off her channeler, adjusted the settings so all messages would go to the chief, then handed it over. "Put that on him so he can communicate."

Though the chief frowned, he strapped it over the man's hand, and his opposing fingers were soon tapping away.

"He's used one before," she said.

"Kynigos wear vambraces." His channeler buzzed. "Void's Embrace."

"What'd he say?"

His gaze rose to the man in the machine. "The mission is an ambush."

He'd passed out after sending that ominous message two hours ago. Since then, Chief had widened the opening, and Eija paced the bay. Now, Shad was examining the man to decipher if it was safe to extract him. She shifted back to them, her expression grave.

"Well?" Chief asked.

"As far as I can tell," Shad said, studying her patient, "he was healthy when he went into this modified crash couch. The wiring makes absolutely no sense—I thought the nostril cannulas were for oxygen, but they actually snake into his nostrils and are embedded in his piriform cortex."

That sounded . . . painful.

"Which means what?" the chief asked.

"The piriform cortex is where sensory information from our olfactory bulb is delivered before it's sent to the thalamus, then on to the hippocampus and amygdala," Shad explained. "I've taken a sample of the liquid in his IVs. It's a strange cocktail. There are antibiotics, anti-inflammatories, but there are also steroids and a couple of compounds I'm not familiar with. They intubated him, likely to make sure he could breathe even if his brain started shutting down."

"And if we remove those tubes?"

Shad sighed heavily. "I don't know. It's delicate because the tubes are attached to his brain, so it gets tricky fast. One wrong move, one wrong *anything,* and we do irreparable damage. Or kill him."

"Let's start simple," Chief said. "The cuffs—can we remove those?"

Shad squinted at the steel braces. "There doesn't seem to be any purpose in having his arms elevated other than restraint. But I can't be sure." She waved at the contraption in disgust. "This is just inhumane. I can't even . . . If we bring him out, I suggest staggering the de-wiring, taking one out at a time until we're sure it's not harming him."

"Agreed. Let's give it a go." Chief motioned Shad to her crash cart. "Monitor his vitals closely." He used the drill to free the man's hands from the bulkhead brace then lowered his arms to the sides of the couch, which they'd angled out of the bulkhead so it could be reclined. "Vitals?"

"Steady. Well, as much as possible for this poor man," Shad said.

Eija gently laid his hand along the gel still buffering his body. His hand twitched, drifting toward his center. She guessed he wanted to type into the channeler and helped bring his hands together.

His fingers spasmed over the device. Their units buzzed.

THANKS.

She smiled, feeling an enormous weight lift, yet, also doused with grief for what he'd been put through.

"We're guessing at what to do here, Marco," Chief said. "We'd like to get you unplugged altogether, but we don't know what will injure you or—"

Her channeler buzzed again.

FORGET LECTULO AND ME. SHIP. AMBUSH. He wheezed a breath, his eyelids drooping heavily.

"Lectulo?" Eija asked.

"I think that's what they call this couch-like contraption," Shad said.

"You said ambush earlier. Can you tell us more?" The chief turned to Shad. "C'we get that tube out of his mouth so he can talk?"

"We need to take it slow," Shad said. "Reclining the couch created a slight heart arrhythmia."

Marco's fingers tapped out a message.

SHIP NAV. ME.

Eija furrowed her brow. What did that mean?

"Navigation?" Chief repeated. "It's been out of alignment since we entered the slipstream. Zac"—he thumbed over his shoulder to her—"is our Engineer. She's been trying to fix it."

STOP. NAV RESET ME.

The nav reset him? How did that make sense? Eija thought about how the trajectory had reset each morning, how she'd thought it was someone sabotaging them. "It was you," she said. "You've been resetting the navigation?"

A faint nod.

"Why?"

AMBUSH.

Frustration coated her muscles. "I don't understand. Resetting is one thing, but I don't think that'd login as me—and how? He barely has strength to tap out waves."

Chief scratched his chin. "I had Jadon look into that—Aoki had a flex screen he used to log in. I think he was working to hide Marco from us."

"And I thought he was changing the course direction." She glanced at the man.

Weary eyes held her. He huffed breaths. His hands twitched like— Suddenly, he grabbed the tube down his throat and yanked.

"You probably—"

He jerked upward, vomiting as the tube came out, his hands pulling. He vomited again—then went limp, still gripping the tube in his drifting hand. Sick floated around them.

Covering her nose and mouth, Eija winced, then froze. "Is he dead?"

Shad looked from Marco to the crash cart and back. "No. Pulse is there, but irregular. He's breathing. I think . . . He could've killed himself with that violent extrication."

"Slag me," the chief said, dodging globs of floating vomit. "Guess he wanted it out."

LAMPROS CITY, KALONICA, DROSERO

"She's a haughty thing, don't you think?" Kersei stood before the mirror.

Darius sniffed. "Did you see the way Ixion called out Khaul for leading her to guest quarters?"

"I told you she should be set up in the medora's residence," Kersei said. "When Marco returns, can you imagine his rage if he found her in *guest* quarters?"

"Is that your concern? Marco's rage?"

Ignoring his quarrelsome tone, she slipped on a pair of earrings. "She is the kyria, Darius. What did you think would happen?"

"I thought *Marco* would bring her here. But he is gone, and we have little hope of his return."

Kersei tucked her chin, heartsick.

"I know it pains you, but we must be realistic."

She glanced at the still-glowing brand and found fledgling hope. "We must be prepared—there is a difference. There has been too much loss already." She saw irritation pinch Darius's face. "Our new kyria is raw and vulnerable, and we must be her allies, not her enemies."

"She was wearing the crown!"

"Likely the machinations of Mavridis, yet it is her right." Kersei started for the family dining hall. "You told Marco to take her as his bound, and he did. She is kyria. You wanted a war, and now that we have one and your brother is a casualty of it, you want to sweep the crown from his bound's head?"

Darius stopped, scowling. "You do me an injustice."

"Do I?" Kersei felt their son thump against her ribs and rubbed her belly. "In earnest, since we go to sup with her, we must not go with the presupposition that she is kyria to a medora now dead."

His gaze shifted to something behind her. "Isaura."

Kersei turned and drew in a breath.

With two Stalkers and regia at her side and dressed for dinner, Isaura stood, her face white, her eyes dark with disapproval. "He is *not* dead." Her gaze glittered. "You, his brother, and you, his one-time love—I would think your regard for him would have been more enduring." Her chin lifted, not in arrogance but a subtle confidence. "Regardless, I would thank you not to speak of him as such." She turned and started back for her quarters.

Arching an eyebrow at Kersei, Darius hurried after her. "Your Majesty, please—" He caught up, but when he went to touch her, Kaveh intervened, making Darius back off. "We beg your mercy, my kyria. I would reassure you of our regard for my brother, no matter his presence or absence."

The angry flush that rose through her cheeks accented her golden hair. Kersei knew not what to think of this woman who had captured Marco's attention and heart. She did not seem more than Kersei's one and twenty cycles, but she was taller, more . . . elegant, though clearly not used to noble life. And there was a directness about her that was becoming. Was that what had attracted Marco?

Isaura gave Darius a disbelieving nod that said she also would not argue further.

"My kyria." Tone deferential, Darius inclined his head. "Let us sup together so we can be better acquainted."

Hesitating, Isaura looked at Kersei for the barest of seconds before giving a nod. "Very well." With an awkward side-glance to her regia, she started into the hall.

Kersei followed, noting regia and Stalkers within the room straighten. Mavridis peeled from the corner and moved to the table. A sergius drew out her chair at the head.

"Thank you." Isaura words were soft, considerate. Her gaze danced around the room, never landing on anyone in particular as she took her seat, allowing the guests to take theirs. Was she too good, or too insecure?

Another woman entered and hurried to a seat near Isaura and sat down, offering an apology to the kyria.

"I do not believe we have met," Darius said to her. "Might I have the pleasure of your name, ma'am?"

Isaura set down her glass. "This is my friend, Kita Lasdos, and she has graciously agreed to be my lady's maid. We both survived the attack in Moidia."

"Camp of the Lawless?" Kersei exclaimed, incredulous. Then saw the hurt that splashed the kyria's face. "I beg your mercy . . ."

Spine straight, Isaura lifted her fork. "Moidia bears that name for a reason, I concede. However, it is unfair to assume that all Moidians are lawless or savage simply because we grew up there, just as one would not assume a noble is snotty and presumptuous from being raised in a castle."

She thinks me snotty?

The color in the kyria's cheeks brightened. Golden curls draped her face, and the coral gown she wore complemented her tawny complexion. Aye, it was quite easy to see why this natural beauty with no airs and little adornment had caught Marco's eye. Not just his eye, but his heart. His love.

Something raw and feral twisted through Kersei, forcing her to swallow. A somber quietness draped the hall as they ate.

"Are you ready for the morrow?" Darius asked.

Isaura hesitated with a chunk of meat on her fork. "For?"

From Kersei's right, Mavridis spoke up. "To secure the line of succession, you must be formally crowned as kyria. Tomorrow we hold a meeting to prepare."

The kyria's full lips stilled, open, then pressed closed. "What am I to prepare?" she asked innocently. "I am . . . who I am. Bound to Dusan and—"

"Dusan?" Kersei gave a laugh, and when others glanced at her, she shrugged. "That was his Kynigos surname."

Isaura held her gaze, but said nothing.

Setting down her fork, suddenly feeling unwell, Kersei cursed herself once more for ill-spoken words.

"The medora chose anonymity while touring the lands," Mavridis said curtly. "It is the name he preferred among the people, so they would know him as a man. He wanted nothing to impede developing a kinship and trust. It was under this guise he came to know our kyria."

Every new revelation of Isaura deepened the connection the winsome beauty had to Marco. Another connection Kersei did not have. It hurt and smarted more than she wanted to admit.

"I am again at your disposal, my kyria," Ypiretis offered, shifting the conversation back to the planning. "I can bring the vestments for the coronation."

"I would be glad for your help again, Ypiretis."

"Perfect," Darius said. "Ypiretis is a good ally. Know you he was an iereas?"

"I do," she said. "He was gracious enough to oversee our binding in Trachys. You were his friend, were you not?"

"Of course," Darius said with a laugh. "Our medora is not fond of iereas, though."

"The greatest of ironies," Ypiretis said with a shrug. "But I daresay he tolerated me well enough."

"He named you friend to me," Kersei said, resenting that Isaura felt she knew Marco so well.

"I am glad it is so, Princessa," Ypiretis said.

"How did you come to know him?" Isaura asked, setting down her fork.

As Ypiretis related how he and Marco had met, the journey to Iereania, something pinched at Kersei's core. This was her story with Marco, and it angered her to hear it so openly shared without her approval or participation. Just when she thought she had conquered the green-eyed monster, she found him lurking in every shadow, in every smile and word spoken by a woman she had just met.

TSC-H *PREVENIRE*

Marco had never known a pain like this existed. Weight pressed against him. He wanted to cry, but it was a futile effort when his body, with each breath, wanted to surrender. It took every morsel of strength to focus. Not to slip into the nether-sphere that had claimed him since being snatched from bed.

Isaura . . .

He blinked away tears, remembering—

"Welcome back," a voice said, drawing his attention to the side. The Eidolon pointed to a red-haired girl. "This is Eija Zacdari—your savior who found you in the bulkhead. Sorry for the rude awakening. We spun up gravity again, and that seemed to pull you to."

Marco's gaze fell on the girl, recalled seeing her face appear with a burst of light in the dark. Emotion rose, but he squelched it. "Thanks." Talking felt like breathing fire. It seared and burned. He coughed, tensing at the pain.

"I know they scuzzed you bad, so take your time," Rhinn said with a nod. "When you're ready, tell us what you can about all this."

Marco didn't know where to start. It was hard to think and even harder to *want* to think. Fighting against the overwhelming ache to fall into the Void, be mentally with Isaura, escape the pain, he tried to focus. Because escaping— dying—that's what Xisya wanted, for him to forget what he'd heard. What he knew.

"Is there a way to get you out of this contraption?"

"No," Marco wheezed. "Take me out—" Holy Fires of Hieropolis, it seared to talk.

"Take you out?" Eija's voice pitched, her scent hopeful.

"No," Marco grunted. "No . . . take me out . . . dead." Why couldn't he talk straight?

The girl's bright eyes held his, then she looked to Rhinn. "I don't understand."

"If we take you out," Rhinn said, "who's dead?"

The will to stay awake was slipping. It was so much easier to let it take him, let the drugs do what Xisya designed them to do—turn him into a seeing-eye dog.

"Marco?"

His shoulder shook and he blinked. Looked around, pulled back to the people on this ship. People counting on him. The people Xisya was using as bait.

"Who dies if we take you out?"

"You," Marco rasped, hating that he was so useless. That he was the only chance to save these people.

"But if he stays in there," a spritely girl said from the side, "he'll die. His vitals are holding, but they're not strong."

Words chased Marco down a long, dark tunnel that slowly filled with the resonant melody of Isaura's laughter. Her warm embrace.

"So," the gruff voice followed him, "take him out, we die. Leave him in, *he* dies."

The preparation meeting with the elders was insignificant and quick. It left Isaura with hollow assurance, for she quickly realized they did not see her as a kyria, but as an adornment for the arm and bed of their medora. Oh, they did not speak such to her face, but their hesitations and sly glances spoke it loud enough. Though angered and humiliated, she had kept her peace, fearing if she spoke, she would dishonor Dusan.

Now, a fortnight later, they who showed little more than fatherly condescension toward her were dressed in finery and gathered at Kardia to crown her kyria.

Bedecked in every bit of ridiculousness imaginable, Isaura stared out at the ocean, aching for Dusan, for his return. She wore the green embroidered coronation dress and jewels. Already her head ached from the plaits and coils piled atop it, arranged just so to support the heavy crown.

Dusan should be here. At her side. Leading her into the throne hall. But he was gone. Ripped from her arms. Turning the light-blue sapphire ring on her finger, she ignored the silent tears slipping down her cheeks. *Please come home. I need you.*

The wiry little priest, who had guided the sergii from the apartments, joined her. "He would be so proud of you."

There was a kindness about the former iereas that she saw in few people. She considered him, his fastidious manner and calm countenance. "You knew him well, so I will trust your words."

A smile creased his face. "I did, yes, though for but a short time."

"It seems we all bear that affliction." She swallowed her grief. "Could I ask you to tell me of him? What you remember most about him?" It renewed the ache in her breast for Dusan's courage and confidence, his smirk. "Please." She chewed her lower lip, fending off more tears.

Tenderness rose in the man's gaze. "He was honorable. And . . . gruff."

Isaura laughed. "Yes, that is certainly his way." She fingered the royal order nestled at her sternum. The heavy livery collar of sparkling gold and emeralds, draped her shoulders. Over her breast hung the Kalonican Heart, and a similar piece hung around her waist. The bliaut was embroidered with gold aetos around the trim.

"Intense, but not brash. He seemed to make decisions in a blink, yet as if they had years of contemplation behind them." Ypiretis smiled. "And he did not go lightly into a relationship with . . . anyone."

Isaura lowered her head. Though it had been but months that she knew him, it felt as a lifetime.

"When he ventured beyond acquaintance it was with the entirety of his being."

A tear defied her attempts and slipped free as she recalled his words: *No man can bend my will.* "I would give anything for him to be returned to me. It would make this day bearable."

"I think we all know that, my lady, and I believe he would do anything to be here, again." He eyed the north lawn, where sergii prepared tables and seating for the feast with hundreds of guests from around the country and continent.

A rap came at the door, and Ypiretis went to answer it. He returned a moment later. "I am informed that High Lord Kyros is here. It's time."

Fingering the fur trim at the wide sleeves of the green duster, she turned to him. "An iereas?"

He inclined his head. "It is tradition to have a religious leader anoint a king or queen—kyria." He motioned to the door. "They are ready, Your Majesty."

Bolstering her courage, Isaura left the serenity of the balcony and crossed the solar.

Theilig and Kaveh escorted her down to the grand foyer, then to the throne room, which made her stomach churn. High ceilings and chandeliers seemed to emphasize the grandeur of the moment. The elders then walked her to the chair that sat alone in the middle of the room, facing the—

Her heart climbed into her throat, seeing the throne. It was the chair from her dream. What did it mean? Was it a bad omen?

High Lord Kyros read the petition set by Dusan's hand and witnessed by two of the five elders of Kalonica and Prince Darius. Ypiretis affirmed he had performed the binding ceremony. Officially accepted as the medora's bound, Isaura was summoned to the dais and set on the throne, where she received the chalice of purity, the orb of honor, the sword of Eleftheria, and the crown. She recited the oath of her title, and as the crown was set up on her head, an ache bloomed for Dusan. This would have been for him to do.

Bells rang, heralding the new kyria upon the throne.

A collective stomp of regia and aerios boots thundered in the throne room, mingling with their shouts of exultation. In response, a deafening roar erupted from the lawn and city from the people gathered outside. Flower petals released from the ceiling and fluttered to the marble floor as she sat there, aching for Dusan.

Regia lined the green carpet, and she strode beneath their swords to a carriage, which bore her through Lampros City with an escort of regia. Hours later, returned to Kardia, she changed into a luxurious white gown with a green bliaut emblazoned, this time, with a single golden aetos—representative of the medora, Dusan—whose wings touched her shoulder and thigh as it screeched across her torso. White fur trimmed her neck, sleeves, and hem.

In the grand hall, windows and doors open to the expansive lawn, Isaura mingled and received guests for what felt like hours, all with the promise of a lavish feast afterward.

"A drink?" suggested Kita, who had tended her throughout the afternoon.

"Please." When Isaura looked upon the next guest, her heart lurched. "King Vorn, Queen Aliria."

"Kyria Isaura," Vorn said with a nod. "Queen Aliria and I pay our respects on your investiture." His dark eyes glanced around her. "I am glad you are well tended, but I confess it pains me not to see your king."

"Thank you. Your pain mirrors my own." Isaura's stomach rumbled.

He grinned. "A good meal would solve *that* pain."

"I have long been in want of food." She clasped his hand. "Thank you for making the journey. It is good, a relief, to see friendly faces."

Intent marked his expression. "Later, I would speak with you about . . . that thing your king witnessed."

The ships. "I welcome the time to talk."

TSC-H *PREVENIRE*

"The machines are auto-adjusting," Shad said. "It seems that even when he slips into a coma, the machines keep going—he's still navigating. But there is so much with these cables, that contraption, and the cocktail he's getting that I cannot even begin to fathom."

"He mentioned he kept resetting navigation," Eija said. "How can he even do that? Why would anyone need to be wired into something like this or the ship? We have the course plotted."

"Like he said—it's an ambush, so the course they plotted could be wrong. Maybe to hide their real location from Symmachia and the TSC." Chief shrugged. "Why him? Besides their honor, the only unique thing about Kynigos is that they hunt by smell." He narrowed his eyes, apparently thinking. "Those tubes in his nose—they're connected to the part of his brain—the olfactory. It processes scent. What if . . . what if that's how he's navigating?"

Eija laughed, then realized he wasn't. "Seriously?" she asked with more than a little mockery, glancing at Reef, who had come out of the nanopod a few hours ago, his injuries and burns healed.

"Just hear me out," Chief urged. "You said navigation was rerouted—and even with the cables damaged, we haven't gone off course or fallen out of the slipstream. So *somehow* there's navigation." He shrugged. "Maybe he's acting like a homing pigeon."

"That sounds unfathomable and also offensive." Yet, it made peculiar sense.

Reef leaned against a crate for support. "Do we take him offline?"

"No way!" Eija balked. "He said that if he dies, we die. And vice versa!"

"That's not what he said."

"But that's what it means," Eija countered. "He said it's an ambush. The trajectory we're on will put us a few light-years from our intended location. Maybe that's what he's been up to—trying to get us there, but far enough from danger."

"What danger?" Bashari asked. "We have no proof of anything."

"Really?" Eija snipped. "We find a *man* plugged into our ship like an electrical socket, and you say we have *no proof*? And what else could *ambush* mean? Its very definition implies someone is lying in wait on the other side."

Bashari lowered his head.

"Jadon, Ashan," Chief said, moving between them and Eija, "get back to your stations. Find a way to conserve fuel. Run analysis on our new trajectory and speed. See if there's anything to Zac's supposition."

"He's awake," Shad called.

Marco eyed them from beneath hooded lids. "The Sentinel." His rasp sounded so painful. "Gate . . . way . . . not for . . . us." He drew in a ragged breath and eased it back out. "It's for them. Their army."

"What army?" Chief stalked over to where the modified couch now poked halfway out of the bulkhead.

"How would he even know about the Sentinel?" Eija asked, feeling unsettled over this man who knew way too much.

"*Her* army," Marco expounded. "I saw them. Xisya—not a victim. She's . . . queen." The machines were making that noise—*vrrrp thump-thump*—as it pumped nutrients into his body. "When she hit my neck—I saw . . . what she saw. She couldn't . . . hide it."

Eija stiffened, panic trilling through her. "I . . . that happened to me. When she accessed my PICC-line, I suddenly could tell what she was. And I heard her later—she said I wouldn't come back."

"She said what?" Chief barked, scowling at her. "And you didn't tell anyone?"

"You already thought I had Void Sickness. Telling you before would've sealed my fate. But now you believe me because of"—she motioned to Marco—"him. This."

"That's why you always looked spooked," Reef muttered.

"I *was* spooked." Eija shrugged. "I had no idea what was happening."

"Plan," Marco said. "Need a plan. How's the ship?"

"We've had problems," Chief said. "Boat's still moving, thanks to inertia."

"Crew?"

"Down two—one dead and one deathly sick."

The two men had fallen into a natural rhythm for an informal briefing. Marco closed his eyes and went still.

Eija deflated. How were they supposed to trust him with nav when he couldn't stay awake? "Marco?"

"Pods?" he whispered not opening his eyes.

"Escape pods." Chief nodded, then frowned. "We're in the middle of nowhere. Intel says there's nothing outside Kuru, so—"

"Wrong," Marco croaked. "I can smell them."

Eija shot the chief a look but didn't say anything. "Smell what?"

"There's . . . others."

"Allies?" Chief asked.

"Unknown, but . . . not Khatriza."

"Okay, so our plans and course are clearly scuzzed," Chief growled. "So, we don't reach Kuru—which is probably the case anyway with our fuel and nav stats."

"Can't . . . go to Kuru. They're . . . waiting at the Sentinel."

"Her army—they're waiting to attack us?"

Marco gave a clipped shake of his head. "Destroy." He breathed heavily. "They need . . . coordinates . . . to come through—destroy quadrants. Wipe out humanity."

Eija was going to be sick. She hugged herself, thinking through how they'd have died if this mission had gone according to plan.

"Scuz me," Chief muttered. "So, we stop short of Kuru, then what? We'll be out of fuel and short on supplies to sustain us."

Marco stiffened. Drew in a breath that sounded like an animal dying. His back arched.

"What's wrong?" Eija asked, reaching for him.

Shad lurched toward the machine. "His vitals are spiking."

As fast as it started, it stopped. Marco slumped, breathing raggedly. Struggled to pull himself up. His eyes were glittering silver discs. "Pods . . ."

"Yeah," Chief said. "You mentioned them—"

"Go!" Marco growled, straining to stay upright. "In the pods—now! They know . . . they know we're off course. Late. That we aren't . . . coming through the expected Sentinel."

"How can you possibly know that?" Eija backed away, disconcerted by the splotchy pallor filling his face. Like he was straining, fighting something.

"I can smell them."

"But they're light-years away," Reef said. "We beat them back. We—"

"No. They're advanced. Very. With their technology, they'll reach . . . the quadrants in days, not weeks. They're an enemy . . . we can't survive." From beneath a hooded brow, those silvery eyes fixed on them. His breathing moved his chest so heavily it was an effort to expel the words that sealed their fate: "They're coming for us."

After the feast, Isaura felt replenished. With Mavridis, Theilig, Edvian, and Kaveh at her side, she met the people by mingling around the garden, speaking with the guests. Though Mavridis kept his gaze on the crowd, he chatted with Kita, who remained close to Isaura and saw to her needs.

Even as she straightened from accepting a bunch of wildflowers from a little girl, Isaura glanced around. Appreciated a subtle breeze, a thing so rare in the wastelands. A sound vibrated the air, and she searched the skies—for what, she could not say—then noticed the long curtains hanging between the great hall's marbled columns billowed violently by an unseen force. Shouts clawed the air.

This time, when she glanced up, she saw a dark shape descend from the clouds and alight on the other side of the castle. A ship!

"On your kyria!" Mavridis shouted, then rushed toward the threat.

As Stalkers and regia materialized around her, cutting her off from everyone, Isaura watched her father rush toward some unseen threat. More aerios huddled around her.

A ship—here. Was Vorn responsible? Was this what he meant when he said he wanted to speak to her later?

"Kynigos, what do you here?" someone demanded.

Through her hedge of regia, Isaura saw more than a dozen black-clad men stalking across the east lawn, their clothing so much like Dusan's.

Heart alight, Isaura pushed forward. Was there word of him? Hope wriggled through her chest, itching to know what news or trouble they brought.

"No, my kyria," Theilig held out a protective hand.

"Stand aside!" she said, breathless.

"I cannot, Your Majesty. There is a threat—"

"There is no threat! Those are the same as your medora, and Elder Sebastiano asked them to come!" At least, she assumed he had. In Trachys, he said he intended to contact them via a device Dusan had. "Stand aside, please."

When they complied, she hurried toward the newcomers, joining Mavridis and Darius who met the hunters.

The tallest Kynigos lifted his gaze to Isaura, and his visage lightened. With brawny shoulders and a lean but powerful build, he so resembled Dusan that Isaura's heart tightened.

"Kyria Isaura." He inclined his head. "I am Roman deBurco, Master Hunter of the Kynigos."

"You are his master." Awe fluttered through Isaura. Impressed by this arc of men so brooding and forbidding, she felt as if she had a piece of Dusan back this day. "You have my great thanks for coming. There is now hope."

Roman arced an eyebrow. "Thank you, my lady. We would have come sooner—" He seemed to rethink what he would say. "We have urgent need to speak with you, Kyria Isaura. Privately, if you please."

She was so happily reminded of Dusan. "I would be glad of it." Where would she take them? She turned to her father. "A room for privacy, Mavridis?"

"At your will." He acknowledged Roman. "This way."

When Darius moved to join them, Roman placed his hand on the prince's chest. "Afraid not, Prince." Blood and boil, the master hunter had a powerful presence. "This matter is with Marco's wife alone." He tucked his chin, severity in his blue gaze. "We will speak later of your treachery." His words had their intended effect, pushing Darius back a step.

Isaura averted her gaze and started across the lawn as Mavridis led them into the house and up the stairs. A strange silence hung in the air despite being accompanied by more than a dozen Kynigos. In a large library, Isaura stood by the fire pit and clasped her hands as the hunters filed in. Her heart leapt, watching their movement, their prowling strides. "Seeing you all—I so much better understand who he was."

"*Was?*" Roman cocked his head, towering over her. "Do not give up on him, Isaura."

Disbelieving the unconscious slip of her tongue, she recoiled. "I . . ." How could she make such a mistake? Her heart crumbled.

Roman moved to her, his words quiet. "You loved him."

Tears, hot and fresh, struck her cheek as she nodded.

"We will not fail him. Or you." His hand rested on her shoulder. "We know who took him and intend to strike back. They have hunted and driven us from our home on Kynig."

"Why? Why would they take him?" She hugged herself, feeling so very tired.

"His gifting was his value to them—Marco had the strongest ability seen among Kynigos in generations. Distance did not seem to matter to his ability to anak."

"What could they possibly have wanted that for?"

"Only in the last few days have we developed a theory." Roman guided her into a nearby chair, and she realized fleetingly that he had smelled her weariness. "They intend to couple his ability with alien technology. To what end, we are not yet sure, but regardless, what they have done to our kind is unacceptable and egregious. We stand on the brink of an interplanetary war." The man's ferocity rolled in like a dark storm cloud.

"A war in which we are overmatched, as, I suspect, are you," Isaura said quietly, glancing at the others in the room. "Why do you tell me these things? Drosero has no strength in technology such as these Symmachians have." What could *she* do?

"I have two favors to ask of Marco's wife. But first . . ." He went to a knee before her, the Brethren arcing around them as he handed her a box.

Surprised, she accepted it. "Thank you." Something pricked her finger. "Oh!"

He took it back with a smirk. "I apologize for the discomfort."

She glanced at blood on her finger, then at him. "What . . .?"

Roman stood and handed the box to Mavridis, who would not meet her gaze. "Kynigos once numbered in the hundreds. We are now no more than fifty, thanks to these attacks. What is happening, I believe, is connected to an ancient blood battle."

And Dusan was linked to that? "His brand."

Roman nodded. "It will be our life and breath to find Marco and hunt down those responsible, starting with Baric, who snatched him once before." He shifted, hands casually at his sides. "Now it is incumbent upon us by our Codes, an oath sworn before Vaqar, to protect our own—to protect you because you belonged to Marco."

The Codes that had so fiercely guided Dusan through his life. And yet, what did the box have to do with that? Rubbing her pricked finger, she again eyed Mavridis, who set aside the box.

"I make a bold request of you," Roman said, his deep, gravelly voice formal once more. "Since the attack on Kynig, the Brethren are without home. Not long ago, Marco offered shelter here if we had need. I fear that time has come. Since Kardia is a fortress with seaside access, our scouts could come and go without interference and possibly without notice. If you grant this request, it will free us to resume the hunt for Marco."

"There is no technology allowed on Drosero," Mavridis said.

"And yet I am not the only one who knows that there are scores of ships on this planet already." When Mavridis scowled, Roman lifted his palms. "My intent is not to argue but to speak that change, whether Kalonica or Drosero would have it, is already here."

"Since Medora Marco invited you—then, of course, you are welcome," Isaura said, not willing for these men to be refused. "And I believe if any can succeed in locating Dusan, you will." Trying to absorb everything, yet ready to topple from the revelations, she again traced her pricked finger. "Mavridis, there are quarters here for aerios, aye?"

Reluctantly, he nodded. "There are barracks berthed within the perimeter wall, my lady." His expression went grim. "With the loss of Stratios, there are empty quarters."

"A sad loss," she said, thinking of the princessa as she turned her gaze to the master hunter. "Would that suit? Not luxurious and likely uncomfor—"

"We look not for comfort but for vengeance."

"Refuge you have here, Master Hunter. Seek your vengeance." The words felt good, perhaps a little too good. Isaura should probably speak with the prince about this, but she would not allow him to refuse the Brethren. "And your second favor?"

Roman glanced at the box, then Mavridis, who nodded. "As you suspected."

When, head down, her father turned away, Isaura came to her feet. "Please. Do me the respect of speaking to me, not around me."

With a smile, Roman quirked an eyebrow. "I see well why he chose you." He lifted a hand. "I have few regrets in my life but Marco is one of them— knowing I never told him the truth."

Hesitancy guarded her. "What truth?"

"When Kynigos enter the Citadel as pups, we are trained to forget families, so that the Brethren become our family." His cheek twitched. "I took Marco when he was but six from within these very walls. From the arms of his mother." He lowered his head, then met her gaze again. "My sister."

Isaura swayed at the revelation. "You are . . . his uncle?"

Roman steadied her. "Marco does not yet know, and I will not let him die until he does." His expression softened. "So, Isaura, I would ask"—his voice went strange—"that you tend yourself well. My nephew loves you, and I would have him find his way back to you." His eyes pinched with a near smile. "Have you an understanding of how we hunt?"

She looked at his sigil, recalling Dusan asking a very similar question. "He explained." She thought of the ambush in the forest and the way he detected her attraction.

Another smile as Roman nodded, no doubt sensing her thoughts, likely her nerves, too. "Good. That—*you* are what will draw Marco back. As his bound, your Signature is as life to him, and I would have you tend yourself carefully so he will find it."

Her heart thundered, making her eyes burn and her throat raw.

"Yours"—his gaze slid to Mavridis and back—"and his child you carry."

Breath snatched, Isaura strangled a cry and stumbled back, not daring to believe. The chair clipped the back of her knees and dropped her onto its cushion. Her hand went to her stomach . . . Could it be? But they had been together such a short time. "You are . . . *How* can you possibly know? Did you smell it?"

He indicated to the box. "A blood test confirmed the presence of human chorionic gonadotropin—the pregnancy hormone. You are newly along or I would have anak'd the babe."

Babe. The word rattled her. "Why did you not simply ask me to take it?"

"That was my doing," Mavridis stepped in. "I feared you might refuse, so new and overwhelmed by events of late. More than that, I feared doing you an injury if the test was negative."

Babe. A babe. Isaura wilted, gulping grief that Dusan was not here. But now, she would always have a piece of him . . . What if he did not return? What if he died never knowing . . .?

An arm came around her shoulder, the master hunter kneeling again at her side. "Isaura, grieve not for a man not yet dead," Roman whispered, his cheek to her ear. "The child will strengthen your Signature and guide him home. *You* are his beacon in this storm that consumed him, so *live!*"

"That's your *plan*?" Chief gripped the contraption that held Marco. "We get in the pods and eject, drop on the nearest planet?" He snorted. "Wait for those aliens on the planet you detected to pick us up? *Hope* they don't want to kill us like the Kuru aliens?" He grunted. "I think that contraption did something to your brain.

Marco gave him a hooded look.

"What about you?" the chief asked. "This ship? You can't fight them off—it has no armaments."

"I'll jump," he rasped, and it made Eija's own throat hurt hearing him speak.

"To *where*? We don't have a map of this system or—"

"There are Sentinels . . . dozens. I . . . detect them—we are exiting . . . alternate one."

That made sense. "That's why you adjusted the navigation, why we still have a stream." Eija had wondered about that.

He nodded. "I'll pick one. Jump. Buy time . . . you reach the planet." The wiring was draining him. "They want the . . . coordinates on this ship, so we . . . destroy it."

"No way." Eija had not found Marco to let him die. "If anything goes wrong, they'll capture you *and* have the coordinates for Kedalion!"

"He won't survive," Shad murmured.

"I think that's his point," the chief grumbled.

"No, I mean—he won't survive jumping the ship."

Chief's gaze sharpened on her. "Why not?"

"His body's too weak," Shad explained. "Taking my wildest guess—it's one thing to navigate a ship in motion, but if I'm reading this contraption right, it's using his neuroelectrical impulses to navigate, which is also sending the ship's feeds to his brain. It takes less fuel to keep a ship in motion than to launch one, so it follows that the same would be true of the cost on him." She bunched her shoulders. "In this condition, his body can't handle a mega-jolt. It'll kill him."

"My choice," Marco hissed.

"No," Eija said, stunned at what kind of man would be willing to do something like that for people he didn't know. "I didn't find you to let you die."

"You found me because She wanted *you* saved," he growled.

"Who? Xisya?" The very name made her recoil.

"No." Marco gave a low growl that betrayed everything he felt about the alien. "She's darkness and corruption. Violence." He drew in a long, ragged breath and let it out. "Light and Truth sent me. Violence of a different order with a higher purpose."

The words thudded against her pounding heart. He spoke so clearly, so forcefully, when all this time he had struggled to whisper. It was as if someone else spoke for him.

Weary eyes held her hostage. "I am not here to live, but to die so you can live."

"No." The objection felt small as it slipped from her tongue. *She* felt small and insignificant beside this man now dependent on IVs. She looked to the chief. "His judgment is impaired—we can't let him make this decision."

Anger blazed through silver eyes, and a rush of something washed over Eija, making her lurch and gasp.

Everyone lurched.

It wasn't mind powers—the ship powered down.

"What?" Eija snapped her gaze to the Kynigos. "You did th—"

"Decision's made." Resolute, he eyed the chief. "Enemy's en route. Get them out."

"Chief! Chief!" Reef shouted from the corridor. "Long-range radar is lit up."

"Now," Marco growled, vibrating with anger and something else. Strain? "In the pods!"

"We can't abandon him!" Eija's throat thickened with emotion. "It's madness!"

"Do it, people. Jadon, get Tildarian in her pod." The chief stared at Marco with something she hadn't seen from him before—vulnerability.

With a faint nod, Marco relaxed against his couch, which suctioned him. His eyes drifted closed.

Like he was falling down some dark, fathomless hole. She couldn't let him disappear, die. Who had he been before this that he'd give up his life for strangers?

"Don't you have someone who wants you back?" Eija wasn't sure why this even mattered when there were ships coming and an enemy bent on annihilating them.

His lids fluttered open. That silver gaze quickly focused on her.

Annihilating . . . That . . . *That* was why . . . why she'd been led to him. So he wouldn't give up. She moved closer. "Isn't there someone you love? Someone who wants you to come home?"

Like a pond glider, emotion glimmered across his handsome face, just beneath the surface of his pain and exhaustion.

A tender swell ran through her, and she started, realizing that she was sensing what he felt. She reached up to brush back the hair from his face, not in a romantic way, but because of something she saw in her mind's eye. A memory. A woman.

She could not know. Yet, he anak'd from the girl the same agony that beat in his own chest. What she'd spoken of . . . Marco had given up on that in the lengthening days of excruciating pain, barricaded in the bulkhead, alone, cold, and terrified. His only solace had been thoughts of Isaura—the melody of her laughter, her soft kisses, her wit, her ability with the moon discs, the thrill of making her his own.

That morning, amid the terror of being stolen away, seeing the second light in her eyes . . .

A daughter.

My daughter.

The young woman from the ship swam into view. "Your tears tell me I'm right."

"Having loved . . . and being loved . . . does not mean I live eternally," Marco ground out. "I was told by the Lady Herself that I would know pain and cruelty." His lips tightened. "There is no other path before me." Not here in the black of space, in a system with terrorizing images of what they were to face—ones he'd seen and felt thanks to Xisya. "I will not give up your lives or our quadrants in the vain hope of saving my own."

"Yet She sent me to find you," she said softly. "Only to make sure I see you die?" She sniffled. "No way."

"We each have a purpose. I cannot know yours, but I know mine." He nodded to someone behind her.

"Zac," Rhinn said, his tone heavy. "We need to go."

"No."

Marco settled back into the *lectulo*. "I've sent the coordinates of a nearby planet to the pods. When we clear the Sentinel, we'll flip and burn to slow, drop the pods. Then I'll power back up and re-enter the Sentinel. Jump away."

"No!" Eija was crying. "We can't let him do this. It's cruel—wrong."

The other pods were powered up—he could smell them, feel their pull on the system, on *his* system. The technology didn't give his mind control over them, but the electrical impulses in his fingers and hands were enough to send commands through the ship.

Rhinn secured the girl in the pod, though she fought it, angry. Grieving for Marco.

She does not even know me.

Isaura . . . Did she grieve for him? He ached for her, to hear her voice. Their love started reluctantly and ended as one of the most powerful influences in his life.

Ended. Was it truly?

He would not survive this . . .

Why . . .? Why give him love from Isaura only for it to end? And their daughter . . . *My daughter* . . . His heart ached.

The Sentinel . . . in three . . . two . . . one . . .

Marco gritted his teeth, and with a growl, he flipped the ship and fired reverse thrusters, slowing them in the new system. Even as he did, the ejecting *whoosh* of pods launching vibrated into his chest—one gone. Then two, three . . .

He reset coordinates for Kuru.

Panic spiraled at him. He glanced at the pods. Wild eyes came to his over an oxygen mask. The girl slapped the shield—*distress*.

The second bank of pods—something was wrong. The girl and two males remained.

Thunk!

What happened? Marco eyed the countdown and felt a twinge of concern. If they didn't launch now, they'd drop into Kuru with him—into the trap. They'd die.

Seconds now. "*Go*," he willed the pod.

Her kicks thudded her panic, his receptors burning with her efflux. Then came the man's. All frantic. Marco searched the system, found a faulty cable that had malfunctioned, preventing the second bank's drop-hatches from opening below the pods.

Shouldering aside the acrid scent, Marco tried to stall the jump. He wasn't fast enough. The process too long. Vibrations shook his head, his neck, and legs as the ship thrummed beneath the hyper-engines.

The *Prev* lurched. It felt like someone ripped his heart out from behind. Gray blanketed his vision. He struggled to find the girl's scent. It was there, but dull, quiet. Afraid he'd never wake up, he fell into an abysmal silence.

Waves slammed themselves into the boulders far below. Isaura savored the brief respite in the days since the appearance of the Kynigos and the raucous reaction to her writ that the hunters would be housed among aerios. She had no regret, especially when Darius questioned her on the writ, reminding her—as if she did not know—that technology was not allowed on Drosero. Holding her ground took more courage than Isaura had mustered in cycles. Being kyria was exhausting, a taxing role that left her with little at the end of each day, especially with the life growing within her. Dusan's heir.

It had been but five weeks since he was taken. Hand on her belly, she marveled at the technology Roman had used to tell her she was with child, something the royal pharmakeia could not confirm because the pregnancy was yet so new.

The way they had revealed what she had not yet guessed . . . It was an unfair intrusion upon her privacy, upon something she would have preferred to learn alone—with Dusan. Not in a room crowded with men who knew Dusan far better than she did. She appreciated her father's desire to protect her—it would truly have been shattering to knowingly take the test and learn she was not pregnant.

Still, she had demanded their silence regarding the child until she could come to terms with it, and until she passed the danger of the first few months. She feared losing this child, an occurrence far too common among those enduring distress. And of late, that was all life entailed.

"My kyria."

She sighed as she came off the chaise and stood. "You are more regular than the rise of the moons, Ypiretis." She turned and immediately noticed his submissive demeanor. "What is it?" Her hand flew to her stomach. "Is there word—"

"No." He held out his palms. "Please do not distress yourself, though I do come to you with a grave matter," Ypiretis said softly. "The Council of Elders has been called, and you are required."

"Council?" Should she not have been informed of any gathering of the elders—*before* they gathered? But she knew so little of law and politics. "What do they address?"

"Prince Darius."

She sagged. Though expected, this had taken longer than anticipated. "Very well."

Kita appeared from a side room. "Let us get you changed, my lady."

Isaura hesitated and looked to the aged priest. "What will they expect of me? I know the basics of our laws, but not the whole of them, especially where the crimes of Darius are concerned."

He gave a rueful smile. "You are allowed an advisor in such circumstances, and upon the recommendation of Elder Mavridis, I have been studying since your arrival here at Kardia. Though no expert, I am read up on the laws."

"Why does not Mavridis serve as my advocate?" Even as she asked, she realized it would look as if they conspired. She waved. "The answer comes to me." She joined Kita in the other room where already her official green garments were laid out. She chose the one with the silvered brocade.

"When you enter," Ypiretis called, "it will be upon you to open the trial. It is also important you inform the gathered that I am your advisor and then allow Grand Duke Rhayld to conduct the inquiry."

Trial. Inquiry. Her stomach squeezed as she looked to Kita, who shared a grim smile as she worked the buttons along her spine. "Must it be me?"

"You are their sovereign," Ypiretis said. "The grand duke is arbiter. I am told Rhayld rarely casts a vote in matters of the Council, but he does conduct them under the direction of the ruling monarch. You have final say."

"Are you sure you are well enough for this?" Kita asked.

"I must be." After the family order was pinned, Isaura nodded her thanks to Kita and left the residence with Ypiretis. "I thank you for your guidance and . . . friendship." Even as they reached the stairs, she saw Kersei pacing inside her solar and recognized her distress. She could well enough imagine her pain. She did not know what to say, only that she must say something.

"Your Majesty." Kaveh shifted into her path. "You should not. It could compromise the integrity of the Council."

Isaura glanced over his shoulder to the princessa, who watched intently. Her desperation, one borne of fear and feeling powerless, pulled at Isaura. How well she knew that feeling.

Kersei stepped into the corridor, a hand resting on her rounding womb.

It made Isaura aware of her own child budding within—a cousin to Kersei's. From the other side of the aerios, she nodded. "I would have you know . . ." She had thought to say she understood, but that would be presumptuous. "I sense your pain and know the . . . helplessness, feeling powerless to stop a nightmare."

"I thank you," Kersei said quietly.

"Your Majesty," a stern voice called from the stairs where Theilig appeared with two aerios. "The Council awaits." His gaze hit Kersei, and something played through his expression.

Isaura looked at Kersei once more. "When this is over, perhaps we could have a meal together. Get to know one another."

"I . . ." Kersei glanced at the aerios. "I would be honored."

"As would I." With that, Isaura headed down the stairs to the grand hall.

"Stand for your kyria," a caller announced. Chairs and boots scraped within.

Isaura entered the throne room, which had been fitted for the trial. The greens and golds always inspired, but the tables flanking the throne unsettled. All eyes turned to her.

The thirty steps to the dais felt an eternity, yet she glided forward, noticing how the gathered inclined their heads in deference as she passed. It was a strange, terrible power the crown created. She was no different today than the day Dusan met her in Moidia.

No, not true . . . The babe.

Feeling comforted at the thought, Isaura stepped onto the dais and faced them, then gained the seat. "Our land has been in turmoil for many weeks, and now we deal with another grievous trouble." She scanned the room of elders and warriors. "This matter was important to Medora Marco, and he made plain to me his distress. Let us do justice here. Honor his name and pray continually for his return."

"Huzzah!" The simultaneous bark of the gathered aerios resounded loudly.

"This inquiry will be presided over by the grand duke." She nodded to Dusan's uncle. "Lord Rhayld, if you please."

"Thank you, Your Majesty." His words were as ice. "I see at your side a recused iereas. Are we to assume he is your chosen advisor?"

Though embarrassed she had forgotten to mention Ypiretis, she nodded. "You are correct."

"Very good, Your Majesty." Rhayld's tone neared sugary now. "Let the court record that present at this inquiry are all elders of Kalonica save Stratios. Princessa Kersei, though representative of her father's people, is deemed to have a conflict of interest, as she is bound of the accused. Now we are here to consider the accusations against Darius, third-born of Zarek and brother to Medora Marco, including treachery, treason, and murder."

Murmurs carried along the murals of the gallery.

"Aerios, bring in the prince." Rhayld nodded to the captain of the guard, who opened the door.

Prince Darius entered, his countenance so like Dusan's in every respect save the color of his hair and his defeated demeanor. Over the next several hours, he stood in the sectioned-off area of the accused as Rhayld laid out the charges and their details: Darius had been complicit in the attack on Stratios Hall, acting against the realm and the crown, conspiring with the enemy, lying to the crown. "And of the charge of treason against your own country"—Rhayld's gaze veered to Isaura—"and your brother, the medora, this evidence comes to light."

She made herself not react, but her heart disobeyed violently as Rhayld passed around a device that must have been borrowed from the Kynigos or from Vorn himself. It showed a moving, albeit silent, picture of Darius with King Theule of Hirakys and High Lord Theon.

Head down, Darius did not argue his guilt.

Rhayld continued. "It has been suggested that you provided the intelligence about the medora's movements and his location, both in Jherako and then back in Trachys, where he was snatched from his bed in the night. What speak you of this charge?"

Darius looked at Isaura. He gripped the wood rail before him. "You do not understand—they threatened harm against Kersei and our unborn child!"

"Answer the charge, Prince Darius," Rhayld said blandly.

Darius huffed. "I only gave them location—"

Shouts went up.

Isaura stiffened, not wanting her pain or distress evident at his obvious betrayal of Dusan. But the torrent, the grief, pushed her from her seat. She moved behind the throne, out of sight, as tears spilled. She covered her mouth and fought the tears.

Feet hurried toward her, and she knew she must rally, but the shock— the abhorrence that he would betray his own brother, that Dusan might die because of him!

Feeling her morning meal rising up her throat, she gripped her stomach.

"My kyria!" Ypiretis was at her side.

"I need a moment," she whispered.

"Let us remove you," Mavridis said, his voice hot against her ear. "This is too much."

"No," she bit out, straightening, her back still to the hall, where terse murmurs raced up and down the marble. "I must . . . stay."

"You must *rest*," he insisted. "The ba—"

"No," she ground out, looking at him. "You promised not to speak it." She did not want this entire hall to hear of her child. "Water, please. I will be seated."

Mavridis looked toward Theilig, who hovered. "Water for the kyria."

After the water, she gave a slow nod, feeling more herself with each moment. "Better?" Mavridis asked.

Standing tall, she let her hands fall to her sides. "Thank you." She returned to the throne, limbs weak. Hand on the arm, she took a shuddering breath and finally looked again upon Darius.

His countenance was pale—likely as much as hers—and his expression tormented.

"May I speak?" he asked, his expression earnest, anxious. "I beg your mercy, Kyria Isaura. Might I have the floor to speak to these charges?"

Her stomach churned, not wanting to hear anything he would say. But then . . . she recalled Dusan's patient thoughts toward the brother he knew had betrayed him. Yet because of him, Dusan was not here. "No," she said firmly, trembling with rage. A thought came to her that greatly confused her. "But you will answer this question, Darius: in Trachys, did you not encourage Marco to set petition for me?"

He hesitated. "I did."

"Why?" she asked. "It does not follow then . . . I know not what to make of it. Had you not encouraged him in this, the throne would have gone to you when your collusion resulted in his abduction. Why would you do this? Did you think to use me to your ends as well, that because I am born of Moidia, I would here act as lawless as you?"

"I beg you not to think these things." His brows knotted above glossy eyes. He pressed his palms together and touched them to his lips. "I encouraged Marco to set petition because it would strengthen our stand against Hirakys. I did this knowing it would anger the Symmachians and that I would likely be killed at our next encounter for offering such advice.

"Never did I know that they intended to take *him*," Darius continued. "I have made many errors and done wrong, betrayed this realm and the name I bear, but I tried to right them." He tucked his head, taking several long moments before continuing. "At the beginning, I thought to strengthen the position of Kalonica with the Symmachians, but I was thoroughly disabused of that notion when they leveled Stratios, murdering my father and brother and so many other innocents. As I recovered on Iereania, I plotted how to let them believe me bought, my adunatos theirs, while I sought a way to break their grip on this planet from within."

"You were a fool!" Rhayld shouted at his nephew.

"Aye, every bit the fool." Darius's words were raw with emotion. "Early on, when I first learned Achilus yet lived—and not only lived but captured the heart of the woman I had been bound to months earlier—I was desperate to reassert my claim to the throne and Kersei. But it was not long before I resolved he could have the throne but not my bound." His unruly light-brown hair shook around his face. "There is no excuse, and I deserve death for what I have done to Marco and Kalonica." His gaze lifted to Isaura. "I beg your mercy for stealing the one happiness you had found, my kyria. The one hope Kalonica had of fighting off Symmachia."

"Sweet, honeyed words," Mavridis growled from the elder table on the right, his gray eyes bright with anger. "Sweet words meant to yet again ply your will and the soft heart of our young kyria. Is that it? Still trying to manipulate?"

"Nay!" Darius started. "Nay, that was not—" His gaze flicked to her. "On my honor, it was not my—"

"You have no honor!" Elek barked from his seat near Rhayld.

Shouts of agreement riddled the room. The tension was thick, the anger rank, the division . . . monstrous. It broke Isaura's heart to the point of rending. Tears slipping free, she could take no more. She stood, and the hall fell silent at once. "Are all charges laid, Grand Duke?"

He straightened, surprised. "Yes, my kyria. They are—"

"Then a break," she said, lowering her tone that had risen. "I believe one is in order."

"But—"

"We will adjourn and resume in the morning." Without another word, she left the dais.

Two aerios rushed forward and yanked Darius from Isaura's path. Apparently, they deemed him a threat, though she did not. Theilig, Hushak, and Kaveh fell in step behind her as elders and guards rose to their feet as she exited the hall. She strode across the grand foyer and up the stairs to the royal residence.

Guards opened the door. She hurried past them and straight out onto the balcony, seeking the solace of open air and sea. Gulping the salty breeze, she dropped onto the chaise, buried her face in her hands, and wept for the broken realm at her feet. That Dusan was not here to carry this burden, or at least to share in it. That she was pregnant and he could not know it. That his brother was the traitor who delivered this tragedy.

The fool. The conceited, arrogant fool.

Curled on her side, she became aware of a presence. Only Mavridis—and Dusan—could sneak with such stealth. "I suppose you think me a simpering weakling."

"Nay." Coming into her view, Mavridis leaned against the balustrade. "It is a wretched business dealing with treason, especially one so ill conceived."

"I could not take any more," she confessed, "hearing his pleas, their mocking of him—he is a prince!"

"He stands to lose that title and his head. He will speak whatever it takes to keep them both."

Isaura recoiled at the bald truth of that.

"The people were very happy with Marco, and the tour—once word spread that he was Dusan, they loved him all the more. Now, he is gone and possibly dead—"

"No!" She surged to her feet and felt a wave of dizziness. Sickness.

Mavridis lunged to catch her. "Give care!"

She waved him off. "I am not weak!"

"No, but you are with child, and that will put a strain on your body."

Hurt, angry, distressed, she marched into the apartment and poured a glass of water.

"Have cordi. It has nutrients."

She fingered the jug of cordi. "He loved cordi—warmed." Her thoughts again bounced to Darius. "What will happen if the prince is found guilty?"

He lifted the cordi, dumped some into a glass, and handed it to her. "Darius will be stripped of title and removed from all responsibilities and property, then he will be sentenced to execution."

"Execution?" She took the glass, numb at the prince's fate. "Must it be?"

Somberly, he nodded. "It is the punishment for treason and crimes against the crown. Next to the medora, Darius held the most powerful position and violated it egregiously. They will make sure he cannot make another attempt against the realm, neither he nor his heirs."

"Heirs!" Isaura drew up sharp. "Kersei?"

"She will not be executed, but she will be stripped of title and power."

"No," Isaura breathed, her gaze roving the table, as if she could find an answer there. "There must be some . . ." She jerked to Mavridis. "He made mistakes but sought to rectify them. The situation was unfair—it should not affect Kersei or their child!"

"Do not listen to the soft plying of his slick pleas, Isaura. He is a practiced politician. Having been raised in this very house, he knows how to wield impassioned words to twist hearts to his will." Nostrils flared, he paced away. "Terrible is this thing he has perpetrated against those who depend on him, including Marco, who like his father and brother, may have paid the highest cost for that selfishness." He glanced at his drink, then gulped it.

"Do not say it. I will not so easily accept that my child will grow up without a father as I did."

Guilt hollowed his expression.

Isaura started at how that affected him. "I beg your mercy, I never—"

"No," he said in his gravelly way. "You have ever been a gracious child. But you are right—I was not there." Acknowledgement was more than she expected. "I wronged you, made you question your worth, and I see the shadows of that already haunting these halls." His gray eyes held fast to hers. "I thought I was protecting you—"

"Aye," she said with a sad smile. "And you did."

"I did not. I am Plisiázon." It seemed as if that should be answer enough, but when she gave him a confused look, he huffed. "I could have—*should* have—easily dealt with the grumblings. Handled directly your mother's indiscretions. I let fear control me, drive me to consider their"—his lip curled—"approval over doing right by my own blood."

Isaura's heart seized. She dared not move for fear this bubble would burst.

"I pandered. Placated their bloodlust, and it drove your mother into a worse state, leaving my daughter to fend for herself. What kind of father does that?"

Though pained—and yet relieved—by his words, she understood now. "This is why you are so vicious about Darius's actions."

"He thinks not of Kersei or that babe," he snarled. "I have learned much traveling with this bound of yours. I had the power in my hands to do something that would have defied the very edicts of our society, yet still would have been the right and honorable thing." He stared hard at her, and it seemed a point dwelt between his eyes and his words. "Do you hear me, Isaura? My words?"

Indeed, he was conveying something. He spoke of defying edicts and honoring blood ties . . . Did he speak of Darius? Or was he saying he accepted her?

He set a parchment on the table and fingered it, slowly bringing his gaze to hers. "I wish you good rest and will see you in Council on the morrow." He took another sip and set down the glass, then gave a curt nod. "Good rest, my kyria."

"No," she said softly, striding over to him. He was strong and powerful, proud and mayhap more than a little arrogant, but he was her father. She stood before him, and how strange that her heart beat so wildly. She thought to say something eloquent, but instead, she tiptoed up and planted a kiss on his cheek. "Thank you."

"I have not earned your thanks, Isaura. There are leagues to go before I can repair what I have done to you."

Warmth surged inside her. "There is nothing to earn, Mavridis."

He grunted, a grim smile slipping out of his weathered visage. "Therein lies my grievance with myself—you do not call me father."

"I . . . was not allowed."

"Ladies forgive me." He gripped the back of her head and kissed her forehead. He stepped back and cleared his throat. She would have sworn there were tears in his eyes. "Read it well. Good rest, Isaura." He nodded to the table, then started for the door

"Good eve . . . *Father.*"

Step faltering and head ducked, he hesitated, then left.

With a fresh cup of warmed cordi in honor of Dusan, Isaura lifted the parchment and stilled at the heading: *Duties and Responsibilities of the Kyria.*

Eija drifted on a pillow of darkness, surrounded by a presence powerful yet so gentle she could do nothing but remain. Laid out and feeling a calmness she hadn't experienced before left her with a sense of euphoria.

Light bloomed to such magnitude that closing her eyes did no good. It intruded, invaded, overcame. A hand reached through the brightness and touched her chest. With it came a preternatural sense of . . . purpose. Like she had something to do.

Boom!

The world shifted and rattled.

Boom! Boom!

Her head jerked to the side, snapping Eija awake amid yet another jolt. She groaned, lifting a hand—and striking something. As she took in her enclosed environment, sudden clarity zipped through her mind. The pod. It hadn't ejected, and the air coming through was . . . leaking. She pulled the release handle. It hissed its surrender but didn't open. With a growl, she tried to kick it. To her chagrin, the light flickered off. A wisp of panic stabbed through her.

Boom! Boom!

Shadows skittered over the hull. Eija stopped straining to open the pod. *What . . . ?* She glanced to the bulkhead. The lectulo's glow dimmed. Marco wasn't moving. She jiggled the release again—to no avail. "So much for protecting me, Patron. And my purpose? Purpose, huh? I can't even get out of—"

A repetitive thump carried into her pod, vibrating her boots and teeth. Shook her senseless. With a loud clank, the *Prevenire* dropped into quiet.

Her gaze rose, finding only darkness. An ominous swirl of emergency lights splashed across the bay. Eija jostled the door again. An erratic panic had her thrashing against the door with a shriek. She slumped against it, fighting tears. The chief, Gola, and Shad had ejected. Bashari and Reef were still here—something was wrong.

Marco must be unconscious again.

Clanging echoed, indicative of something very large and very powerful colliding with the hull. A sound that reminded her of a drumroll that never ended.

From her pod, she peered down the corridor and past the medbay, where the entry hatch opened. Large, black shapes ducked through. The blood thrashing in Eija's veins went cold when the things straightened.

Lavabeasts.

No no no. She shuddered a breath, taking in the all-too-realness as the creatures stomped toward the bay. This was no dream. No vision. They'd found them. Found the *Prev*. Just like the training video of the creatures who decimated Xisya's kind on her ship.

Draegis. The name trilled in her brain. Shards of terror speared her courage at the sight of the ruthless, violent beasts.

A black shape blurred past her pod. Its skin looked so much more violent in person with red molten trails snaking beneath armor. She found it difficult to discern armor from flesh. Its face seemed half mask, half lava with red Y-shaped eye slits. Crimson threads pulsed from the chest upward into the well-muscled, segmented neck.

Six Draegis managed to clog the bay, all dark and forbidding. These creatures had an agility one wouldn't expect. They moved effortlessly. Without suits. Without helmets to ensure their ability to breathe. One shook something, then pitched it. Whatever it'd thrown hit a supply crate and dropped hard to. Then it shifted.

Bashari! He drew himself onto all fours, his face bloodied. Two Lavabeasts assaulted him. One drew back its arm as if cocking an old-fashioned gun, then shoved his arm forward—and a different appendage appeared there. A warming, orange glowing thing with heat wakes coming off it. A volley shot out.

A terrified Bashari lifted his arms to block the strike, but it was futile. Red engulfed his body. Reduced him to ash.

Eija clamped a hand over her mouth and sank back into the pod, as if she could hide. Tears burning, she noticed a symbol glowing on their black-as-night bodies. One Draegis had a blue icon on its cheek, and another silver. Two others pounded on Reef's pod beside hers. Death felt too close!

Silver shifted to Marco, then aimed a weapon-arm at him. Unexpectedly, Silver turned away.

Wait. What did that mean? Was Marco already dead?

She cowered as Silver stalked toward her pod, his movements too lithe for such a monstrous creature. When he passed by, she noticed Blue turn suddenly and stomp over to—

Oh no.

Marco! He was stirring—awake!

Blue jerked his elbow to his side, powering his weapon arm.

Eija could not let them kill him! No matter what Marco said, she didn't believe his purpose was to *die*. Especially not like this! "No!" she shouted. "Leave him alone!"

Crack! Thunk!

Her pod door ripped away, shocking her. Thick and black, a hand snapped in and closed around her throat. A pungent odor stung her nostrils as the thing hauled her from the pod. Struggling, she could do little against this beast, though she kicked and thumped the abrasive armor. Grappling, panicked, she gritted against the searing agony and terror.

Behind her captor, Draegis converged on the lectulo . . . Eija fought to see past Lavabeast. Begged the Ladies for Marco to be alive.

The drone of a drumroll hammered in her head as the Draegis squeezed from her both air and life.

59

LAMPROS CITY, KALONICA, DROSERO

What do you think I am made of?

Understanding what her father meant was one thing, but to act with the intention he indicated last evening, for him to suggest she do the very thing he, a noble and elder of Kalonica, had not been brave enough to do . . .

She—a woman of two and twenty cycles, never acknowledged, always having to fight for every scrap of decency and honor—was used to the cruelty of men, their thoughtless words, feckless actions. Yet she had always seen the good in people, the reason behind their actions. While it did not excuse them, it helped her understand and leave her anger over their actions at the feet of the Ladies. Here, at the end of the inquiry against Darius, she sat in a position to deliver judgment.

Or mercy.

Prince Darius stood at the wood bar again, his expression blank.

Princessa Kersei was allowed in for the reading of the verdict and stood with a hand on her belly that bulged with the heir her body produced. Ah, the cruelty of this hour.

"Your Majesty." Rhayld's voice boomed in a way that said he very much liked the sound of it. "I would ask that, considering the delicate nature of today's proceedings, we clear the room of those not directly involved with this matter."

Isaura's heart thumped. She knew well he meant the man standing at the back of the room in his black trousers, shirt, and cloak. "Master Roman is here at my request."

With a huff, Rhayld looked to the elders, but none chose to argue with the unorthodox inclusion of a skycrawler.

Isaura stood her ground. "At your will, Duke Rhayld."

"*Grand* Duke," he said with a sniveling noise.

"Is that more important at this ora, sir?" she challenged, wearied with the entire affair. In truth, her insides squeezed in anticipation of what was coming. Her concern over the princessa and the babe. Her ache to have

Dusan with her—no, in her place—she anywhere but in this chamber.

Her father stiffened at her rebuke, and she felt Ypiretis lean closer. "Please—read your judgment," she insisted of the grand duke.

"As you will," Rhayld said. "Make it known and written in the annals that on this day, the twenty-third rising of the sixth month in the first year of Marco, the first of his name, the Council of Elders pronounce their judgments regarding Darius, third son of Zarek and his bound, Athina." He shifted to deign to look upon the prince. "Stand ready to hear the judgment of your peers and elders."

"I stand ready." Darius somehow managed to sound like Dusan just then.

Clearing his throat, Rhayld snapped the parchment in hand. "On the count of colluding with an enemy of the realm of Kalonica, Tyrannous Darius is found"—the grand duke gave a long pause for effect—"guilty."

Crying quietly, Kersei lowered her head.

Darius stared straight ahead, which put his gaze directly over Isaura's shoulder.

She held fast, watching, gauging, monitoring. Then shifted her gaze almost imperceptibly to the hunter.

Rhayld continued. "On the charge of treason against the realm of Kalonica, Tyrannous Darius is found . . . guilty."

This time, Kersei yelped, and a woman wrapped an arm around her.

Darius's gaze dropped but not his head. He gripped the wood rail he stood behind.

Isaura watched him as the next charges were read, two dismissed for lack of evidence, and one judged neutral due to a dispute among the Council.

"Elders of Kalonica," Rhayld called, "please rise."

The punishment phase.

Isaura looked from Kersei, with her blood-red eyes and trembling frame, to the elders standing ready to hand down their decisions.

"For the judgment of guilt in the matters of colluding with the enemy, accepting bribes for personal gain and influence, Darius is stripped of all title and lands, as are his bound and heirs," Rhayld pronounced. "In the matter of treason against the crown, against his own brothers and father, against an entire entoli and its people, the punishment is execution."

"No!" Kersei let out a strangled cry, and others gathered close to console her, but she shrugged them off. "No, you cannot. Please!"

"Commander Theilig, take Darius into custody until—"

"Nay," Isaura said, her heart pumping hard.

Rhayld looked as if she'd struck him. "Your Majesty, the verdict has been delivered. He is judged guilty. You cannot argue the law."

Quavering, Isaura straightened on the throne. "Did I speak to that effect, Grand Duke Rhayld? That I would argue the law?" She gave him a smile she did not feel. "I fear you are mistaken, sir."

Murmurs filled the gallery. Theilig hesitated.

Isaura rose and drew in a shaky breath. This would test their willingness to support the throne upon which they had set her. "Master Hunter." She clasped her hands. "Please approach, so I may inquire of you."

Roman unfolded his arms with casual grace and strode toward her. By the Ladies, he had the mannerisms of Dusan. It swelled an ache in her breast for him. When he reached the dais, he inclined his head.

Isaura moved to the lower step so they could talk with privacy—what could be had—and steeled herself against the murmurs and wary glances from the gallery. "What do you detect, sir?"

Standing sideways to avoid any hint of impropriety, he bent his head toward hers. "Anger, grief."

She stared into his eyes, sad that she did not hear the one—

"Regret."

Shuddering a relieved breath, she nearly buckled.

He caught her arm. "Are you well?" he asked quietly.

She smiled around another exhaled breath. "Very. I thank you. Would you please remain here?"

Again, he inclined his head, then pivoted and took up a position next to the dais, a spectator once more.

Isaura resumed the throne seat and set her hands in her lap. "I would beg your patience but a little longer." She slid her gaze to Kersei, who seemed to have lost all color. With a breath for courage, Isaura steeled her spine. "'Uncertainty remains about his character—is he a good man, acting under some misguided sense of right? Or is he corrupt?'" She stared at Darius, who seemed confused. "These words were spoken to me by Medora Marco in Trachys as he wrestled with the truth of his brother's betrayal." Though her words sounded clear and calm, there beat a frenetic pace in her chest, and she saw the same in Darius as he lowered his head. "The medora believed that the reason our enemy sought out Darius was to undermine Kalonica."

The elders shifted, nodding. Clearly, this was not news.

"Do I speak true, Elders?"

They glanced at one another, then Bazyli rose. "Aye, Your Majesty. He spoke very forcefully about that belief when we held council in Trachys."

"The medora has experience with this enemy who has sought to influence and alter relations and spur wars in Kalonica and across Drosero." Isaura probed them further, but this time she turned to Roman. "Is it not true, Master Hunter, that Marco has experience with Symmachia?"

Roman clearly did not like being drawn into this. "Aye. Firsthand—they kidnapped him and did horrific things to him. We believe it is Symmachia who has again taken him."

Isaura struggled through a few breaths but then faced the gallery. "To honor Medora Marco's stated wish, I hear, grieve, and understand the judgment delivered against his brother. It is . . . deserved."

Darius hung his head.

Roman shifted, glancing to her. "Grief," he rumbled. "Deep regret."

Those words firmed her resolve. "Yet . . ."

The prince peered from beneath his brow.

"As Kyria of Kalonica by all rights and set in authority by this very Council, I deliver a stay of execution."

Shouts of outrage went up. From Rhayld. From another man—Shau'li elder, she believed—saying she had no right. Elek and Bazyli argued it was well within her right. As the argument continued, her regia and the aerios formed in front of Isaura, a preemptive measure that made her knees weak. She had expected argument but not violence. Would they resort to such?

"I object," Rhayld shouted. "You have no authority to overrule our judgment."

"I would have—" She could not hear herself over their shouts and objections.

A shrill whistle streaked into the air. The Council covered their ears, effectively silencing the rancor.

With a nod, Isaura thanked Mavridis. "Ypiretis." She turned to the wizened priest. "Would you please come forth?"

He slowly rose and shuffled into the open. "Yes, Your Majesty?"

"You told me, did you not, that you had been reading the law books of this great realm since my arrival."

"I did." He cast a nervous glance at the grand duke.

"And I have heard it from some that you have perfect recall. Is that true?"

"Yes . . ."

"Would you cite for me from the constitution regarding the duties and responsibilities of the kyria. Section 5, paragraph 2?"

Rhayld went white. Then crimson. "We do not need it cited," he grumbled. "Certainly not from a recused priest of the very order that colluded with Prince Darius."

"So, his guilt is by association?" Isaura inquired. "Is not then your guilt also determined, Grand Duke Rhayld, by being uncle to Darius?"

Sniggers rattled the air, and Isaura considered she might have gone too far. "Very well," she said. "*I* will tell you what it says. The law allows the kyria to act in all matters of state where the medora is unable to do so. Not only that, but when acting in the best interest of the realm, it is an imperative that the kyria always respect first the wishes of the medora."

Isaura took a slow, measuring breath. "As such, Prince Darius, I cannot adjudicate all your charges. You have grieved the crown—your brother—and I ache for the wound you inflicted upon him, upon your bound, and your people." She looked to the master hunter. "I requested Roman's presence so he could tell true what feelings you harbored. Considering the crimes, words could not be trusted, but as Marco told me often, the nose never lies."

She paused for a moment, considering those gathered. "Our country—our very world—is in troubled times, and the counsel of good men is needed. Our medora trusted your counsel, Darius. He spoke highly of you in that regard, even when he knew your treachery. And I would trust it, too. To that end, I have asked the Kynigos if one of them would attend me at all times. Until such a time as you regain trust or our medora is returned to us to alter this edict, all dealings with you will be handled in the presence of a hunter, so one will remain with you as you go."

"As I go?" Darius frowned.

"I am told that Stratios Hall is being rebuilt," Isaura said, looking to Kersei, who wore an expression of bewilderment. "When it is repaired and livable, it is a gift to you and Lady Kersei from myself and Medora Marco. Until that time, you may retain your apartments here in Kardia. All appointments and visitors will be cleared—through Mavridis, myself, or Medora Marco when he returns—and held in the presence of a hunter."

An objection lobbed into the air.

Isaura glowered at Rhayld, silencing him. "Darius, since your regret is known to me through the master hunter, I feel it a waste of resources in the future not to hear your thoughts on political matters. Would I have your honest, loyal counsel?"

Darius jerked straight, stunned. "I . . . Of course, my kyria. You are gracious."

"I flatter myself I am, but only insofar as I would see no more loss," she said with a smile, then turned to the master hunter who stood to the side. "If you please . . ."

He pivoted and strode to a side door, which he flicked open. Murmuring shrouded the man who entered the great hall.

"King Vorn, I appreciate your patience. Twice in the last month, and thanks in part to your . . . ventures, you have journeyed to a city not entirely friendly to you or your queen. I would beg your patience more and ask that you remain a while longer." She addressed the elders and nobles gathered. "It is a time for us to rally together, to set aside grievances for the sake of Kalonica, for Drosero. We have an enemy wielding enough destruction, and as Medora Marco said to me, we have war at our doors and heavens. Our enemy seeks to cripple Kalonica from within, to destroy a planet defiant of their ways. They think us weak, pliable."

Sunlight streamed in through the stained-glass window, glinting in her eyes and spearing her with a warmth that made her feel as if Dusan stood at her side . . .

Return to me, Dusan. Please.

"Honor is our hallmark," Isaura said, "and rather than handing them our very adunatos, this day—for our children, our world—we must unite and bring them the dawn of vengeance."

EPILOGUE

Tigo wrenched awake, blinking rapidly against the sudden brightness. Against some heavy . . . heaviness . . . Wet. Cold. His mind jolted—water! *I'm drowning!* He tried to jerk free, thrash, but his body would not obey. Panic lit anew.

You are not drowning, Tigo. Be still. Be at peace.

Tigo slowed at Jez's voice, but the viscous, oily cocoon suffocated. Where was she? He knew water amplified sound, but this was slagged. His heart thumped hard, lungs screaming for oxygen.

In the sanitatem, *you do not need oxygen.*

Scuz that! How was he supposed to breathe?

Relax!

Right. You try to relax while drowning.

He heard a laugh, and awareness struck him—he hadn't spoken any of that aloud.

A heavy thunk sounded. He dropped hard. Water trickled away. Then came the uncontrollable urge to . . .

Tigo pitched to the side and vomited—right onto shiny black shoes. "Oh man," he said, then spit to the side. "I'm sorry."

The man standing over him sighed and rolled his eyes. "You were supposed to do that in the *sanitatem*. Now I must cleanse."

Hands slick from whatever he'd been submerged in, Tigo tried to wipe the sick from his mouth as he looked around. Hues of blue and purple bathed the chamber hewn of some type of smooth stone. "Where am I?"

"Come out of the *sanitatem*," the man insisted. "Then we can talk."

Tigo wasn't showing his jewels for all the world—or this stranger—to see. "How about a towel first?"

"You don't need one." The man went to a tall station and used a pelting spray to clean his pant leg, then shook it . . . and it was dry.

"Impossible."

"Out, Mr. Deken," he said, a millimeter short of angry.

Tigo gritted his teeth. "Maybe you haven't noticed, but I don't have any clothes."

As if amused, the man smirked and lifted a hand. "Please. Rise."

"I'm naked!"

"Rise!" Something about the way the man barked seemed to pull Tigo straight up.

Panicked, he clasped his hands over himself for privacy but felt a sudden covering of . . . something. His gaze strayed from the man to his own body. Clothed. Fully clothed. He stumbled back. "How in the Void . . .?"

"Carefu—"

Understanding the warning too late, Tigo flipped backward out of the tub. Whacked his head against the stone. He groaned, working like never before to get a bead on what was happening. On all fours, he lifted a hand and rotated it, staring at the strange clothes. Only . . . it wasn't clothing. Whatever it was *coated* his body and moved with his muscles. As if a part of him. Yet not fabric. But it had to be. Right?

"Your vestments are provided by the Ancient now."

"I think I hit my head harder than I realized." Or maybe he *had* drowned. No, he'd crashed on Drosero . . . "I died in the pod." That was it. "This is what comes . . . after." Some sick, twisted After. "Punishment."

"For us? Yes, quite." The man's jibe was not lost as he helped Tigo to his feet. "You, who are very much alive, have been granted mercies by the Ladies."

"What ladies?" He felt the need to cover himself again.

Irritation skidded through the man's features.

"Give him time, Garai," came a melodic voice from behind.

That lilt, the singsongness of it, spun Tigo around. He gaped at the woman who'd never looked more beautiful—or forbidding. Her dark hair had grown impossibly long and dangled in tiny braids. "Jez," he breathed.

"*Triarii Rejeztia*," Garai corrected. "Learn to address your Lady correctly."

She smiled. "Come, Tigo. We must prepare."

"For what?"

"War." Her voice and visage were sad. "It is time. He has reached his destination, so we must train. Ready ourselves to help him."

"Help who?"

"Marco."

ACKNOWLEDGEMENTS

THANK YOU to my amazing readers from the Droseran Saga Facebook group who offered their ideas for a forest experience. Y'all are so brilliant and creative! Special thanks to Toni Shiloh, Jane Farrelly, Katie Donovan, Fiona Barenfield, and Lizzy Hite, whose artistry left me in awe. Also: Madeline Roush, Necee Lomelino, Terri Sweetland, Amy Etner, Renee Leach, Mary Foster, Jessica Baker, Susan Poll, Lilah Mast, Marylin Furumasu, Kristen Tallau, Laura Shuck, Kiki, Andi Tubbs, and Halita Wilson.

Special thanks to Trissina Kear, not only for the use of your name for the Tryssinians, but for the gorgeous instrumental album you gifted me. It was such a help on a rough night working on *Dawn*.

Also, many thanks to Katie Donovan for early help during the Great Culling, when this book was powering its way toward 200K words. Whoops!

Last, a hundred thousand thanks to you amazing readers who have come to swoon over Marco as much as I do. Seek peace!

ABOUT THE AUTHOR

Ronie Kendig is an award-winning, bestselling author of over twenty-five titles. She grew up an Army brat, and now she and her Army-veteran husband live a short train ride from New York City with their children, VVolt N629 (retired military working dog), and Benning the Stealth Golden. Ronie's degree in psychology has helped her pen novels of intense, raw characters.

Ronie can be found at: www.roniekendig.com

Facebook: www.facebook.com/RapidFireFiction
Twitter: @RonieKendig
Goodreads: www.goodreads.com/RonieK
Instagram: @KendigRonie

Greenwillow
Read-alone

PEGGY PARISH

AMELIA BEDELIA HELPS OUT

pictures by
LYNN SWEAT

GREENWILLOW BOOKS
New York

Published by Greenwillow Books,
A Division of William Morrow & Company, Inc.
105 Madison Avenue, New York, N.Y. 10016
Printed in the United States of America   10 9 8 7 6 5

Library of Congress Cataloging in Publication Data
Parish, Peggy.   Amelia Bedelia helps out.   (A Greenwillow read-alone book)
Summary: Amelia Bedelia shows her niece Effie Lou how to follow instructions
to the letter as they dust the potato bugs and sew seeds.   [1. Humorous stories]
I.   Sweat, Lynn.   II.   Title.   PZ7.P219Ap   [E]
79-11729   ISBN 0-688-80231-1   ISBN 0-688-84231-3 lib. bdg.

For Rebecca and Amanda Freedman,
two special young friends,
with love
–P.P.

For Elynor, my wife
–L.S.

"Have a good day,"

said Mr. Rogers.

"And you help your aunt,

Effie Lou."

"I will," said Effie Lou.

"I'll come back for you

late this afternoon,"

said Mr. Rogers.

He drove off.

"What a grand house," said Effie Lou.

"Miss Emma is a grand woman,"

said Amelia Bedelia.

She went to the door and knocked.

"Come in," called Miss Emma.
Amelia Bedelia and Effie Lou
went inside.

"I am glad to see you,"
   said Miss Emma.
"Sumter is sick
   and my garden is a mess."
"Don't you fret," said Amelia Bedelia.
"We will take care of that.
   Just tell us what to do."

"First," said Miss Emma,

"weed the garden."

"All right," said Amelia Bedelia.

"Is there anything else?"

"Yes," said Miss Emma.

"But go ahead

and start

before the sun gets hot."

"Come on, Effie Lou,"

said Amelia Bedelia.

"Let's get busy."

They went to the garden.

"It does have a lot of weeds,"

said Effie Lou.

She started to pull one.

"Stop!" said Amelia Bedelia.

"What are you doing?"

"Trying to get the weeds

out of the garden," said Effie Lou.

"Get them out!" said Amelia Bedelia.
"She said to weed the garden,
not unweed it."
"Oh," said Effie Lou. "I wonder
why she wants more weeds."
Amelia Bedelia thought.

"Those weeds are little," she said.
"Maybe vegetables get hot
just like people. They need
big weeds to shade them.
That's why Miss Emma told us
to weed before the sun gets hot."

"That makes sense," said Effie Lou.

"I see some really big weeds."

"Let's get them," said Amelia Bedelia.

They did.

Soon that garden was weeded.

13

Amelia Bedelia and Effie Lou
went back to the house.
"The garden is weeded,"
said Amelia Bedelia.

"Good," said Miss Emma.

"Now I want you to stake the beans.

 Here is the string to tie them.

 You can use this saw

 to cut the stakes."

"All right," said Amelia Bedelia.

"There are bugs
on the potato plants.
Take this bug powder
and dust them,"
said Miss Emma.
"If you say so,"
said Amelia Bedelia.

The telephone rang.

Miss Emma went to answer it.

Amelia Bedelia found
all the things she needed.
She and Effie Lou
went back to the garden.

"All right," said Amelia Bedelia.
"We will steak the beans first."
"Have you ever done that?"
said Effie Lou.

"No," said Amelia Bedelia.

"But she just said to steak them.

Anybody can do that."

"Can I help?" said Effie Lou.

"Yes," said Amelia Bedelia.

"You count the bean plants."

Effie Lou counted and said,

"There are fifteen."

Amelia Bedelia
unwrapped a package.
She shook her head and said,
"That's a mighty little bit
of steak for fifteen plants.
But it was all she had."

She took the saw
and cut the steak
into fifteen pieces.

"I could have cut better
    with a knife," she said.
"Why didn't you use one?"
    said Effie Lou.
"Didn't Miss Emma say to use
    this saw?" said Amelia Bedelia.
"Yes," said Effie Lou.

"Then that's why," said Amelia Bedelia.
"Now hold the steak while I tie it."
Amelia Bedelia and Effie Lou
steaked those beans.

"All right, beans,"
said Amelia Bedelia.
"Enjoy your steak."
Effie Lou laughed.

"Your work is fun," she said.

"That it is," said Amelia Bedelia.

"Now those bugs
   are waiting to be dusted."

"How do we do that?"
   said Effie Lou.

"I'll catch and you dust,"

said Amelia Bedelia.

"Here bug, here buggy, buggy, bug."

They caught and dusted every bug.

"Why did she want us to do that?"

said Effie Lou.

"Most people want bugs killed."

"But Miss Emma is not most people,"

said Amelia Bedelia.

"Those bugs may be her pets.

They are pretty little things."

"If you like bugs,"

said Effie Lou.

"That takes care of that,"

said Amelia Bedelia.

"Let's go in."

"I made lunch for you,"

called Miss Emma.

"After you eat,

throw some scraps

to the chickens."

"All right," said Amelia Bedelia.

"And Amelia Bedelia,"
   said Miss Emma, "my garden club
   is meeting here this afternoon.
   Please make a tea cake."
"I'll be glad to," said Amelia Bedelia.
"I do love to bake."

Amelia Bedelia and Effie Lou
ate their lunch.
"I wonder where she keeps
her scraps?" said Amelia Bedelia.
"I'll ask her."

She went to Miss Emma's room.

She came right back.

"We will have to look for them,"
said Amelia Bedelia.

"She's asleep."

They looked and looked.

"Here's a whole bag of scraps,"
said Effie Lou.

"Good," said Amelia Bedelia.

"Take some and we'll throw them
to the chickens."

They went out to the chicken pen.

Effie Lou threw the scraps.

The chickens came running.

"Look at that!" said Amelia Bedelia.

"I never knew chickens

liked to play."

"Aren't they funny?" said Effie Lou.

"They sure are," said Amelia Bedelia.

"But I've got to get

that tea cake made."

"I never heard of tea cake,"
   said Effie Lou.

"Neither have I," said Amelia Bedelia.

"Then how can you make one?"
   said Effie Lou.

"Well," said Amelia Bedelia,
"I know what tea is and I know
   what cake is. I'll put them together
   and I'll have tea cake."

"That's easy," said Effie Lou.

Amelia Bedelia got a mixing bowl.

She put a little of this

and some of that into it.

She mixed and she mixed.

"Now for the tea," she said.

Amelia Bedelia opened some tea bags
and mixed the tea into the batter.
"It looks awful," said Effie Lou.
"Different folks have different tastes,"
said Amelia Bedelia.
She poured the batter into a pan.
Soon that cake was baking.

Amelia Bedelia began to mix
another cake.

"What kind are you making now?"
said Effie Lou.

"Nut cake," said Amelia Bedelia.
"Miss Emma loves that."

Finally the cakes were baked.

"Are you going to put icing
on them?" said Effie Lou.
"That's a good idea,"
said Amelia Bedelia.
"It will fancy them up."
She mixed white icing
and pink icing.

"You ice the tea cake pink," she said.
"I'll ice the nut cake white."

They finished the cakes

and put them away.

Miss Emma came into the kitchen.

"The cake is ready,"

said Amelia Bedelia.

"It smells good," said Miss Emma.

"There's one more thing

I want you to do.

There is a bare spot in my front lawn.

Please sow these grass seeds on it."

"We will be glad to," said Amelia Bedelia.

"Come on, Effie Lou."

They went out front.

"That spot is bare," said Effie Lou.

"It sure is," said Amelia Bedelia.

She sat down and took two needles

and some thread from her bag.

She threaded the needles.

"Here is yours," she said.

"Now, let's sew."

Amelia Bedelia and Effie Lou

sewed those grass seeds

on the bare spot.

"Tie the ends together,"

said Amelia Bedelia.

"We don't want the seed to fall off."

They went into the house.

Miss Emma was in the kitchen.

"Let's walk around some," she said.

"Show me what you've done."

"All right," said Amelia Bedelia.

They walked by the chicken pen.

"Land sakes!" said Miss Emma.

"What are those colored things?"

"Scraps," said Amelia Bedelia.

"Those chickens did have fun."

"My quilting pieces!" said Miss Emma.

"My good quilting pieces!"

"Did we use the wrong scraps?"
 said Amelia Bedelia.

"Go get them, Effie Lou."

Miss Emma walked to the garden.

She stopped and stared.

"Those weeds!" she said.

"Those big weeds!"

"We got the biggest we could find,"
said Amelia Bedelia.

Miss Emma looked at Amelia Bedelia.

"Thank goodness Sumter
will be back soon," she said.
"Why didn't you stake the beans?"

"We did!" said Amelia Bedelia.

"There just wasn't much steak
   to give them.
   Show her, Effie Lou."
   Effie Lou held up a bush.
"There goes my dinner,"
   said Miss Emma.

She looked at the potatoes.

"I see the bugs are dead," she said.

"Dead!" said Amelia Bedelia.

"Did we dust them too much?

I'll get you some more."

Miss Emma laughed and said,

"I can live without them.

You've done enough."

"We enjoyed doing it,"

said Amelia Bedelia.

"I've seen all I want to see,"

said Miss Emma.

They all went inside.

"The ladies should be here soon,"

said Miss Emma.

"The table is set.

The tea is made.

You can put the cake on this tray."

"All right," said Amelia Bedelia.

"I'll let the ladies in,"

said Miss Emma.

She left the kitchen.

"Let's get the cakes ready,"
said Amelia Bedelia.
"I hear the ladies coming now."

Soon Miss Emma called,
"Amelia Bedelia,
  please bring the tea."
"Coming," said Amelia Bedelia.
"Bring the cakes, Effie Lou."
  Amelia Bedelia set the tea tray
  in front of Miss Emma.

"Go ahead and pass the cake,"
said Miss Emma.
Every lady took some cake.
"I'm starved," said Mrs. Lee.
"I can't wait for the tea."
She bit into her cake.

"Delicious!" she said.

"I've never tasted this kind before."

"You've never tasted nut cake?"
  said Miss Mary.

"This isn't nut cake," said Mrs. Lee.

"Try the pink kind."

"It is good,"
  said Grandma Wilson.
"Hand me another piece."
"There," said Miss Emma,
"your tea is poured."
"Who cares about tea?"
  said Mrs. Mark.
"I want more pink cake."

"Emma, do tell us what kind of cake
this is," said Mrs. Bloom.

Miss Emma took some cake.

"My favorite," she said. "Nut cake."

"No, the pink kind," said Ella Jean.

"Try the pink kind."

But all of the pink cake was gone.

"Stop keeping secrets,"
said Grandma Wilson.

"What kind of cake was that?"

"Ask Amelia Bedelia,"
said Miss Emma.

"She made it."

A car horn honked outside.

"Mr. Rogers!" said Amelia Bedelia.

"Come on, Effie Lou."

Miss Emma followed
Amelia Bedelia to the kitchen.
"What kind of cake was
the pink one?" she asked.
Amelia Bedelia looked puzzled.
"Tea cake," she said.
"That's what you said to make."
"Tea! You mean–" said Miss Emma.
She began to laugh.

Amelia Bedelia saw something.

"Oh, I plumb forgot," she said.

"Your grass seeds."

Miss Emma looked at them.

She laughed harder

and put them around her neck.

"Amelia Bedelia," she said,

"you are really something.

Effie Lou, you are lucky

to have Amelia Bedelia for an aunt."

"I know," said Effie Lou.

"Amelia Bedelia knows everything."

The horn honked again.

"Hurry, Effie Lou,"

said Amelia Bedelia.

"We can't keep Mr. Rogers waiting."

PEGGY PARISH is the author of many books enjoyed by children of all ages. Among her easy-to-read books are the seven previous books about Amelia Bedelia (including *Good Work, Amelia Bedelia* and *Teach Us, Amelia Bedelia*), *Too Many Rabbits, Dinosaur Time, Let's Celebrate*, and *Mind Your Manners*. For a slightly older group she has written *Key to the Treasure, Hermit Dan*, and *Let's Be Indians*. Originally from Manning, South Carolina, Peggy Parish taught school in Texas, Oklahoma, Kentucky, and New York. She is living once again in Manning.

LYNN SWEAT is a serious painter as well as a well-known illustrator. His work has been exhibited in New York, Texas, and California. When not at the drawing board or easel, Mr. Sweat is outside, running. He finished seventh in the Nationals in the Master's Pentathlon in Raleigh, North Carolina. He runs in both long and short distance road races and says that if he had Amelia Bedelia to help him he would win even more often!
Mr. Sweat has illustrated a number of Peggy Parish's books, among them *Good Work, Amelia Bedelia* and *Teach Us, Amelia Bedelia*. He lives in Weston, Connecticut.